Amaresh Misra is a [...]
poet, doing his Ph.D in Modern History from Allahabad
University on the social and cultural attitudes of the
middle classes of north India. He is a political columnist
for the *Economic and Political Weekly of India*, besides
contributing regularly to *The Times of India*. He is also
a scriptwriter and is set to direct a television serial on
1857 for a reputed channel.

The contemporary photographs are by **Ravi Kapoor**, a
prominent photo artiste of Lucknow with a special
interest in architecture and heritage.

Amaresh Misra is a freelance writer, historian and poet, doing his Ph.D. in Modern History from Allahabad University on the social and cultural attitude of the middle classes of north India. He has political columns for the Economic and Political Weekly of India, besides contributing regularly to The Times of India. He is also a scriptwriter and is set to direct a television serial on 1857 for a regional channel.

The contemporary photographs are by Ravi Kapoor, a prominent photo artist of Lucknow with a special interest in architecture and heritage.

Lucknow: Fire of Grace

The Story of its Revolution, Renaissance and the Aftermath

Amaresh Misra

Rupa & Co

Typeset in Garamond by
Nikita Overseas Pvt. Ltd.
1410 Chiranjiv Tower
43 Nehru Place
New Delhi 110 019

Printed in India by
Saurabh Printers Pvt. Ltd.
A-16, Sector-IV
Noida 201 301

To,
the people of Lucknow, Avadh and U.P.
so that they feel
good, bad and smug the world over

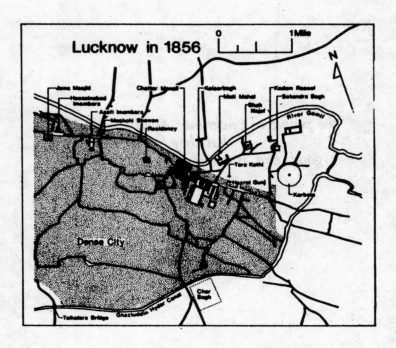

Lucknow in 1856

0 · · · 1 Mile · · · N

Jama Masjid · Hoosainabad Imambara · Chatar Manzil · Kaiserbagh · Kadam Rasad · Sekandra Bagh · Asafi Imambara · Machchi Bhawan · Moti Mahal · Shah Najaf · River Gomti · Residency · Tara Kothi · Hazrat Gunj · Karbala · Dense City · Char Bagh · Talkatora Bridge · Ghaziuddin Hyder Canal

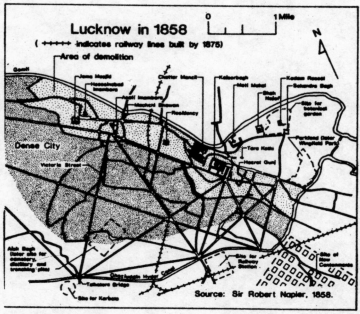

Lucknow in 1858

(+++++ indicates railway lines built by 1875)

0 · · · 1 Mile · · · N

Area of demolition

Gomti · Jama Masjid · Hoosainabad Imambara · Chatar Manzil · Kaiserbagh · Kadam Rasad · Sekandra Bagh · Asafi Imambara · Machchi Bhawan · Moti Mahal · Shah Najaf · Site for Secandad garden · Residency · Tara Kothi · Parkland (later Wingfield Park) · Dense City · Victoria Street · Hazrat Gunj · Alah Bagh (later site for cemetery, military and trenching pits) · Site for Railway Station · Site of New Cantonments · Talkatora Bridge · Ghaziuddin Hyder Canal · Site for Karbala

Source: Sir Robert Napier, 1858.

The Avadhi Nawabs and Kings

Burhan-ul-Mulk	—	1722-1738
Safdar Jung	—	1738-1753
Shuja-ud-Daula	—	1753-1774
Asaf-ud-Daula	—	1774-1798
Wazir Ali Khan	—	1798-?
Saadat Ali Khan	—	1798-1814
Ghaziuddin Haider	—	1814-1827
Nasiruddin Haider	—	1827-1837
Muhammad Ali Shah	—	1837-1842
Amjad Ali Shah	—	1842-1847
Wajid Ali Shah	—	1847-1856

The Awadhi Nawabs and Kings

Acknowledgements

Pankaj Mishra for giving me a break as part of the resurgent Kanyakubja brotherhood

Raaes Agha for being the teacher with the authoritative Lucknowi perspective

Ali Mehndi for the eagle eyed love of precision

Amir Naqi Khan for the refined interpretation of Mahmudabad history

Mr. AK Das for that brilliant sense of detail about twentieth century Anglo-Indian life

Dr. JK Misra and Dr. Rama Misra for being the best of parents, north of the Vindhyas

Anand Misra, IAS, Muzaffar Ali, Shahid Asqari, AR Kidwai, Ramzi Khan, Parveen Talha, Prof. SK Narayan, Raja Salempur, the Larkins, Manas Mukul Das, Advanis, Dr. RP Rastogi for those crucial pegs of information and support

Salahuddin Usman, Yasa Rizvi, officials of the information department, state museum, Lucknow, state archives Lucknow, Archaeological Survey of India.

Contents

Contents

Introduction

Right from colonial times, the privilege of shaping India's destiny was grabbed by the giant port cities. Norms of progress and civilisation were set by them even after the end of the British rule. For decades Calcutta remained, as of now, the quintessential city of the Indian 'renaissance'. Similarly, Bombay, now Mumbai, carried the caste mark of an Indian city of wealth, opportunity and 'gold'.

Situated at the far end of the peninsula, Madras, now Chennai, seemed to combine a provincial reproduction of the two. She led the laid back intellectual ambience of the East and the dynamism of the West into the passionate embrace of an ancient, regional impulse. The urban landscape of India mushroomed within the east-west-south triangle formed by these cites. Economic growth, middle class formation, modern values were seen, first, to take shape in their environs. The LA, Paris, Milan of India, they mirrored, in native eyes, images of a Western culture ascendant in South Asia at least from the latter part of the last century.

But there is something more to India, perhaps a paradox, manifest in the wide chasm between the apparent and the real. Logically, the metros ought to constitute the mainstream in politics, culture and social life. Influences emanating from their portals should have set the tone of contemporary happenings. And yet, this has not been so.

The region which defines the socio-political agenda of the country is located further up north. Stamped forcefully on the heart of India, it is better known as the Hindi-Urdu belt of the Indian subcontinent. Comprising, roughly, the four states of Uttar Pradesh, Bihar, Madhya Pradesh and Rajasthan, this area has traditionally formed a solid, turmoil ridden bastion of the status quo.

Known in common parlance as Hindustan, it provided an indivisible cultural-political identity to India, Pakistan, Bangladesh and parts of Afghanistan before the onset of British rule.

A zone of power, the Hindi-Urdu belt provided, in the medieval as well as the ancient past, the fertility, resource of men and material and the socio-political context to sustain major Empires. British power consolidated only after a series of conquests and re-conquests of the area from 1764 to 1858. Anti-British nationalism of the twentieth century became a political threat only when it reached the Hindi-Urdu heartland. And for decades after independence, Indian political elites drew their mandate to govern the country from its Indo-Gangetic core of Uttar Pradesh. Recently, a battle for caste based reservations and 'social justice' in Uttar Pradesh and Bihar raised the issue of status quo change at the national level. Around the same time, the demolition of a medieval mosque by right-wing Hindu groups focussed world attention on South Asia. The incident came close to toppling the constitutional regime in India and took place at Ayodhya, just a few miles from the medium sized city of Lucknow, the present capital of Uttar Pradesh.

The very fact that it held the vaziriet of Uttar Pradesh for over fifty years, running back to the time of the United Provinces of British India, makes Lucknow the next most important political centre of the north after Delhi. But the city's historical identification has been with something different: for generations it has occupied a pre-eminent position as the cultural capital of north Indian society. The Urdu language acquired its baffling vazan, phonetic nuances and suave perfection in Lucknow. Here the most recent, and arguably the most advanced, of all the classical Indian dance forms, the Kathak, took shape. The origins of the mass popular Parsi theatre, whose basic structure was taken over by Hindi films in the twentieth century, are traced to the Urdu theatre of Lucknow, as also modern innovations in musical instruments like the tabla and the sitar.

Inadvertently, Lucknow is the land *savoir vivre:* the place where indigenous etiquette and manners were sculpted in baroque. It is also, surprisingly, the den of *savoir faire.* Bred on a mixture of tact, responsibility and polish, the 'pehle aap' tehzeeb of the city once startled the conventionally minded. It reflected the competitive ideal of the Indo-Persian gentleman vis-a-vis his European rival: a person steeped in refined manners, unassuming sophistication, love for poetry, ideas, wit and letters, but equally well versed in subterfuge, valour, scepticism, spunk, style, wanderlust, and the Asiatic gesture of 'emotional power'. The ideal was once the preserve of all sections of the society. But even after the cultural inroads of British colonialism, it surpassed sectarian loyalties to spruce up the elite corners of Muslims, Hindus, Sikhs and Christians across the subcontinent.

Lucknow's richest spoil, however, is its 'composite culture': that cultural strain which, for centuries, welded together diverse communities, religions, ways of life and thought to finally showcase an idea and praxis of 'Indianness'. Ironically, the concept of composite harmony, projected by Indian ruling elites as the basis of national unity and secular temper, found an echo in the Indo-Gangetic plain, a perceived centre of religious discord.

The 'Indo-Persian' legacy of the area, nurtured by centuries of Mughal and the earlier Delhi Sultanate rule, embodied the cosmopolitan face of 'composite culture'. Uniting elements drawn from the high society of West Asia to the folk culture of the Indo-Gangetic plain, from Perso-Arabic legends to Hindu mythology, it produced an entirely new, turbulent and awe-inspiring synthesis. The cultural movement of the new ruling classes unleashed a grand experiment of social engineering and change which displaced old forces. Radical humanist ideas were encouraged introducing the day of enterprising individuals, suppressed social forces and women. A professional-entrepreneurial ethic combined Islamic-Turkish-Afghan-Mughal traditions with living Brahmin-Rajput-Vaishya-Shudra conventions, and the Arthashastrian-Mauryan-Gupta etymology of secular, ancient India, to transform social values. Landmark achievements in accountancy, medicine, astronomy, astrology, chemistry, mathematics, political science and philosophy altered, for good, the normative picture of Hindustan.

After the decline of Delhi in the eighteenth century following the raids of Nadir Shah, the legacy faced a crisis of patronage and identity. To the Persian raiders from afar, 'Indo-Persianism' was too remote. And to the emerging power of the British, it was simply alien. At that point, Lucknow, until then the capital of the Mughal suba of Avadh and a major entrepot of trade, emerged as the seat of a regional dynasty. Consequently, cultural and political syncretism shot to a position of official fusion and experiment. This was a throwback to the days of Akbar, Jehangir and Shahjehan complete with the incidence of Indo-Persianism touching the indigent at the grassroots. The venture got a boost due to the ancient temper of Avadh, the rural political base of the Lucknowi nawabs. Embroiled in a heroic, epic history of grandeur, ferment and change, the Avadhian landscape proved receptive to new age sounds emanating from the war and peace drums of the nawabs.

A fresh statement of political and civilisational 'power' was born. It began with the sensational charge of the aristocracy — sword in one hand and the banner of Ram, Muhammad, Krishna and Ali in the other held alike by Hindus and Muslims. Dazzling the world with their energy, these aristocrats arrived at international markets in their full syncretic regalia as cosmopolitan entrepreneurs and factory owners. The shock was further intensified by Lucknowi capitalists and administrators. Donning the aristocratic cap, they rode into the ferocious rural frontiers of Avadh and other native states to meet the heat of scorching minds and bodies with the heat of wealth, conflict and opportunity. Peasants celebrated their religion and secular freedom by wearing arms, noble garments, hopes of fortune and the code of chivalry to township or qasba markets. Hookah smoking queens, courtesans and lay women put on tough, material, business-aristocratic airs to arouse the romantic and cow down the wimp.

Avadhian scholars of the qasbas rewrote the rational sciences syllabi of reputed West and Central Asian universities while mystics came up with advanced concepts of being and becoming. Performers, entertainers, artists and playwrights exploded genres to communicate a Lucknowi mizaj of fun, irreverence, doubtism, indulgence, contemplation and the mixing of emotions, tragedy with comedy, anger with banter. The world was stumped by another nawabi-

Avadhi subterfuge when the Lucknowi synthesis appropriated Western features in architecture and technology. An 'Indo-Persian-Italianate-French-Egyptian-Turkish-Chinoiserie-Anglican' rococo style evolved which made the classicist 'Anglo-Indian' fusion, then going on in Calcutta under British tutelage, look like a downmarket, tawdry, philistine affair.

In the annals of Indian history, the city formed the vital link between tradition and modernity, the fall of the Mughals and the emergence of the British. The timing of its rise, in the second half of the eighteenth century, was rather unique. By then, other great empires of the West Asian mainland, like the Safavid and the Ottoman, were also in decline along with their cities. The Indo-Persian legacy was, after all, the subcontinental extension of a larger Asian impulse. Lucknow became, for a brief tantalising moment, the envied repository of a continental memory passing through a phase of rapid transition.

The city's story, therefore, provides the key to the psychological and social depths of a lost, and probably the last, impulse of an Asiatic modernity. The experience which it arrests in glimpses extends over a grand penumbra of emotion and humour. Full of idiosyncratic details and historical insights, sensual flourishes and philosophical despairs, old world ambience and new world outlook, the tale has few parallels elsewhere. Lucknowites always found it difficult to exclaim 'Oh this is so much like our city!' in the Asian metropolises of Constantinople, Isphan or Turan, or in Delhi, Peshawar, Lahore, Surat and Hyderabad.

Burdens of uniqueness aside, Lucknow, as a personality, did not get cramped or isolated. Her forte lay in the multidimensional leitmotif of the Asiatic dastaan and grand, polyphonic tunes. These works of subjective history encompassed a whole era of poetry, literature, art, fashion, forms of footwear, culinary delights, domestic furnishings, industry, leisure activities, game, entertainment and medicinal advanced. Her 'structure of sensual feeling' ended, significantly, with one of the most cataclysmic episodes of Indian and Imperial history — the 140 days siege of the British Residency in Lucknow during the great revolt of 1857. The siege ended in Indian victory which succumbed before the force of British arms and counter revolution in 1858.

Battles of Lucknow entailed a gigantic, civilisational clash and decided the destiny of India. But not before implanting in the victors a trauma of terror and incomprehension. Colonial and Western historians never came to terms with an 'oriental' culture that passed away through the travails of a 'modern' upheaval, reminiscent of the French revolution and the German peasant wars of the sixteenth century. A veil of silence, or a whimper of white journalistic sympathy, accompanied the wanton, wilful, conscious and murderous vengeance which the British extracted from the city.

Post-war years were terrible as a pro-British 'bonne' bourgeoisie held a ghost city hostage to its hybrid, 'stolen' and pretentious nawabi manners. English and French novels then were just beginning to satirize this class in Europe, busy in laundering its dirty linen on the world of *haute* culture left desolate by defeat of the revolutions of 1848. But the last 'heavenly' city survived, like the spirit of 1857, the defeat of her revolution. In course of changing seasonal and attitudinal cycles, she opened out a window to the zeitgeist of the late nineteenth and early twentieth century.

Her famed evening mood changed to accommodate new idioms befitting the agenda of anti-British, Congress and Muslim League led, composite nationalism. In the '30s, Lucknow was windswept by a Leftist 'storm and stress' in modern Urdu literature. The resultant Progressive Writers Association pushed the sickle carrying Avadhian peasant to the position of a hero in novels of Hindi literature. Musically, thumri and ghazal artistes twisted conventions to bewilder connoisseurs. New infusions transformed Kathak into a ballet form and the dadra, or the fast tempo thumri, into a lyric of the even metre. These experiments shook the film industry of Bombay, then deep in throes of expounding a new style of music and dance. Migrant communities of Parsis and Anglo-Indians found spunk, ambience and employment in ice-cream soda and cake joints, small scale trades, the bustling parties of elegant hostesses and the big publishing houses of indigenous magnates.

From Lucknow's bursting localities, a genteel, restless middle class sallied forth to stamp the '20s and the '30s with an indigenous mark. The process was shortchanged as much by the narrow vision of the post-1857 nationalists as by the events of 1947. Partition threw the unconventional city of pulsating harmony back by decades. But Lucknow refused to collapse. Despite enjoying the nostalgia built around a past glory, she moved on through the crimes and smiles of contemporary politics, society and administration.

Obituaries are ruled out because Lucknow's tragedies were acted out in a thin and restless twilight zone, 'between' past and present. Even aborted possibilities did not become museum pieces or part of official rhetoric. They hung out, eluding fixed definitions and predictions, which, like those made by stymied British troops in 1857, tend to falter on reaching Avadh. No wonder then, that when other great urban centres are facing the problem of 'overdefinition' and repetition, discourse on Lucknow is just heating up. Political change in Uttar Pradesh and India has foisted those forces to power who were responsible for the demolition of the Ayodhya mosque. Their rule promises to raise anew, in several complex ways, the issue of a theocratic state, or Hindu rashtra, in India. Liberal-radical trends know that the rearguard action of secular constitutionalism will be fought out in Uttar Pradesh and are busy sharpening their weapons in preparation for the coming war. Behind this central conflict rages the larger battle of old and new social forces for political, economic and social power. Political uncertainty in Uttar Pradesh is determining the course of political instability at the centre. Once again, the premier city of Hindustan faces a titanic battle which may decide India's future in the twenty-first century. The sad narrator of the past, the raucous cynic of the contemporary present, the historian-biographer of a lost era and the lay adventurer of the modern times would be advised to put on a pair of spectacles in the very beginning. For one is not quite sure what may come up in the middle and the end.

1

❧

Evenings, Gomti, Henna and the Bagghi

*In the beginning there was the city. Then the moonless night.
Crows swooped for prey, armies swept mansions, but battles did
not cease. For, there was still the light.*

There is something undeniably feminine about Lucknow. No other
city invites like a courtesan of yesteryears — without inhibitions,
pretensions or lewdness. It is a city with a skyline devoid of frown-
ing bastions, vain battlements of huge fortresses or the harshness
of the skyscraper. From one end of the city to the other what one
sees is a long line of slender minarets, small chattries, parapets, gold-
plated, sky-aiming spires, broken occasionally by the running columns of medium sized buildings. But the view from the sky is
nothing compared to that from the ground. Great sacrifices and a
lost trail of the blood of martyrs haunts every nook and cranny of
this city. A gloom hangs over its towers and minarets to register
a permanent tragedy.

Lucknow is where people like to stay after a long day's journey.
The city has not been a stop gap rendezvous of political and cultural
caravans. Tales and legends and true-to-life accounts speak of travellers coming from as far as Constantinople, St Petersburg, 'Toledo',
Peking, Tashkent, Bokhara, Kon and Mandalay and terminating
their journeys here. It was as if there was no more to see or
experience after Lucknow. But Lucknow did not attract the traveller

with the promise of the final, mystical destination. He arrived to whet his appetite for power, authority and sensuality.

Many of Lucknow's descriptions are linked with taste, scents, aromas, touch and sounds of the flute. Yet the 'exotica' could not acquire a permanent form. Every visitor to the city was compelled to create his own image of Lucknow, from the legendary explorer Ku Chin Wu to the nineteenth century *Times* correspondent William Russell, from that early mapper of the colonial dilemma, Rudyard Kipling to its later purveyor, V.S. Naipaul.

These images have been so central to Lucknow's thematic evolution that it is hard to recall any other city based, primarily, on imaginative fantasy. Recall Delhi and at once, the ponderous image of heavy structures, soaring ambitions and the devastating beauty of an arid landscape takes over. Think of Benaras and dark, snaky lanes sneak behind the rundown Gothic architecture of common buildings to present a blend of mystery, remoteness and frail progress. Aligarh, Patiala, Lahore, Bareli and Bhopal, the other centres of genteel decline, remind one of a few derelict poets who huddle in equally derelict buildings, bathed in the fading light of a long-lost moon.

But imagine Lucknow and one hears sounds of carefree laughter. An unveiled beloved darts across an open courtyard to rest on the rampart of a balcony. Gilded crowns and ornamented pediments embellish the roof like precious jewels dangling in the sky. Evening descends below on the shores of the Gomti and a soft wind blows along the banks, the orangish hue of the water dissolving into a dusky shade of purple in the late hours.

The scenario unfolds: evening calm, a soft but firm breeze, the quiet ripples of the Gomti, domes, arches, the grey Moorish backdrop, the red 'French' haze — and the beloved. Not the estranged one of yore or the quintessential object of desire, but the exciting, amorous, earthy and urbane lady. Instead of making her paramour pine, she plays with him. Instead of hiding behind her mystique, she displays the mole on her navel. In the background, a portrait of Akhtar Piya[1] looms large with the sounds of thunder. It reflects neither the pompousness of a haughty lover nor the obsession of a devotee. It is mellow, romantic and detached: capable only of gently urging the beloved to uncover herself and withdrawing, if she refuses, to a world of fantasy. The lady moves with a dancer's grace, and the forms of love are superseded by that of art. The swirl of her skirt becomes a blur which invokes a lost thumri celebrating the delights of unencumbered desire.

Akhtar Piya, thumri, Kathak, the changing colours of buildings and moods are just some of the many pictures of Lucknow which carouse in and out of the pages of history. Lucknow's senses come alive when set against her everyday 'texture'. The 'evening' feel in Lucknow is not limited to a particular time or experience. It hangs in the air, and on the roads, as a continual quality of Lucknowi ethos. Whether it is the well-known Hazratganj crossing at the heart of modern Lucknow, or the long semicircle around the city to the other side of the Gomti, Lucknowi passages develop in short strides. They instil a feeling of calm pleasure, a kind of association with the slow arrival of dusk.

The same feeling is aroused further, in the lush quarters of the city's well-to-do, or in the paths on the outskirts, which remind one of groves and orchards. Lucknow has been described as a city of gardens and even her main railway station bears the name Charbagh[2]. Yet the gardens are more like orchards rather than conventional lawns with flowers and waterfalls. Exuding a cool, dense luxury, they fill one's memory with the glow of orange, gold and red. Similar sensations are linked to evening and its fading light, described by the phrase 'sham-e-Avadh'[3].

Like a dazzling gem, this catechism has served to incorporate all aspects of Lucknowi life, in the same way that 'subah-e-Benaras'[4], meaning a cultural milieu of morning gaiety, has denoted for centuries the essence of Benaras. The milieu of the sinuous Ganges at dawn, of the bath, bhang, paan, raand and the folkish poorvi thumri. With Lucknow, it is difficult to think of a dip in the Gomti. The river exhibits a motion which is neither free-flowing nor still and grand. It does not lend itself to a kind of seamless, aimless sift through the shores, still less to a spiritual interpretation like the Ganga and Yamuna. Pauranic sources are almost silent about it, preferring to celebrate the mythical sources of the Saryu, the river of Faizabad, Lucknow's sister city.

The Gomti appears to be the least ancient of all rivers. Its stately, silent, luscious flow is characteristic of rivers associated with pangs of secular love, splendour and refinement. Its entity is not mirrored in the self-image of a peasant, transcendental love common to the Jhelum or Chenab[5]. Its comparison is to be sought with the rivulets of late medieval cities which saw a cosmopolitan culture growing on their shores in the West. In France and Spain, people hark back, even today, to the era of town citadels where many a chivalrous love story was born.

In Jaunpur, a few miles downstream from Lucknow, the Gomti retains the look of the past. It is visible from the dignified ramparts of Jaunpur fort as a knight's fantasy carrying the fading perfume of his princess. As in Jaunpur, the Gomti flows through the city in Lucknow, dividing its urban settlements in the north and south. There are very few rivers which divide cities in India, as town civilisations have come up either beyond or along the river banks. But the Gomti creates, in long contemplative distances, the culture of the slow, casual walk, weighed down by the silk of the flamboyant Lucknowi achkan, setting the emotional context for an ashraf's passion, expressed in urban formality, delicate zaban and fiery desire.

On this path, orange and ochre-red seldom stood out as the only determining patches in the city's personality. In keeping with the old days, when the rustle of the Lucknowi wide-legged ladies' gharara left behind a shimmering upheaval in the calm of evening, a dark backdrop has always lurked behind the city's bright colours. This sensation has had little to do with the blackness of untamed desires. On the contrary, it is the dark landscape of a fair setting: the acres and acres of dark green foliage that contrast with the light hue of orchards and groves of cypress, mangoes, datepalm, oranges and custard apple, in and around the city's environs. More importantly, it is the brown red glaze of henna, that perfume of Lowsina flowers which has symbolised the city's industry and poetry. The colours of henna express the cultivated wildness of a caged beauty, standing as the mysterious 'other' of Lucknow's fairness and breaking the song and roses stereotype.

Over centuries, the dual shadow of this intoxicating hangover has followed the city through romances and heartbreaks. The pavements and the lime washed walls that lead to the innermost lanes of Lucknow, carry a greyish underbelly of their own. Stories of the ashraf's hopes, the fatal commitment of individuals to lost ideals and love, the slow eclipse of a way of life still floating on the periphery of the present age. Like the lustre of Lucknow's famous stucco paint, which retains its whiteness in the midst of worn down calcite deposits, the lesser known formal symbols have a more complex account to render. The now silent entity of the Lucknowi bagghi, or carriage, bears testimony to a history more ambivalent than the Gomti or sham-e-Avadh.

Bagghis are identified as aristocratic vehicles of the nineteenth century, when palanquins and royal elephant rides went out of fashion. In nawabi Lucknow, the royalty still used the traditional means of transport but for the common ashraf citizenry, the bagghi was fast becoming the new status symbol. With the back portion drawn behind, and no space in the front to conceal the view, the Lucknowi bagghi was more open than the English phaeton. Its plush seat made of velvet was the perfect vehicle for the ashraf to announce his entry into the contemporary era. It reflected a flash of dandyism which encouraged his lady to cross the zenana and overlook the blowing away of the veil by a gust of wind during the bagghi ride. The bagghi was to Lucknow what the single horse with a saddle was to the American West — a synonym of action, lifestyle, individuality, triumph and failure.

Old city photographs show the Lucknowi carriage standing aside chateaux, palm tree gardens, Greek pillars and the long winding verandah. In stories retold over the years the visit to the courtesan's gate lacked dignity and grace if not made in the bagghi. Without the slight tap on its wood, which signalled the kochvaan or the carriageman to move on, the final parting with the beloved lacked regal poignancy.

But perhaps, without the bagghi, there would have been no

adventurous sojourn — that final moving out, towards the Lucknow-Faizabad road or the north bank of the Gomti, in search of a new destiny after a long spell of sensual exuberance. From here the ambiguity of the city's poetic tone was born, which led the heart to express the multifaceted beauty of a culture thus:

> *In this devastated world a drunkard's pleasure is bitter,*
> *that is the secret in the bitterness of wine.*

2

❧

A City Comes into Being

The almost habitual blend of the base with the sublime, the philosophical with the physical, has also been Lucknow's catastrophe, her so-called 'decadence'. In most other cultures the spiritual has followed the sensual as a kind of an over-compensatory gesture for a life spent in neglect of some higher meaning. Lucknow's angst has produced the opposite effect: higher meaning has arrived through everyday pleasures and pains associated with the sight of the moon and the blemish on the face of the beloved.

This has been the city where the material world achieved the same status not only as that of poetry, but philosophy as well. The exploits of Gods and supermen retreated before the tinkle of a woman's anklet. Cynicism and pessimism too have led, not to the lessening, but the heightening of involvement with the world of the here and now. Its decadence has resided in a surrender to material sensations, in a way quite uncharacteristic of those periods and cultures which have gone into an irretrievable spin of decline because of this reason. For Lucknow, even after seeing the end of a dynasty and many dramatic changes, has yet to be totally engulfed by decay. Many elements which distinguished it have certainly vanished but new ones have sprung up; there is no evidence of a lifestyle caught in the warp of time.

It is remarkable that a city with such a distinctive ethos going back in time, is still so alive. Lucknow, unlike the typical modern or traditional city, is not the prisoner of a rarefied, glorified history. Nor is it a victim of haphazard growth. Perched between new and old worlds, Lucknow stands counterposed to both. However, it is not merely a city where different ethnic worlds coexist. Rather, where layers and layers of cultural lifestyles are superimposed on a certain clockwork of time.

There is the Lucknow of myths and legends, alive today because of one enduring symbol, the Lakshman Tila. The tila, or the famous hillock, is the highest point of the city situated at the extremity of the south bank of the Gomti. This is also the oldest surviving remnant of the mythological time of Lord Ram. The Avadh countryside, with its seat at Ayodhya, constitued the domain of the Ramayana's hero and nearly all its important cities bear some form of pre-ancient association.

Avadh, previously, was the 'Brahmavarta' of yore: the purest and least contaminated abode of post-Vedic Brahminism. Brahmavarta marked a demarcating boundary between the influences accumulated during the years of Aryan expansion in the deep east, and the heathen survivals that continued to prevail amongst the tribes in the western portion of the old and larger Aryavarta. The Lakshman Tila links the city to the central impulse of Brahminical religion. Yet the hillock with its ancient cave is now known more for chivalrous legends than sacred memories. Religious claims to the site have been few and random and recently, an effort to change Lucknow's name to Lakshman-puri'[1], drew little response from the general citizenry. Today, the Lakshman Tila stands also as the Pir Muhammad hill, the place where the first Sufi saint of the city, Shah Mina, pitched his tent in the early half of the fifteenth century. The Pir Shah Mina became, both literally and figuratively, part of Lucknow's landscape and his tomb is still a revered pilgrimage site for both the Hindus and Muslims. Later, Aurangzeb built a Jama Masjid at the spot, the tall minarets of which remain the most imposing sight of Lucknow.

The Lakshman Tila also opens the floodgates of the city's early history. Its lower half carries the remains of the original Panch

Mahala, the first officially recorded royal building of Lucknow. It was built sometime during the reign of Akbar before Lucknow actually became the capital of the new Avadh Suba under the third Mughal in A.D.1580. By that time, the city was already a thriving settlement with dwellings of traditional Hindu upper castes alternating not only with the Muslims but Bhars, Pasis and Ahirs[2].

But pre-Mughal Lucknow had yet to acquire an enduring place in history. She was eclipsed by the fourteenth-fifteenth century rise of Jaunpur, a late-Delhi-Turkish Sultanate, pre-Mughal replica of Lucknow. For nearly a century, it brought together the advanced development of the Slave, Khilji and Tughlaq Sultanates and reproduced their achievements in a provincial setting. Its rulers, the Sharqui kings, enjoyed many similarities with the Avadhian nawabs. They too were the first governors of Delhi who took advantage of the unsettled conditions of their time to carve out an independent principality. The instability at the centre then was caused by the raids of Timurlane in A.D.1398. The fierce and learned Mongol-Turk conqueror left behind a vacuum in the Indo-Gangetic plain which was filled in by the Sharquis.

Whenever Delhi grew weak, its political heartland, the Indo-Gangetic plain, acquired an independence of its own. The seat of power shifted, as it were, closer to the real base where imperial developments received a new shape and content. Jaunpur, under Sultan Hussein Sharqui the colourful, licentious, erudite genius of Hindustan, gave final form to the early experiments of khayal music and Rajput-Jain painting[3]. The crude blend of Hindu and Islamic elements, characteristic of Tughlaqi architecture and statecraft, were refined, providing the much needed basis for the full flowering of Mughal composite culture. The city attracted the attention of the Asian mainland and was called the 'Shiraz of the East', a term ascribed to Lucknow in later years.

Jaunpur's rise was also poised between two worlds — the decline of the early Arabic-Persian impulse due to the Mongol raids and the future rise of the Mughals, Safavids and Ottomans. Without the backdrop of Jaunpur, Lucknow's true character is difficult to grasp, though today, Jaunpur is a forgotten backwater of Uttar Pradesh

(UP) with only a few old monuments to remind the historian-biographer of its past importance.

Even during the later years of the Sharqui reign, Lucknow was fast developing as a district market town. In the 1540s Humayun halted in the city to replenish his dwindling resources after being defeated by Shershah Suri in Bihar. The help extended to Humayun at Lucknow was the work of the Sheikhzadas, the earliest surviving peer group in Lucknow. Arabic in origin, the ranks of these wealthy merchants and landholders were soon swelled by a sheikh from Bijnore[4]. In Akbar's time, Sheikh Abdur Rahim went to Delhi to seek his fortune. He returned to Lucknow as the governor of Avadh, encountering the lucky sign of mahi maratib, or the two fishes, while crossing the Ganga. This was the beginning of the Piscean impact on Lucknow. Soon, the symbol of 'two fishes in water', the ultimate mark of tropical sensuality as opposed to the Mediterranean passion of Venus, became the crowning motif of Lucknow.

The symbol was given the status of a royal insignia by the Avadhian nawabs. They took it from the first building which Saadat Khan or Burhan-ul-Mulk, the Persian adventurer from Nishapur, Persia, and the first nawab of Lucknow, wrested in the 1720s from the Sheikhs. Saadat Khan was acting on behest of the Mughal emperor as the new governor of Avadh. That building was the Macchi Bhavan, with the Panch Mahala and the famous Shaikhan gate, bearing the sign of the fishes.

The Macchi Bhavan was destroyed in 1857 and is today linked with a number of past events. It is associated with memories not only of pre-nawabi days, but of a time when Lucknow was perhaps dominated by indigenous tribes and groups on the lower scale of the Varna system. Its construction is attributed to an architect named Lakhna, who was an Ahir by caste. Legend has him playing several roles, principally as the master mason of Abdur Rahim. The ultimate reward for his craftsmanship came when the city adopted his name. Whatever be the truth in the statement, it is fairly certain that the current name dates from the time of Sheikh Rahim. Present-day Yadavs of Avadh also link themselves with Lucknow through

Lakhna. Some claim that Lakhna belonged to a Yadava dynasty which once ruled the area. Though this has yet to be corroborated, historical sources do allude to the rule of the Bhars, still present in Uttar Pradesh and Bihar as backward caste peasants. Pauranic mythology speaks of a time when the area was given by the last Pandava king Janmejaya, to the Rishis. Their power was later usurped by an unknown tribe. The Bhars actually came from Bundelkhand and by the time of Mahmud Ghazni's invasion of north India in the eleventh century, they had independent principalities of their own. Some were feudatories of the Rathore rulers of Kannauj and fell to the superior forces of Muhammad Ghori and Qutubuddin Aibak in the early thirteenth century.

The first dent in Bhar power was made by Syed Salar Masud Ghazi, the mercurial general of Mahmud Ghazni's army, now the revered Ghazi Baba of the countryside of Uttar Pradesh. With one foot in history and one in myth, his tomb in Bahraich, in northeast Avadh is a famed pilgrimage site for both Hindus and Muslims. Ghazi Baba's stature equals that of Hercules or other such epic figures of Western and Semitic lands. He was said to be very tall, a warrior who fought by hand as well as by the sword. He possessed the rough edge of a hunter and the civilised grace of an Islamic civilisation then attempting to introduce a new purpose and meaning to the world — one God, one universe, one brotherhood of man. It was a missionary impulse devoid of the sermon or the exploitative arm of monetary extraction. It was an adventure, a junoon backed by force and the scent of liberation. For Lucknow it produced perhaps, the earliest tomb of the city — that of Malik Adham, one of Syed Salar's lieutenants. He fell fighting somewhere near Lucknow and is buried at a spot sequestered in the heart of the city. It is awe-inspiring — more than seven feet long, tough and large, a reminder of the Herculean stature of the men of those days.

Ghazi Baba's ambiguous position as a conqueror and a saint, someone who subdued the indigenous population yet won them over with devotion and heroism, is typical of Avadh. It is a place where diverse religious and ideological trends came together in unity and conflict to thrash out a single, dominant, stable social-political current. Creative innovation, therefore, went hand in hand with solid conservatism. Here, before the complete triumph of Brahminism, Buddhism enjoyed immense popularity. The Buddha himself hailed from a place in Nepal not far from the Avadh terai. Shravasti, the capital of ancient Koshala at the present day border of Gonda and Bahraich, was his favourite resting place during the era of the first sixteen republics of pre-Mauryan India. Ayodhya itself was a very important centre of Buddhism and during the medieval period, the area could boast of the widest Sufi influence. The Bhakti movement also achieved its classical form at the hands of the saint-poet Tulsidas in Avadh and so did the secular literature of the period. The *Padmavat* of Malik Muhammad Jayasi transformed Avadhi from a local dialect to a refined language, capable of giving secularised and elite expression to the hitherto hidden, and rapturous reflections of the Bhakti impulse.

By the eighteenth century, the Mughal suba of Avadh enjoyed the intractable reputation of a formidable fortress impenetrable to outsiders. Between 1707 and 1722 about thirteen governors were sent from Delhi to Lucknow to secure the province for the crumbling Mughal empire. None succeeded in accomplishing the feat. Instead, successive subedars slowly eroded the central authority and kept on introducing various innovations in the post of the governor. At that time, the relationship between the Mughals and their subordinates was being redefined. There was a demand for greater decentralisation as province after province began breaking away under the overbearing weight of the old Imperial framework[5].

Based on principles of progressive absolutism, this framework rested on the balance of power between regions, status groups, classes and social forces. It also depended on the person of the emperor whose handling could restore, or upset, the whole balance. The Mughal era monetised India's peasant economy and elevated local handicraft production to the artisan-factory level. Cottage industries were integrated in thriving regional and national markets leading to the explosion of entrepreneurial tendencies. The *tour de force* was the linkup of peasant and town economy with world trade and foreign investment[6] in India, a bargain in which the country ended up enjoying an economic surplus. A monarchical, state-backed, peasant-artisan[7] path of commercial capitalist development, it unleashed prosperity and new social forces.

With time, these forces began demanding a share in political power. Revolts by zamindars, peasants and traders made the earlier Mughal arrangement untenable. Change, however, was resisted by old habits and notions and two patterns emerged. Mughal authority was either usurped temporarily or there developed more decentralised extensions of Mughal power. Lucknow provided the model of the latter; here, before anywhere else, concessions were wrenched from the Mughals for a greater role and authority for the governor, including the rights of subedari in other provinces.

The two pioneers in this regard were subedars Chabeele Ram and Girdhar Bahadur[8] who anticipated the exploits of Saadat Khan. They were the first to defy the central authority and create a new independent space for the post of the governor. Their marks are still evident in Lucknow in the form of references to old mohallas and buried buildings. Without their influence, Saadat Khan would have found himself without a legacy to build upon. In A.D.1722 he was neck deep in a sea of revolts and instability and had to virtually fight his way to the heart of Lucknow. Resisted stoutly by the Sheikhs, he won the battle by a combination of diplomacy and military strength. Saadat Khan mobilised the Sheikhs of rural Avadh and made them partners in the new power arrangement that included other Hindu and Muslim zamindars of the province. This meant recognizing the position of groups who had risen recently from village society at the expense of the old Mughal nobility.

But the founder of nawabi Avadh could not stay on in Lucknow. He rented the Macchi Bhavan from its owners and went on to win over the countryside. For this, he pitched his camp near the Saryu — a move which proved crucial for the development of Lucknow. On its banks grew the twin cities of Ayodhya and Faizabad, the first creations of the nawabs, which pioneered the concept of a new township. One, developing, not through the haphazard construction of market places and dwelling quarters in concentric circles, but along roads interspersed with gardens and mansions. For the old town, typical of the Mughal era, the large fort was the natural corollary of the medieval ganj. For the new concept, a large bamboo pavilion with a thatched roof laid the basis of what altered forever, the nature of the royal seat. In Lucknow, no Red Fort was ever built; the nawabs occupied Farhat Baksh palaces, chattar manzils, and Qaiserbaghs. Similarly, the nobles, instead of constructing havelis, built bhawans, kothis and the Avadhian bungalow, a rival of the British inspired Calcutta bungalow.

Faizabad was actually called 'bangla' in the early days, an indication of the primeval impulse it gave to a very cosmopolitan development. For many years, the city remained the capital of Avadh. Saadat Khan's successors, Safdar Jung and Shuja-ud-Daula, stayed in Faizabad, decorating it with new embellishments which soon out-rivalled Lucknow. These were the years of nawabi consolidation when the Nishapuri house was still shaky and a centre proximate to the wild, untamed areas of the northeast Avadh was needed. Later, when stability and political intrigue dictated the final shift to Lucknow in the time of Asaf-ud-Daula, Faizabad remained the outlying inspiration for Lucknow — a city from where it drew much of its exalted recruits in men, women and material design. Even later, it remained the site of the ashraf's adventure and temporary repose: a place where the bangla still retained its pristine innocence and raw energy, much like the river Saryu, in the twin area between the town and the countryside.

Thus, when Lucknow re-established its position after 1775, she carried a fresh world atop an old one. The tortuous lanes of the old city quarters and the chowk, along the mid-west portion, continued to grow with minor modifications. But long, winding and fairly broad avenues with spacious villas and gardens, were established in the eastern, northern and southern parts. These did not constitute an exclusive enclave but the common centre, thereby altering the traditional picture of the Asian city. The change was monumental and not noted by contemporary Western chronicles. Only one French traveller left behind an unnamed account which was to prove prophetic for the future of the city, in ways unintended by its author. It spoke, unnervingly, of a fairyland emerging more beautiful than anything achieved in Europe which if *not checked* will attract like flies men of adventure and intelligence to the Orient.

3

❧❧

The Making of a Culture

In the spring of 1775, a young man stood on the Faizabad-Lucknow road with his entourage. Before him were miles and miles of deciduous shrubs broken intermittently by dune-like mounds. This expanse afforded a strange sight — it resembled the aridity of the desert and yet it was clothed in grass and mud. The river bed had a roughness to it similar to mountainous desert tracks left desolate after a trek. The terrain was broken at points by clusters of trees huddled together in neat rows of unfathomable depth. In the further reaches of the expanse could be seen trees of great beauty, not of peepal, neem or the bargad but of juices, nuts and dates. The sight combined a breathtaking vision of the desert, beach and the marshiness of swamps arousing feelings both of adventure and repose.

The man was Asaf-ud-Daula, the fourth nawab just installed on the masnad of his father Shuja-ud-Daula, who had died in 1774. Shuja-ud-Daula's reign was marked by a combination of violence, subterfuge and suffering — in keeping with the movement of Indian history at that point in time. The years 1754 to 1774, during which Shuja-ud-Daula occupied the seat of his father Safdar Jung as the governor of the Mughal provinces of Allahabad and Avadh, were the decisive years of native and colonial destiny. These were the years which saw the Battle of Plassey. The reformist nawab, Siraj-ud-Daula of Bengal, was defeated by the arms of a force just emerging from its position of trader vassals to that of king makers and eventual kings of Hindustan.

That event in 1757 marked the beginning of a conflict between native and foreign powers for the control of the country. It shifted focus away from the earlier phase which began from Aurangzeb's time and the consequent break up of the Mughal Empire. By the time of Plassey, the main struggle was no longer between the weight and might of the Mughal rulers and their former subordinates. The Marathas had already carved out a principality for themselves and were fast on their way to becoming a paramount power. The Sikhs too, despite their factional differences, were consolidating behind the revived power of the misls or brotherhood, later to provide the basis for a regional kingdom. Smaller forces like the Jats and Rajasthani Rajputs had also established their principalities. Breakaway Mughal provinces like Avadh, Hyderabad and Bengal were autonomous subas and new forces had emerged in the Indo-Gangetic plain, the heartland of the Mughal Empire. Rohilla Pathans and Bhumihars had anchored themselves towards the west and the east, first as revenue collectors and then as petty nawabs and rajas.

On the eve of the Battle of Plassey, the class struggle within the Indian subcontinent, encompassing the Mughal state, jagirdars, merchants, zamindars, peasants, traders, intellectuals and artisans had come full circle. Many of the erstwhile rebels were now in power and the Mughal state was a dismal image of its former self. A new class base of zamindars, traders, townsmen, professional soldiers, peasants, entrepreneurs and portfolio capitalists competed for a stake in political power. Spread over the length and breadth of the subas and petty kingdoms, they were redefining the very nature of Indian polity.

In the middle of the pre-Plassey, post-Mughal period, the erstwhile contenders of the Mughals, however, were caught in a paradox. The breakdown of the old political order had impaired the political unity of the land leaving the field wide open for foreign interventions and attack. Supporters of pax-Mughalia also realised that the Empire could not be revived on the earlier basis. The turbulent situation began unleashing radical thinking. It was around this time that Shah Waliullah, the scholar-polymath-theologian of Delhi, came up with his penetrating analysis of the decline of the Mughal Empire. He specifically mentioned the over-taxation of the peasantry in his economic treatise and urged for a more equitable social order.

When French liberals were hedging their bets on democracy, 'the queen of all concepts', in the salons of Paris, Shah Waliullah was building a theory of Asiatic revolution in the madarsas of Delhi. He envisaged great civilisations passing into a stage where power begins to alternate between one rich person and another, and where the traders, the poor, the helpless and the labour class are deprived of their economic and political rights as the government becomes corrupt and dictatorial. It then becomes legitimate for the exploited and over-taxed subjects to proclaim 'inquilab' (revolution) against the state power. First protests and demonstrations are organised, followed by meetings, and raising of issues in the press. If everything fails, direct action and an armed fight to the finish is sought. After immense sacrifices and bloodshed, the government is overthrown and peace and prosperity reigns in place of chaos and confusion[1].

Here was a bold example of a radical Islamic framework analysing contemporary historical and social problems, and coming close to a concept of bourgeoisie-peasant revolution. On religious issues, Shah Waliullah took the path of research, enquiry and ijtihad (independent thinking), committing the then heretical act of translating the Koran into Persian. He established the historical basis of Islamic traditions and commended evolution, rather than closed thinking, in this sphere. Reformist enquiry by the Sunni Islamic Ulema had reached the point of allowing contraceptives with the consent of the partner by Aurangzeb's time[2]. But Shah Waliullah went a step further by attempting a reconciliation between Shias, Sunnis, Sufis, the four schools of jurisprudence and various other Islamic sects. He recognised the validity of the Hindu path to knowledge, God and truth and probed into the nature of other religions of the Indian subcontinent. A number of hostile, Muslim and non-Muslim opponents developed whom he combated with the force of ideas, arms and a glittering litany of followers. His was a progressive fundamentalism which unleashed a political movement for the liberation of the peasantry and the country in the nineteenth century from the yoke of British and native feudalism.

Shah Waliullah also attacked the contemporary ruling classes for their weaknesses — a theme which was to later echo in poetry through the pen of Mir Taqi Mir and Sauda[3]. Mir even came close to offering a socialist critique of the rich:

> *Na baith ab ameeron ki sohbat mein mir*
> *Hue hain faqir inki daulat se hum*
> (Do not sit in the company of the rich o' mir
> We have become beggars because of their wealth)

Mir's flamboyant alter ego in Agra, Nazir Akbarabadi, took poetry to the streets in the same period. This 'peoples poet,' was also a born actor. He wore the Toshdani cap, smoked the twirled hookah and celebrated everything from ata to 'Bal Krishna' of the common street gentry. His only parallel was the radical street bards of the Latin America of the '60s.

Parallel to these radical critiques the current of modern, indigenous rationalism was also emerging. Its seeds were sown in the Mughal empire from the time of Akbar. The rationalising and reforming policies of his state provided the context for the pioneering work of a team of economists, adventurers, statesmen, artists, scientists, doctors and men of wisdom. Khwaja Shah Mansur, the physicist-polymath Fazlullah Shirazi, Hakim Abdul Fateh Gilani, Abul Fazal and Raja Todar Mal wrote financial treatise, went into the field as activists and conducted experiments in physics, astronomy and medicine. They revived secular traditions of ancient India in a way that a straight line ran from *Arthashastra* to *Ain-i-Akbari* and from Kamasutra to the Mughal nude. Mahabharata and Ramayana, Brahminism and non-Brahminism, Charaka and Panini, Maurya and Gupta came alive in a new version of cultural, political and economic nationalism. But Mughal modernism was not the secularism of Pandit Jawaharlal Nehru — it looked neither towards the West, nor towards an abstract 'idea' of India, for inspiration. Caste and religion were neither manipulated nor swept under the carpet. From Kabul to the Deccan, the Mughal non-religious, non-casteist, non-regionalist traditions carried, in full measure, the spunk of the Bhumihaar, the spine of the Turani, the pride of the Multani, the mark of the Mewari, the akkhadpan of the Bihari, the stubbornness of the Dakhani. Based on a reduction of caste, religious and regional feeling to practical social 'gestures' and symbols, it celebrated, rationalised, secularised and universalised deep primeval and emotional impulses. This trend spilled over to the seventeenth century in the form of writer-philosophers such as Mulla Mahmud Jaunpuri, Abdul Halim Sialkoti, Mulla Muhammad Harafi and Danishmand Khan.

These men did not merely improve upon the works by Arabic, Persian, Moorish and Central Asian scholars. They developed extraordinary, almost unbelievable insights of their own. This churning produced the 'scientific', Persian verses of Mirza Abdul Qadir Bedil, the noted mystic, prose writer and poet from Delhi and Patna who lived around the time of Aurangzeb. He was to enjoy, later, the status of a national hero in Afghanistan and several Central Asian countries. His 'mysticism', in the best traditions of Sufism, was the visionary path to secular knowledge, truth and this-wordly grace. A hundred and twenty-five years before Darwin and Marxism, and quite a few years before the onset of French enlightenment and materialism, he wrote:

> *Haich shakle be hevalli qabil soorat na shad*
> *aadmi hum pesh azan aadmi bood bozeena bood*
> (Nothing takes shape without raw material
> Man, before he became man was a monkey)

Echoing similar sentiments and temperament, Mir Taqi Mir was to say later in the eighteenth century in Urdu:

> *Ab aese hain ki saneh ke mizaj upar baham pahunche*
> *Jo khatir khwah apne ham hue hote to kya hote*
> (Such as we are, God fashioned us close to His heart's desire:

If we had been what we had wished, what might we
not have been!)

Hain mushte khaak lekin jo kuch hai mir hum hain
Maqdoor se zyadah maqdoor hai hamara
(Made from clay — but what we are, we are
Our power is greater than the power God gave us)

The seventeenth century also saw an unprecedented expansion
in trade and industry and the growth of 'modern', erotic poetry in
the regional dialect. This was the reetkala poetry of Jehangir's court
and the Mughal 'city'. Written in Braj — the dialect of the middle
Doab of the Indo-Gangetic plain comprising the countryside of Agra,
the then capital of the Mughal Empire — it catered to the refined
demands of an urbane society. As if commemorating its times and
deeds, a poet exclaimed in a moment of unusual candour — 'my heart
rests upon the amorous time, my head on its lap. The beloved asks
not my destination but follows her own in lovemaking'.

Reetkala gave voice to the needs of women and fulfilled a very
important social and economic function. It reflected a growing
sensuality of taste which in turn stimulated the market forces of the
Mughal economy by increasing the demand for luxury goods. At
the same time, women were freed from traditional roles of wives,
mothers and sisters. In the seventeenth century, Mughal princesses
owned fleets of ships and Radha made love to Krishna as a 'subject':

Radha Hari Hari Radhika, bani aye sanketa
Dampati rati biparit sukha, sahaja suratahum leta
(Exchanging clothes Radha and Krishna came to the
rendezvous for love making
She was on top but dressed as a man
So they got the thrill of novelty, even while seeming to
make love in the normal way)

The fillip given to rational and sensual feelings emboldened the
further growth of radical currents at the grassroots. Lower caste
saints donned the mantle of Bhaktism, edging out the domination
of old, upper caste figures. The Bhakti movement itself had

evolved as a response to the new conditions of the fourteenth and fifteenth century. In this period, the Indian subcontinent woke up from a long slumber to the new ideas of Islam and the Indo-Persian, Turkish sultanates. These sultanates, especially from the time of the Khiljis, were trying to modernise the native ethos and indigenise Central and Middleast Asian influences. Their interest was the creation of a subcontinental empire — a dream realised by Akbar — based on modern notions of citizenry, accountancy, politicking and geography. They unleashed a great humanizing drive which saw a personality like Amir Khusro[4] underwriting the voice of the suppressed woman with a tone of desire:

> *Shabane hijra daraz chun zulf va roze vaslat chun umra*
> *kotaah — sakhi piya ko jo main na dekhoon to kaise*
> *kaatun andheri ratiyan —*
> (This night of separation is as long as a tress but the
> day of meeting is as short as an age
> O' my friend, if I don't see my beloved how will I
> spend these dark nights?)

Khusro wrote the first line in Persian and the second in Hindi. The first denoted a restrained, sensational, desirous 'manner', the second a pretty and raspurna bhaav. The first blended philosophy with poetry — 'the night of separation as long as a tress, the day of meeting as short as an age'. The second blended practical empiricism — 'if I don't see my beloved' — with emotion 'how will I spend these dark nights'. One was a 'statement'; the other a complaint. Both had no connection; and yet they were intimately linked. Between dialectical logic and sentimental metaphysics, Khusro created two lines which alone could stand up to the best poetry produced anywhere in the world and summed up what the effect of Indo-Persianism in culture was going to be.

Born at Etah in the middle Doab[5] and bred in Delhi, Khusro's sensuality anticipated reetkala. His humanism embraced every relation: pupil and master, husband and wife, son and mother. When his friend, philosopher and guide Nizammuddin Auliya, the great Sufi of the Chishti order, who accomplished in the realm of intuition and ideas what Khusro achieved in the real n of letters, died, Khusro said:

> *Gori sove sej par mukh par dhare kes*
> *Chal khusro ghar aapne rain bhayi chahundes*
> (The fair one is sleeping on a bed of flowers, hair strewn on the face
> Go, Khusro, to your house, night has fallen in every direction)

A late thirteenth, early fourteenth century warrior, statesman, Sufi, mathemetician and diplomat, Khusro was the first to codify Indian music. He invented the tabla and the sitar apart from celebrating and theorising the earthy world of masti, logic and passion. 'Tarana' was another of his inventions, perhaps the first musical form to classify the non-religious feeling of pleasure. He rescued classicism from stultifying meditativeness by laying down the foundation of the khayal — a form of cerebral, mood music. Khusro rediscovered the rugged, spunky gesture of ancient Indian art in the qawwali, the epic musical form of valorous oath-taking (qaul or vachan). Arriving in Hindustan on the sensual and spiritual bandwagon of the Sufis from Arabia and Persia, the qawwali soon became synonymous with Khusro's Indraprastha or Delhi school of music. Khusro blended the seven tone, modal, Persian scale of the qaul with the five tone music found in the Deccan to produce the khayal. His classification was picked up by musicians of Vijaynagar and Tanjore who later formulated the seventy-two modes of Carnatic music.

Projecting the tenets of medieval Indian culture from Jaunpur to Lucknow to the south was also Khusro's contribution. He gave Indo-Persian refinement a rural and vernacular base and dehati languages a Persian 'manner'. He was the one who discovered Khari Boli with its straightforward yet angular structure — *Jaise lathi aur phool* (like a stick and a flower). This he called Hindawi which became the basis of both Urdu and Hindi. He was truly the first modern personality, a supra Dante, of the new age.

Amir Khusro's stress on the vernacular anticipated the Bhakti movement and the assertion of local languages against the formal use of Sanskrit, just as Bhakti anticipated the assertion of the middle and lower social orders against older secular and religious hierarchy. The combined thrust of these two movements was not only critical but also negative. Bhaktism gave the image of a new humanist ruler exemplified in the figure of Rama and a new personal god, Krishna. Tulsidas's *Ramcharitmanas* is a long treatise on the virtues of humane, valorous and universal kingship which comes close to the ideals set by Akbar, a contemporary of Tulsidas[6]. Habituated to the 'deen-heen- dukhi' (poor and sad) image of Tulsidas, later generations found it hard to digest the valour and pluck of this visionary Brahmin whose original gesture was preserved in thinly extant tracts of Indo-Persian literature.

By the seventeenth century, Bhakti had embraced the atheistic and the rebellious in the form of Pran Nath and Bab Lal, two Shudra poets of north India. However, the eighteenth century turned out to be even more remarkable. The rationalist school was institutionalised under the aegis of the Firangi Mahal of Lucknow, that great centre of Islamic thought. Theology brushed shoulders with science in the two rooms bequeathed to the descendants of the great scholar, Mulla Qutubuddin Sihali, by Aurangzeb. Qutubuddin Sihali[7] was linked to the school of Shaikh Daniyal of Chaurasa and through him to Abdus Salam Dewa, the chief mufti (religious scholar) of the Mughal army in the seventeenth century, and Abdus Salam Lahori, the direct disciple of Fazlullah Shirazi himself.

These intellectuals of Avadhi qasbas established Dars-i-Nizammiya, the curriculum of Mulla Nizammuddin[8], Mulla Qutubuddin's son. The world of learning was not the same thereafter. Dars-i-Nizammiya gave more emphasis to Islamic rational sciences, as opposed to the revealed sciences. Logic, philosophy and dialectics gained precedence over the study of the Koran, traditions and law. This rationalism under Mughal patronage invoked parallels with the radical Mutazilite current of the Abbasid caliphate in ninth century Arabia. But Mulla Nizammuddin's aim was also to create an Indo-Persian professional: a person trained to be a lawyer, judge, administrator or a businessman, with skilled expertise in the complex and sophisticated bureaucratic and commercial systems of seventeenth and eighteenth century India. Scholars of Dars-i-Nizammiya spread the torch of enlightenment to Hyderabad, Arcot and Bengal. Students arrived from Sinkiang, Afghanistan and Central Asia making the school a cosmopolitan centre of Asia. In the nineteenth century, when universities sprang up in Egypt, Iraq and Turkey, post-classical commentaries on rational sciences in their syllabus were mostly of Avadhi origin.

Mulla Nizammuddin died in 1748, and Shah Waliullah in 1763. By then the old order was all but gone. Nadir Shah invaded India in 1739 and ransacked Delhi. His invasion announced the beginning of a post-Mughal situation, but his target was still the old imperial seat of the Mughal empire. When Clive attacked not the Mughal emperor but the new man of the eighteenth century, Siraj-ud-Daula, he signified a new phase. From now on, the chief contradiction was between the Mughal empire, the host of post-Mughal states deriving their legitimacy from the Mughal name, and the East India Company representing Great Britain, the emerging European imperial power.

The reign of Shuja-ud-Daula was informed by the vicissitudes of this new situation. While conflict raged on with the Marathas and the Rohillas, a war with the Company was becoming more and more inevitable. The time of kingly adventure, of kingdom making, territory grabbing and political entrepreneurship, so typical of Shuja-ud-Daula's father Safdar Jung, was coming to a close. Safdar Jung was probably the last full-bodied figure of the previous era — a man steeped in the valorous traditions of the Mughals, a figure who relied on the cavalry rather than the infantry and open conflict in place of subtle politicking. Like his father-in-law, Burhan-ul-Mulk, he was involved in the intrigues of the Mughal court and at one point camped outside the capital in order to physically fight his claim as the Wazir of the empire. Unlike his son years later, Safdar Jung aim was to acquire the highest position at Delhi and establish a pan-north Indian influence. He was the last figure of the Nishapuri dynasty to link his dominions in Avadh and Allahabad with ambitions in Kashmir, Punjab and Malwa.

In Safdar Jung's time, the affairs of Avadh were looked after by his naib, Nawal Rai, a Saksena Kayastha, well-schooled in the art of Indo-Persian administration. Nawal Rai was a powerful man and so was Atma Ram Khattri, the favourite administrator of Burhan-ul-Mulk. Both Nawal Rai and Atma Ram symbolised the early generation of qasba Hindu professionals — people who could wield the pen as well as the sword, who were as adept in the vernacular Avadhi as in Persian and Urdu. In the Mughal period, these men patronised reetkala poetry, dhrupad music and gave shape to Ilmus-us-Siyaq, the Islamic-Vaishya syncretic school of Mughal accountancy.

This composite culture, which separated personal faith from social and political calling, ended up redefining the tradition of Muslims and Hindus. Many of the rites and rituals that later became an integral part of Brahminical society were actually codified and created by the Mughals. The evidence for this is sketchy and lost in family memories and some surviving customs. But it is suggestive enough to alter the whole notion of an exclusive caste-Hindu, village society remaining largely untouched by Turkish and Mughal currents in religious and social matters.

The base of Brahmins, since the time of the Gupta dynasty, was Kannauj, just a few hundred kilometers west of Lucknow. Along with Kannauj, northwest Avadh constituted the paramount belt of the Kanyakubja Brahmins: the centre of their secular and not religious power. This was the region with the maximum land grants to the Brahmins, where they ate meat, trained as warriors and married outside their caste[9]. When Akbar occupied the throne in Agra, Abdur Rahim, his governor in Lucknow, brought and settled a few Brahmins in the city[10]. They were called Vajpeyis on account of the 'Vajpeyi yagya' which they performed. Soon they established themselves as townsmen. But Akbar's greatest innovation lay in creating a landed hierarchy of Kanyakubja Brahmins. The now famed and exclusive Bees (20) Biswa, Unees (19) Biswa Brahmins of Kannauj[11] and Avadh were a product of Mughal social engineering. Mughal political science altered the social structure by creating and legitimising non-traditional professional castes, the Kayasthas and the Khatris. It also introduced new, non-caste groups, such as the Jais disciples[12] of Din-e-Ilahi, who bore absolutely no links with ancient Hindu or Muslim traditions.

This fact and circumstance played a great role in Avadh during the nawabi period — it created a class of Brahmin and Kayastha landlords, moneylenders, businessmen, professionals and intellectuals who affected modern north Indian life down to the British period and after. Similarly, in the Maithal region of north Bihar, Maithal Brahmins adopted the title of Thakur in Akbar's time and emerged as rulers and professionals all over east and north India.

Nawal Rai's loyalty and professional calling led him to lay down his life for Safdar Jung in a battle against the Rohillas. But this was the last instance of a major battle being fought at home, in Avadh, without the presence of the nawab-vazir himself. When Safdar Jung died, his son built a mausoleum for him in Delhi. The tomb of Safdar Jung was the first and last Avadh style building in Delhi. It remains one of the few examples of walled columns, turrets and pavilions existing on a tomb. These features were to later become the standard marks of the Delhi haveli design. This was also the only Avadhi building constructed in the classical haveli style — Shuja-ud-Daula in keeping with the times was to adopt a form of baroque romanticism in Faizabad while building the pioneering Gulab Bari.

Shuja-ud-Daula was placed firmly in his seat by the Mughal emperor Alamgir-II. But Delhi had become unsafe and constricted. With Plassey the drama had shifted to the east. Intrigues in the former Mughal seat led to the blinding of Shah Alam-II, the successor to Alamgir-II. Yet, this represented no unremitting picture of misery or Mughal decline. New equations were being forged at the Mughal court and the emperor himself was gearing up for the eastern theatre. Until then, Avadh had had to look towards Delhi but now the latter sought the protection of the vassal. Soon, Shuja-ud-Daula became the main force behind the emperor. After Plassey, it was inevitable that a second, more decisive round of battle was forthcoming. The concessions being wrought by the British from the Mughals amounted to a virtual usurpation of sovereignty. The British may have used the Mughal name, at least till 1857, while perpetuating their rule. But indigenous powers knew from the beginning that temporary compromises notwithstanding, there could be no permanent alliance with the 'firangi'.

The Battle of Plassey was followed by the Battle of Buxur in 1764. An alliance of Shah Alam, Shuja-ud-Daula and Mir Qasim, the governor of Bengal, confronted the Company forces under the leadership of the Avadhian nawabs. The significance of the coming together of three indigenous powers who were previously divided was not lost on the victors or the vanquished. The alliance was defeated after a bloody fight which saw thousands killed on both sides. For Avadh, it was a day of calamity— folklore kept alive the 'fact' that in a single night, 1700 wives broke their bangles in one area of Barabanki alone. They belonged to the Qidwai clan whose 1700 warriors preferred to lay down their lives at Buxur rather than retreat and show their defeated faces. The Company made Shuja-ud-Daula pay the cost of the war and forced him to sign a pact of mutual defence. Trade concessions were wrenched and Allahabad was taken away to serve as Shah Alam's virtual jailhouse.

Officially, Shuja-ud-Daula acquiesced to the wishes of the Company and the Marathas stepped in as protectors of the Mughal house. But the anti-British struggle did not cease in Avadh. It only assumed a subsumed and concealed character. From now on Avadhian nawabs would never clash with the British in the open, there was going to be no repeat of Buxur. But every treaty, every clause, every gesture of friendship was accompanied by a silent veil of violence, conspiracy and one-upmanship. In this, neither side brooked any quarter and the nawabs often paid with their lives. Right from Shuja-ud-Daula's time this was to be a battle of shadows — a fight without the clang of swords or the fire of muskets, manipulated through the smooth and deadly weapon of political diplomacy.

It began right after the defeat at Buxur when Shuja-ud-Daula began improving his army. He set for himself a modern European standard, knowing fully well that the days of decentralised Mughal armies manning defensive forts and then routing the enemy through a cavalry charge were well nigh over. It was now the time of drilled infantry supported by cannon fire in the open field— a tactic which had won for the British the fatal hour of Plassey and Buxur.

Shuja-ud-Daula succeeded in re-building his army by the late 1760s. It was so strong that contemporary travellers went on record to state its superiority to Company troops. Sensing the inevitable, the British immediately ordered the nawab to demobilise his forces. Shuja-ud-Daula dithered — his mind was as much on the military aspects of the struggle as on the political. The balance of forces at that time was not favourable. The Mughal emperor was still in exile in Allahabad. The Marathas had yet to come out from their defeat in the Third Battle of Panipat to resume their ascendancy under the leadership of Mahadji Scindia. And in the south, Indian powers were locked in a struggle from which Mysore emerged later as a clear leader. Inappropriate also, was the situation nearer home in the subas of Allahabad, Agra and Rohilkhand. Shuja-ud-Daula's friend Muhammad Khan Bangash, the nawab of Farrukhabad who had advised him to stay on and consolidate his forces at Faizabad instead of moving to Lucknow, was now dead. The other power on whom he could rely, that of Hafiz Rehmat Khan of Rohilkhand, a warrior-statesman in Shuja-ud-Daula's league, was inimical towards him. Later Shuja-ud-Daula was to fight a battle against Hafiz Rehmat with the help of the British and seize his territories. Hafiz Rehmat was to lose his life and Shuja-ud-Daula condemned as a tool in the Company's hands. But reality was more complicated. Before the conflict, Shuja-ud-Daula had sent a letter to Hafiz Rehmat Khan suggesting a joint war against the Company. The letter found its way to the British. Somehow, through the deft manipulation of a sympathetic munshi, Shuja-ud-Daula saved his skin. But he got the notion that it was Rehmat Khan who had leaked the letter. He demanded money owed to him by the Rohilkhand nawab as part of compensation for help in a previous anti-Maratha campaign. Rehmat Khan was taken aback and Shuja-ud-Daula presented before the Company the pact of mutual defence[13].

But the outcome did not imply victory for Shuja-ud-Daula. It reflected more a tragedy of epic proportions where two similar men with more or less similar visions became entangled in a web of betrayal and lost sight of the larger political objective. This was a tragedy of the Mughal military-warrior ethic of which both were a part — an ethic which had provided the basis for both to modernise. Shuja-ud-Daula died soon afterwards leaving behind an expanded Avadh and unfulfilled dreams of combating the British.

The man who stood surveying the plains of Avadh in the spring of 1775 inherited this troubled legacy. His accession was confirmed by the British who celebrated the onset of the new ruler in public with an array of adjectives in private. The incumbent prince was described as obese, a pervert, juvenile and a sodomist. This judgement persisted to such an extent that contemporary scholars, Indian and European alike, have quoted verbatim from an opinion which originated from such a messy and dubious source such as East India Company officials. They, in accordance with the constant wails of the British government itself, were charlatans and opportunists of the worst sort. Condemning easterners while indulging in heathen pleasures was a convenient way to get into the good books of the Parliament in London. British politicians too fanned their partisan probity as it suited their plan of defaming and controlling Avadh.

The making of Asaf-ud-Daula and his personality set off a trend of cultural and political conflict which persisted till 1856. One of Asaf-ud-Daula's first acts as nawab was to further exacerbate his defamation. Mirza Amani's[14] personality remained, all through, a deliberate spectacle of pagan outlandishness. Unlike his father, who hid his amorous passions behind the sombre-warrior ethic, Amani was an exhibitionist untrammelled by an outward show of moral behaviour. In many of his juvenile acts, he struck a posture of being foolish and clownish. But all the while he was laughing surreptitiously at the fools he made of others. During the spring tours, when he introduced himself to his subjects, he often got drunk and his friends displayed behaviour which shocked the Company officials. But the Company mandarins, interested in renewing his father's treaty on more favourable terms than before, overlooked an important factor. The spring tour also marked the beginning of Asaf-ud-Daula's famous munificence and accessibility to the people. In fact, Mirza Amani's unpopularity with the Company stood in direct proportion to his popularity with the subjects. He was the one who gave the culture of Avadh and Lucknow its present status — scholars, poets, adventurers, entrepreneurs, hakims, engineers, soldiers had started gathering at Faizabad during the time of Shuja-ud-Daula. But it was under Amani that the capital was shifted to Lucknow. The city was then a backwater compared to Faizabad, yet her disadvantageous, uneven topography and irregular spread was turned into a primary raw material for a modern township. This style of construction, which refined the crude, followed the sensational eighteenth century boom in town building, then in vogue from Travancore to Jaipur via Poona and Saurashtra. All of these places had renaissance men as their leaders. And all of them were touched by some form of Indo-Persian vermilion.

Shuja-ud-Daula and his uncle Salar Jung, the chief cultural patron of Burhan-ul-Mulk's and Safdar Jung's time, belonged to a period of transition between Delhi and Lucknow. At a time when the Avadhian capital was still in Faizabad, Salar Jung invited Khan-e-Arzu, the ustad of Mir Taqi Mir and Sauda, to Lucknow. A Persian scholar, Khan-e-Arzu also pioneered Urdu poetry, expounding the tradition of Quli Qutub Shah, Pandit Chanda Bhan 'Brahmin' and Wali, the first architects of Urdu. Many of his experiments in linguistics were conducted in Lucknow. Khan-e-Arzu died during Shuja-ud-Daula's reign which saw other masters like Ashraf Ali Khan Fughan, Mir Zahik and Mir Fakhir Makhan arrive from Delhi. It appears that by that time Avadh was already becoming a centre of Urdu poetry, but though the form took on a distinct Lucknowi tone, the thematic material harked back to Delhi. Khan-e-Arzu's experiment with rekhta, the mixed, refined form of Urdu, were also confined to introducing the personal voice and the more correctly rhyming metrical structure. The content of his poetry, as developed by his legendary pupils, was based on the great interplay of ideas which characterised the Delhi school.

Western critics were to later reduce the ghazal to a poetic form mired in the medieval form of love. They were to see its panegyrics as an artistic equivalent to despotic thought. In this view, sentiments of pain and separation were a response to societal constrictions and unrequited love.

To them, Mir would have replied — 'how could I tell my tale in this strange land, I speak a tongue they do not understand'. For Mir was first and foremost a poet of the 'idea' of love. His poetry encompassed the positive, amorous, imaginative side of passion, painting a 'full' picture of the bodice—

Gundh ke goya patti gul ki voh tarkib banayi hai,
Rang badan ka tab dekho jab choli bhige pasine mein.

(As if a plan has been hatched by plotting the petal of flowers — see the colour of the body when the sweat soaks through the bodice)

The impact of this school was also felt in the poetry of Mir Hasan, the son of Mir Zahik and the composer of the masnavi '*Sihr-ul-Bayan*', literally, *The Enchanting Story*. The masnavi was a revolutionary form in its day as it introduced the long narrative and loosened the verse for freer interplay of the senses. Mir Hasan hailed from Delhi and the bayan was still about emotions, feelings, longings and descriptiveness of 'ideas'. Yet, its style throbbed and pulsated with the erotic. Meaning was communicated not in a single whole but through fragmentary parts. Its instant popularity marked the mid-point from where the Delhi school passed into Lucknow — from where ideas and emotions crossed over to gesture and sensuality.

The cultural synthesis forged by Asaf-ud-Daula took off from exactly this juncture. By his time the Sufi ideal of personal suffering, love for nature, simple living and high thinking was long since over. It was a time of celebration and the appropriation of things material. The period of Asaf-ud-Daula's high culture was also marked by revived interest in the fabulousness of the East by a Europe passing through wealth, opportunity, innovation, enlightenment and romanticism. There was a new youthful energy in the air compromised in Lucknow only by the increasingly constricted political position of the nawab. Looking back, it seems extraordinary how he survived the first few years of his reign. Treaties, which made the nawab pay several times more than his father, were renegotiated and a huge Company force, plus a 'resident', was imposed on him. In addition, he had to turn a blind eye to the depredations of the traders and the officials of the Company hell bent on tapping whatever source of wealth they could find. Often, it was the Company, and not the nawab's men, who directly exploited the people. At one point, the Company officials began to bleed the treasury dry while monopolising leading articles of trade at the expense of Avadhi traders. But Mirza Amani too replied in an ingenious way. He closed the areas of revenue demand, which appeared to the Britishers as the most profitable source of wealth, by expressing his helplessness in making his subjects pay. From here stemmed the myopic literature about the Avadhian countryside being in constant revolt due to the severe exactions of the nawab's amils.

This was one amongst the many ruses played by the court of Lucknow on the British. Another form of subterfuge rested in hiding areas of trade and appearing parsimonious, even miserly. Asaf-ud-Daula attracted notoriety for not paying foreigners who visited his court in search of fame and fortune. They were often treated with nice words, plenty of work but little money. The nawab made favourites of Europeans and then did not pay them as they could have escaped to Europe with his money!

These tactics paid off and the Company was forced to review the treaty. Governor General Warren Hastings came down personally to Lucknow the demands on the nawab were lessened and the interference of the resident curbed. The new treaty gave the nawab relevant power to bring foreign influences under his control. From now on, Europeans looked to him for favour and redressal. Many Europeans were packed off while travellers from Asiatic countries participated more and more in the glories of the Lucknow court. Asaf-ud-Daula crowned his 'triumph' with the completion of a commercial treaty in 1788 which ended the Company's monopoly on saltpetre. It also imposed restrictions on the Company's license of duty free trade. Exemptions from Company laws on nawabi territories were won for Indian traders. This was vital as it unleashed the long suppressed local potential in commerce.

Trade by Indian merchants had never stopped even during the worst days of Company depredations. But the lessening of British influence did something more than allowing Avadhi traders to participate in the lucrative plying of goods from Lucknow to Calcutta. Political initiative once again passed over to the Lucknowi court. Suddenly, the real significance of Asaf-ud-Daula's reign began to be felt. This was a reign which initiated a conscious policy of commercialisation. An open, internal economy based on the specialisation of articles, from the polishing of the ruby to the feathers of a cap came up. Here, each and every item, however useless it may have been, was raised to the level of industry. This specialisation resulted in production of various types of the same article — seven or eight varieties of shoes accessible even to the ordinary man, fifteen types of perfumes suitable not only to the seasons but also to the vagaries of mood. More than a dozen designs of chandeliers, dressing tables and mirrors were available, alongwith a whole range of clothing to meet the demands of every class. This was no medieval artisan production as it centralised skills developing at isolated, local centres.

The market responded immediately — ganjs sprang up all over Lucknow to supply the city with the adequate amount of foodgrain and to take its product into the countryside. In small towns, officials and courtiers of the nawab created their own mini Lucknows with local traditions and cuisine. The famed eighteen[15] towns of Avadh sprang up and the nawab was able to consolidate his hold over the province of Allahabad. Towns in Avadh and Allahabad soon began to carry their own brand of trade, industry, school of thought, sport, festivity and poetry. The portly man sitting at Lucknow was now having the last laugh. On the one hand, he compromised politically, showed his preference for foreign goods and enhanced his reputation as a decadent eastern king. On the other, he encouraged oilseed and ghee production in Sandila, sword and 'talvaar paani' manufacture in Sandi, the making of bamboo sticks, chairs, durries, carpets in Balrampur, Shahbad, Khairabad and the production of 'baandhs' or bed material in Leharpur. His hakims and amils build sarais, constructed bridges and provided land for the town ganjs. They also set about discovering cash crops and the potential which existed in each region for a marketable fruit product.

A lot of adventure went into the making of this history. Various patterns were added to the bridges out of the love for a beloved. Ganj patterns were changed in order to accommodate the mood of local talent. Export-import depots linked domestic consumption with external impetus. In this way, a situation was created in which the tanda jamdani textile cloth, an erstwhile Company monopoly, took on the characteristic of both a local speciality and an object of wonder in European capitals. Till that time, the malmal of Dhaka had inspired awe in the subcontinent and beyond. Based on a special type of hybrid cotton, its beauty rested in skills of weaving and spinning. Tanda cloth embarked on a different path— it was made from a new type of imported Egyptian cotton and Japanese silk. Softer and malleable with a transparent sheen, it was lit up by the exquisite Avadhi 'kadhai' or embroidery which became a primary quality in itself; perhaps, the famed chikan work of Lucknow also originated in this fashion. Lucknowi embroidery pre-dated the nawabi period, but its evolution as a style of clothing was a specific contribution of Asaf-ud-Daula. Compared to the printed shades of the Benarsi style, chikan embroidery was less luxurious. Yet it produced a unique mix of rich texture and easy flamboyance — luxurious but impressionistic, displaying more sheen in appearance than in material.

The same combination and effect was repeated on buildings where plaster work gave an impression akin to the white marble of the Mughals. This, then, became the hallmark of Lucknowi culture — it began with the minimal and created the grand, it began with tradition and created modernity. This was a culture which produced a new mode of architecture with the locally available lakhauri brick. The building material was made up of urad ki daal (lentils) besides other such unconventional materials, and the building foundations were kept moist instead of dry.

This was how the great Imambara came to be built. In the early part of the 1780s, north India was hit by the catastrophic Chalisa famine. It wiped out many hapless Indians caught between the decline of an order which had provided relief during such calamities in the past and the uncertainties of the new Company raj. The famine was no less severe than the Bengal famine of the 1760s which was brought about by the policies of the Company. A saying went around in north India in those days that fate was playing a trick on the Hindustanis for having lost the Battle of Buxur just as it had made the people of Bengal suffer a decade earlier for the defeat in Plassey.

But fate had not envisaged the shrewdly innovative and sensitive ruler of Lucknow. Mirza Amani's response to the crisis was very different both from the past rulers and the fumblings of the East India Company. He came up with a quintessentially Lucknowi response — instead of keeping a low profile and letting the crisis blow over, or initiating relief in the old kingly style, he embarked on a plan of 'building in the time of famine'. British officials sharpened their pens for another round of attack on what was bound to appear as the best proof of Asaf-ud-Daula's callousness and anti-public sentiments. But they were surprised and outwitted once again in the battle of shadows. Mirza Amani enrolled the services of the great Iranian architect, Kifayat Ullah and opened the very process of construction to the public. In Lucknow, during the days of the famine, there were no sights of wailing beggars, famished citizenry and dying hordes. Who could have perished unsung when a great task was on just a few miles away in the western end of the city? There were scenes of the Shureifa — the distinguished middle class — composed of lower level officials, pensioners, courtiers, doctors, employees and maulvis, bearing their suffering with dignity, working during the night with torches. People who thronged from the countryside were first fed in the makeshift alms houses and then directed to workplaces where the building of the Imambara proceeded according to plan and constant innovation.

Asaf-ud-Daula was constructing a religious building; yet his interest was in duplicating the concept of a hall. At that time in Europe, behind the classical architecture of Palladio and Christopher Wren, was emerging the style of the majestic indoor. John Adams had already arrived with his artistic 'floor' and the ceiling; a long way off in Persia, buildings around Isfahan exhibited the feel of the warm, luxurious room full of pearls and flowers.

In Lucknow, without the direct impact of Adams, an entirely fresh experiment was conducted. Three great halls, with front portions extended by the open aangan or courtyard, were created. A flight of steps was added in the style of a modern country house. In the central hall there stood a rectangular ceiling, while round domes occupied the same space in the two adjacent rooms. The floor spread out to the same angle — the middle one like a straight walk on a pathway, two adjacent ones like round posts. From the exterior, the building looked like a long column of brick, similar to the beautiful, long vault of the cupboard. The interior was like a restaurant of the early 1960s — the same baroquian hangover of darkness in light, the same effect of tinkering chandeliers in cave-like depths of an angular dance floor. The ceiling of the central hall was shaped like a Persian tray; that of the two other halls like China porcelain and the curved lines of a kamkhira or melon. The big vault had a roof-top corridor for audiences, with an intricate labyrinth of stairs, snares and passages.

This bhulbhulaiya or maze gave Indo-Persian architecture a quality of the labyrinthian mind, reminiscent of Borges, Poe and the explorer-detective of old Arabic-Persian literature. A logician could get entrapped in this complex world, for one flight of steps did not lead to the next one above, though appearing to do so. One was endlessly in the pathways without a clue of what came before and what followed after. The way to unravel the intricate plot was to think with the mind etched backwards. So if one had to go down, there was no way but to go up; if one had to turn right, the surest way was to turn left.

Even the gate which flanked the Imambara from the left was an exercise in experiment and sport. In ancient architecture, there was the frieze, architrave and cornice. This was the classic design of the gateway to the Buddhist stupa at Sanchi and the model for all ancient gates. The Attala Masjid of Jaunpur and the Buland Darwaza of Fatehpur Sikri supplanted ancient pillars with the arch and the architrave and the cornice, with jharokhas and pavilions. But the Rumi Darwaza of Lucknow came up with the concept of an arched cornice, a surprising, almost shocking development where the building arose in a uniform folded pattern, like a huge, wavy cornice. Designs of musical instruments jutted from all sides exposing the hidden elements of the frieze while cutting down the architrave and embellishing the jharokhas and pavilions. This was certainly post-modernism much before its time.

These buildings projected a style older and subtler than their western counterparts. It was a style that extended outwards to embrace society as well. In Lucknow, the Hindu-Muslim synthesis did not require a combination of dome, arch and the drooping ends of 'Hindu' brackets. It was based on an integrated concept of an indistinguishable mass — during the making of the Imambara, the separate religious identity of participants was lost. Distinctions of rank and order were also blurred. There was the 'mass' and the 'benefactor' locked in a common aesthetic experience. In Asaf-ud-Daula's time, there was no spurt in temple and mosque building of the old type. What came to the fore was a sudden rise in pan-community fairs, festivals and local celebrations. In fairs of ancient temples, deities became the object of play and sport. The gods started coming down to earth to become beloveds of Muslims and Hindus alike and public figures with secular qualities. The cult of Lord Hanuman in Aliganj was established by Bahu Begum, Asaf-ud-Daula's mother. In this form, the Lord became a symbol of loyalty and gusto, a playful, brawny kid of a strong, loving mother. The teeka or vermilion of Hanuman, the fragrance of Sheetla Devi's fair, the aroma and the militant wail of Muharram all dissolved in the Avadhi 'aestheticisation of ritual' and 'emotionalisation of belief'.

These two features formed the basis of Lucknow's modernity, its famed 'jadidiyat'. In later accounts of the city, the stress was more on its 'qadimiyat', by which authors meant its traditionality. But right from Asaf-ud-Daula's time, the jadidi spirit comprised the emotional core of the city. Soz, Mushafi, Insha and Jurrat, the brewers of the Lucknow school of poetry, were hopeless jadids. Soz was Mirza Amani's Ustad and the first one to introduce a youthful strand, a pulsating energy of immediacy, in verses. Mushafi too, was steeped in the voluptuous spirit of the here and the now. In Delhi, belief was a matter of faith and ideas; in Lucknow, it was an issue of feeling and common sense. In the former it could take on the form of a conservative or radical body of thought. In the latter, it took on the attributes of old and new practices. Lucknow's jadidiyat was defined in terms of a strange 'emulsion', or a tendency to drown oneself and yet swim around in a pool of views and praxis. Here was an example of a believing mind, not sceptical in the Western sense, but evolving its own 'cunningness of honesty', 'ruthlessness of compassion' and 'doubt of belief'.

This was a culture which knew how to respect tradition and yet move on. The school of Delhi poetry was forever respected here, but Mir remained an outsider. Sensualists of Delhi, normally derided there, found their mark in Lucknow in the 'non-poetic' arts of Vasokht, Rijal and the Phabti. Vasokht was an 'ironic' form of erotic verse where angry remonstrances supplemented physical descriptions. Rijal was a method of stating dialogue in rhyme with the object of subverting authority and non-authority alike. It was Lucknow which created both the etiquette of 'pehle-aap' implying meaning after you and the vagaries of one of the most subversive forms of address, the 'danda'. 'Aap' was a form of 'drawing room' address possible only in the Lucknowi setting of the jheena kurta, the carved serving table of wood and the andaaz or art of bowing down to respect the elder.

Lucknowi apparel converted the angarkha into a flowing garment even as a new ethos developed around women's clothing. Here, long flowing robes were replaced by prim ghararas and the slender ghutannas. Items ranging from food, confectionery to martial arts were touched by the blend of jadidiyat, watanparasti, nazakat and nafasat. The martial arts of Lucknow drew on all available and extinct forms of Avadh. 'Binaut', patronised by Brahmins as the skill of fighting with gold coins wrapped in a handkerchief, 'bank', or the art of knife combat, archery, the 'weapon' of Pasis and Bhars, and lakri bhanjana or lathi wielding, were mixed with traditions of Indo-Persian valour. A 'mass' form of martialisation emerged where respectable citizens, musicians and poets carried arms, an individual being incomplete without a martial skill.

As an ideological frame, Asaf-ud-Daula invoked traditions of Shia liberal humanism. These were then universalised as a general humanism incorporating society in a code of 'insaniyat' or humanism. The Shia ethic, interpreted and understood in this form, provided the basis for cultural integration, while Sunni traditions of rational knowledge remained relevant for educational growth. In formal Shiism, the Usili rationalistic branch was given preference over others. Shiism was also used to lessen the impact of the 'official' Hindu-Muslim religions and leave the path open for a wide variety of heterodox activity. In time, the Lucknowi brand of composite culture came to be called the Shia-Hindu, Shia-Brahmin Ittehad. Centuries ago, the Brahmins of Kashmir had sent help to Imam Hussein, the son of Hazrat Ali and the first Shia martyr, in the Battle of Karbala. Long before the coming of the Muslims, a Husseini Brahmin subcaste existed in Avadh which combined Hindu and Muslim practices. More than a coincidence, thus, lay behind the specific features of Asaf-ud-Daula's composite culture. By the 1780s, the Persian new year, the Navroz, was being celebrated as a Hindu festival and Shia families were celebrating Holi and Diwali in villages. Mirza Amani patronised the sensational, militant side of Hindu religion too, elevating Baba Jagjivan Das of the Satnami sect to the position of a close confidant. Jagjivan Das grew out of the anti-status quoist Prannath and Bablal led trend of the Bhakti movement. His sect, like Banarsi Gosains, dealt extensively in trade and comprised a commercial-warrior brotherhood[16]. Rebel Brahmins were also given land grants and one such figure, Baba Hazari, emerged as a wealthy citizen of Lucknow by the 1790s.

Around the blossoming of culture, the city kept growing. Mohallas were named after trades and professions and the structure of the city became circular. Starting from the area around the old Macchi Bhavan to the southwestern portions to the eastern limits, the city formed an irregular semicircle. The uneven topography of the land was kept in mind while constructing mohallas. Towards western Lucknow stood a glittering new palace complex, the daulat khana. Built in a style best described as country house baroque, so typical of Bramento if a Western parallel is required, its roofs and walls curved at several ends. The eastern side was adorned by the Bibiapur Kothi built in the classic style, with Greek pillars and the Romanesque arch. The former recorded a statement of grandeur, the latter signified a retreat to rest.

4

❦

A Countryside in Turmoil:
the Avadhian Aristocracy

Asaf-ud-Daula was one of the greatest hunters of his time, but his
peer, Shuja-ud-Daula, represented a combination of strength and
wisdom before which all hunters bowed in respect. Six feet tall, with
striking Persian features, he had a drooping moustache which he
flaunted as the insignia of his fierceness. His hunting expeditions,
on which he wore his characteristic shining, robe-like angarkha,
were the stuff of legends. He was said to have killed a buffalo with
his bare hands, while another claimed he shot a tiger disguised as
one. His favourite haunts were in the far reaches of Faizabad,
Bahraich and Gonda. These were wild areas, known for the tigers
who roamed freely near the Rapti river, neelgais, stags and deers
who though deceptively peaceful and carefree, could mount a
dangerous attack.

The hunters of Avadh were led by a group of people who
matched the Lucknowi nawabs in strength, valour and fortitude, but
they possessed some characteristics which the Nishapuri nawabs did
not. This was a rustic chivalry, which brought out a desperate
gallantry in men.

These acts of courage were seldom impetuous. They reflected
a premeditated design and a readiness to upturn convention that
could overcome the most perilous obstacle. Their manner was
courageous but calculative, faithful but rational, loyal but enterpris-

ing. It sculpted the ethic of the great rural aristocrats of Avadh: the most stable hunting and political partners of the rulers of Lucknow who symbolised the 'wild belly' of Avadhi culture. The famed talukedars of Avadh were not directly linked to the city. They were neither an appendage to the culture of Lucknow, nor its excluded vestige. Their history of colonisation dated back to the thirteenth and fourteenth century, but their adventures had not lost their appeal. They were a class with both ancient and contemporary elements. They could unexpectedly colonise new areas, set up trade depots and enhance their position from zamindars to rajas. They could also leave their ancestral lands, held with great emotion and passion, for new adventures in far off areas. Ideals were fiercely preserved but nothing restricted them from embracing new religions, lands and other material possessions

By Shuja-ud-Daula's time, Avadhian aristocracy was already evolving its own distinct culture. There was little room for an inflexible hierarchical structure which blocked the way of innovation and social mobility. Rajputs constituted the ruling class and spread their honour, privilege and culture in many villages of Avadh. But the Rajput code extended universally to Muslim Sheikhs, Pathans, Brahmins and lower caste clansmen. From this emerged something close to an aristocracy of 'attitude', possessed by all sections of the rural populace, including the working peasantry.

If there was a peasant aristocracy anywhere in Hindustan, it was within the mud baked fortifications of Avadhian villages. Steeped in traditions of pride, valour, dignity, compassion, generosity and entrepreneurship, this was a peasantry which recounted the story of Lord Ram with pride. Avadhi folk culture was not in the tradition of bhakti common to Bengal or Maharashtra. Instead, the voice of prayer was peppered with militancy, exemplified by *'bhakti ras jaise lath baanchna'*; recounting devotion like one wields a stick. The most popular folk form was the non-devotional, valorous Aalha — a long, endless ode mired in myth and reality. It told the tale of two Rajput brothers who combined bravery and wisdom to outwit villainous and crafty rulers of a rival kingdom. The tale of Aalha and Udal had its origins in Bundelkhand, beyond the Ganga-

Yamuna Doab, but its next important centre was Avadh. Aalha combined the ethos of the peasantry and the landlord, but beyond that, it represented the code of the adventurous, valorous 'individual', who would battle for the 'wronged'.

This sense of justice drew much from the maryada purshottam image of Lord Ram of Ayodhya. More than a preserver of the social order, he was for the people of Avadh the 'ladaku raja', the fighter with a purpose and a rule of honour which respected the enemy. The twin elements of honour and respect for the enemy were integral to the Avadhian aristocratic code. So was the attitude towards the lower classes and women. The weak were protected but with the realisation that, one day, they too may rise in status. Women were respected and their protection was paramount. But a sense of their autonomous, female power persisted. They were not expected to be compliant creatures to be kept behind a veil. On the contrary, whether Hindu or Muslim, they often crossed traditional boundaries to embrace the aristocratic code. Women who partook in state affairs or who listened to the call of their hearts and did what suited their dignity or iman were immensely respected.

Under Shuja-ud-Daula, rural Avadh underwent a major change. Aristocrats who were middle ranking revenue payers during the Mughal period, began to emerge as the new ruling classes of the countryside. The peasants in turn were being transformed into the new middle classes and the nawabi power structure depended heavily upon this life equation. Soon the village aristocrats found their way into areas hitherto closed to them — trading and the core army of the nawab. As part of the reverse flow, the professional soldiers, many of whom had turned into free-booting samurai in the post Mughal era, started taking on the features of a settled aristocracy.

Shuja-ud-Daula put a final seal to this process by raising Rajput regiments. A legendary figure who rose in this fashion was Hindu Singh, the Bisen Rajput of Mangalsi, Faizabad. In the early nawabi period, Mangalsi was a small pargana, dominated more by Bais Rajputs than the lower caste Bisens. Bais clansmen, along with the Sheikhs, were instrumental in colonising the area in the early days. They were the ones who fought against the native Bhars, set up

hutments, farms and rural communities. Their feats inspired numerous stories of intercaste marriages, flouting of tradition and acts of
courage. These areas had their own culture reminiscent of the
American wild West of the 1860s and '70s. Women and natives also
formed part of the 'team' of adventurers out to annihilate their
opponents, whether for personal or community gain. Chronicles of
Gautam Rajputs, who founded Mangalsi, boasted of one Mangal
Sen, the subduer and protector of the Bhars. He held sway over the
region till the coming of the Sheikhs and Bais Rajputs, after which
he became a fugitive, formed a gang with Bhars, and created a fierce
brand of dare devilry.

Hindu Singh himself was an adventurer of the highest order.
At first, he commanded a small regiment which was sent to subdue
the recalcitrant zamindars of Faizabad. On one occasion, he commanded a charge on the fort of Bangarmau even when his immediate
superior, the commandant of all regiments, was unwilling to grant
permission. The fort was taken at the point of the sword in a burst
of unanticipated, 'hurricane like' energy. In reality, the attack was
planned and relied on the charge of the infantry instead of the
cavalry. Thus was born the legend of Hindu Singh and he was
granted land and the rank of general by Shuja-ud-Daula.

From hereon, Hindu Singh began his rise as an aristocrat,
known more by his own name than that of his clan. He fought in
Rohilkhand and earned the grudging admiration of British officers.
In Asaf-ud-Daula's time, he emerged as an expert in tiger shooting
and the nawab's trusted confidante on the other side of the Ghagra.
The favourite hunting ground of the nawab was in Butwal, Nepal,
an area considered particularly dangerous because of the marshy
lands. High platforms were difficult to construct, and most of the
hunting was done on elephants.

Once when Asaf-ud-Daula was out hunting with Hindu Singh,
he was startled by a tiger who suddenly appeared before him. Before
anyone could react, Hindu Singh made his elephant lie down on
the ground. The tiger's attention now turned towards him. As if
by instinct, the beast jumped on the huddled figure who had drawn
out his scimitar. The tiger landed straight on the sword, and as

legend goes, was 'cut into two'. Hindu Singh got up smiling— a valorous deed was accomplished once again by a deft combination of brain and brawn. For this brave act he was rewarded with villages in the pargana of Mangalsi. Later, with the help of his son he set about introducing cash crops, building ganjs and arched gateways in the area[1].

More dramatic were the fortunes of the great military adventurer, Faqir Muhammad Goya[2]. His career included zamindari in Malihabad, a life of constant travel while fighting battles for different kings, a love of poetry, and the setting up of a flourishing agro-business in his village. Faqir Muhammad Goya was called to Malihabad, probably from Rohilkhand, by the Aminzai Pathans of Malihabad who, along with the Yusufzai Pathans, colonised the area. He was given land by a prominent Aminzai. He then joined the Qandhari horse regiment of Asaf-ud-Daula who was trying to better the British game by dividing the cavalry into blocks of regular drilled regiments on the pattern of infantry. Soon a dispute, one of the many that were to occur in the life of this turbulent personality, made him leave Avadh and join the services of Amir Khan, the ruler of Tonk in Rajasthan. The Tonk nawab was just beginning to settle down after leading the life of a wanderer. A Pindari free booter, who was now establishing a principality, he attracted wanderers and fortune hunters like a magnet.

Faqir Muhammad built up a formidable reputation all through the last quarter of the eighteenth century. He was sent by the Amir as an ambassador to the court of Saadat Ali Khan, the brother of Asaf-ud-Daula and the sixth nawab of Lucknow. But the nawab expired when Faqir Muhammad was still at Kanpur. He changed his route and went back to his native place in Malihabad. In the course of a few months, he gained access to Agha Mir, the prime minister of Saadat Ali Khan's son, Ghaziuddin Haider. He got to command his own regiment which became known for its new troop movements. During Ghaziuddin's son, Nasiruddin Haider's reign, Agha Mir fell out of grace. However, Faqir Muhammad was requested, both by the British and the new ruler, to throw in his lot with the new regime. He acquiesced but never gave up attempts to smoothen out differences between Nasiruddin Haider and Agha Mir. The British resident wanted to keep these two apart for political reasons, but was upstaged temporarily by the manoeuverings and tough diplomacy of the 'hot headed' Pathan. But Faqir Muhammad fell out with Nasiruddin Haider as well. He got into a dispute with Dhania Mehri, the ruler's favourite maid, courtier and confidante. In this case, he let his heart rule his head. In response to Nasiruddin Haider's strictures, he got ready to leave Lucknow. He lined up his belongings on the streets of the city and did not look back to see what became of them.

After leaving Nasiruddin's service, Faqir Muhammad set about improving the breed of Malihabadi mangoes. The famous Malihabadi 'Dassheri' mango, of exquisite quality suited to the Avadhi temperament, was actually his discovery. Its extra-sweetened yet delicate, stately taste, different from the earthy and slightly khatta aftertaste of the Benarsi 'Langda' mango, symbolised the Lucknowi tastebud. Its unmatched quality resulted from scientific grafting, undertaken by Faqir Muhammad after painstaking research. Both in mango grafting and construction activities, which he undertook in Malihabad, Faqir Muhammad represented the innovative-aesthetic strand of the Avadhi Pathan. In the rural areas of Avadh and Allahabad, Pathans were perhaps the best connoisseurs of poetry and architecture. Their building style was a combination of Lucknow and Jaunpur embellished with slender, dainty pillars and arches. In Faqir Muhammad's time, areas from Bilgram and Kakori in northwest Avadh to Rudauli and Faizabad in the east were being beautified with large gateways, English-style villas and the sturdy sarais of Sheikhs and Sayyids. But the countryside was witnessing the growth of elegant Pathani country mansions with open verandahs, courtyards, playfields and the baoli, beautifully arched in the form of pavilions. This legacy extended in Faqir Muhammad's family to include warriors of 1857 and poets of modern India and Pakistan.

The great melting pot of the Avadhian countryside threw up a brand of entrepreneurs in Baiswara, a region cutting through the districts of Rae Bareli and Unnao. It rose in prominence through the industry of the legendary warrior-trader breed of Bais Rajputs[3]. These Hindu Rajputs had a Muslim as the chief of their clan. Marriages were solemnised by Rajput priests in the presence of the Muslim-Rajput Bais family of Hasanpura and the same family arbitrated in hereditary disputes. Inter-religion marital alliances were not uncommon[4].

The Bais were landlords who believed in improvement and reform — they not only collected revenue for the state but ploughed back their profits into the soil. They grew cash crops and set up cotton plantations in the region. Tenants and agricultural workers were brought under rigid professional and centralised control which increased their bargaining power and level of freedom. Under these men of enterprise, Baiswara attained a high level of prosperity and became the prized area of the Lucknowi court. But things did not stop here. The capital thus generated found its way into trade. These Rajputs, who till two or three generations ago fought in ill-clad clothes with rough-edged swords, were soon wearing the most expensive Dhaka and Tanda cloth during trade expeditions. They took Avadhi cotton to Calcutta while bringing Kashmiri shawls to both Avadh and Lucknow. The Bais traders also exchanged elephants from Tipperah, salt from Jaipur and Bharatpur, plus many other luxurious articles. They set up depots of trade from Kashmir to Bengal where Bais settlements became indistinguishable from other trading communities. The income of the Bais's which was remitted to Avadh gave a push to the local economy and encouraged market forces in the Avadhian countryside. A general, quasi-capitalist atmosphere saw Brahmins and people from low castes turning into money-lenders and traders.

These aristocrat-traders loved wealth and combined a sense of honour with a broader vision of life. Their ancient disputes went hand in hand with a political understanding of the happenings in the Indian subcontinent. They were ardent supporters of Nasiruddin Haider in some of his social reforms and extended the impersonal code into polities as well. This was something common to the other Rajput clans, the Raikwars of Bahraich, the Palwars of Faizabad and Sultanpur, the Janwars of Rae Bareli, the Bisens of

Gonda and the Kanphurias of Pratapgarh. Kanyakubja Brahmin lineages, such as the Sukuls of Balan, Pandeys of Khor, Misras of Majgaon, Ganj-Muradabad and Meerasarai (Kannauj), and the Tiwaris of Jehangirabad, also contributed to the aristocratic churning. They wore the Persian jama at weddings, fought against the Pathans and the Rajputs and died with them swearing everlasting friendship.

Over time, there developed the legend of the fierce Brahmins of Unnao, Rae Bareli and Barabanki. Dissenting Brahmins of Maharashtra, Bengal and the south were beaten with a stick if found using the affix, 'Muslim blood of Hindustani Brahmins', in a derogatory sense. The bond with Pathans and Sheikhs was loudly proclaimed, Muslim martial tradition finding easy familiarity with the secular (laukik). Brahminical martial tradition of the Gupta period. The priestly class too followed the lure of arms. But this did not mean that the Brahmin-Hindu moral authority slipped away from this quasi-secular class. They knew how to enforce the writ of 'power'. Puritannical, anti-Muslim currents were weeded out and militant bhaktism from below, as well as the cult of Shiva, Hanuman and fiery goddesses, was encouraged[5].

Kurmis, Ahirs, Koeris and Pasis participated in this code of behaviour and graduated to the ranks of rajas and traders. Perched between the purer clans of the northwest and the 'impure' lineages of Bihar in the east, the Avadhi Rajputs took the best of both worlds. The Avadhi language too treaded this 'middle path', being neither 'straight' like the Khari Boli of the west, nor sentimental or full of vowels, like the Bhojpuri of the east. Though derived from the rugged and gestural Khari Boli, its structure gave an overall feeling of sweetness, and clarity of pronounciation.

The Avadhian aristocracy bemused and excited the Britishers but they were unable to build Rajasthan like myths about it. They found its deft advancement and level of politicisation disconcerting and uncomfortable. During the late 1840s, when the British resident Sleeman undertook his famous tour of Avadh, he shared some opportune moments with its agitated men. Sleeman's report was to provide the basis for the annexation of Avadh and it derided native culture and institutions without compunction. But beneath the cavalier, stiff upper lip attitude, Sleeman was stumped. He was thrown off gear by the contrast of generous hospitality and stoic distance in the countryside. He was warned by a leading talukedar,[6] whose words proved prophetic, that in the event of an anti-British war, peasants would fight alongside Avadhi landlords, bound as they were both with a common rule of honour. Sleeman could not comprehend the coexistence of valour and tact, the presence of daring and civilised behaviour, in one culture. Later, he also could not understand why this aristocratic code exploded into a revolution.

5

❦

The Lucknowi Bourgeoisie

Branding rosy scars across their breasts
your lovers testify fidelity
there is hot trade these days
in camphor dressings

—Atish, in the first half of the nineteenth century

Camphor dressing and the labour of love were only two of the several
articles of commerce that crossed the bustling bazaars of Lucknow. By
the 1780s, the city was fast on its way to becoming the foremost tijarat-
mandi of north India. From the moment Asaf-ud-Daula eased the
exactions of the East India Company, there was a sudden spurt not only
in the traditional trades but manufacture as well. But something more
important than an increase in the volume of commercial goods and the
mushrooming of workshops occurred. An institution or an attitude,
arriving not with a loud cheer but with the fatal buzz of the parvana
bhaura, or the love-sick honey bee, gained ground.

This was the 'market'— a source of economic power which transformed the very look, approach and poetry of the city and its environs.
During the reign of Shuja-ud-Daula, the writer Munshi Faiz Baksh saw
something strange outside Faizabad[1]. He was coming towards the city
after a tiresome journey when he chanced upon a collection of makeshift
tents over which a fair-like atmosphere prevailed. Goods were being

auctioned, courtesans strolled about in their finery and a brisk business was being conducted. Munshi Faiz Baksh at first thought that this was Faizabad. But it turned out to be neither Faizabad nor Ayodhya but Mumtazganj, a qasbah between Lucknow and Faizabad. Along with adjoining areas like Nawabganj it was an offshoot of the new bourgeois culture which had begun sweeping Avadh.

This feeling began to pervade everything from Asaf-ud-Daula's time. The sale in revenue rights had already become an accepted practice. From now on, any daring spirit was open to a life of risk, failure or prosperity. An assignee who had failed to assess the political and economic yield of a region correctly could be replaced by a more enterprising rival. The new incumbent had the freedom to create his own private domain — an exercise which could be both permanent and impermanent. For this was no fiefdom of the old type; he had unlimited power but only for a short time. His power grew out of the traditional function of an agricultural capitalist who had to see that the fallow land got transformed into a double cropping unit, and the cycle of rabi and kharif crops gave way to a season of fruit, sugarcane, indigo and opium production. He had to sit in the self created ganj to see that traders got their money's worth in the market, day labourers got paid and the regular sarai brawls did not interfere with the smooth transaction of affairs. This man was a pioneer who set up towns, villages and even the concept of law. Sporting the early, rough edged angarkha with the makeshift topi, he rode on a horse or a bagghi, built mandirs and masjids and married Hindu and Muslim women. While citing and composing Urdu poetry, he could spot a woman of character and then set her up as the influential courtesan of the qasba.

The antecedents of these men rarely mattered. Like Afrin Ali Khan and the great Amil of Asaf-ud-Daula, Almas Ali Khan, they could be eunuchs or Khwajasarais. Their ranks included respectable Kayasthas like Tikait Rai, conventional Muslims like Mehndi Ali Khan, Khatris like Surat Singh, or Kurmis and Brahmins like Darshan Singh and Bakhtawar Singh. They inhabited a world where fortunes rose and fell with rapidity and where agricultural wealth was not immovable. It depended on the returns on investment made in a particular region, office and enterprise, whether through money, faith or heart. These men were different both from the aristocrat-talukedars of rural Avadh and the courtiers of princely dispensation and comprised in part the nawabi-bureaucratic-capitalist class.

If the aristocracy was a product of adventure, they earned their worth through entrepreneurship. Their Indo-Persian capitalism was far removed from the ethics and life style of the Indo-Persian trader of yore. The latter was known to operate double entry account books with a knowledge of cross country trade routes behind the doors of the family system. Quite often these men had no family — Beni Bahadur[2], the Brahmin Naib of Shuja-ud-Daula, was brought up in the Khatri family of Atma Ram.

This family had gained the favour of Burhan-ul-Mulk and was firmly entrenched, all through the eighteenth century, in the office of the diwani, or the financial branch of the government. Its first generation produced administrators and warriors but the second generation came forth as bureaucrats entrenched in a single office and its related branches. A third generation man, Beni Bahadur did not remain in the diwani for long. He went on to make his fortunes elsewhere, retaining ties with the family but getting away from the image of a traditional bureaucrat. He developed Munshiganj, Nawab Ganj and Mian Ganj, the crown lands near Unnao. A diplomat and politician as well, he gained the confidence of the nawab to finally capture the post of the naib. Yet, Beni Bahadur did not build a stable, landed base for his own family. The crown lands and the ganjs which he set up passed on to other entrepreneurs when Beni Bahadur fell out of favour.

People like him and Almas Ali Khan or Tikait Rai were restless seekers. Fiercely loyal, they, however, could not be taken for granted. While appearing acquiescent, they could hold their own as great dissenters. At the same time, they could sacrifice an individual interest, not for honour, but for a larger benefit, 'cause' or a long term investment project.

Avadh's history is riddled with the exploits of these men who were close to the rulers and yet kept a distance. Almas Ali Khan was not deliberately castigated and made an eunuch. Contrary to myth, eunuchs were not victims of dubious royal designs. They included in their category those who were either born hermaphrodites or those who chose to live as transvestites. Yet, instead of being ostracised, they were accepted as normal human beings. Often, their exceptional abilities made them rise in an environment where merit took precedence over caste, creed or gender. A contemporary saying summed up the situation: *aadmi ki bisaat kya, koi nek sarai, koi khwajasarai* (What is the value of man; someone may be a good man, someone may well be an eunuch) almas Ali Khan attracted the attention of Asaf-ud-Daula and soon got the revenue assignments of lands belonging to Beni Bahadur and other amils. Fulfilling his obligations to the Lucknow treasury, he deceived the British by not disclosing the real amount of revenue due from his assignment. But real glory arrived when he laid the foundations of large scale capitalist agriculture in Mianganj, Hasanganj, Merajganj and Navalganj. He transported Kurmi and Kacchi cultivators from Bundelkhand and the western Doab and had them settled in large farms[3] Raising capital from Armenian and local capitalists, he set up indigo factories, supplementing agriculture with real industrial manufacture He was fond of his cultivators who by the next century had risen a prosperous peasants, landlords and small factory owners in Lucknow Unnao and Barabanki.

Almas Ali also pioneered changes in Lucknow. He set up baghs sarais, mohallas, hotels and tanks which completely changed the nature of the city. Earlier, the city carried the pockmarks of early generals and officers of Burhan-ul-Mulk and Safdar Jung who had set up katras, or residential market places, and a few ganjs. This work continued in Asaf ud-Daula's time but now regular residential complexes, with little or no immediate economic function, came up. Tikait Rai, the nawab' divan, set up the Raja Bazaar — a mohalla capable of housing a wid variety of the new city crowd, traders, labourers, courtesans and th shuriefa. Built in neat rows with a gate pointing towards the main road it had several alleys with straight pathways. The houses were situated on each side and small crossings acted as the main markets of the alleys Here, a traditional family of a physician, with roots spread in Lucknow lived side by side a neo-rich trader of Kashmir. The moneylending caste of Rastogis, then dealing in 'loi chadars' and petty trades, established their quarters alongwith ironsmiths and toymakers. Jailers lined up beside courtesan quarters and Mullahs brushed shoulders with Brah mins. In the cosmopolitan environment of Raja Bazaar, the shroffs and sonars constructed houses with richly decorated doors of teak wood standing in rows, like small arched gateways straddled together. The small verandah in front helped in minimising the imposing edifice of a haveli and completed the neo-exotic picture. The pattern fitted in perfectly with the colour and elan of the new middle classes emerging as a force to reckon with in the city.

Tikait Rai himself was a revenue contractor, engaged in establishing market centres. He connected the Avadhian hinterland with the capital and the qasbas by constructing bridges in places like Kakori and Mohan over the Beta and Biganwa rivers. These bridges were quite novel for their time as they fulfilled a functional, philanthropic and aesthetic purpose. Arched posts of elegant lakhauri and small towers embellished the entrance beyond which the weary traveller, trader or journeyman could always find a small brick hut for rest. The roofs of these huts were slanted in the Bangla pattern and a hexagonal Shivalaya while a Kamkhira dome stood at one end of the bridge. It gave the appearance of a well cut, multi-sided black pearl. Nearby stood a masjid in the same style. The qasba of Mohan, which seems to have been established in the time of Safdar Jung by Newal Rai, was renovated by Tikait Rai. It was developed by other nobles like Haider Beg and Almas Ali Khan who implanted domes, shikharas and arched gateways on temples, mosques and sarais.

Multifaceted individuals like Tikait Rai met their foil in Abu Talib, known also as Mir Londoni. Born in Lucknow sometime in the 1750s, Mir Londoni hailed from Isfahan and began his career in Bengal as an amil under the British. He represented the other trend of the Indo-Persian bourgeoisie — someone who got early access to the British and the new world emerging in the West. His dynamism did not rest in building bridges, sarais or tea or coffee houses but in perfecting the technical art of administration, science and commerce.

Abu Talib was recalled to Lucknow by Mukhtar-ud-Daula, the naib of Asaf-ud-Daula in the 1770s. His arrival coincided with the rise of Afrin Ali Khan, the gentleman-scholar close to the nawab. Abu Talib came to Lucknow with Saiyyad Zain-ul Abdin Khan and was drawn into the vortex of politics which led to the assassination of his mentor soon after. He administered an area called Phaphund near Lucknow and migrated to Gorakhpur under a new assignment with the blessings of the British. There he began mastering the European languages but was disturbed in his reading of classical Latin by a different call. He was asked by the court of Lucknow to subdue the recalcitrant raja of Tiloi. In a famous incident, he out-manoeuvered the raja and killed him by tact and strategy.

Abu Talib supplemented his mastery of foreign languages with an interest in mathematics and classical European, Persian and Indian art. His successes increased the intrigues against him and his stipend was stopped. He then left for Western shores along with an Englishman, Captain Richardson. The captain was a lover of the Orient and represented the tradition of men like William Hodges and William Jones. These enlightened individuals did not believe in the manifest destiny of the white race. They were in awe of the east— not only the east of the Vedas and the Upanishads, but that of Kalidas, nautch girls, colour, food, valour, language and the glorious memory of Mughal arms and painting.

Asaf-ud-Daula's court fulfilled the desire of many Europeans wanting to understand and share with the east. For them, Abu Talib represented a similar quest for the West going on in the Indian subcontinent. This search produced Tafazzul Hussein Khan Kashmiri, Khwaja Fariduddin and in a different vein, Azimullah Khan of Kanpur, the hero and political strategist of the great revolt of 1857. The first two were residents of Lucknow more or less in the time of Abu Talib, who set upon a voyage for the 'land of the Franks' in 1799 from Calcutta with Richardson. Crossing Asia and Africa, he landed at Nantes. His stay was marked by scintillating observations about the French — remarks which often ended in ironical comparisons with the English. He then went on to Ireland and England; in the land of the 'master race', he became an instant celebrity and an object of wonder. His 'amazing' scholarship in Persian and English led to a meeting with members of the royal family. He was also invited to the annual dinner of the Lord Mayor of London where he shared the seat of the most honoured guest with Lord Nelson, the future hero of the battle of Trafalgar.

But Abu Talib was not the only Indian visiting England at that time.

Two other notable personalities, Itisam-ud-Din of Delhi and Munshi Ismail of Bengal, also became early Indian chroniclers of the West. But the accounts[4] left by the three differ in important respects. That of Itisam-ud-Daula is basically factual. He had arrived in Great Britain as a messenger of Shah Alam, the king of Delhi, to the queen of England. In that capacity, he recorded details without adding his own views apart from some very interesting and subtly humourous barbs directed at his hosts. Munshi Ismail was a clerk in Kalna, Bengal and his account bears the wonderment of a small man of opportunity descending upon a land of plenty due to God's grace. But Abu Talib's account is political, opinionated and aesthetically informed. It dwells on the strengths, weaknesses, frailties and the beauty of the West. It is critical of the narrow and intolerant aspects of British national character while appreciating British efficiency and adaptibility and urges Indians back home to adopt modern ideas and reforms.

Abu Talib, however, was not alone in his reformism. His exploits were evenly matched by that of Tafazzul Hussein Khan. Belonging to a family of northwestern traders who had settled in Delhi, Tafazzul Hussein became a pupil of a Delhi-based firangi mahal scholar. His family then came to Lucknow on a trade mission and settled down in the city. Tafazzul Hussein emerged as a trader and a devout Shia, very much a product of the Shia Renaissance then sweeping Persia and Hindustan. In Lucknow, the rational Usuli school was becoming dominant and Tafazzul Hussein gained an entry into the court through its office. But he left Lucknow following an assassination attempt on Asaf-ud-Daula. He spent the next twenty years in Calcutta where he studied Latin, Greek, English, mathematics and physics. He translated the works of Newton, Emerson and other scientists and mathematicians into Arabic and then returned to become Asaf-ud-Daula's chief minister. This ministership, however, was an exercise in subtle force, Tafazzul Hussein being the friend and tutor of Saadat Ali Khan, the nawab's brother and rival. He thus suited the British policy of counterbalancing the nawab. But he remained the favourite of the British connoisseur rather than that of the British administrator — he and his tutor both were unable, ultimately, to fulfill the political demands of the Company.

Khwaja Fariduddin was another distinguished pupil of Tafazzul

Hussein. Kashmiri by birth, he came down to Lucknow because of its reputation as a centre of modern learning. He was the one who rediscovered the value of the proportional compass, which judges relative distances. He established the fact that its use and science was known to Asians and Indians much before the arrival of the British. Saadat Ali Khan took a liking to him and the British appointed him as the superintendent of the Calcutta madarsa. There he worked further on the compass and after astounding foreign men of letters with his scientific knowledge, settled down in Delhi.

Khwaja Fariddudin was not a political man but the generation of scholar-entrepreneurs which came after him linked learning with politics. From the 1760s onwards, there was a great ferment in the Firangi Mahal as learning got disseminated to wider circles. Middle class libraries and discussion groups came up and an exchange of talent from Lucknow to outlying areas began in earnest. Mulla Nizammuddin's son Syed Bahr-ul-Uloom went to Madras to teach at the Madrasa-i Kalan founded by Shah Wallajallah, the nawab of Arcot. Shah Wallajallah was also an Avadhi entrepreneur, a virtual prince in their rank. Hailing from Gopa Mau in Rae Bareli, he went to the Deccan in order to seek his fortunes and ended up carving out an Indo-Persian kingdom in the deep south. Here the Mughal impact was superficial and it was left to Avadh to export the high culture of the north right upto the shores of Kanyakumari.

In the city itself, the ranks of the Lucknowi bourgeoisie were swelling with hakims, calligraphers, cooks, artists and barbers. Skilled persons were respected no less than scholars and this was a constant complaint of those attuned to the old culture of Delhi. How could physicians, nastlikhs or ordinary craftsmen acquire a status comparable to that of the adibs?

In Lucknow, poets themselves became linguists, grammarians, hakims, even jesters and clowns. Insha, Mushafi and Jurrat, and before them, Qatil and Rangin, competed with Hakim Masih-ud-Daula, Hafiz Nurullah, the calligraphist, and ordinary lithographers for honours. Sometimes they had to compete with palanquin bearers like the incredibly talented Raja Mehra. This figure rose meteorically under Asaf-ud-Daula to don the title of 'Raja' on account of his sporting skills. Qatil, formerly a Hindu, bore a carefree attitude — 'I became a Muslim because of the smell of the kebab'. And the poetry of Rangin took on the voice of a 'bazaaru woman'— free, amorous, enjoying the present, unhampered by the past and the loss of economic status.

6

❧

The Company and the Kingdom

Jisko na de maula
Usko de Asaf-ud-Daula

Holi khelen Asaf-ud-Daula vazir
Rang sohbat se ajab hai khurd aur pir

The Holi of 1798 was not so colourful. The sohbat, or company of the nawab-wazir was missing. Asaf-ud-Daula died that year, the way he had lived — behind a cloak of suspense. His favourite hakim had been treating him for a mysterious and deadly illness. Hushed whispers from the palace claimed it was 'Isthisca'.

This morbid end, however, was not the work of chance. It was Asaf-ud-Daula's protest against his helplessness: a position of desperation brought about by the manoeuverings of an alien power. For the man who was the virtual sovereign of the Indo-Gangetic belt had failed to save his best friend, Jhau Lal, from the Company Bahadur.

A. Saksena Kayastha, Jhau Lal[1] had some influence in Faizabad before he attracted the nawab's attention. He was close to Bahu Begum, Asaf-ud-Daula's mother and had protected her treasure from the depredations of Warren Hastings. The notorious governor-general had tried in Faizabad what he was best at: taking advantage of a local dispute to fill his coffers.

Asaf-ud-Daula and his mother were locked in an internecine conflict during the 1770s. But Warren Hastings's attempt to take advantage of the situation came to naught. The nawab refused to go against his mother beyond a point and people like Jhau Lal acted to ward off Company designs. Soon after, Jhau Lal was called to Lucknow as an officer in charge of the artillery. He was then elevated to the coveted position of mir bakshi, the manager of the crown lands. Jhau Lal constructed bridges, mohallas, imambaras, mandirs and houses for the general public. He also became unpopular and a *persona non grata* with the British. He was getting extremely close to the nawab, both of them sharing a deeply personal bonding which the British found hard to understand.

One day, the Company handed over some documents to Asaf-ud-Daula. They proved that Jhau Lal was corresponding with the king of Afghanistan and other Indian princes for a coalition against the British. This meant that he was also plotting against Avadh, the nawab being bound by a treaty to the Company. Asaf-ud-Daula was presented with no choice but to hand over his closest friend to the British. The nawab complied but Jhau Lal, instead of being hanged, was exiled to Patna on a pension. Why did the British pardon a *de facto* baghi? Apparently, due to two factors. Firstly, they suspected that Jhau Lal was not acting alone. He had the blessings of the nawab who was turning bitter towards the Company during the 1790s, regretting his earlier refusal to side with Shah Alam, the emperor of Delhi. The latter had called upon him, as his nominal wazir, to reconquer the subcontinent for him in the 1780s. The communique jolted the British and they prevailed upon the nawab to make them a party in any dealings with the Mughal emperor.

Secondly, there was the fear of social unrest. Jhau Lal was a popular man and harsh treatment would have evoked a grave reaction in Lucknow. So he was sent to Patna but the nawab never forgave himself. His hakim was called over and asked to suggest an illness which had no cure. The hakim mentioned 'Isthisca', incurred by taking a bath after lunch for days on end. The nawab began working on the suggestion, killing himself step by step.

This version never became a part of 'official' history. But in the late 1790s, Lucknow was seething with disturbances and a hostile spirit. Far away in Seringapatam, the tiger of Mysore, Tipu Sultan, had died fighting the British. Inspired by radical Islamic[2] and European-American[3] thought, this modern personality of the post-Mughal age had celebrated the French revolution in Mysore. When his courtiers expressed sympathy for the slain royal family of France, he replied as an Indo-Persian republican, 'Don't worry, now the people will rule.' He corresponded with Benjamin Franklin and sent aid to the anti-British, American War of Independence. Revamping his administration, he set about introducing capitalist features[4] in the economy. After defeating the British several times, he did not flinch from fighting the last battle in which defeat was certain due to betrayals and a change in the balance of forces. He preferred to die to set an example for future generations.

Back in Lucknow, another turbulent man of the 1790s occupied Asaf-ud-Daula's masnad. This was Wazir Ali, his son, for whom he had performed the most elaborate wedding in recent history. Hindu ceremonies mixed freely with Muslim rites and kathaaks and bhands came from Allahabad, Benaras and Kashmir. The wedding was a statement of cultural pride which Nawab Wazir Ali took to heart. He dismissed pro-British nobles and courtiers and fired missives to the resident asserting his independence.

Alarm bells went off in the Residency, the seat of British officialdom. This building was designed by Claude Martin on the west side of the Gomti with funds from the Avadh treasury. Claude Martin was the last obscure figure to play a role between the Company and the Lucknow raj[5]. Martin, a Frenchman was liked by the British in Lucknow as a 'friend' of Asaf-ud-Daula. He arrived in Lucknow on Company favour as head of its arsenal. From here he built his fame and wealth, bribing Company officials, as was the normal practise at the time. He became a personal contractor to Avadh and Company troops in contravention of his official duties and robbed the nawab by selling European articles at inflated prices. But he was a talented man and the nawab saw in him a corrupt genius essential to offset Company influence. Martin too needed Asaf-ud-Daula to keep alive his bargaining position with the Company.

Thus both became 'friends' and Lucknow benefited by some beautiful buildings in the bargain. Martin was an artist by instinct and displayed his mettle by interpreting classical European architecture in the eastern fashion. His buildings were peppered with verandahs, turrets and flat ceilings inside a castle or cathedral-like structure. But Martin could never recreate the magic of Farhat Baksh or the Bibiapur Kothi, the mansions he made for the nawab, in his own La Martiniere and the British Residency. Less eclectic in style, La Martiniere was still a momentous affair. Tigers roared at the sides of huge staircases, Vatican style pillars stood as columns and successive storeys looked straight out of a French chateau. But the colourful flourish was missing and a rustic look contrasted instantly with the grand expansiveness of Indian buildings. The Residency, on the other hand, represented the kind of crude functionalism which Martin, the Frenchman, considered appropriate for the British.

Wazir Ali's accession did not quite please men like Martin. For officials seated in the Residency, it spelled disaster. Challenge in Lucknow was sure to effect British designs on Delhi, the ultimate prize of their expansionist plan. Sensing the urgency of the situation, the governor general himself stepped into the act. An elaborate plan was made to depose the young nawab and install Saadat Ali Khan, the exiled brother of Asaf-ud-Daula. Saadat Ali Khan was in Benaras and seemed to have given up hope of governing Avadh. He was surprised when the opportunity fell in his lap. A coalition of nobles, especially people like Tafazzul Hussein and Tehsin Khan Sr., who were close to the British, joined hands against the young nawab. Many old Asaf-ud-Daula loyalists were either dead or ineffective and the new nawab had yet to consolidate his position. A British backed plot declared Asaf-ud-Daula impotent and therefore incapable of producing an heir. Wazir Ali thus became an 'interloper' — someone who had usurped the throne, through trickery, and by falsifying his inheritance. He was deposed and offered a pension for life which he refused. Saadat Ali Khan became the sixth nawab-wazir of Avadh and Wazir Ali was packed off to Benaras.

The Wazir Ali episode was an open and unabashed act of fraud on the part of the Company and its highest officers recognised it as such. The governor general himself spoke of the fact that even if Wazir Ali was only an adopted son of Asaf-ud-Daula, he still stood as the legitimate heir. Moreover, the proofs summoned for his deposition comprised crude hearsay.

The new nawab was immediately slapped with a treaty, which increased the subsidiary amount to be paid to British troops. Subtle force was applied to amend the commercial treaty of 1788. The company established its compulsory mediation between Avadh and other powers, and imposed a condition whereby the resident was to have a say in the administration of Avadh.

This meant a setback to the gains achieved by Asaf-ud-Daula. Saadat Ali Khan resisted. He made prompt payments and kept up a pretence of pleasing the Company. But he resented British interference in administrative matters and began initiating reforms of his own.

Before he could streamline his offices, he was given an ultimatum by the Company. An angry nawab went to the extreme of proposing a royal abdication. Acting hastily, the British resident drew up a plan of annexation which allowed the nawab to keep his treasury. Saadat Ali Khan responded strongly against this degrading show of munificence and the Company beat a hasty retreat. Too much pressure on the nawab was considered counter-productive, especially when the British had yet to understand fully the cultural milieu in which they were operating.

British moderation, however, also resulted from the renewed threat in the east. Wazir Ali revolted and killed Mr. Cherry, the resident of Benaras, along with several British officers. The anti-British war was joined by Rajput landlords and peasants in the countryside and the traders of Benaras city. Wazir Ali raised a strong force of a thousand armed men who launched a full scale offensive against the Company. The guerrilla struggle combined courage with foresight, the Wazir Ali episode anticipating 1857 by about fifty-eight years.

After suppressing the revolt in Benaras, the British worked out a compromise with Saadat Ali. The Company took half of his territories and reduced the army to one-tenth of its former size. It also kept the right to a moderate role in administrative matters. The areas of Doab, Rohilkhand and Gorakhpur passed out of the hands of the Nishapuri house, which was now left mainly with the original lands of Burhan-ul-Mulk. With the addition of a few districts of the Allahabad suba, Saadat Ali Khan's suzerainity extended to the twelve districts of Rae Bareli, Sultanpur, Pratapgarh, Hardoi, Unnao, Barabanki, Lucknow,

Faizabad, Sitapur, Lakhimpur-Kheri, Bahraich and Gonda. This now became the new Avadh.

By acquiring lands located between Delhi and Lucknow, the Company cut off links between the Mughal emperor and the nawab. But the 'deal' only began a new round of confrontation. Saadat Ali accepted the agreement with a rider — 'I have been 'induced' to cede the districts for the charges of the British government merely to gratify his lordship (the governor general) — '[6]. Saadat Ali's veiled missive was directed at the governor general and his populace. Immediately after its issuance, he became an obsessed figure, tormented by the Company and his desire to win back his territories. He embarked on a plan of administrative reforms, trade expansion, ganj formation and the modernisation of Lucknow. Isolated from all sides, he went about improving conditions in Avadh so that the lost territories could be brought back from the British. This was no idle dream — Saadat Ali was a 'rational man' by European standards. He was a scientist with an expert knowledge of physics and mathematics. Close to Tafazzul Hussein and Khwaja Fariddudin, he wanted to revive the lost traditions of Arabic and Indo-Persian science.

But the 'reform conscious' British reacted strangely to the nawab's zeal. To centralise the revenue system, Saadat Ali Khan located jagirs and redirected the flow of agricultural surplus to the Lucknow treasury. Instead of supporting him, the British sided with the same dispossessed nobles and courtiers whom they would normally have dismissed as degenerate eastern potentates. The nawab was ridiculed, Tafazzul Hussein resigned and Khwaja Fariduddin left for Calcutta. All trusted men of the loyal nobility came under suspicion while the nawab's opponents received favour.

But Sadat Ali did not surrender. He cut down expenditure and filled the Lucknow treasury. The British game of eroding his support base in Lucknow was countered by recruiting men from low castes and from areas beyond Avadh. Captain Fateh Ali, Rai Ratan Chand, Bakhtawar Singh and Darshan Singh were the great personalities of his age. Fateh Ali was a household slave, purchased by the nawab in Benaras. Ratan Chand belonged to Moradabad, Bakhtawar Singh was a Company trooper and Darshan Singh hailed from a Kurmi, labour class origin.

All four rose in the face of hostile and conservative British opinion. Fateh Ali took charge of the nawab's treasury and commanded his troops, earning the title of 'Captain' in the bargain. He modernised the nawab's arsenal and formulated a new policy of land revenue. His engineering skills saw him constructing a large well on the western side of the city and laying down the foundation of modern water works in Lucknow.

Raja Ratan Chand's multidimensional personality had to overcome several handicaps due to his Bhatnagar Kayastha-outsider status. But Bakhtawar Singh and Darshan Singh[7] faced vehement opposition — the latter was even given a number of derogatory epithets in traditional chronicles. His father had come to Lucknow from Faizabad and worked as a labourer in one of the nawab's buildings. Saadat Ali had an eye for a good body and talent — somehow Darshan Singh attracted his attention and was co-opted in the new personal corp which the nawab was raising. He found his way into the financial department, and then from there to the military. By his time, the earlier division between the amils or revenue contractors, service elite and troop commandants was breaking down. Darshan Singh· had no roots in the Mughal service traditions, he was not even a part of the prosperous Kurmi families of the countryside. He entered the closely knit department of the Indo-Persian finances without a formal education and commanded a platoon right from the beginning of his military career. He then became a land entrepreneur, bringing new areas under the plough and overriding the protests of old zamindars with a history of rigid, unbending practices. His exactions against the raja of Balrampur gained him both fame and notoriety as a feared figure. He did not care much about rank, encouraged new men of poor background and patronised his own style of art and music. Falling in and out of favour with successive rulers after Saadat Ali, he succeeded in springing back on each occasion.

But Darshan Singh's crowning glory was his foray into the world of engineering. He supervised the setting up of a steam engine in the Farhat Buksh palace which pumped Gomti water into the building. Steam engines had been brought into regular operation by Watt in England just a few decades ago. The smooth transplanting of this technology in Lucknow in so short a time without explicit British aid required men of genius like Darshan Singh.

Bakhtawar Singh also played a similar role. Employed first as the head of a cavalry troop, he graduated to land revenue management and acquired zamindari rights in Shahganj and Faizabad. With help from his brothers, he built up an estate while remaining a warrior. Bakhtawar Singh too possessed engineering skills, fast becoming a hallmark of Saadat Ali's reign. Quite unsurprisingly, this was the period when the construction of an iron bridge was conceived.

Iron bridges were relatively recent in Europe. Lucknow had a number of stone bridges built during the time of Newal Rai and Safdar Jung and the need for a more secure mode of transport was being felt both by the British and the nawab. The British wanted one for security reasons, as their cantonment lay across the river in Mandiaon. On the other hand, the nawab yearned to improve the image of the city by a scientific feat. The famous engineer John Rennie, who had designed the Waterloo bridge, supervised the project. Recast in England, the structure was soon ready to adorn a city coming out from the last vestiges of the eighteenth century.

By the 1800s, Asaf-ud-Daula's Daulat Khana was already wearing a dated look. It conformed to the image of the eighteenth century princely palace immortalised by Mir Hasan in 'Sihr-ul-Bayan'. Made up of bhavans, havelis, fountainheads, rest houses, arched columns and boundaries, it ran irregularly with the curves of the Gomti. This was the fantasy land of the shahzada still clad in the silver studded angarkha and the long pyjama with big flares and the large, turban-like topi. Its building complexes existed in panoramic continuum with a large imposing gate in front. The Daulat Khana included such innovations as the 'Gend Khana', a huge oval shaped wall, used by the nawab to play ball. The exact nature of the game has yet to be determined but the ball was struck with a hard instrument and bounced back to the other participant — maybe a bit like present day squash?

The British did not participate in this form of recreation, so it was either an invention of the nawab or an extension of an earlier Mughal sport. The Mughal period also conceals a history of Indo-Persian sport seen in numerous inventions in athletics, polo, riding, swimming, card games and chess.

The Daulat Khana actually was the last mahal, a quintessentially

Lucknowi invention. Elsewhere, nawabs continued to stay in palaces and forts with the nizam of Hyderabad only improving upon old Deccani traditions of architecture till the 1850s. But by 1810, Saadat Ali was improving upon the concept of the mahal. His palace complex was called the Chattar Manzil — a term technically used for describing a multistoreyed building. It evoked romantic associations not of princely lore but memories of one's family or one's beloved. Chattar Manzil was built for the preservation of this very feeling. It had three buildings with arched doors and a plethora of rooms on the upper floor. The rooms were reached through a spiral staircase, which also led to an open roof. Huddled columns, appearing more like lamp shades, surrounded the roof from two sides with porches in the front and rear. The Chattar Manzil faced the Gomti and soon became the seat of Saadat Ali's government. It was followed by a smaller Chattar Manzil near other buildings like the Darshan Bilas and a Lal Baradari with long columns built like the legs of an Indian bed. A wide road separated these plastered and painted structures.

Similar buildings came up all along the central and eastern part. Manzils faced one another separated by roads, which ran parallel creating a huge, horizontal, mosaic like view of the city. The Khurshid Manzil ran parallel to Moti Mahal, a pearl-like domed structure. Beyond it came up the Begum Kothi. Romanesque arches and porches flanked the Khurshid Manzil from four sides. The same style was applied to the Noor Baksh palace, the Hayat Baksh and the Badshah Manzil which appeared like lodgings of a wealthy merchant rather than that of a king.

But nothing compared with the Dilkusha palace. An 'Egyptian' temple with long steps, imposing towers and large windows, its open interior resembled the altar of yore. The gate was camouflaged as a huge Romanesque arch with a festooned cornice; it was ancient yet modern, an Arabic-African design reformulated as the feel and sensuality of the Indian subcontinent — it shocked and belied definition. Dilkusha, surrounded by a lake and a garden, was designed by Gore Ousley, one of the last non-official Englishmen still retaining an attitude of wonder for the east.

Avadhi gardens originated in Faizabad but their altered, perfect shape was achieved in Lucknow. Mughal gardens, with their classical grid-like spread of flora and fountain, had set the norm in this sphere. Paths in all four directions, laid out like the four flaps of a chess board, ran from a central core. Rows of flowers adorned the centre of the paths while grass lawns lay along the side, enclosing a central tomb or pavilion. This garden pattern flourished in Rajasthan, Delhi, Haryana and the western parts of the Doab. Its style spread to areas like Allahabad in the lower Doab as well. But the Khusro Bagh, built during Jehangir's time in the city, was walled. It possessed a dense, jungle like, eastern feel with canals spread in a haphazard manner.

The Faizabad-Lucknowi Bagh modified the provincial Allahabad-Jaunpur style. A new concept evolved with walled enclosures, centre spaced grass lawns and flower beds and canals at the outer limits. Flower beds were not cut by passages but flanked by a mass of lush greenness, cut by trees from four sides. The concept excited a sense of adventure and mystery; this was the basis on which the rough edged, hilly, garden style religious shrine, the Qadam Rasool, came up. The more sedate lawns of the Badshah Manzil bore a look of wilderness. The Dilkusha garden was actually a hunting ground. Twisted trees, invisible paths and a predominance of the chameli and bela, in place of the traditional rose, completed the picture of tempestuous beauty.

But Saadat Ali was unable to enjoy the fruit of his innovations. He died under sinister circumstances, poisoned to death by his cook, allegedly on Company instigation. The person commissioned by the British to write Avadh's official history mentioned in his account that the royal cook, Jawahar Khan, went to the British resident to announce the 'good news'[8], while Darshan Singh hurried to Ghaziuddin Haider to give the 'sad news', (a subtle difference existing between the Urdu usage of good and sad). Even under the unsympathetic scissors of the British censors, this deadly double meaning was passed on to history.

The masnad now passed on to Saadat Ali's son, Ghaziuddin Haider. He transformed the nawabi into a kingdom. On 9 October 1819, the seventh nawab of Avadh became its first king. The British were particularly keen to force Avadh into kingship in order to erode the legitimacy of Mughal rule. Ghaziuddin himself, it appears, had no choice but to accept the inevitable. The East India Company now constituted an alternative power centre in Avadh. It began controlling a section of government officials and appointed, in extreme cases, royal household servants as well. Ghaziuddin was, at first, apprehensive about the outcome; he knew the turmoil it would cause in Delhi. But he told Fateh Ali that if he failed to take the plunge, his rivals might strike a bargain with the British⁹. Behind the pomp and show which accompanied his coronation there was an element of fear, and in security.

After accepting the inevitable, the king tried to put his position to good use. The crown for his coronation was designed by the British, but between the insignia of the lions he pushed in the symbol of the Nishapuri family, the two fishes. The coins were designed by Kayastha officials who translated Mughal features and kept up the facade of continuity with imperial Delhi. The throne mixed Mughal, British and Hindu features and Ghaziuddin Haider himself did not make much of his coronation.

The finale to the whole show was not without humour. The Company supported the coronation because of its anti-Mughal political import. But Ghaziuddin Haider did not take the issue so close to his heart — he even 'forgot' to assert his royalty to his people. Conversely, kingship embroiled the British in petty squabbles with Ghaziuddin Haider over forms of etiquette. Instead of Lucknow and Delhi tearing each other apart, the resident was complaining to the governor general that he was being stopped from accompanying the padshah to the gate of the palace as it did not befit the calling of a sovereign.

The new king turned back the policy of centralisation — with British influence so firmly established he reverted back to Asaf-ud-Daula's 1770s approach. Revenue collection was left in the hands of local potentates and administration to the mind and schemes of Agha Mir Wazir. With Agha Mir began the domination of the wazir in the affairs of Avadh. Ghaziuddin Haider concentrated on the inner life of the city turning it into an evening fair of food, light, lamp, tea, tappa and the mesmeric fights of animals. The musical form, tappa, lyricised the classical 'rhythm' of northwest camel caravans. It then spoke in the 'addha taal' in a staccato meter, beguiling the connoisseur with its hard boiled, 'non-lyric'. Mian Shori, its inventor, was a Punjabi but he found the atmosphere to match his rough edged musical score only in

Ghaziuddin's Lucknow. Tappa forged the low with the high, the gut, sweat and heat of the caravans with the sophisticated 'bulandi' of an Indo-Persion count — a rare mixture unavailable in the history of Western music.

Economic activity too got a boost — the fifty-two new ganjs established by Saadat Ali were organised so distinctly that each one of them catered to a specific market. The Nakhas specialised in leather trade and Sadaatganj in the movement of namak, rui, saunf and zarda. Similar occupational localities went by the name of Bawarchi tola and Haiderganj where tea was served with a longish bread in the shape of a cow's tongue. Export was encouraged in textile and embroidery while local industry embraced the luxury art of meenakari and bidri as well as shoe making, hukka, betel nut and paan masala manufacture. The king constructed the Shah Najaf on the pattern of Hazrat Ali's tomb in Iraq. But inside, sombre symbols of Islamic warriorhood coexisted with Belgian mirrors, Hindu taziyas and rows of chandeliers which glittered in the dark. Shah Manzil and Mubarak Manzil were built as platforms on the bank of the Gomti for the staging of giant animal fights, which took place on the other side of the river. A tiger would be pitted against a rhinocerous or an elephant against a panther. This violent drama spilled over to the city itself. Cock, quail and goat fights began to extend the meaning of normal 'sport'.

This legacy was inherited by Ghaziuddin's son, Nasiruddin Haider, the second and most controversial king of Avadh. On the surface he cohabited unabashedly with the British and allowed his English barber to fleece him dry. But it was he who began the era of science in Lucknow, setting up an observatory, a khairatkhana, a couple of hospitals and a government press. His two unpredictable sides bemused and disconcerted Asian and European observers. But right till the end, while revelling in wine and women and indulging his sartorial fancies, Nasiruddin remained the elusive, Indo-Persian modernist. Sensual and scientific, reformist and lavish, indulgent and thrifty. He basked in the sight of beauty and colour; he married, first, a lady of good breeding, then a Kurmi woman of taste, then a sweepress whose graceful bearing captivated him, a dancer and a grocer's daughter, and finally an Englishwoman.

This was Mrs. Walters — a married woman. She wore skirts, the 'aastin ka shaluka', or the blouse with short sleeves, and enticing garments that fitted her like a second skin. Well versed in Persian and Urdu, she taught English to the king in private. When Mrs. Walters took Lucknow by storm, she was living in the Residency along with her father, Hopkins Walters. The king began wooing her and won her over with 'attitude' and style, calling her 'mukhdare-aaliya', literally the mistress of ceremonies, after marriage.

While building the observatory, or the Tarawali Kothi, the king chose the austere Greek classical tympanium with the round hemisphere on top. His hospitals had separate branches for research in European, Unani and Ayurvedic medicine. The lithography government press did not rush into bringing out religious texts. One of its first productions was the *Taj-ul Lugat,* a dictionary of Urdu. Nasiruddin updated libraries, including Asaf-ud-Daula's massive private collection of books. Foreign journals arrived regularly in the observatory which propagated advanced ideas in astronomy with the help of the latest telescopes.

Behind him stood Hakim Mehndi, the genius nawab-wazir of Avadh. A former nazim of Khairabad, he supplemented his entrepreneurial talent with the devotion of the service cadre. This combination made him both loyal and experimental. He encouraged the king to initiate social reforms and tighten the rule of law to compete effectively with the British.

It was around this time that Governor General William Bentinck banned sati and Raja Rammohan Roy's Bengali renaissance began to arouse new passions and ideas. Nasiruddin Haider also launched a tirade against female infanticide, sati and other outmoded customs. In this he was following, as were Bentinck and Roy, the example of Emperor Akbar who had banned sati way back in the sixteenth century. But the reformist zeal of Bentinck and Raja Rammohan ended in creating a new legitimacy for British power, while Nasiruddin Haider and Hakim Mehndi were responsible for further unleashing revolutionary currents in the countryside.

Courtesans received a place of honour in the king's time during which the Ghaziuddin Haider canal was also sought to be completed. Conceived during his father's reign, the canal was to link the Gomti and the Ganga, Hakim Mehndi and Bakhtawar Singh acting, respectively, as the executive-in-charge and contractor of the operation. William Ticket was the director of the project, meant to irrigate parts of Avadh. But the survey conducted by Company engineers reported that the gradient was four feet higher towards the Ganges. The report arrived when digging had proceeded to well over four or five km from the side of the Gomti. With problems mounting by the day, the project had to be abandoned. It was found out later that the Gomti stood on a higher ground level than the Ganges and the survey had misconstrued facts. But it was too late — by then Hakim Mehndi, who was also pursuing the building and completion of the iron bridge, was no longer the wazir. He fell to Company and court factionalism; soon after, Nasiruddin Haider disappeared behind a smoke of Company and native intrigue. The iron bridge, of course, was never completed.

7

❧❧

A Sensuality Pleases: Arts and Culture in Transition

During the reign of Ghaziuddin Haider, a merchant from Iraq arrived at his court. The new entrant from the ancient Arabic centre of learning, politics and trade was announced with great fanfare. Though much feted, he was not impressed by what he saw. With an arrogant flourish, he took out an object d'art — a plate of agate embellished with a floral design.

The court was shocked; this, after all, was a specimen of 'yashab': a rare piece of finished work on a rare stone not found beyond the Persian Gulf. Some said it originated in Egypt, some traced its appearance to the divine inspiration which infused the masonry work of Cordova and Granada, the erstwhile centres of Muslim Spain. How could Hindustan, for all its riches, gold and diamonds, produce a stone moulded like thick glass?

Or so the merchant thought.

The next day he was invited to a feast by the king. With the confidence of a man who had just won over a new audience, he picked up his plate, and grew pale. The plate was made of yashab, bathed in violet and blue. In nervous trepidation he inspected the glasses, vessels, even the spoons which lay near. They were all made of yashab. The king smiled. Without saying a word, he gestured to the merchant to begin his meal. The courtiers noticed nothing, and the meal proceeded uninterruptedly. But at a distance, the merchant's gift lay amongst a pile of similar items, nondescript, like a drop in a sea of marvels.

This dramatic anecdote carried all the ingredients of a Lucknowi autumn. Amongst all the provincial cultures in the Indian subcontinent, it was Lucknow which imbibed to the hilt, the incoming 'Western influence' of the nineteenth century. It evolved head gear, round caps, outdoor shoes, sleepers and an Avadhian band. Yet it remained mysteriously old, reviving ancient forms of jewellery and anguthis. The history of the anguthi encompassed the discovery of the khooni neelam, virtually a bloody 'cats eye'. Gleaming dangerously, it worked as a talisman of luck and betrayal. The naginas, or gems, formed the plots of detective novels, later to become an integral part of the city's pulp literature. The diamond also stood out as a messenger of death and fortune. In Lucknow, traditions of astrology, numerology and the occult sciences acquired an element of doom, prophecy, fun and heartbreak. Tantra, an ancient form of material, biological and sexual science, came to be practised in elite houses as a sort of multipurpose, underground aphrodisiac. Its fanatically cultist and ritualistic aspects were pruned and integrated into a refined cultural ethic.

Astrology passed on from the Brahmin to the Muslim as a science of wisdom, speculation and mathematics. The native cooling system produced ice refrigerators and the Indian 'ice-cream', the kulfi. Made by combining the earth's natural cooling process with ice and thick milk, it left a rich, heavy, but delicate after taste. The same creativity led to the preparation of the sheermal, a bread kneaded in flour and honey, and the rogni roti. Even the system of Unani medicine came up with novel combinations which astounded the sedate Delhiwallahs.

While opening its doors to the West and simultaneously asserting indigenous forms, Lucknow blended diverse influences into a pattern of development and 'subversion'. Soon the West spoke freely, through architectural design, in the 'hostile' climate and habitat of Kakori, Barabanki, Faizabad and Rae Bareli. The 'General' cap, which became popular amongst the British during Nasiruddin Haider's time grew out of Mundel. The Avadhi rounded cap, almost like the base of a sitar stitched in velvet, developed from the earlier chaugoshia or the panchgoshia cap of Indo-Persian headgear. From the raw elements of the dupalli topi with its seam in the middle, emerged the 'nukka daar' — a cap small and narrow, pointed from front and behind, which appeared bewildering to the firangs.

The period of Ghaziuddin and Nasiruddin Haider actually marked a decisive 'break' from the ideological predilections of earlier nawabs. In the arts, emotions went beyond a secular, humanistic stirring, let alone a religious one. The 'woman' of Nasikh, Atish and Khalil, premier post-Insha, post-Mushafi poets, edged past the symbolic subjectivity of reetkala to become a flesh and blood creature. Ferocious cheetahs in bed, they demanded, dominated and desired for more in pleasure:

> *Vasl shab ki palang ke upar*
> *misl cheetah ke voh machalte hain*

— Khalil

(On the night of union atop the bed
she struggles like a cheetah)

Full-breasted and voluptuous, they showed off the forbidden navel:

> *Mujh se hilvata hai ab lezim junun zanjir ki*
> *aur koh-i ishq ki kahta hai to mugdar utha*

— Nasikh

(The chains of madness
I have lifted up like a barbell
and raised the mountain of love
in the manner of a dumbbell)

> *Tune mugdar hilaye kyon na karen*
> *bagh alam men iftikhar darakht*

— Nasikh

You shook (your) dumbbells
Why shouldn't the trees bask in their pride
in the garden of love

> *Tune dekhi shab-i-vasl naf us ki*
> *roshan hui chashm arzu ki*

— Khalil

(On the night of union I saw her navel;
The eye of my desire lit up)

Shakh ahu hai bhaven ankhen hain chashm-i ahu
mashk nafa tha koi naf men gar til hota

— Nasikh

(Your eyebrows are soft, fuzzy antlers
Your eyes those of the soft gazelle:
Were there a mole on your navel
It would be a gland of musk.)

But this free indulgence in the world of eroticism came with a price.
The people who constructed these images were informed by a deep sense
of social commitment and personal sacrifice, by the value of 'wazedari'.
Lucknowi eroticism owed a lot tó the scepticism and sensualism of
belief. Every gesture of 'masti' was interlaced with a deep struggle going
on in the hearts of Lucknowi poets — a struggle with prevailing norms,
personal relations and themselves. From this conflict emerged a sweet
stab of pain:

Voh mast hun khumar se jab dard-i sar hua
sandal lagaya main ne ragar kar sharab men

— Atish

(I am enthralled by the hangover as the headache took over.
I applied a paste of sandalwood after rubbing it in wine.)

Ranj se rahat nasib-i tab-i shirin kar hai
Bar lata hai qalam hone se nakhl angur ka

— Atish

(Experience of pain gives comfort
to things which are sweet in nature
From being cut, a grape sapling
bears a load of grapes)

And an insight:

Hai baja nazdeek vale mujhse gar vaqif nahin

mere shuhre ne kiya hai ab Irada dur ka

– Nasikh

(Its fitting that I remain unknown
to those close to me:
My renown has set its sights
On more distant horizons)

Political comments appeared between the lines of passion: a jab at the pro-British ustad who liked 'grapes' and the juices of life, but had forgotten that without the pain of the native, he will get only sour grapes in life. This trend stretched back to Mushafi and Jurrat both of whom made direct and indirect references to British rule. Much before the onset of the 'drain of wealth' theory, Mushafi wrote:

Hindustan ki daulat o' hashmat jo kuch ki thi
Kaafir firangiyon ne batadbir khech li

(All the wealth and splendour that India had
The infidel Englishmen have squeezed out by treachery.)

Jurrat, the erotic funster, directed his biting sarcasm at the pro-British section of the Avadhian ruling classes, including Saadat Ali Khan, when they failed to side with Wazir Ali. He blasted them for preening as European rich men, losing their Avadhian-Hindustani gesture in the bargain and becoming 'like a Bengali maina'.

Samjhen na ameer unko ahle taukeer
angrezon ke haath se kafas men hai aseer
jo kuch woh padhayen wahi muhn se bole
Bengal ki maina hain yeh Europe ke ameer

'(Consider them not rich and worthy of value
They have been imprisoned in a cage by the British
Whatever they teach is repeated by them
They are like Mainas of Bengal, these European rich.)

Poems of Nasikh and Atish took the critical dimension to the realm of psycho-sexual politics — the constant war of 'upmanship' between man and woman, friends and friends, friends and enemies, for control and domination. Each line of normal pleasure and innocence — the stance in lovemaking, the smile after a humiliation, the sneer after a victory, the attitude of the rose — bristled with perfidy and power. But unlike European art, Urdu poetry celebrated the material energy of everyday life. It did not lapse into purposeless epicureanism, guilt, fear or the pessimism of the intellect. This was an enlightened materialism based on a positive notion of power. Its sex appeal was as uninhibited as the history of Indo-Persian sexology. Lucknow in Ghaziuddin Haider's time produced a micro history of sophisticated pornography which carried forward the traditions of Sahab Qiran and Jafar Zatalli, the great seventeenth and eighteenth century sex poets. Sexology existed alongside politics, aesthetics and philosophy as a 'normal way' of reason and passion, nerve and judgement in Mir Taqi Mir's autobiography. This was in keeping with the Indian subcontinental attitude towards sex as an open, healthy, serious attribute of life 'at par' with other vocations. Practice ordained the organisation of separate sessions of erotic poetry in 'all' respectable houses. The cult of the virgin was not celebrated here. In sexual tales the fruit snaked unabashedly up the beloved's thighs to make a girdle of desire. The night of lovemaking was the night of velvet — an unsentimental journey of style, art and mood.

Saadat Ali Khan's tomb, built at the future site of Qaiserbagh alongside his wife Khurshid Zai's tomb, also reflected the quality of Indo-Persian subterfuge. Completed by Ghaziuddin Haider, it showcased a decorative mayhem of pavilions and towers on the outer side. But the sprawling inner floor was made up of black and white blocks, spread out in the manner of a huge chessboard. The fizzy exterior hid a cold interior; beyond establishing the mood of the tomb, this double-edged symbolism revealed the Avadhi attitude.

Trends in fashion saw women adorning the bade paiche or the flared pyjama, often tied below the navel. This was also the period of the farshi gharara — a gheredar lehnga worn below the navel, but parted between the legs which left behind a rustle of silk and fabric with each movement.

Lucknowi feminism produced its own form of poetry in the 'rekhti': perhaps the only example in the world of a separate genre of women's poetry. Uninhibited in attitude and spoken by men, its lyrics were different from the 'woman's voice' found in the ghazal, khayal or sohars and kajris, the folk forms of Avadh. Its very gesture was womanly — the poems heaved, sighed, panted, wisped, tantalised and abused. In these, the female expressed her individuality — 'there she went, corner of dress in hand, dangling her bangles — she is there on the roof getting wet in the rain, getting crazy; is it for her husband or someone else?'

The two creators of rekhti were flamboyant creatures — Rangin, the son of a risaldar, had undergone army training before dabbling in verse. Both Jan Sahab and he dressed up as women in performance, encouraging the fairer sex to break taboos. The womanly gestures which they adopted were bold and forthright, bearing none of the syrupy sentimentality accorded normally to women[1]!

Indeed, this was the period during which Lucknow witnessed a total feminisation of culture followed by an aristocratisation of the feminine.. A 'femalian' dialectic, in which in an instant, anger turned to passion, suffering to revenge, stamped the arts with its 'stigma'. Just as the ghazal gave way to rekhti, the masnavi was extended by the marsiya and the soz — two early examples of the non-narrative poem where an elegy was broken up by the heightening of emotions. Suddenly, a cadence of valour began to interrupt the tale of Imam Hussain's martydom in Kerbala. A despairing note followed, lifted by a slow bar of mellow dignity. The soz weaved magical movements out of a dream which aroused Abdul Halim Sharar many years later in Lucknow[2].

On Chehellum, the fortieth day of mourning, he saw a procession of bare headed, loose haired women carrying a taziya of Imam Hussain in the early hours of the morning, when the rays of the sun mingle with the darkness and the night is chillingly bright, while chanting a soz in Raag Parach:

> When the caravan of Medina
> Having lost all
> Arrived captive in the vicinity of Sham
> Foremost came the head of Hussain
> Borne aloft on a spear
> And in its wake a band of women
> with heads bared —

The song, the sight, 'the mood' bore testimony to the 'sansanikhez', sensational tumult of the marsiya and the soz. Its long chant of heroism, martyrdom, beauty and death was immortalised by Mir Anis and Mirza Dabir, two names who shone like stars on the poetic horizon of Lucknow:

> My style is simple, interesting and full of salt
> People have stopped talking after listening to my magical style
> The colour vanishes, so colourful is my writing
> The one whose name is in the winds is a flowing river and that is my temperament
> My life was spent traveling in these very forests
> This is my fifth generation which is praising the deeds of Imam Hussain

— Mir Anis (Marsiya)

The deeds of Imam Hussain in the Battle of Kerbala:

> Then tabors were struck, and did amplify
> The vibrant drum note, till it shook the sky;
> Death's trumpet sounded at the prince's cry
> And the farthest wilderness made reply.
>
> The martial clamour from above the ground
> Startled the dead in their slumber profound;
> With noise of stallions the cohorts rushed;
>
> The air like an hourglass was filled with dust.
> The sun's shining face was awestruck and flushed
> As it sank to earth in the gathering dusk;
> The combat waxing with doubled roar,
> The sky grew thicker, and it showed no more.

— Mir Anis

Lament on the death of Hazrat Ali Asghar, the six-month old martyr son of Imam Hussain:

> O' God if someone sees through the eyes of justice;

How a child went to his death from the mouth of the
cradle
He is separated from Sughra (his sister), the beloved of
Bano (his mother)
He cries on seeing their face and the gesture of departure
Other flowers too are young but they are well bred
Asghar just arrived and he is departing from the world

— Mirza Dabir

The 'structure of feeling' introduced by the soz and the marsiya
effected the style of sitar, tabla, humour, bhands, phabti, vasokht and
danda. It also embroiled the Asiatic junoon of itinerant story telling as
a 'way of adventure and aesthetic' in the fatal irresistible embrace of
non-tragic drama. Dastaans were Arabic in origin but in Lucknow
dastaans recited tales of Amir Hamza as 'Tilism-e-Hoshruba' in
Chandukhanas, the dimly lit Indo-Persian opium houses. Villainy
cohabited with heroism in these dens of vice, virtue, crime, punishment
and renaissance. Tradition sanctioned the recitation of dastaans in
workplaces as well. As the ironismith struck a blow and the seamstress
fixed a corner, their gesture of minute, laboured precision and
professional aesthetic achieved a literary high in the painstaking exploits
of Amir Hamza. The dastaans hide the pulsating smell and narrative
of the Indo-Persian-Lucknowi karkhana which constituted its most
potent audience.

The working classes and the maverick rich, vagabonds and shuriefas
all shared the 'Khwaja Nasiruddin' ethic — 'cunningness of honesty',
'ruthlessness of compassion' — of the Chandukhanas. This super-
Candide of Bokhara typified the medieval Asiatic bourgeoisie-socialist
— never staying at one place, he constantly harassed feudal amirs and
mullas. Never forgetting to con the rich, he made it a point to sleep
and strike an alliance with their wives. Principled and unprincipled, as
a true revolutionary, he used his mind and skills in trickery to earn a
fortune. And then blew it all away while providing justice to the
labouring and middle classes.

In the Lucknow of Ghaziuddin and Nasiruddin Haider, there was
a Khwaja Nasiruddin in every mohalla. The rich were lampooned while

the poor were entertained. In the same period, Lucknowi scholarship was able to shed off the last vestige of the old Indo-Persian verbosity and introduce the new method of practical, empirical writing. Issues became concise and ideological preaching gave way to brevity of expression. In fashion, the heavy nathani, a form of a nose ring, was discarded for the precise and pointed 'keil'. Rounded bunde , or earrings, emerged in the form of slim, long hanging ladis, ujtrajs and untians. In place of the traditional red vermillion, married women laced their forehead and parting of the hair with sandalwood paste. Pyjamas and angarkhas got transformed in such a way that there was little to demarcate between a female and a male dress.

As if to complement style with wit, the high and the mighty were ridiculed in the 'danda', addressed primarily to middle and lower class people. Danda performers were like joke show artistes in night clubs with a streetwise, impromptu dimension. There was also the tradition of reciting chirkin — Avadh was perhaps the only culture in the world to elevate scatology to an art form, where the 'motion of refuse' acquired rhythm and tonality. The phabti dealt exclusively in smart jibes or innuendoes, especially between men and women. Standing at the edge of the market place, a bunch of 'bankes', the flamboyant street smart guys of Lucknow, passed a phabti at a woman —

> *Jaan jaate kisi ne dekha hai,*
> *dekho ankhon se,*
> *jaan jaati hai.*

(Who has seen ones life to go past, see with your own eyes, life goes by)

After a pause the woman replied —

> *Ji haan yeh jaan mushtari ki hai,*
> *murda jismo mein jaan laati hai.*

(Yes, this is mushtari's life, she puts life back into dead bodies.)

8

❧

A Sensuality Emerges: the Life and Times of Wajid Ali Shah

Nasiruddin Haider too met a violent end. Some say he was poisoned by Dhania Mehri. Jealousy may have been the motive but the Company's hand was widely suspected.

Haider's death was followed by widespread violence. The succession of Munna Jaan who was his legal heir, was contested by the resident in a court of law. On losing, he resorted to a show of arms. The throne room, the Lal Baradari, was attacked with cannons and troops, and many lives were lost before Munna Jaan surrendered along with Badshah Begum, Nasiruddin Haider's fiery mother.

One of Saadat Ali Khan's brothers, Muhammad Ali Shah, was literally 'woken up' and crowned third king of Avadh. His accession was supported by the same clique of the 'leisurely nobility' which had opposed Badshah Begum and Munna Jaan. They were mainly courtier-pensioners, who were on the pay roll of the Avadh treasury via the good offices of the Company. Comprising of both Hindus and Muslims, they had little in common with the entrepreneur nobility spread over the length and breadth of Avadh administration. Bound by the treaties which committed the kingdom to the East India Company, this section constituted a silent, opposition-in-waiting.

The new king was immediately slapped with a treaty; he was also made the victim of a big fraud. The treaty increased the subsidiary amount payable by the nawab and specified that the Company would take over the administration of Avadh should it deem necessary. But it was struck down by the directors of the East India Company who considered it unjust and hardly an improvement on the treaty of 1801. Officially, no treaty existed — but it so happened that the governor general 'forgot' to inform the king of this very obvious detail. So unofficially, the treaty continued to be enforced. The king was unaware that the threats under which he was issuing loans to the Company — loans which were seldom paid back — had no locus standi[1].

But beneath the harassed frame of a frail king also lay a brilliant mind. The buildings of Muhammad Ali Shah did not follow the Saracenic baroque style. That phase ended with Roshan-ud-Daula who was Nasiruddin Haider's prime minister after Mehndi Ali Khan. A mixture of flamboyance and scientific sternness, his famous house had a dainty masjid besides giant, Acropolis-style Doric columns. The brooding, grand and scholarly look was broken by floral patterns on the pillars, brackets on the walls and the panoramic, non-linear structure of the building.

Muhammad Ali Shah's buildings leaned towards the rococo. He constructed the Sat Khanda, a giant observatory tower fit for observing the moon with the aid of a telescope. Situated near the Bara Imambara, it was a 'mood' and 'attitude' building resembling the architecture of Moorish Spain. While the structure rose like the leaning tower of Pisa, the columns danced in the manner of the palace of Cordova. Palladian tympanums stood atop Romanesque arches in all the four storeys. It gave a raw, energetic, darkish-red look, a precursor to the pure rococo of Hussienabad or the Chhota Imambara.

Polished with white limestone, the embellishments of the Chhota Imambara looked like frills of the khayal — the tinkering 'zamzama', the gliding 'meend' and the hanging 'taans'. The Muslim crescent stood atop the Hindu kalash and a flight of steps led to a small courtyard. The Chhota Imambara invoked parallels with the nearby Bara Imambara, but between Asaf-ud-Daula and Muhammad Ali Shah, the 'big vault' had given way to a 'cottage', and splendour to elegance. Both the Bara and the Chota Imambara were traditional Shia buildings with a touch of the contemporary. But while the former was a 'farrashkhana' with a Persian tray, the latter seemed like a pearl dropped from the sky. Angels, cast in the colour of gold, stood on each side of its gateway and a miniature Mughal garden was interrupted in the middle by a rectangular pond.

But Muhammad Ali Shah's Baradari, built near the Sat Khanda, went beyond the rococo. It had an arched balcony with pillars resembling the legs of an Indian bed. The space between the arches was curved like the space between two rods of the bed, making a 'C' shape with the two arms curved inwards and the two ends jutting outwards. The balcony top was occupied by three triangular 'huts', in the manner of rest houses on a hill side resort. Muhammad Ali Shah's style combined Greek, Moorish, Persian and even 'household' features, while always keeping close to a multiplicity of visions.

But the Sat Khanda was never completed. Muhammad Ali Shah died a premature death, leaving behind a Lucknow which appeared more and more startling to foreigners. Provincial styles of Europe, which had yet to grace the capitals of the occident, had found their way into the alleys, lanes and bylanes of the city. One could see Mughal, Jaunpuri, Rajput, Pahadi, even Japanese and Chinisorie features existing side by side, exploding all notions of stylistic continuity.

A rococo phase was qualified by the sudden emergence of a Rajput haveli, a Turkish dome or a Masjid with pagodas. Ganjs and roads intermingled to establish elite shopping centres. After coming to power, Amjad Ali Shah, the son of Muhammad Ali Shah and the fourth king of Avadh, laid down a ganj. By his time, the road from the Rumi Darwaza to Dilkusha, from the west to the east, already marked the luxuriant arm of the city. What it needed was a modern reach into the inner heart of the city — a path linking the Zahoor Baksh and the Begum Kothi to the dense quarters of Aminabad. Thus emerged the Hazratganj — a market centre with a straight, wide road running uninterruptedly from one end to the other with pavements on the sides. The road resembled the grid like streets of Shajahanabad, Istanbul, Isfahan and the British dominated centres. It signified Lucknow's coming of age and her varied, cosmopolitan base. Saadat Ganj now looked like a busy market centre of Kanpur, and the chowk wore a walled, festive look on the pattern of Faizabad. The baghs, mini forests, waterfalls and canals reminded one of Nainital, Dehradun and Kashmir, the fiza bringing close the open, lush smells of the Punjab.

The city, however, was no disordered maze of streets, alleys, markets and environment. Her irregularity represented the sajavat, or beautification, of a Krishna Janmashtmi jhanki. The multilayered spread of spaces approximated to the burada of the jhanki, frayed on the sides with passages, leaving in the middle a wide mass of dense and uneven edges. The city thus emerged as a swinging tapestry, running ten to twelve miles from Charbagh in the south to Aishbagh in the north and Takia Bodhi in the west to Kothi Bibiapur on the east, on a circumference of 152 villages. As in a jhanki, the complex of palaces with their many storeys gave way to thinly populated spaces surrounded by open fields, baghs and ponds. These again were cut by roads, more palaces and densely populated portions. The main streets were linked at vertical and horizontal points, seldom bulldozing through the living quarters. The city's drainage system linked seven big underground canals with the Gomti. These were constructed keeping uneven slopes in mind, low points to the east being supplied by small canals to prevent waterlogging.

Amjad Ali Shah completed a modern, pucca road linking Lucknow and Kanpur. Hazratganj became a thriving market place of the new sort, housing foreign luxury and consumer goods plus smallscale workshops of shoes, candles and toys. Parsis, Afghans and Tajiqs comprised the new breed of traders who introduced new occupations. The art of building carriages acquired a market orientation as Parsis began making bagghis for the middle class gentry and the British. Local ittar factories sprang up and so did paper mills and workshops for producing dyes and printing blocks.

By Lucknowi standards, Amjad Ali Shah's reign was a 'puritan' one. But the importance given to religious disciples was offset by a stress on secular learning and the cultivation of library science. His minister, Amin-ud-Daula, a man of learning himself, inhabited the new locality of Aminabad. This area was formerly the property of Prince Suleiman Shokh, a son of King Shah Alam who settled in Lucknow in the latter part of the eighteenth century. The Avadhi nawabs upto Saadat Ali Khan respected his superior status, allowing his personal court to became a centre of patronage and culture. After Ghaziuddin Haider's coronation, his status was undermined and he had to give away one of his daughters in marriage to Nasiruddin Haider. But his family had become Lucknowites to the point of adopting the poetry, dress, customs and language of Avadh. They inhabited the area near Maulviganj in the southern part of the city which had evolved as the exclusive resort of the town nobility.

However, by Amjad Ali Shah's time, the old Indo-Persian nobility was on the decline. A 'mass level' composite culture came to the fore going well beyond Persian manners. Revolving around Urdu and Avadhi, it was led by the middle classes made up of shopkeepers, sportsmen, employees of private, Shahi and Company firms, educated youth, educationists, proprietors of printing presses, maulvis and professional artisans. These forces were present from before but now they took on the features of a 'citizenry' with an autonomy of their own. A large number of lower level courtesans came up as individuals in their own right. The courtesan salon was now witness to conflicts between the neo-rich and the old nobility, or middle class aspirations based on love and the older standards of etiquette based on distance and restraint.

Aminabad became the exclusive haunt of these middle classes. The transfer of property from Suleiman Shokh's family to Amin-ud-Daula signified the transfer of a social milieu. The new Padain ki Masjid, which came up in the locality, was patronised by Amin-ud-Daula's Brahmin mistress. She broke down restrictions of gender and religion to allow both Hindus and Muslims, men and women inside the prayer hall. The masjid adopted many Hindu customs, common hitherto, only to the Sufi dargahs. Aminabadi culture foreshadowed a new age — the age of Wajid Ali Shah.

When the young son of Amjad Ali Shah ascended the throne in 1847, he already enjoyed the reputation of being a 'rasiya'. Oscillating between the company of religious and intellectual scholars on the one hand and musicians, courtesans, dancers on the other, he also showed, in those early days, a keen interest in mathematics and other rational sciences. Two sides were apparent from the very beginning — one of the organiser, the man interested in the world of ideas and politics, the other of the literary genius who saw the physical realm as a path to knowledge, experience and spirituality, and outwitted senior maulvis in the theory and practice of religion.

Wajid Ali Shah's age was one of tumult and greatness. Under the Delhi trio of Momin Khan Momin, Zauq and Ghalib, Urdu poetry reached its pinnacle of gesture, mood, language and ideas. The Mughal court of Bahadur Shah Zafar finally departed from past nostalgia to inaugurate a phase of mature political and cultural diplomacy. Momin, a confirmed Waliullahite[2], composed verses which extolled martyrs fighting for an anti-British egalitarian society in Punjab. Zauq, who was Zafar's ustad, used the metaphor of the 'morning breeze' to comment caustically, on the 'enlightenment' promised by the British and how it would snuff out the Bahadur Shah Zafar's candle:

> Ae shama ek chor hai mauje naseem subah
> Mare hai koi dam me tere taje zar pe haath
> (O'candle, this gust of morning breeze is a thief
> Anytime, it may snatch away your golden crown)

Ghalib spoke of the dimensions of pain — how emotional expressions require a full age to be effective. 'Aah ko chahiye ek umra asar hone tak'. All at once, lament gave way to historical and political themes. A realisation that the power of the East India Company could no longer be negotiated peacefully became obvious. In Calcutta, a new governor general had arrived with a new weapon. Called the 'Doctrine of Lapse', doctrines lapsed with impunity following its application.

Lord Dalhousie's most ardent and passionate victim, the city of Lucknow, kept passing through an unusual crisis of development and opportunity. Sleeman began his Avadh tours and the office of the resident became a means to empty Lucknow of resources and money. Elliot, the governor general's secretary, started a drive to empty Lucknow of learning[3]. Arriving in 1847, he began collecting rare manuscripts by persuasion and coercion, finally destroying the priceless library of Asaf-ud-Daula.

People grew restive as cultural authority collapsed. Young boys began correcting disciples of Nasikh, the 'zila' and the 'tuk bandi' (forms of versified satire) torpedoing puritanical strictures against the play of the material. In the countryside, Sleeman heard ominous portents of a possible revolt. In the city, there was a sudden spurt of men carrying arms. The traveller Bishop Hebber described[4] the amazing sight where stern looking maulvis, dark skinned labourers and the fair skinned nobility talked in the language of armed forces.

Wajid Ali Shah entered an environment where the colour of Mir and Sauda had turned pale, and the ideas of Nasikh and Aatish were passing through a phase of transition[5] — noble aristocratic suffering and noble approval of the market was out. The 'market' with its labourer, trader and the rebellious noble, had come centrestage. Disciples of Aatish and Naiskh, Rind, Sava, Rashk, Aseer now arrived with a new kind of post-Mir Hasan, post-Daya Shankar Naseem[6] Masnavi.

Slowly and subtly, society was being ripped apart by contradictions. Suppressed passions between the rich and the poor, the firangi and the native, the rich and rich, the middle class and the urban landlords, the nobility and the neo-rich, the criminals and the police, criminals and dacoits, the underclass and the shareef, were coming to the surface. In keeping with the spirit, the new king understood the upheaval inside him. Younger than his contemporaries, he lived the 'ideas' which others only spoke of.

Wajid Ali Shah was an unusual man of an unusual time — when everything was possible he did the impossible. He preserved for posterity what it meant to be a true Asian in the best and worst of periods. Beneath the rapidly spreading tentacles of Western might and culture, he upturned the very meaning of tradition to create a concept of Asiatic freedom. This was a freedom which followed the mind and the heart according to the need of the situation. It did not take anything for granted, believing in the transitoriness of all phenomena. And yet every moment was captured in its entirety.

Wajid Ali Shah, in this form and content, was the greatest enemy of the British. He was the exact opposite of their puritanical, positivist, pugnacious and metaphysical value system. When they called him indolent, he involved the people in his sensual pleasures. When they termed him capricious, he shamed the British with his humanism. Charged with over indulgence, he institutionalised his love for music, dance and women.

On account of his previous reputation as the heir apparent, the

Company did not expect Wajid Ali Shah to take an interest in the affairs of the administration. But on assuming the throne he mounted a horse and began conducting infantry parades at the Musa Bagh in an army uniform. In the early hours of the morning, the Corinthian pillars and brick huts of the Musa Bagh built by Asaf-ud-Daula shook to the sound of European drill in Persian terminology. But there was no compromise in style. The regiments had fancy names, cavalry troops being called Banka (Dandy), Tircha (Fop) and Ghanghur (Dark), while the infantry was given titles such as Akhtari (Lucky) and Nadiri (Rare). This was a revolutionary concept as it did away with the earlier practice of naming regiments after troop leaders and regions.

The British were alarmed. They were doubly perplexed by the king's intention to effect reforms in every sphere. To gauge the 'people's mood', complaint boxes were placed near roads. In them, most of the complainants expressed their satisfaction over the existing judicial system founded on the principles of Mohammedan and Hindu law. So the king set about strengthening the existing judicial system and did not pay much heed to the British advice of introducing European style courts[7]. He also stopped the practice of holding lavish durbars, finding them inconvenient and a burden on valuable resources. To tighten professional conduct, people were encouraged to seek redress in the Avadh courts and come to the king only in cases of emergency. In land revenue management, the state established direct contact with the cultivators and the Ijara, or the contract revenue system, was abolished. The king also transferred responsibilities to a set of trained officials, instead of concentrating autocratic power in his hands. He bade the district collectors to take into account the specifics of an area and public opinion while assessing the revenue. Justice on economic matters was dispensed in special courts and criticism was encouraged in the king's personal durbar.

The British condemned Wajid Ali Shah's system of justice, stopped the morning drill and placed barriers in the way of revenue reforms. They began complaining against the collectors, entangling the king in petty and inconsequential details while subverting his state machinery. The king simply ignored them. The British then began hitting below the belt. Wajid Ali Shah's experiments in music, arts and personal ethics became the butt of scathing, personalised attacks. He replied by setting up the Parikhana, a hostel of dance and music. There he expressed his ideas on mass culture and initiated new festivals while setting up exclusive fairs for ladies. His master stroke rested in creating an Urdu theatre, the crystallisation of a concept which had begun in the time of Nasiruddin Haider.

Wajid Ali Shah stamped the Indo-Persian cultural tendency, unleashed by Amir Khusro, with a last point of definition. If Khusro was the subconscious of the Indo-Gangetic belt, Wajid Ali Shah constituted its self-consciousness. Khusro entered deep within the Indian household with his loris[8]. Wajid Ali composed pahelis, or riddles, which taught wit and manner to children right upto the post-independence period:

Hari thi man bhari thi nau lakh moti jadi thi,
Raja ji ke bagh men, dushala odhi khadi thi —

(She was green, she was heady, and was embellished with nine lakh pearls, she was standing in the king's garden encased in a shawl)

What is it? A corn on the cob.

His palace complex, the Qaiserbagh too marked the culmination of something begun as far back as the building of the Qutab Minar. In this sense, his character was assimilatory as well as singular. He wrote in Avadhi, Braj, Marwari, Punjabi, Bengali, English, Deccani, Urdu, Hindi and Persian. In over a hundred books[9] he included his poetry, writings on literature and theories of art. The literature written on the art of love, or 'ishkbaazi', was biting enough to rival De Sade and Henry Miller.

Amir Khusro mixed Persian with Avadhi, Braj or Hindi, to create a fresh montage:

Zeehale miskin makun taghaful
Doraiye naina banaye batiyan

(Don't ignore this poor and down and out You turn away your eyes and try to fool me through your talk!)

Or

Ketabe hijra na daram ae jaan
Na leo kahe lagaye chatiyan

(O' my love, I do not possess the capacity to bear the pain of
separation
Why won't you press against me your chest?)

The inclusion of 'batiyan' and 'lagaye chatiyan' changed the whole
tenor of the qawwali. It provided the emotional break in the lyrical flow.
It was like introducing a bit of 'khameera' in a beeda of paan, making
it 'tadak', sweet and mellifluous. But Wajid Ali Shah overturned the
whole structure of the paan. He began his compositions in Avadhi, even
Bengali, before going on to Urdu:

Asho bosho na bolon banagalin meri jaan (Bengali-Urdu).
Aankhen teri ras raseelin, bhauen chadi kaman (Urdu).

Wajid Ali's leitmotif combined gesture, humour and emotion. It
could adopt the stance of a suffering woman, a proud tormentor, a rustic
rasiya, a sophisticated gentleman. He could write in an emotional,
melancholy voice so typical of the ghazal mood —

Ravish chanegi gulshan me saba mere baad
Bulbule bhulengi phoolon ki dua meri baad

(The morning wind will search for small pathways in the garden
Nightingales will forget the grace of flowers after me)

And immediately adopt the 'sringar ras' with an 'irony' —

Gesu pe pari ru ke rasai hai kisi ki
Sar pe ye bala aaj bulai hai kisi ki

(Someone's tresses are entangled like a fairy's today, trouble will
come calling on someone's head!)

Irony entered his love poetry too:

Pada hai paanv men ab silsila mohabbat ka
Bura hamara hua ho bhala mohabbat ka

(The chain of love now encases the feet
As if I suffer and love prospers!)

Or

Ishk kya kam tha aina ki kholi kalai
Ek hairani zyada hui hairano men

(Was love not enough, that you had to expose the mirror's secret?
This was one more astonishment amongst many astonishments.)

These lines joined dissimilar metaphors with a 'bang' by
attitudinalising the physical excitement of doing so. Poetry had acquired
the tone and timber of the 'akhada' where two profiles clash with elan.
There was no contemporary example to rival Wajid Ali Shah's duel.
Its legatee appeared later as the non-idealist working class poetry of the
twentieth century.

Akhtar Piya exploded genres to introduce the narrative in the ghazal
and the singular idea in the masnavi. This 'something' between the
ghazal and the masnavi included a wail of patriotism (composed when
he was leaving Lucknow, never to return):

Doston shaad raho tumko khuda ko saumpa
Hamne apne dile nazuk ko jafa ko saumpa
Qaiserbagh jo hai usko saba ko saumpa
Daro deevar pe hasrat se nazar karte hain —
Khush raho ahle watan hum to safar karte hain
Sare ab shahar se hota hai akhtar rukhsat
Aage bas ab nahin kahne ki hai mujhko fursat
Ho na barbaad mere mulk ki ya rab khilkat
Daro deevar pe —

Friends, be happy, I consign you to God
My tender heart I consign to the virtue of faithlessness
This place called Qaiserbagh I consign to the morning wind
I look at my house and walls with the look of aspiration —
Be happy, my nation, I journey ahead Akhtar departs from the whole
of the city
Beyond this I do not have the patience to state anything
That the people of my country should not get destroyed O' God

I look at my house and walls

When the Parikhana laid out the rudiments of Kathak, ancient Indian dance forms, hitherto centred around temples, were also being updated in the secular courts of south India. But they still relied on ancient moods. The Bharatnatyam leaned on grand posture and the Odissi on the supple sway of the body. Kuchipudi undulated on the elegance of rhythm while Manipuri on the grace and fixture of abstract, mathematical movements. Only Kathakali was driven by narrative and gesture. Kathak, formerly the Allahabadi[10] art of story-telling and secular dance, moved faster than the Kathakali. Despite revolving around gesture and rhythm, rather than mood or posture, it drew its energy from emotion and meaning.

These emotions, however, were not confined to the traditional navrasas. While evolving the nritta, or pure dance, and nritya, the thematic movement, Wajid Ali Shah and his dancers subsumed single blocks of emotions into a montage of pure pleasure. Simple taals and intricate footwork broke all naturalistic-thematic rules common to Bharatnatyam or Kathakali. A celebration of style for its own sake, Kathak nritta introduced the new attitude of freedom and individuality, seen in the American tap and the Spanish flamenco. But its pure speed and technique also had a story to tell and in that sense it came close to the European classical ballet.

The gestures of Kathakali and Bharatnatyam invoked deep, primitive forms of energy. Wajid Ali Shah's 'gatens', or compositions, spoke of modern functions, physical attitudes and material objects: Salami (salute) gat, naaz (care) gat, fariyad (request) gat, mukut (crown) gat, banke (flamboyant) gat, ghunghat (veil) gat, bhainga (twisted eye) gat, lehnga (garment) gat. This gesture ended up energising the tradition of khayal, thumri, dadra, tappa, hori and dhrupad. Thumri evolved out of the nritya but expressed feelings in a quasi staccato form, pitting pain, complaint and masti in a competitive whole:

Gori lat khol de, lat men kala nag
Chati ki tu bani bajhi, akhtar sunao rag —
(thumri in Rag Jhinjhauti).

Wajid Ali Shah's khayals became 'un-khayalised', following the abstract conventions of classical raags but producing shock, 'special effects':

Kahi hovat bijli, chamak chamak akhtar
Dhak dhak chatiyan bajat
Chaundh chaundh man lapak lapak.

This style changed the mood of his 'heroines'. He had a number of nikaahi and mutahi[11] wives, as well as liaison women, some of whom were part of his Parikhana. They were all titled differently, as per their ada. One day, a begum who was quite vocal in her protests said to the king: 'You enjoy life whenever you feel like, we are engrossed in only one occupation, there is very little application of our dance', and so on and so forth. The king came up with a solution: how about a play on Radha and Krishna? There were raas mandalis of Braj in Lucknow adept at performing Krishna's dance with the gopis. But their art had no plot. Wajid Ali Shah created events before the dance in the manner of the 'jalsewaliyan'[12] of Lucknow and the folk per. ...ners of Maithal[13]. He then transformed the dance itself into an 'epic manner' to produce a full fledged drama or 'rahas'.

Soon Radha appeared on a proscenium stage speaking in Persian and Urdu. Krishna became the Avadhian peasant — lusty, rugged, witty and full of life. This was the 'proletarian' interpretation of Krishna, present in the original Mahabharata or in later Vaishnavite texts. The Krishna who caught the hand of bhakt Raskhan[14], about to leave Mathura thinking that Krishna would no longer visit him, and said — *Kahan jaat ho, saar* (Where are you off to, you sod?).

In a 'rahas'[15], a jogan wants to see the raslila of Krishna. Her servant sets out for the purpose and reaches Radha after several encounters with pariyan, sakhiyans and funsters. The Radha he meets acts tempestuously, like a regular heroine of the burlesque.

Before Radha enters, Wajid Ali Shah issues stage instructions: 'After the completion of the previous scene all sakhiyan, or friends of Radha, should say Raja Ramchandra ki jai. After that, the competition of Radha and Kanhaiya should commence, half the sakhiyan should stand on the side of Kanhaiya, half on Radha's side, question and answer should commence between Radha-Kanhaiya and meaning of the reference to the context ought to be elaborated alongside according to the already established custom through the right side of the circular stage after each sher and each dohra'.

Radha enters and says:

Majmaye gair men aisa sitam ijaad kiya,
katila bhool ke humko na yaad kiya (Urdu).
Dohra: Main virahni sanjog sang na koi saath,
Nari chuvat bed ke fafla ho gaye haath (Braj-Hindi).

Krishna replies:

Naam mera hai kanhaiya main tujhko janat hun,
Radha ji jaan se main tumko yahan maanta hun.

Dohra: *Radha ji ang par bindiya iti chavi det,*
Mano fuli ketki bhor basan let.

Radha: *Main teri ishk men diwani hui ae kanha,*
Maine ji jaan se tujhko yahan pahchana.

Dohra: *Aao pyare mohan palak dekh tohe leun,*
Na main dekhun auran ko na tohe dekhan deun

At one point, Radha gets angry with Kanhaiya; she suspects that he has given his flute to Kubri, or the other woman. Kanhaiya is in a fix; what to do now? He calls Ramcheera, the eternal jester, and the jogan's servant. Ramcheera arrives; from the beginning he is irreverent towards Kanhaiya. The rahas changes tone from verse to pure conversational dialogues, mainly in Avadhi.

Ramcheera: *Hazir Maharaj Hazir Raja ke Raj Adhiraj Maharaj Shiv Pradhan Chattrapati batao to kya hua?*

(I am here great king, I am here kingdom, of the king, great king Shiv Pradhan Chattrapati, do say what happened?)

[Why was Chattra Pati Shivaji, the Maratha ruler, being compared to Kanhaiya?!]

Kanhaiya: *Radhike khafa ho gayin. Janat hain main murli kubri ko de aaya hun.*

(Radha is angry. She knows that I have given my flute to Kubri).

Ramcheera: *Maharaj, fir manao.*

(O, king win her over again)

Then Ramcheera tells Kanhaiya to enlist the help of a sakhi. Kanhaiya calls a sakhi.

Kanhaiya: *Ae Lalita, hamri Radha hamse nahin maanat hain. Kya karun?*

(O, Lalita. My Radha refuses to get won over by me. What should I do?)

Lalita: *Vinti karo. Naak ragro. Paiyan paro. Mood ghiso. Chirauri karo, jab to manihain.*

(Pray to her. Rub your nose. Fall at her feet. Rub your head, grovel before her, then she will agree.)

Then, after a long exchange with interludes full of dadras and thumris, Kanhaiya decides to go in search for his flute.

Kanhaiya: *Hamri murali kisi ne dekhi hai?*

(Has anyone seen my flute?)

Ramcheera (mocking the tone of Kanhaiya): *Hamri murgi kisi ne dekhi hai?*

(Has anyone seen my hen?)

Kanhaiya plants a blow on Ramcheera and drives him out. Then laughs and says: *Hum murali dhoondhat hain ki murgi?*

(Am I searching for the flute or the hen?)

The rahas was followed by the nakal, or the one act, one scene imitative, realist, story-drama. It drew parallels with Moliere's satires, American slapstick and twentieth century gestural theatre. Nakals were also set to 'humorous' music, a convention used by Bertolt Brecht from *Three Penny Opera* onwards. One nakal, set in Band Raag, sets out to enact the story of a thakur and his servant. The servant had not received his salary from the thakur for months and was nursing a grudge against him.

One day the thakur told his servant: *O' Ramcheera, my mind is restless to hear the faag* (the music of spring). *Bring me a raag.* Ramcheera replied: *Very good, Maharaj. I will entertain you with a Band Raag.*

He went and brought an empty vessel from the market. He then climbed a tree on which there was a beehive. He filled the vessel with the hive, closed its mouth and kept it inside a small room of the house. He told the thakur that he had brought the Band Raag. The thakur was very happy; he went inside the room, the Ramcheera bolted the door from the outside. The thakur shook the vessel; the bees hummed — *ae bhan bhan bhan bhan bhan bhan* —

The thakur was extremely happy. What excellent service by Ramcheera, what an excellent raag. Ramcheera egged him on to open the mouth of the vessel to hear the raag in its full form. As the thakur did so, in an instant his body was covered by a swarm of bees. Ramcheera had bolted the door and he could only tear his clothes, shout and beat himself.

The moral of the story — never wrong a heartless, 'unpaid' servant. Laughter.

In another nakal, Wajid Ali Shah gave instructions at every step, to imitate, put on the gesture, and make the face of particular characters. 'Make the face of qazi thus', 'that of the mufti in this way'. The enactment tells the tale of an amir who asks his servant to send horsemen in search of the new moon in the month of Ramzan so that Id can be celebrated. The horsemen catch hold of a musafir, a traveller, and ask whether he has seen the moon. The musafir replies that yes he has seen a moon near the Jamuna, behind the leaves of the peepal tree.

The musafir is brought before the amir. The amir is happy and tells his servants to take him to the qazi. The qazi sends him to the mufti. The mufti sends him to the big court. The big court sends him back to the small court. The musafir shuttles between various 'offices', gives evidence about the moon, time and time again, and swears that he will not see 'the moon' again in his life.

The musafir then goes off and sleeps in a broken masjid. There he begins to talk in his sleep — the moon is at the qazi's place, the moon is at the mufti's place. Some religious Muslims pass by — one of them thinks he is a ghost, one is of the view that he is a martyr, the other admonisher tells him to read the kalma. But the musafir, too tired and stupefied by his experiences, continues — the moon is in the big court, the moon is in the small court. The Muslims wake him up and on seeing their faces, the musafir runs off swearing again that from that moment on he would never speak about the moon.

In these slapsticks, the author undermined authority and poked fun at institutionalised sacredness. They fell under the dramatic conventions of the non-Aristotelian, non-Victorian, non-Ibsenian, non-Stanislavskian theatre represented chiefly, by medieval European drama, German baroque comedy and Brechtian didactics[16]. As if this was not enough, the rahas and the nakal soon inspired the first 'opera' of Lucknow, the 'Indar Sabha' of Amanat.

In contrast to the bawdy burlesque and the irreverent slapstick, dramatic forms of the elite and the working class, the opera grew out from the world of the middle class, bourgeoisie 'citizenry'. Amanat himself belonged to the breed of the 'Lucknowi bourgeoisie' — he even used to call himself 'citizen Amanat'. In Indar Sabha, the gods came down to the earth and the public stage of Lucknow in front of ordinary people. It unleashed, in a short while, a revolution in attitude, fun and social life. Amanat himself wrote[17]:

> *The moment when Indar Sabha was presented in a sequence, the whole world listened to it and praised it without a sequence.*
> *Idols cried Allah! Allah!, each line is a line or a gift from God!*
> *Whoever remembered whatever, flew away with it, it was on everyone's lips.*
> *Some remembered it, some wrote it down, some searched for meaning, ad infinitum.*
> *When its fame 'flew' in Lucknow, 'Amanat', everyone presented their righteous wish.*

The sabha revived the post-Sanskrit tradition of Indian theatre, begun in the time of Jehangir in Rajasthan and Agra through the medium of the Braj language[18]. The sabha posed stiff competition to the purely English theatre of Bombay and provided the standardised formula for a new genre.

Realist conventions, tragic twists and the sensational, akkhad gesture balanced the fantastical plot in Indar Sabha. The play was translated in Marathi, German and Sinhalese and influenced the development of

Parsi theatre. But before Indar Sabha became a raging box-office hit, Wajid Ali Shah had himself adorned the jogiya dress with his begums in a display of mass festivity. He had begun organising festivals during the spring and monsoon on the Gomti, when the river was lit up near the Chattar Manzil. Rows and rows of boats of every conceivable size cruised to the accompaniment of dance, music and revelry on board. Fetes by women, the meena bazaars, first organised by Akbar, were held at Qaiserbagh, the huge complex which the king had created in the heart of the city.

Enclosed by a wall of Romanesque arches and Greek pillars, Qaiserbagh had four gateways. Apart from the symbol of the two fishes, a number of angels stood as primary motifs at the gates. Baradaris, pavilions, manzils, waterfalls, gardens beautified the inner space. A huge, tent like structure, the lanka, was constructed near the white baradari as a massive auditorium. Some of the plays staged here by the king's friends and courtiers showed sword fights and combats in precise realistic detail.

Qaiserbagh housed the peepal tree under which the king sat as a jogi near the the big house of Chaulakhi. From a distance, the palace-complex looked like a never-ending carnival. All its arches were elliptic and the baradaris had big round 'burj' like structures at the ends. Appearing as pen castles, they were adorned by sculptures and surrounded by bridges.

Qaiserbagh summed up the history of Indo-Persian architecture, seriously and humorously. It tamed down and absorbed the romanticism of Rajput and Sur[19] pavilions, the openness of Mughal gardens, the brooding elegance of Jaunpur and the Tughlaqs, and played a joke by making the pavilion work like a rest house near the gates. Gateways, also camouflaged the famed optical illusions of Golconda and Bijapur forts.

But Qaiserbagh was no garden of paradise. It stood forth as the king's open house, or more appropriately the resort of an explorer who could go visiting a courtesan at night, disguised as a commoner. Indeed, Wajid Ali Shah met his future wazir at one such gathering. He represented the open, uninhibited culture of the Indo-Gangetic plain where even the most unconventional acts were permissible if done with valour, in full view of the public. Exuding male power and nazakat, Wajid Ali gave voice to the peasantry and introduced the post-sensual, sexual sign in poetics of love. To him women were faithful but 'conscious' individuals, capable of shifting 'allegiance' with the changing balance of power.

Lovemaking under him was shorn of mystery or romance, becoming scientific and casual. His code of cultural sexuality complemented his ideological code of post-humanist politics and philosophy. He cultivated talents like the painter-architect Kanshiram who blended the hand of the Lucknowi calligraphist, seen in khat-e-bahar, khat-e-gulzar, khat-e-nastalikh, with the Company school of painting. Popularised by the lithographs of the Daniel brothers, this marked the culmination of the Avadh school of painting classified earlier by Juan, Jofeni, the internationally renowned German painter, during Asaf-ud-Daula's time. Though drawing on the epic, gestural, non-Western perspective of Mughal painting[20], Kanshiram painted 'dotted' figures in the manner of Monet.

His art showed that perspective, far from only being three dimensional, could also be epical. The observer's eye, instead of receding to a vanishing point in the centre, could well savour a narrative in three or four successive stages. Mughal scenes did not cleanse or present the viewer with lofty ideals. Colliding idea with idea, emotion with mind, drama with drama, they planted surrender, loyalty, submission, tact, battle, retreat in a single, 'multipart', whole. This epic style is unparalleled in the history of European, Chinese and Japanese art, being the handiwork of ordinary workmen like Balchand and Payag in Shahjahan's time.

Kanshiram, along with Dayanat-ud-Daulah, the king's courtier, was also one of the architects of Sikandar Bagh. A big walled garden built for Sikandar Mahal, one of the principal wives of the king and a forceful personality in her own right, its gates had semi-circular 'dalans' with Greek pillars. The second floor was adorned with Romanesque arches, interpreted more like the round, non-European or Asiatic-European arches of Cordova. The top floor was fragmented with pagoda-pyramid style pavilions on either side. The main gate itself had a big arch flanked by elephants and two fishes.

It was this vision which applauded the new trend in fashion and literature. In Lucknow the Delhi style angarkha evolved out of combining the jama and the balabar while doing away with the bodice. The two lapels were fixed to each other in a way which exposed the left side of the chest. Wajid Ali Shah wore the Lucknowi angarkha with the semi-circular jabot and the crescent shaped necklet, unmasking the left nipple. Modern men's wear has yet to beat this pure, unadulterated Asiatic-Lucknowi flamboyance, before which contemporary Western fashion must have paled into drab, philistine, peasant insignificance. Ghetle shoes and the 'kulah' topi imparted a gorgeous look to the achkan, now captured not in oil paint but the still image. The reign of Asghar Jaan, the photographer of Lucknow, had begun, which brought latest European technology right into Lucknowi homes.

Wajid Ali Shah's rule was marked by an aggressive de-Westernisation and full-bloodied assertion of Indianness. This was the culture of the gut, power, mind and humour which blasted all idealist, heathen, Western myths about India. In contrast to the clerical-Bengal, and the comprador-Bombay, mentality, it showed the pride, self-respect, thanak and thasak of the Indo-Gangetic belt. Its realism saw Mirza Shauq's masnavis[21] departing from the stories of fairies and houris to portray the trials and tribulations of khangins or ordinary women. This shift encouraged Wajid Ali to write an early work of Urdu prose — an account of his love life or ishkbaazi ki dastaan. Brutally frank and guiltless, the work spared neither the beloveds nor the lover. It also revealed a dim desire for a community of love, a concept, at once Shiite and universal where relations are struck and broken on the basis of passion and style without jealousy, possessiveness and narrow restrictions of social-legal laws. In the end, there was a note of uncaring sadness, about a suffering life that was lived and enjoyed, but in which the search for faith, love and more suffering has yet to cease.

9

A Sensuality Fights —
Lucknow: 1857

On 21 November 1856, an item appeared in *Tilism*, an Urdu weekly newspaper of Lucknow:

> "On Mondays and Wednesdays, a crowd collects at places, fakirs sprout fire from their mouths, neither their mouth gets blisters, nor do their clothes get stained."

The editor of the newspaper was Maulvi Muhammad Yakub Ansari, a firangi mahali. Only a few months had passed since its first issue was published from the city's leading printing press. *Tilism* was the second newspaper to hit the newsstands — *Lucknow Akhbar*, edited by Lalji, had been in publication since 1847.

But the language of *Tilism*, and its presentation of news, was unmatched. It mirrored truly, the special, embellished, spunky flavour of Lucknowi Urdu. The item was about a series of alarming incidences rocking Avadh — bands of fakirs and agent-provocateurs speaking out openly against the British and spreading the gospel of revolution.

Surreptitiously, the *Tilism* smuggled a political message, establishing the fakirs as revolutionaries, as people who were playing with fire and yet not getting burned. The message was so coded that it could also be read as an ironic, derisive comment on the fakirs.

In Urdu prose, irony, twists and the exhorting tone entered the realm of diction and vocabulary itself—

'*In dino galle ki girani hai, giraniye khatir ki arjani hai, goya mufassil men aata gila hai, khune dil bajaye sharab hai, tarje dil kabab hai — *'

In this new use of language, satire, pun and emotion found their way into everyday speech. The structure of Khari Boli, which lay at the base of Urdu, underwent a strange twist of outlandishness, sweetness and sourness in the bargain. This 'coexistence of opposites' gave a new charge to political and social commentary. The 'idea' in the above-mentioned extract, published in the Urdu weekly, *Sahre Samri*,[1] expressed the simple fact of a shortage of foodgrains, a problem hitting the city with increasing regularity[2]. The reporting was factual but prosaic twists were drawn out of the objective text. Inflation was high so the market must be down. A down market suffers from shortages; so instead of foodgrains, it receives bags of complaint. The heart is (normally) full of blood. But (due to complaints) it gets drowsy, like the effect of wine; and then angry like a fried kebab!

The additional use of zabar and zer, the 'a' and 'e'; in Lucknowi Urdu stretched words and made them pukhta and rounded in comparison with Delhi. Linguistic extensions brought a change in lip movements which in the mid-1850s expressed a momentous event in the history of the Indian subcontinent — the annexation of Avadh.

On 9 February 1856 Wajid Ali Shah was informed by the then resident, General Outram, that the Company was assuming charge of Avadh's civil and military administration. The king was allowed his title, claim to a generous pension and possession of prized buildings. He was to put a seal on a treaty, specifying his consent in the matter.

The terms were generous; what had the king to lose in signing it? As it is, fighting the British was out of the question. Hadn't his forefathers tried and failed in this endeavour? Had not all the native powers, from Satara in 1846 to Nagpur in 1854 to Tanjore in 1855, proved ineffective in resisting Company encroachment on their sovereignty?

These arguments were fed to the king by Ali Naqi Khan, the controversial wazir of Avadh. Ali Naqi was presumably acting at the behest of the British on the promise of a jagir and other rewards. The king's seal on the treaty was very important to the Company as it would have conferred legitimacy on a document of doubtful legal validity. The treaty of 1837, which had mentioned the possibility of a Company takeover, was not in force. And no such clause existed in the treaty of 1801. In fact, the king had to be informed that the treaty of 1801 had become redundant[3]; the Company in effect, had to rescind, arbitrarily, its own agreement. An Indian territory was being siezed by a foreign Company still, theoretically, a vassal of the Mughal emperor[4], on the issue of maladministration, without the consent of that emperor! Even on the scale of the informal relation which had evolved between the Company and Avadh, the king's side tipped heavier. Wajid Ali Shah had tried to implement reforms suggested by the Company and observed all norms of 'special friendship' with cordial sincerity.

The annexation of Avadh was thus a political move; its 'irrationale' and history of fraud was compiled, blow by blow, with intense precision, by a servant of the East India Company. R.W. Bird, an assistant of Sleeman, fell out with the British administration on the Avadh policy and after its annexation wrote an expose — *The Spoilation of Avadh*. It detailed the rapacious exploitation of Avadh by the Company with satirical relish. The titles of chapters were: *With what Means did the Company come to Know about the Wealth of Shuja-ud-Daula and How Soon it Grew Close to his Kingdom and Treasure; How did the Company Turn Ghaziuddin Haider into a Treasure of Benevolence; Col. Sleeman as the Basic Tool for the Spoilation of Avadh; General Outram Finishes the Unfinished Task of Col Sleeman*, and so on.

The book was published in early 1857 and brought into focus the irreconcilable conflict between the British and the native powers. At that point, other social forces, from the bourgeoisie and the peasantry to the modern soldiery, held the fragile levers of social and economic power. But political legitimacy still rested with native rulers. Even after decades of direct and indirect Company rule, they housed the memories, struggles, hopes and despairs of the people. So long as there was a Bahadur Shah Zafar, a symbolic 'Sovereign of the World', 'Pride of Hindustan', in Delhi, a hope for an indigenous 'renewal' remained. So long as dupalli topis, angarkhas, shalukas, ghararas and dhotis remained in force, why would clerks and sepoys of the East India Company be interested in pants and tunics?

Deep cultural, economic and psychological reasons worked behind British attacks on native rulers. Qaiserbagh's rahas and Amanat's Indar Sabha portrayed the psychological and contemporary urges of the native mind with all their splendour and tradition. Who would then be interested in the measly outputs of the European stage put up by stiff-lipped realists? When women had their own rekhti and fashion, courtesans their exclusive salons and housewives their exclusive interiors to lord over, who would be interested in the drab look of an European woman?

The native Hindus had a religion in which aesthetically pleasing human forms of the divine were worshipped without an innate concept of guilt. The native Muslims bowed their heads to the one and only Allah with pride and freedom unencumbered by stern injunctions of natural suffering. Who would then be interested in a Christian god whose unity was split in three? A god who, on the other hand, could never be a playmate, or a valorous hero like Krishna and Rama?

This historical mindset of the Indian people on the eve of 1857 landed the British in a dilemma. The time for accessibility to native culture was running out. Tainted with exploitation, European modernity also sounded less appealing to Indians.

A court like Lucknow enjoyed a particular type of legitimacy — it was the repository of tradition but it was also the centre of innovation. A Mughal badshah or the Avadhian king could change the time held traditions of the Hindu religion — the temple of Hanuman at Aliganj on the north bank of the Gomti was endowed and further developed by Mallika Kishwar, the wife of Amjad Ali Shah and mother of Wajid Ali. She placed a crescent over the kalash, which too become a sacred symbol of Hindu culture. Similarly, a Hindu talukedar could introduce changes in Muharram celebrations. In Gonda and Rae Bareli, the taziya had to pass the deorhi of the Hindu raja before the annual procession.

The ruling class did not regard itself as Hindus or Muslims in their social calling. Indeed, dharma was more concerned with one's virtue and calling as a 'man', rather than with being a Hindu or a Muslim. For an Avadhian peasant of that period it would have appeared strange to be told that he was to deal with two persons, one Hindu and one Muslim, as men of separate dharma. He would have replied, 'deen to ek hi hai, chahe Hindu ya Musalman ('faith' is one whether Hindu or Muslim).

This mass secularisation unnerved the British. Their reforms were rejected but the modern injunctions of native rulers received wide popularity. More dangerous was the possibility that indigenous courts, if kept alive, could well become the hub of political activity should the native decide to switch his loyalty.

There were two ways open — either the destruction of courts as independent places of affluence and influence, or their 'redefinition' according to colonial versions of tradition and modernity. The court of Lucknow resisted the latter trend by mocking the British version of Bengal modernity and upturning the Western view of the east. It conformed to no specific view of caste, of the eternal separatedness of Hindu and Muslim 'nations'. It also subverted the very idea of the east as a backyard of knowledge whose science, astronomy and medical sciences were 'fit to be laughed at by girls at an English boarding school, and disgrace an English farrier and its geography made up of seas of treacle and butter'[5].

The British first set about destroying and appropriating for themselves India's scientific and intellectual achievements. The Mughal empire competed with Europe in the age of the commercial revolution but the Industrial Revolution saw England and France edging past in the eighteenth century. During this time, the Indian subcontinent too moved towards an industrial renaissance through a period of great social turmoil and political flux. This process was enhanced, interrupted and distorted in stages due to England's intervention. Colonial designs reduced India, the premier power in world trade of manufactured goods to the status of a vast, revenue drawing agricultural machine of primary export and foreign import.

But prevailing trends set by native courts, made it difficult for Manchester cotton to be widely and culturally acceptable. The end of the Company's trade monopoly in 1813 terminated the period when its primary aim was loot accumulated through the circulation of Indian goods. Under the new scheme, India was to act as an entrepot to balance

Shahnajaf — the Lion Gate.
(top) The Begum Kothi, destroyed in post-independence India.
(Courtesy - State Museum, Lucknow)

1

The Choti Chattar Manzil Darshan Bilas.
(top) Sikandar Bagh with the scars of war.
(Courtesy - State Museum, Lucknow)

2

*Wajid Ali Shah in posture, a statement of material
and gestural art of the Avadhi school.*

*(top) Lanka – the great Lucknowi auditorium, a statement of
anti-Aristotelian, epic aesthetic – destroyed by the British deliberately.*

(Courtesy - State Museum, Lucknow)

Qaiserbagh, the mermaid gate.
(Courtesy - State Museum, Lucknow)
(top) The sack of Qaiserbagh.
(Courtesy - State Archives, Lucknow)

Mallika Zamaniya's imambara, a woman's
demeanour in stucco — vandalized.
(top) Begum Hazrat Mahal —
cunning and compassionate — The Woman of India.
(Courtesy - State Archives, Lucknow)

The young Akhtari Bai Faizabadi,
Avadhi cosmopolitanism in profile.

Nana Saheb leaving Lucknow.
(Courtesy - State Archives, Lucknow)
(top) Birjis Qadir — riding to battle
"Jai Avadh — Down with anti-1857-ites".
(Courtesy - State Museum, Lucknow)

7

Panch Mahalla, the sturdy, earthy origin of Lucknow's enterprise.
(top left) Nasiruddin Haider, the drill before the muse.
(Courtesy - State Museum, Lucknow)
(top right) Mirza Amani's modernity, hated by the British,
destroyed in 1857.

the British world export-import trade bill. Indigenous commerce and industrialisation had to take secondary place; industrial centres like Mirzapur, developing with British and native capital, collapsed when the East India Company withdrew its patronage. On the face of it there was a crisis of demand. But demand in any economy is a product of market and political factors; native capital, which could have supplanted the flight of British capital, was discouraged in Mirzapur due to the absence of a supportive state power.

The 1820s and '30s were very crucial for the subcontinent for they marked the beginning of the end of the possibilities that had emerged in the eighteenth century. After withdrawing their capital in large measure, the British began closing down the native courts which provided the source for investment and development. Within a few years, places like Bundelkhand, Agra, Doab, Rohilkhand, even Mathura, Bharatpur and Rajasthan turned from great cotton, opium, salt and other luxury production centres to backwaters of starving peasants and insurgent landlords[6].

But Lucknow remained the one pebble in the eye. The British did not have full control over its resources and the court still encouraged local industry. Lucknow capital was also invested in Kanpur. In the years after the 1830s, population from the Company territories had actually crossed over to Avadh which they found more prosperous than the miserable conditions in the Doab and Rohilkhand.

The destruction of Avadh and Lucknow was imperative. The British did not fear Wajid Ali Shah as a decadent king existing in splendid isolation. They dreaded his presence as a man of free will in touch with the people. This was why it was important to make him sign the treaty; and that was why Wajid Ali Shah refused to do so. He called his treasurer, Miftah-ud-Daula, and told him not to hand over the royal seal even if asked for. When Outram arrived, he found a king making a show of handing over his articles of kingship without putting his seal on this act.

Behind Wajid Ali Shah's action was a covert political pattern. He neither sought armed confrontation with the British nor did he succumb to their demands. He also made a show of the fact that he was being wronged. On the surface, his behaviour confirmed his 'weak' character.

But his uncomplaining attitude, his meek surrender before a 'higher power', without conceding ground, sent a different message to an Asian audience. It generated suppressed anger at the sight of a tormentor assailing a proud victim. This was classic passive resistance, Asian style, and the British understood this. They were doubly perturbed when the former king decided to embark on a tour to Calcutta while his mother, brother and a number of vakils, went to England to plead with Queen Victoria. Cracks had appeared in the British camp too — R.W. Bird had openly thrown in his lot with the former king and his book was suffering censure by the authorities. This very important document on the annexation of Avadh vanished as a regular source material after 1857. Bird was forced to remove his name from the title and twentieth century English, European and Indian authors on Lucknow continued that censure by seldom alluding to its content.

Back in Lucknow, Wajid Ali Shah's departure to Calcutta turned into a political sideshow — a show of public mourning, anger and protest. A crowd began gathering from Qaiserbagh's exit gate proclaiming loudly that a proclamation from London would come, giving him back his throne. A wail arose from the womenfolk and the villagers. He was, after all, their 'Jan-e-Alam' (beloved of the world). As the royal train left, the gardens and fields of Avadh echoed:

> *Hazrat jaate hain London*
> *Hum par kripa karo raghunandan*
> (Our Hazrat is departing for London
> Now we have only your care left O' Lord Rama)

And long after his departure, a feminine cry was heard from the inner chambers of houses:

> *Tore bin barkha na suhaye*
> *Calcutta vale juya, kab aaoge tum*
> (Without you rains bring no enjoyment
> O' my lover of Calcutta when will you come back?)

The king departed but he left behind an uneasy Lucknow and a seething Avadh — perhaps, the exact intended effect. Wajid Ali Shah, after all, was a king who began his reign with the military drill rather than the muse. Unknown to many, including the British, he had never given up this hobby. When the Parikhana was resounding with the vibrations of the ghungroo and the jhanjhar, his harem reverberated with the clang of weapons being made by the female platoons of the king. These platoons whose Hindu and Muslim members were drawn from the bylanes of Lucknow, practised an army drill with perfect discipline in Persian dress.

But the king had another ace up his sleeve. This was a woman, one of his wives with no apparent special quality. Only, she smoked the hookah with style and struck coins of a type bearing no resemblance with the traditions of the 'harem'. While the coins of all other queens bore the symbols of 'bel-butes' and flowers, hers showed the 'sword' and the 'shield'[7]. She was Wajid Ali Shah's 'mahak pari' who later acquired a name and title that was to resonate throughout India and Britain — Begum Hazrat Mahal.

Before leaving, Wajid Ali Shah indicated that though he did not fight the British, he had left the fate of Lucknow to its avaam or the public. Apparently, he was leaving all options, including the military one, open. He also left Hazrat Mahal behind to guard the interests of the people of Lucknow in their time of trial and tribulation. One of Wajid Ali Shah's couplets written before 1857, praises her 'golden colour', straight nose, black hair, sophisticated demeanour and then goes on to say:

Gharon par tabahi padi saher men, khude mere bazaar Hazrat Mahal
Tu hi bayse aesho aaram hai garibon ki gambkhwar Hazrat Mahal
(Calamity visits houses and families in the city
My markets were uprooted, Hazrat Mahal
You are the only means for comfort
You who shares the pain of the poor, Hazrat Mahal[8])

Implicit in this couplet, which shows how the annexation had ruined a thriving bourgeoisie economy, was also a tacit recognition that in Lucknow and Avadh a new force had gained predominance: the gareeb avaam or the poor public. The Company now directly faced the people as the new British administration set about effecting a land revenue settlement under a chief commissioner. Apart from the talukedars, the land was also settled with the small landlords and the substantial peasantry — that is those who ploughed their land but also lent it out on share cropping and lease. It was from this section that the East India Company drew its Thakur-Brahmin sepoys. They were not exceptionally well off at this point, constituting a rural lower middle class. Mangal Pandey, the first sepoy to train the gun on the British in Barrackpore on 29 March, 1857, belonged to Faizabad, Avadh. He, along with his warrior nephew Bujhavan Pandey, was a typical pre-1857 Avadhi Saryu Parin⁹ Brahmin — mercurial, akkhad, rural, passionate and individually oriented, the prototype of the rising new men of Avadh who were as proud of their janaeo as of their trousers and company bonds.

The British land policy, however, differed from the liberal reforms of Wajid Ali Shah. Assessment was higher, there was no immediate ploughing back of investment in agriculture and an alien political apparatus implemented Company laws. But more importantly and crucially, it meant a transfer of property and resources from the landlords and peasantry to new men: outsiders, traders and speculators who entered the rural scene with the protection of British arms and courts. The phenomena was offensive — British rule became synonymous with a radical shifting of social forces and classes. Instead of the much awaited haven of yeoman farmers, Avadh began degenerating into a hunting ground for rapacious outsiders and unscrupulous people. Thus, instead of the lessening of landlordism, there was the emergence of a new type of an extractive zamindari, lacking the benevolence of the traditional nobility. The peasantry and the small landlords, who were supposed to gain, became more dispossessed. The talukedars did not lose much: out of 4,243 villages originally held by them, they lost only 916. But they smarted under the rule of the firangi and the 'bania'. Many of them were Avadhian patriots with unswerving loyalty to Wajid Ali Shah.

In the city, which became the headquarters of the new establishment, the situation was worse. Many of the 70,000 sacked employees of the former king used to collect near the Chattar Manzil, the seat of the government, to curse the British. Unemployment became large scale and dispossessed begums were another source of unrest. The karigars of the kafsha — a special shoe designed for religious purposes — were suddenly without orders or clients. Some of them, like Dulli Chamar, were well known entrepreneurs. Their decline was pathetic — when one of them was leaving the city, a maulvi cried and said, 'there goes my beauty, what will I do without the kafsha?'

The middle classes too, were hit by the increase in prices, insecurity and corruption. In a petition dated 28 March 1857, Lucknowi residents complained to the governor general about a certain Muslim contractor who had been involved in quadrupling taxes, imprisoning people, running a regime of bribes and usurping lakhs of rupees with the collusion of British officers. They also complained about the complete breakdown of law and order in Lucknow and an increase in thefts and dacoities on the Kanpur-Lucknow road. The residents warned that if negligence and oppression on the part of the British officers did not stop, a great rebellion might take place at Lucknow which would not be easily suppressed[10].

Urdu professionals, also, could not be accommodated in the British establishment even though Urdu had become the official language throughout north India by 1836. Traders and merchants, who had depended upon old tariffs, became unsure about their future. Several entrepreneurs in the town had to shut their Urdu presses and ittar factories in face of a hostile market situation.

After 1856, Lucknow was fully drawn into the anti-British mobilisation going on in north India and beyond. Lucknowi resistance had three different shades: petty bourgeois intelligentsia inspired by Walliullahism, aspiring peasants with a tradition of militant Bhaktism and the elite intelligentsia with a schooling in the Tipu Sultan brand of Indo-Persian republican, European-American thought. Remnants of the entrepreneurial nobility, portfolio capitalists, the trend of Almas Ali Khan and Darshan Singh, made up for a ruined, gloomy, anti-British bourgeoisie. Many of their ilk were in British government service, smarting, restively, with slighted pride. The big merchants of Lucknow, Kanpur and Delhi, who had not turned into big landowners, saw their capital blocked between a dying north Indian intermediate economy and a hostile alien power. They needed state patronage for the leap into industrial capital. But in the British scheme, which concentrated heavily on building railways with and for foreign capital, Indians were just junior contractors. In cities like Kanpur[11], the trade and manufacture of nearly all consumer goods had passed into British hands. With the discovery of the German dye, the Indian indigo industry received a setback, something which a sympathetic native power could easily have offset by a protective tariff. A comprador economy was in the making which north Indian merchant capitalists, in contrast to the 'contractor-capitalist' of Bombay and Calcutta, found stifling and unenterprising. British inspired capitalism was already turning out to be a momentous conservative exercise, failing to generate even the rapacious, cheeky optimism associated with the 'adventurous' spread of American colonial capital.

The sepoy army and the small landlords formed a national patriotic guard, energised by native versions of peasant and aristocratic nationalism. The royal houses and big talukedars moved with their own vision of a modern, progressive, monarchical revival. The only sour element in this framework appeared in the form of big princely houses, the Scindias, Holkars and the Rajasthan houses, and the orthodox courtiers of Delhi and Hyderabad, who appeared anxious to maintain the status quo. Their unease was shared by those merchants of north India who had either turned into stable landowners or who were acting as bankers, contractors and treasurers of Indian comprador and British capital. In the hot months of 1857, pro-and anti-British polarisation took place under the weight of these material and sub-conscious factors.

The revolutionary guard drew together a comprehensive ideology; the chief points revolving around the concepts of anti-colonialism, deen, cultural honour, nationalism, azaadi and rajniti. This framework, especially the concept of anti-colonial, deen linked the main instigators to the vast masses of artisans, poor peasants, agricultural labourers and the lower middle classes.

A man evoking these ideas created a major disturbance at Faizabad in February 1857. A posse of British soldiers were sent to arrest a maulvi who had been urging Hindus and Muslims to take up arms. The man had arrived in Lucknow in November 1856 and rented a room in the sarai of Motam-ud-Daula, thus bringing into focus the one institution that was to play a very prominent part in the coming uprising. It was from within the arched gateways, columned balconies and the brick rooms of these sarais that much of the propaganda of 1857 was launched and conducted. These were the centres, often led by bhatiyarins, or the hefty women inn keepers, where three components of the movement met and conspired — the agitators, the sepoys and the courtesans. All the important ganjs and areas in the city had their sarais which circulated sophisticated ideas. How, a hundred years after the Battle of Plassey, an upheaval was going to rock India. How the invincible British were losing the Crimean War to the Russians. Over flickering lamp lights and the aroma of kebabs, paranthe, tea and coffee, impassioned debates about the drain of wealth, native economics and laws of revolution were conducted.

The maulvi in question was Ahmadullah Shah. He belonged to an Avadhian family which had gone to the Deccan with the adventurous team of Shah Wallajalah. Ahmadullah Shah's family seems to have fallen out with the Wallajalahs over Tipu Sultan's opposition to the British. Already under the influence of Shah Waliullah, Ahmadullah Shah began a wandering life which led him to Gwalior[12]. He was feted here by an important personality of Tansen's Senia Gharana, also under the influence of Waliullahism. They had provided shelter to Syed Ahmed Barelwi as well and commanded the loyalty of lower officials inside Scindia's court.

Ahmadullah Shah soon shifted from the sarai to Ghasiyari Mandi in Lucknow where the poor jostled with the middle classes. He was obviously a man with a mission — he soon caught the kotwal's attention who questioned him sometime in January 1857. He asked the kotwal to cross over and join him in the mission to liberate the country. The kotwal went away but left a guard near his residence. The maulvi then left for Faizabad trailed by a British force. He was finally captured there after a bloody confrontation which left many of his followers dead.

The maulvi's arrest seems to have sent a wave of indignation throughout Avadh. This was overshadowed in the city by another incident — the arrival of Nana Sahib from Bithur along with his aide, Azimullah Khan, in April 1857. Ahmadullah Shah was previously in consort with these two leaders who represented the Indo-Persian republican trend in the ongoing mobilisation. Nana Sahib was the last Maratha Peshwa's adopted son, but his claim to Peshwahood was redundant in the eyes of the British. Outwardly, he was the Asian man of pleasure, corpulent and fond of dancing girls. But he was also a member of the secret society of Freemasons in Kanpur — the elite society of 'people of the mind' who exchanged, amongst other things, ideas of Diderot, Voltaire and other heroes of European enlightenment.

Freemasons operated in Lucknow too and Azimullah Khan in particular embodied many of their ideals. He was the one who had gone to England to plead Nana Sahib's case. There he became the protege of a British lady who introduced him to the upper echelons of English society. Soon he won over the minds of men and the hearts of ladies and made them aware of shades of Asian enlightenment[13]. He surprised Russell, the war correspondent of the *Times* in Crimea and Turkey with his agnosticism and casual valour[14]. He drank wine, appeared unconcerned about religion and smoked a cigar while bombs exploded all around him. Azimullah Khan represented the Girondist-Jacobean arm of 1857. He stopped in Crimea on his return journey from England in order to study the military technology of the British. In Lucknow, Nana Sahib and Azimullah Khan consorted with talukedars and the soldiers with active help from Hazrat Mahal.

The British command in the city was headed by Sir Henry Lawrence — a man with a hand on the pulse of the situation. After Governor General Lord Canning, he was perhaps the most important British official in India. After the departure of both Nana Sahib and Azimullah Khan, he faced the first incidence of 'rebelliousness' — the soldiers' refusal to bite the new cartridge prescribed for the Enfield rifles imported from England[15]. A letter addressed to soldiers of the Mandion cantonment was intercepted and disturbances broke out in Musabagh. On 1 May, Henry Lawrence convened a durbar in Lucknow. There he harangued against the possibilities of a revolt and impressed upon local native men of influence gathered there, the invincibility of British rule. The atmosphere was sullen and the people assembled did not give the customary response. By the time of the Meerut uprising[16] on 10 May, the city was in ferment. The cantonment had a number of native regiments[17] but only one European force of note — a highly disciplined unit of the 32nd foot with a cavalry detachment. Unlike Mathura or Etawah, the city was in the firm grip of the British. The districts of the Doab slipped out of British control in the early days of the revolt as long years of unstable Company rule had eroded their administrative framework.

A newly annexed area, Lucknow's officialdom was fresh and well oiled. Avadh's hierarchical society also did not lend itself easily to temporary disaffection. It was not sufficient to take the city by a mutiny of the army backed by an insurgent mob. This was attempted on 31 May when the native regiments revolted in the Muriaon cantonments — but they were repelled by British and 'loyal' native troops. The next day, a civil uprising began in the city — crowds gathered at several points towards the west and marched on to the jail. But the police held firm and so did a large section of the elite. The crowds were dispersed after heavy casualties. The insurgency was a result of a planned conspiracy fuelled by leaders like Kadir Ali Shah who had also sent a letter to the Shah of Kabul asking for help. His 'underground' organisation had enrolled thousands of recruits belonging mainly to the poor, karigars and the lower-middle classes.

Widespread reprisals followed the failure of the operation. Maulvis were hanged near the Macchi Bhavan and the area between the bhavan and the residency was levelled. Thus began the systematic demolition of the city which was to take a horrifying shape after 1857. Many baghs were ruined, houses destroyed and mohallas and ganjs devastated. The only concern of the British seemed to be to secure a line of defence from the west to the centre along the Gomti.

One of the first prisoners to be hanged went by the name of Mir Abbas, a trader who had taken an amount of Rs. 4,000 from the British officer Carneigh for his business. The list included Munshi Rasool Bux, Hafiz Abdul Samad and a havaldar. The early phase of insurgency included hakims, small vakils, traders and craftsmen of Saadat Ganj, Mashakganj and Rakabganj who organised another uprising on 15 June. This too was crushed. It seemed that in Avadh urban insurrection was in urgent need of another component — the armed might of a regular, organised military backed by an insurgent rural population.

This combination was ignited by the revolt of sepoy units in Sitapur on 3 June and in Faizabad on 8 June. Soon other stations revolted and, in a matter of days, major districts came under the control of the revolutionaries. Ahmadullah Shah was freed from Faizabad jail as sepoys began gathering around Lucknow, their ranks swelled by peasants and talukedari forces. Led by Barkat Ahmad and Shahabuddin, the Avadhi army massed its ranks at Nawabganj, Barabanki. It was a little further from this township, twelve miles east of Lucknow, that the decisive engagement of Chinhat, which changed the course of 1857, took place.

In a bid to pre-empt 'rebel' movement, Henry Lawrence took his best force and set out to intercept the insurgents at Chinhat. He had the sound backing of the artillery and a spy network. A masnavi, composed by a Lucknowi eye witness, was to record:

'Lawrence Sahab went to battle, said I'll overcome this hurdle;
as the cannon wagon moved carrying the cannons the white
regiments moved ahead.'

The Battle of Chinhat engaged the British and the Avadhians in an insatiable violence of mind, manoeuvering and subterfuge. The war of Lucknow was fought, consciously, as a bitter civilisational and racial struggle, in which 'no one asked for mercy, and no mercy was given'. It was a chilling, cold and calculating battle of annihilation from both sides, with no scope for 'lesser', humanist concerns. From the native side it was a fight to preserve the culture of Lord Ramchandra, Prophet Muhammad, Hazrat Ali, Krishna, Mahadev and Mahavir, the memory of Amir Khusro, Sher Shah Suri, the Mughals, Shah Waliullah, the emotion of the qawwali and the faith of the mazaars, Qaiserbagh, Wajid Ali Shah, the Ganga and Yamuna; and hopes of national renewal on this basis.

For the British it was a struggle to preserve the virtues of the Christian civilisation and the myth of racial superiority, on which rested the whole edifice of the Imperial empire. Charles Dickens, the British novelist was in the habit of offending the government and the British public with realistic, critical portrayals of conditions in England. He was not expected to be a bigot where a political struggle was concerned. But the response of this liberal humanist to the Indian 'mutiny' was —

I wish I were Commander in Chief in India. The first thing I would do to strike that Oriental race with amazement — should be to proclaim to them, in their language, that I considered my holding that appointment by the leave of God, to mean that I should do my outmost to exterminate the race[18] — '

The international reaction too spoke of a racial dimension that often overrode economic considerations. Dependant on sugar and cotton imports from India, the United States of America was facing economic difficulties at the time of the outbreak. It could have, at the least, adopted a neutral position or kept a distance from what educated, pro-British Indians were describing as 'just a mere local rebellion'. But one of the dispatches of the *Washington Post*, reproduced in *The Englishman* of 15 October 1857, mentioned nervously, its worldwide impact in terms that put a question mark on the 'secularism' of Western democracies: 'We do not believe that the rebellion in India will eventuate in successful revolution...'

'England never was so powerful as she is now, and never so well prepared to carry on war in a distant theatre. Her immense steam navy, aided by rapid communications by mail and the telegraph, makes it less difficult for her to conduct a war now in India than to have carried on one in America 40 years ago. Yet, with all these advantages, the struggle may be protracted; and even when the rebellion is suppressed, consequences will probably ensue seriously affecting, the *weal of Christendom.* Instead of exerting herself, as she has just proposed, to increase the supply, of sugar and cotton, which have become alarmingly deficient, the fact stares us in the face that this deficiency must increase, and the suffering consequent on it be aggravated. But England is alone concerned on this matter. All Christendom — will suffer alike —

'The momentous consequences likely to ensue from the rebellion in India can be justly appreciated when viewed in connection with the deficient supply of slave products which now perplex nations — [19]'

French journals, however, noted the growing anger of the Indians. Sitting between files and notes in London, Karl Marx also spoke of 1857 as an Asiatic racial, civilisational and political war, led by the most modern institution then in existence in India, the Sepoy Army. He linked it with the anti-British Persian war and the anti-Imperialist Opium war being fought in China in the 1850s[20]. He also justified the so-called cruelties of Indians against the British during the revolt as a natural consequence of British colonial policy. Almost endorsing his views, a French ministerial paper, *The Imperial Estafette,* commented:

There is profound panic in London; for in the worst days of its history England has received no more violent check. In fact, the loss of India would be a death blow to her commerce and industry; and once driven out of that country, the former conquerors would find insurmountable obstacles if ever they should think of returning.

In the first instance, they have cruelly oppressed the Indians, who are now taking their revenge and who probably will prefer to be exterminated to the last man, rather than to bear again the odious yoke of the foreigner.

The English have hurt the national feeling, and committed acts of breach of civilisation. They have to answer now a terrible account; instead of civilizing India they have exploited it. They only wanted slaves but they have created Spartacuses — [21]

The reply of the 'Spartacuses' was no less vitriolic. They summed up the breach of civilisation by the English thus:

'To all Hindoos and Mahommedans of Hindoostan who are faithful to their religion know that *sovereignty* is one of God's chief boons, one which a deceitful tyrant is never allowed to retain. For several years the English have been committing all kinds of excesses and tyrannies being desirous of converting all men to Christianity by force, and of subverting and doing away with the religion of Hindoos and Mahommedans. When God saw this fact, he so altered the hearts of the inhabitants of Hindoostan, that they have been doing their best to get rid of the English themselves — Soon they will have been, by the grace of God, so utterly exterminated, that no traces of them will remain. Know that all Hindoos and Mussalmans have become so hateful of them that they will not suffer any to live with honour.'

So 'All you Hindoos are hereby solemnly adjured, by your faith in the Ganges, Tulsi and Saligram; and all you Mussalmans, by your belief in God and the Koran, as these English are the common enemy of both, that you unite in considering their slaughter extremely expedient, for by this alone will the lives and faith of both be saved. It is expedient, then, that you should coalesce and slay them.²²'

After this, there was no question of a middle ground, no mercy from either side; it was either victory or death.

Lucknow and the people of Avadh had been preparing for 1857 for quite some time. But their situation was like that of a combat soldier forced to sit idle, not for one or two months but in this case, since the Battle of Buxar. There is something elemental, almost beauteous and sensual, about the violence of 1857. The veteran Bihar leader of 1857, Kunwar Singh, remarked on the eve of the outbreak of the Arrah uprising in his hometown — 'this bloody revolution had to come so late, when I was past my prime'. It was as if he was waiting for something to happen. Avadhians and Lucknowites must have shared this sentiment — they too were waiting to battle.

At Ismaelganj, a hamlet close to Chinhat, Barkat Ahmad and Shahabuddin first lured Lawrence into combat with a small force. Lawrence thought that the rest of the 'rebels' had fallen back on Nawabganj. But his advance was checked by heavy artillery fire which pinned him down in the village fields. But even then it looked as if the 'enemy' was in retreat. One British officer even encouraged his men to charge, sensing victory at hand. But the retreat was a ruse — soon columns of rebels appeared on the British right flank, ready to charge. A surprised Lawrence saw uninhabited groves and dunes swarming with Indian soldiers, holding green and saffron flags. Then the cavalry charged, lead by someone identified by the Britishers as a Russian —

an Asiatic European who had crossed over to the Indians — and all was over. The great army of Sir Henry Lawrence, now beaten and bruised, was hurrying back to Lucknow. The British blew up the Macchi Bhawan and decamped for the Residency with the Indians on their heels. In a matter of a day and a half, the 'rebels' had become rulers.

The myth of British invincibility lay shattered. Chinhat was an open, fair engagement, not a guerrilla affair. After Crimea, it was the first instance of the defeat of the British army anywhere in the world in a straight combat. The masnavi spoke further of its 'even handed' nature:

First the White regiment chased away the enemy and
returned to their lines, they won and retreated for a while
Then the rebels counter-attacked, surrounding from all sides
The White regiments again attacked in desperate irritation
Swords flew equally from both sides, every cannon spewed
fire
The battle that took place was intense, the British too
fought for every inch of their fame

From Chinhat to Lucknow thus was the situation, that
there were corpses and corpses all along the way
The White Regiments retreated into the Bailey Guard, they
brought the rebels too trailing on their back
Then the battle began again in earnest, blood started
flowing again in sequences
Excitement grew on both sides — corpses fell on corpses on
both sides

As the battle raged, now for the capture of the Residency, a new ruler of Avadh was coronated at the Patharwali Baradari in Qaiserbagh. He recognised the suzerainty of Bahadur Shah Zafar, declaring himself his wazir, thus reverting back to the original position of the Nishapuri house. Birjis Qadar was eleven years old then, a son of Wajid Ali by Hazrat Mahal. The masnavi went on:

Now lend an ear to the story of the prince, he is comely in

his adolescence, he is happy go lucky in attitude
Fairy like, he looks happy, his body is tall and thin, Shah's
son by Begum Hazrat Mahal is not much acquainted with
the world and is reserved in his expressions
His age is just eleven years, this is childhood, these ought to
have been days of play and fun

But in his heart is ingrained, that I will fight the battle
which has been unleashed
He is a child, so he is innocent, his eyes can see where lies
justice and where injustice

So he orders the troops to fall in line, and tells them to
show the drill
And then he fires balls of cannon, he does not flinch even
if he gets burned
He conducts the drill personally, and lavishes the troops
with rewards of money

During the coronation, the prince was called 'kanhaiya' by the
Indian troops who crowded in the assembly hall with naked swords and
loaded guns. The crown was placed on Birjis Qadar's head not by a
religious leader, as was the conventional practice, but by Barkat Ahmad
himself. There was fun and gaiety all around. The talukedars welcomed
the event by firing cannon shots in their villages. A mass of green and
saffron flags engulfed the city as a big procession proceeded towards
Qaiserbagh. Children sang and danced, people wore their best clothes
as if this was *the* Id and Diwali.

   This, however, was a government with difference. Real power of
decision making lay in the hands of the executive and military council,
acting in concert with the Begum. The executive council had important
people belonging to the old regime like the well known Kayastha Raja
Balkrishna, who had refused to hand over the details of the revenue
administration after the annexation. A finance minister of Wajid Ali
Shah's time, he remained so with the new regime. Sharf-ud-Daula, a
Kashmiri Sunni convert, minister under Muhammad Ali Shah and
Amjad Ali Shah, was made naib. A number of new men of low origin

headed the important posts of the paymaster and the darogah of the magazine. The darogah or chief of the diwankhana was Mammo Khan, a close aide of the begum and a true man of fortune.

The military body was led by ordinary sepoys: Ghamandi Singh, Rajmund Tiwari, Jahangir Khan, Raghunath Singh and Umrao Singh. Darshan Singh's son, Raja Jai Lal Singh, assumed charge as the president of a council of ministers, engaged in stipulating and supervising matters of the new provincial government. The council fixed norms for the army to nominate the chief minister and officers of regiments, receive increased pay and decide the treatment of pro-British elements. The high court was ordered to obey the strictures coming from Delhi where Bahadur Shah Zafar headed a national government, once again as the sovereign of the world.

Avadh followed the democratic pattern of Delhi's court of administration in which armed peasants, the ex-sepoys, sat as the new heads of state under the leadership of Bahadur Shah Zafar. Besides establishing law and order on the basis of modern principles of justice, the Delhi court issued firmans promising capital to merchants for trade, industry and ship building[23]. Patriotic landlords were offered light revenue assessments. Perhaps for the first time in the history of Asia, a state announced 'land to the tiller'[24], as its official policy. With this one slogan, 1857 became a movement imbued with distinct revolutionary-democratic features, complementing Bahadur Shah Zafar's thrust on constitutional monarchy. Delhi and Azamgarh proclamations also promised prosperity to the artisans, the latter going far to produce a penetrating analysis of colonial economics and promise respite to the working man.

The elective principal followed in the Delhi Court was applied to Avadh as well. Talukedars and small landlords, hitherto excluded from the power structure of Lucknow, participated in the new government. They began arriving in Lucknow with their levies alongwith a substantial number of low caste peasants, the Pasis and the Ahirs. Many of them were professional miners, sappers and marksmen who led the assault on the residency. This British citadel of defence was now transformed into a fortress besieged by Indians from all sides. The sound tactician that he was, Henry Lawrence took advantage of the lofty slopes of the

Residency to resist Indian assaults. Despite being low in numbers, the British possessed substantial ammunition and guns; forces of Avadhi government therefore decided to combine violent attacks with a policy of wearing down the enemy.

The Residency assaults were led by Maulvi Ahmadullah Shah. Jai Lal Singh, Mammo Khan and the maulvi formed a trio which guided military and state matters. Jai Lal Singh raised the necessary finance and formed the link between various groups and the begum. The maulvi worked on military strategy; a man of vision, he combined passion with precision, deep-dark eyes with an aquiline nose, schooling in theology with radical politics.

The maulvi advocated a normative civil administration in Lucknow and a concert with the talukedars for an offensive towards the east. He subjected the Residency to heavy artillery fire in which Henry Lawrence lost his life, much before the Residency siege turned into a historic battle. In that interlude, Delhi fell on 20 September after a fight in which the British troops covered the small distance from Kashmiri gate to the Red Fort in six days with the loss of a thousand soldiers. Kanpur, which had been won over by Nana Sahib in June, was also lost on 16 July. But Henry Havelock, the 'butcher' of Allahabad and Kanpur, was unable to proceed to Lucknow from Kanpur. Twice he tried and failed, falling back from Unnao. There he was resisted by the talukedars of Mohan and Dhundiakhera, Thakurs, Brahmins and Pathans of Baiswara, the sons of Faqir Mohammad Goya and peasant fighters. He won the skirmishes fought around the villages but was pinned down in the fields and mud baked walls due to dogged guerrilla resistance. The new Indian tactic deflected his forces and wore down their morale by shows of exemplary courage. In one of these battles, Muhammad Ahmad Khan, a son of Faqir Muhammad, continued, even when the rest of the force had retreated, to strike at the enemy with his shield and then his bare hands till he was captured.

This resistance from the villages shook Lucknow and Avadhi society. The traditional caste structure was severely impaired and so were relations within the family. There were cases where a religious father forbade his son to participate in the 'rebellion'. The son taunted the father that he was the one who used to talk about religion and now when a war was being waged in its name, why was he afraid? The father gathered all his logic but to no avail. Finally, the mother came forward. She handed the father a pair of bangles and told him that from that day, he stood abandoned. The father entreated her in the name of religion and the duties of a Hindu wife, to which she replied that her duty to Birjis Qadar and watan was higher than her duties as a wife.

In Hardoi, a Brahmin ran off from the midst of a battle where the British had pinned down a talukedar. His father saw his close friend, a Kurmi, running back towards the house. On learning about the incident, he picked up his gun and told the friend that he and his son would be dead if they showed their cowardly faces. Both of them went back to the battlefield and embraced martyrdom.

Fakirs and sadhus did not worry about religious predilections and women abandoned their veils when they charged the Company cavalry with crude swords. Maulvis and ulemas sacrificed everything, often defying the orders of pro-British superiors and religious heads. In the city, there was great controversy over the proclamation of jihad, or the Muslim religious war. To many orthodox Muslims, 1857 was a not a religious but a political war. It had more Hindus than Muslims and Bahadur Shah Zafar, born of a Rajput mother[25], was not a religious head. He wore the sacred thread on several occasions and welcomed those natives who wanted to convert to Christianity of their own free will. At a durbar at Red Fort, he spelt 'freedom' as God's greatest gift to man and the anti-British fight as a revolution. He also expressed his willingness to hand over power to any man of history as the war was not for the benefit of only the Mughal house.

1857 raised the issue of religion as a political war cry, as a means to assert the value of deen in one's culture and nation. The orthodox and ritualistic religious leadership hesitated to support such a move. But to Waliullahites like Ahmadullah Shah and Maulvi Liaquat Ali, the leader of Allahabad, the debate over jihad was academic. Within Shias too, while the elite family of Dildar Ali Nasirabadi in Lucknow and Maulana Muhammad Baqar in Delhi supported the revolution, the orthodox group of Allahabad helped the British. Non-Waliullahite maulvis also supported the call for jihad; Maulvi Fazle Haq 'Khairabadi' belonged to an Avadhi qasba and was a contemporary symbol of the great rationalist-liberal-intellectual 'country town' churning of the region in the eighteenth century. He signed the jihadi fatwa in Delhi and combined a penetrating economic analysis with religious grievances to present a theoretical exposition of 1857[26].

Begum Hazrat Mahal, the real power behind Birjis Qadar, held court at Qaiserbagh, adding glamour to diplomacy. Combining softness with fire, she personified the political potential of the petite household woman of Avadh. Leading the concord of talukedars in the austere Tarawali Kothi, she impressed upon the elite the 'practical' necessity to remain united during the crucial test between September and November.

The British force under Outram and Havelock managed to break the resistance in the countryside during the third British offensive, launched in late October. They crossed the Ghaziuddin Haider Canal with the intention of marching on to the Qaiserbagh through Naka Hindola in the centre of the city. But heavy firing forced them to retreat towards the Chattar Manzil, from where they passed over to the Residency. Besieged with the rest of the garrison, they were pushed away from the borders of Qaiserbagh in a desperate musket, bayonet and sword fight. The 'great' General Neil, who had made Brahmins and maulvis lick beef and pork meat at Kanpur besides hanging hundreds of innocent villagers at Allahabad, fell fighting near Qaiserbagh's Sher Darwaza.

The residency faced further trouble. Outram and Havelock, despite manning a larger area, had to face constant bombardment from Qaiserbagh. Sorties from fortified positions in Sikandar Bagh and Shah Najaf reduced their number every day. The situation was getting desperate when Colin Campbell's army arrived at Dilkusha in November.

In Lucknow, the morale of the native government was high. Till now, the British had proved superior only when assisted by massive guns, the weak point of the Avadhi army. The begum was leading an anti-status-quoist revolution due to which she was short of funds and resources. The army had cannons and carbines but little access to British howitzers and missiles. They could outsmart the British in tactics, but lacked the power battery to demolish the thick walls of the Residency.

Meanwhile, the revolt spread to the countryside as the city swarmed with soldiers and ghazis from the Doab and Delhi as well. Lucknow became the prime focus of national interest; Khan Bahadur Khan, Bahadur Shah Zafar's representative in Bareli, Rohilkhand and a descendant of Hafiz Rehmat Khan, wrote that if Bareli fell before, it would not amount to much in the overall scheme. But if Lucknow fell, it would be difficult to save Bareli[27].

Colin Campbell's entry into the city was resisted fiercely at Sikandar Bagh. There, in the shade of Egyptian style pyramidical roofs holding the banners of Bahadur Shah Zafar and Birjis Qadar, 2,000 Hindus and Musalmans took a fatal decision — either to win or perish — 'neither to ask for mercy nor grant any'. En route to the garden the British had a foretaste of things to come. On seeing a jogi, a Scottish highlander wanted to do away with him. The staff officer told him not do so as he was a harmless Hindu, the real trouble makers being the Muslims. As soon as he had spoken, the 'harmless', bead-counting jogi, with ashes and sacred marks smeared on his body, took out a blunderbuss from under his leopard skin and shot the officer point blank[28].

At Sikandar Bagh, the British troops made up of Scottish Highlanders and Sikhs, were pinned down for well over three hours. The defenders did not have heavy guns but their firing was so intense that casualties began mounting on the British side. The day was carried by chance, when seeing a breach in the wall, the British force hurtled inside. The native troops fought with everything they had, even their empty muskets and talwars upto a moment when nearly all of them perished. There was heavy resistance at Qadam Rusool and Shah Najaf, which stood almost in a line from Sikandar Bagh, where native guns stood in a better position. Campbell was almost forced to retire but heavy mortar and rocket fire, to which the Indians had no reply, gave him a pyrrhic victory.

Colin Campbell finally caught up with Outram and Havelock, who were coming from the Residency through the Moti Mahal, at Khurshid Manzil. But triumph turned to defeat as Campbell ordered a retreat of all British troops to Kanpur in face of the overwhelming superiority of the 'enemy'. He still had a large force at his disposal but it lacked the back up of guns and howitzers. An open struggle in the city between evenly matched armies was risky; Campbell had almost got defeated at Shah Najaf in a pure artillery to artillery battle.

So instead of storming the Qaiserbagh, the British retreated to the Dilkusha with a wounded and dying Henry Havelock. Leaving a small army in charge of Outram at Alambagh[29], Campbell hurried back to meet Nana Sahib's lieutenant Tantia Tope who had won decisively in the hard fought second battle of Kanpur.

In Lucknow, government forces were re-aligned before the final battle in March 1858. Between December and February, important shifts occurred in north India. While a section of the old leadership dropped out, new areas joined in with a deeper base. The revolt in Bihar, Bundelkhand, parts of the present day Madhya Pradesh and Rajasthan acquired depth and momentum, even as the interiors of Avadh and Rohilkhand became more prominent. Sometime in December, Begum Hazrat Mahal called a meeting of the talukedars in Lucknow. There she convinced a majority of them to stick to the cause, resorting to every possible argument, including the possibility of victory in the countryside. It is possible that the decision to take the battle directly to the people of Avadh, was taken here. This thinking was also echoed by Khan Bahadur Khan, then evolving a theory for the proper conduct of a protracted insurgent war. Kunwar Singh, General Bakht Khan of Delhi, Nana Sahib, Azimullah Khan and Engineer Mohammad Ali too came to assist the begum. From the west arrived a legendary figure — Prince Firoze Shah, Bahadur Shah Zafar's nephew. He was to lead the revolt in Rajasthan and defeat the British in successive engagements at Jiran and Kotah. Lucknow also excited tremendous interest overseas in Burma, China, Turkey, Russia and Persia.

The British forces, now numbering over 30,000, were resisted village by village en route to Lucknow in March, 1858. At Mianganj, the Lucknowi bourgeois town of the eighteenth century, the army of Hope Grant burned down houses and raised the once prosperous markets to the ground. They were defied by old men, women and children as the young had left for Lucknow to defend the city.

Lucknow was well protected with three lines of defence running in a semicircle, narrowing in the third stage from the Qaiserbagh right up to the Ghaziuddin Haider canal. It was designed by Engineer

Mohammd Ali, a product of Roorke Engineering College and an aide of Azimullah Khan, and Ahmadullah Shah. The maulvi took personal charge of the operation, bringing his vast experience of beating back the British at Alambagh and Jalalabad Fort into play.

But the British pressurised the city from three sides. Outram crossed the Gomti and began pounding the lines from the northern bank, Colin Campbell's offensive proceeded from the Dilkusha towards the Begum Kothi, while the Nepalese army of Jung Bahadur appeared on the outskirts ready to enter from the south. General Franks's army also arrived from Gorakhpur via Sultanpur and Amethi, after losing officers and men to desperate village resistance in the two districts. The British contingents had a large number of Sikh soldiers who played an important role in altering the balance of forces. But the Sikhs fought from the begum's side also; previously, they had heroically defended Delhi along with Hindu and Muslim sepoys. They were the first to revolt in Benaras and Jampur and fight with eastern sepoys in the 'mutinies' of the Punjab. The flag song of the 'sepoys' referred to Hindustan as the land of Hindus, Muslims and Sikhs,[30] and Bahadur Shah Zafar appealed[31] specifically to Sikhs on the British side before the fall of Delhi.

Campbell's Sikhs were fresh recruits drawn from the countryside of Punjab, where the revolt had been routed before Delhi fell in September 1857. The British took to heavy repression of army units, besides imposing severe exactions on the Jat and Muslim peasantry of west and east Punjab. The Company officers in Punjab were helped by big Punjabi princes. The original Sikh aristocracy had died fighting in the successive Punjab wars of the 1840s and most of those who ruled now were being propped up by the British. More importantly, the elite Jat Sikh peasantry, unlike the Company and nawabi trained Thakur-Brahmin peasantry of Avadh, lacked long years of military and political exposure. Devoid, thus, of a native aristocratic leadership and the necessary context to emerge as independent power aspirants, the Punjabi kisans or farmers, despite expressing anti-British hostility, could not put up an organised resistance.

In Lucknow, the bloodiest engagement took place at the Begum Kothi, once the Lucknow defence broke down in face of determined

British encirclement. Hodson, the officer responsible for massacring Indians at Delhi, fell to a stray bullet here, meeting his Waterloo at Lucknow. Hundreds of British officers and men were killed beneath the high ceilings of the Begum Kothi, resembling a Roman lodge of yore, defended staunchly and to the last by 900 fighters. Soon Campbell was joined in by the Nepalese army from the south even as Outram continued to advance from the west.

Even before the fall of Lucknow, the loot and wholesale destruction of this Babylon-Paris-Alexandria-Kremlin-Constantinople of Asia, had begun. The native troops kept inflicting heavy casualties and retreating as part of a pre-conceived plan. House to house fighting commenced in which the middle classes and the poor took up arms. The begum moved towards the west with her forces and Birjis Qadar, taking shelter at various houses and exhorting people to fight. Outram sent her a proposal of 'honourable' surrender which was rejected. Without losing courage, she amassed her troops once more at Musa Bagh but lost out to a heavy cannon charge from three directions. The British tried capturing the begum but proved incapable of cutting off her retreat towards Baundi in the northeast. A number of troops also crossed over to Faizabad, dodging Outram and Campbell. The maulvi established himself at Saadat Ganj, then lured the British towards the Dargah Abbas in the heart of the city before catching the Sitapur road.

Summary executions began back in Lucknow. People were blown apart by cannon fire and bare hands tore the limbs of captured soldiers. Acts of despoilation left Nadir Shah far behind in cruelty and savagery. It was as if a barbarian race had embarked upon the 'valorous' task of stripping and raping a fair but defiant damsel. The 'civilised' British became bloody, lusty, gold thirsty mobsters gouging gems from sword hilts, caskets, pipe stems, saddlery, shawls, brocades and muslins. Clothes with zari gold and silver work, which still smelled of musk and sandalwood, were wrapped around smelly bodies. It was as though a low culture had chanced upon the beauties of a higher culture-jade vases were reduced to smithereens and stolen brass pots were paraded as gold items[32].

Qaiserbagh, the symbol of the Avadhi political and cultural power, was destroyed with a vengeance. Ankle deep piles of looking glasses, giandoles, vases, crockery, furniture, glassware and alabaster figurines could be seen in its courtyards. All native records were destroyed. Across the Gomti, Indian 'niggers' were shot at in fun and villagers maimed. Even the servants of the British, who had remained loyal, were treated like animals and objects of a shooting 'game'. The modern masters of India performed a planned genocide for which there would be no Nuremberg.

10

❦

A Sensuality Passes Away: the Women of Lucknow

*Sunate ho mujhe baten hazaron, kahun main bhi kuch apni
zaban se to is dam kirkiri ho jayegi bas, sabhon ke samne meri
bayan se*
*Hui jab Dehli chavni men ae bi, vahan log aa gaye sare jahan
se*
arab tha koi to koi ajam tha, koi sheeraz koi sherwan se
*jo ki aapas men in longon ne baten, to Urdu ki zaban nikli
yahan se*
*Namak mirche mili hain Lucknow men, ki ab tak raal bahti
hai zaban se*
*Vah Urdu thi ki ek lakri ka chaila, na nikle jiske katen
baghban se*
*Kharada Lucknow walon ne isko, tumhen kyon fakhr tum layi
kahan se*
Meri jaan Lucknow vaalon ke aage
Bahut mushkil hai kuch kahna zaban se

Zaban ke mulk ka sikka hai aurat

Zaban ka faisla hai aurton par
Yeh baaten mardduen laaye kahan se

— Rekhti

This poem, by Abid Mirza 'Begum'[1], a Lucknowi practitioner of rekhti, is an angry and satirical retort to the denigration of Lucknowi Urdu by Delhi's Nawab Mirza Khan 'Dagh' — but it ends up constructing the unintended — an alternative history of the language itself. It states:

(You chide me with a thousand complaints, but if I say something through my own speech
Then at the very moment 'yours' will go down the drain before everyone through my statement
When Delhi turned into a camp, people gathered from all over the world
Someone from Arab, someone from Azam, someone from Shiraz, someone from Shirwan
When these people talked amongst themselves, then the language of Urdu emerged from here
Salt and pepper were added in Lucknow, so that even till now saliva drips from the speech
This was Urdu or but a plate of wood, whose thorns never left the garden of beauty
The colour on its plate was put on by Lucknowites, why are you proud, from where did you fetch it?
Before Lucknowites, my love
It is very difficult to say something through speech
Woman is the coin of the nation of speech
The verdict of speech rests on women
From where did 'men' bring forth these 'small talks')

It so happened that the final, unambiguous verdict of language or speech (zaban ka faisla), always rested on women in Lucknow. Speech, as defined by men, was a woman's forte, so how could men have invented speech?

In the immediate aftermath of 1857, this assertion struck a note of epic tragedy. For, apart from language, the final verdict of pain and love too, was to rest on women. The destruction of the city which followed British occupation was to mark the end of an entire way of life. The end of an epoch as cataclysmic as the decline of Egypt after Akheneton's death or the collapse of the Moorish renaissance after Boabdil's defeat at the hands of the Christian-European armies of Isabella and Fernandes in Granada, 1492.

But one 'fact' was not recorded in history books. The passing away of this last bastion of Indo-Persian modernity meant a setback to the power of the zenana, personified in the begum and the courtesan, the sharifzaadi and the khangin. For men, 1857 was a fight for life, death, religion and political power. For women it was a struggle for identity, for the retention of the cultural power which they enjoyed, and for its extension into the political realm which 1857 promised. Proclamations of the revolt made specific references to women and all over Avadh, Kanpur and Bundelkhand, the participation of ladies of all ranks and classes was, and still is, a mystery.

The women of 1857 were not fighting to preserve the throne for either their husbands or sons. This could not have led to the 'frenzy' displayed, and the trust elicited by women leaders. Reasons unknown lay behind Begum Hazrat Mahal striking a defiant pose till the very end, trying her best to reclaim Lucknow. No secondary motive ordained Azeezun Bai to raise Bahadur Shah Zafar's flag at Kanpur, Umrao Jaan Ada to compose songs for Birjis Qadar and the ranis of Tulsipur and Hadha to give up their comfort and life for the cause.

The cultural ethos which these women represented went back to the early days of Lucknowi Indo-Persianism — a time when the zenana of the Avadhi nawabs came to control the fashions of the times and the affairs of the state. During the Mughal era, shehzadees of the royal court dabbled in business, politics, fashion and the marketing of festivals. Noorjehan, a woman of exceptional talent, extended the rigours of state craft into architecture. Her father's tomb at Agra marked the beginning of a new post-Akbar aesthetic style which required no conscious synthesis of Hindu and Persian 'floral motifs'. It combined the jaali work of Gujarat, the dreamy lusciousness of Malwa architecture and the decorative patterns of Persia. A new Mughal-Indian style was set into motion which reached its zenith in the building of the Taj Mahal.

But the women of Mughal India were moving shadows behind the main show, with power dependant on their status inside the royal household. They could be as unconventional as Jehanara who ridiculed her brother Aurangzeb's prohibitions by openly drinking wine. But they didn't have the historical perspective of Shuja-ud-Daula's wife Bahu Begum, the one charismatic figure of Avadh who changed the concept of Indian womanhood. Operating from Faizabad as a centre of power, she set the trend for the later acceptance of Begum Hazrat Mahal as the virtual ruler of Avadh.

Bahu Begum inspired an unusual awe in people. In Faizabad her durbar was attended by powerful Avadhi leaders. At a time when Shuja-ud-Daula was busy fighting the East India Company and other adversaries, Bahu Begum was the one who controlled the strings of administration. One of the first entrepreneurs, she settled the wild ravages of Gonda and Balrampur, before the emergence of Tikait Rai and Almas Khan. These terai areas were a mass of intractable, unexplored forests inhabited by ferocious animals and dacoits. Bahu Begum's alliance with Bisen and Janwar clans was the beginning of an humane and emotional bonding by which the Rajputs came to align themselves personally with the begums.

Bahu Begum built a number of sarais some for charity and some for profit in Benaras and the districts of the Doab. She determined the succession of Asaf-ud-Daula, overruling the wishes of Shuja-ud-Daula who, it is said, preferred Saadat Ali Khan. The way women perceived their power was illustrated by Shuja-ud-Daula's mother, Sadar Jehan's response to Bahu Begum's row with Asaf-ud-Daula. She told the nawab that the kingdom was the creation of her father, not his, (she was Burhan-ul-Mulk's daughter) and the new nawab should be careful before taking any hasty steps against his mother.

Socially, the era of adventure and disturbances of the eighteenth century had relaxed conventional rituals and cultural roles. There was no apparent break in theory, but in reality the purdah was being flouted, women received military training and led men in battle. In love and marriage, boundaries of caste and religion were often crossed, especially at the behest of a strong suitor, say a Pathan willing to take up arms for a Brahminee. These turbulent conditions produced Begum Sumroo of Sardhana who not only loved, left and fought as she liked, but carved out a state for herself.

A certain valorisation of women went alongside a full bloodied assertion of sensuality — a tendency identified exclusively with Lucknow and Faizabad. The period from Bahu Begum onwards was one in which there was an amazing growth in women's fashions, linked not just to luxury, but a thriving market mobility. It was considered not only refined, but hip, to sport exotic clothes, evolve new forms of smoking the hookah and wear amulets and earrings. This sensuality was not just to please men but reflected, first and foremost, a self-conscious mood of raiment and style.

On this path, traditional rights of men over women were challenged through a feminist application of insaniyat or humanism. A broadening of this concept saw a woman's traditional position, of being treated with respect, getting a modern sanction. Strong women, poetesses and 'personalities of letters', bent rules and conventions as and when required, to combine valour and sensuality with wisdom.

Bahu Begum herself did not keep quiet after the compromise with her son. In 1781, Chet Singh, the ruler of Benaras, revolted against the British. In the ensuing battle, Warren Hastings fled the field with such haste that it was said:

> *Ghode pe hauda, haathi pe jeen*
> *Bhag chala Warren Hastings*
> (The horse's saddle on the elephant
> The elephant's on the horse
> Thus ran away Warren Hastings)

Bahu Begum was accused of helping Chet Singh and this was one of the reasons behind Warren Hasting's infamous row with the begums of Avadh. But she was protected by her private army and, ultimately, a disgraced Warren Hastings went back to England to be impeached on the matter.

After Bahu Begum's death, the trust formed by her for royal employees became a means of special charity as it guaranteed women a pension, or wasika, for life. Her benevolence developed into a tradition with noble women giving grants to kerbalas and temples, constructing imambaras and helping scholars, pundits and maulvis. As a unique, late eighteenth century testament of Avadhian individuality, her tomb at Faizabad stood on an open courtyard surrounded by fizzy, rococo columns.

Queens such as Badshah Begum, Mallika Zamaniya and Mallika Kishwar extended her promise. Badshah Begum too managed her own jagir with a personal army of retainers. Politically, she faced difficult times, having to fight the Company on more than one occasion. She introduced new, womanly rituals in the festival of Moharram and re-organised the status of ladies. It was from her time onwards that royal servants were organised professionally with fixed work hours, pays and gradations. Separate work categories were evolved for singing, storytelling, body massage, cooking and hair dressing. Processions began to get named after her even as regular durbars inside the zenana increased the mystique of the spirited lady. In these, educated women from the city, those who had mastered the Koran, calligraphy and the martial arts, were called and honoured. Ghaziuddin Haider and Nasiruddin Haider, her husband and son, did not possess the informal right to interfere in the female domain.

But during her days of ascendancy, a different trend was becoming prominent. The first wives of all the nawabs and kings hailed from high class Delhi families. But their other nikaahi and mutahi wives were almost all drawn from the lower classes of Muslims, Hindus and courtesans. There were also a number of premikayen or women who arrived to entertain the king. Nasiruddin Haider's second wife, Mallika Zamania, was a married woman of Kurmi origin and his eighth consort, Qudsia Begum, a former servant of the household. Both were considered exquisite beauties and the former rose to claim her son from the previous marriage as the heir to the throne — a claim supported by Nasiruddin Haider at one stage. She was also a great builder, introducing the new, Baradari style, 'plaster' imambara. This Shia monument which stood at Golaganj, had open, arched columns running from four corners, with the pulpit visible from each end. People sat in angular rows to hear the Moharram majlis, the imambara having a special provision for mounted guards. Its pillars were like engravings of sculpture emerging from the ground with a primary arch drawn in a semicircular, bungalow-like fashion. A second arch stood over the first one, making a triangular, elliptical pattern. The arches were decorated with plaster work and round, mirror-like engravings on top. On the sides ran floral patterns and abstract decorative pieces, placed between the two arches, resembling Mughal and Moorish frescoes. The quality of play and frivolity was etched dramatically on each piece, in a way characteristic of plaster work.

The feminine talent in construction also produced the imambara of Mughal Sahiba, another unparalleled proof of gajkari plaster. The arched columns of Jama Masjid built during the time of Mughal Sahiba's father, Muhammad Ali Shah, looked like zari work done on stone and plaster. Constructed by Muhammad Ali Shah's principal wife, a brooding, unfinished imambara was left beside the masjid to remind one of a ruined Acropolis.

Nasiruddin Haider's beloveds made fun of the king and blended French designs with jalidar, revealing shoulders in their shalukas or tunics. Transparent shirts and tight pyjamas made of white satin went along with sleeveless blouses and shimmering hairdos studded with pearls and small clips of silver. Later, hair clips became exclusive items of European import. Beloveds enjoyed little formal status, yet they were proud, economically self-sufficient and their pregnancies were seldom looked down upon.

By Nasiruddin's time, the elevated courtesan was no longer limited to the durbar, having emerged as the lady of the city. Her salon was also not simply a place of dance and music, becoming a centre of sukun, humour, manner and letters. Here thumris were fashioned out of difficult raags like Jhinjauti and Jaunpuri and the daadra became a vehicle of sophisticated speed. Debates raged about the difference between Nasikh and Mir and Persian and Hindustani history. Salons disseminated culture, educating children of well-born families in the etiquette of zaban, behaviour and the correct attitude. This comprised a respect for the individual, an indifference to ritual, and an openness to beauty, aesthetics and new ideas. Courtesans acted as arbiters of many a middle class fate, teaching merchants, hakims, pleaders, guests and general men of fortune, the vices and virtues of life.

Before 1857, there was little incentive for these women to aspire for marriage. Though many of them eventually settled down with one man, they moved around freely and cultivated male friends. The tradition of striking friendships with men was not forbidden to respectable, married women, often poetesses of individual worth.

The courtesan was rivalled only by the bhatiyarin, the woman of iron. As an inn manager, she dealt with all sorts of men and commanded influence on the lower middle classes and the poor. She could strip an unpaying customer naked, use her hunter or whip too with effect on a recalcitrant staff, and smoke with abandon. But she had a sensitive heart which endowed the poor and religious concerns with liberal grants. A bhatiyarin was known to recognise a person's worth — she could open her place for the dreamy-eyed poet or the uncertain idealist quietly and discreetly, free of charge.

Bhatiyarins wore thick shades of dark surma in their eyes and participated in the underground culture of feminine secrets. Spread deep and wide, this network supplied the rekhti with anti-men themes told in the form of a woman's description of sexual experiences:

> *The moon told his moon-like heroine, about what happened during the meet*
> *Her stomach is light, it could not retain even for a day what happened during the night*
> *I come within your grasp because I am innocent*
> *You are the preyer, it is your mind which thinks about preying*
> *You will demand lightning from me and then make me cry again Mr. Cloud?*
> *I remember, I have not forgotten that other night of the last rains*

The first two lines speak of qualities which men ascribe to women. The next two establish a woman's 'innocence' in the war of nerves and passion. The third describes the heartlessness of men — how they demand 'the lightning', resulting from the rubbing of bodies, and yet make a woman cry in lovemaking. This rekhti by Jaan Sahib then goes on to reveal how this 'helpless complaint' was just a stance, a daanv or a master stroke in the ongoing game of chess between the sexes. In the traditional ghazal, the woman was the tormentor; here men are equally cruel. Through rekhti, women turned the tables on their stereotyping, transforming men into sensual objects. Suppressed humiliation as wives, mothers, sisters, and 'brides' on the first night of 'arranged' weddings, came out in hard-hitting verse. Erotic themes were charged with lesbian gestures and a sexual, sensual code of female bonding.

Sophisticated pornographic literature circulated in inner female circles which shared a culture of professional 'workmanship'. Of particular importance were the innovations in kite making and fire-crackers which women and lower class workmen established as a tradition for all generations to come. The heroines of the new grade of poets, Shauq and Aseer, inhabited the areas of Maulviganj, Aminabad and Chowk as daughters of the shuriefa. They angled for love through rooftops, tortured by a growing realisation of suppressed passions. Breaking bonds and swearing faith came naturally to them as did constraint, fear, restlessness and revolt.

This rich aroma of 'non-traditional-traditional', 'unconventional-conventional' women reached a strange apotheosis on the eve of 1857. The struggle threw up personalities who represented the different faces of Lucknowi-Avadhi womanhood. Begum Hazrat stood midway between middle class enterprise and the traditions of the zenana. She carried the traditional benevolence of the latter and the keen eye and perceptiveness of the former. Round-faced, misty-eyed with drooping eyelashes, the perfect Avadhi damsel broke household traditions,[2] rode personally to the battlefield and ruled with a strong hand. She bewildered the British with her manoeuvering of the mind and was as adept in the art of love making as in the war of arms.

Azeezun Bai, on the other hand, represented the revolutionary voice of the courtesan. Like her madam, Umrao Jaan Ada, she belonged to a conservative background. Umrao Jaan's father was an employee at the maqbara of Bahu Begum at Faizabad. Her family was not rich but her childhood memories were full of parented indulgence and material comforts. Azeezun was orphaned at an early age and was transferred to Umrao Jan's house as a young courtesan. She symbolised a flamboyant, rebellious adventurism, so typical of tawaifs coming from a lower middle class background. Unlike Begum Hazrat Mahal, Azeezun, who had shifted to Kanpur just before 1857, rode to arms from the start, excelling as a fighter, agitator and a glamourous revolutionary. She mirrored the contemporary extension of the charhari extroverted, non-purdah Lucknowi beauty, in contrast to the petite and introvert damsel. Comely and dandyish, women of her type were identifiable through their tight, punjabi ghutanna and the peshawaz, sometimes worn without the dupatta. An adventurous veerangana, Azeezun Bai came close to numerous ordinary women, like the lower caste aide of Lakshmi Bai, Jhalkhari Bai, who took up arms and fought desperately all over north India. In the battle of Sikandar Bagh, it was a woman who brought down many British soldiers from a tree top after the end of the battle. She died a martyr's death, feted by British soldiers for her courage. Her name was later discovered to be Undi Bai. The African women who guarded the Qaiserbagh and the women of Wajid Ali Shah's platoons all died fighting on the streets of Lucknow, still in their glittering Persian uniforms.

11

❧❧

The Grey Years

Elated, the British camp stepped into 1858. The 'mutiny' was officially over. Major towns had been won and the leaders driven out. The old revenue 'bandobast' was coming back to areas from where it had been swept aside by a wave of revolutionary fervour. More importantly, the remaining rebels were to receive a crushing blow — a proclamation, duly sealed by Queen Victoria herself, was read out at Allahabad transferring rule of India from the Company to the Crown. It removed the major target of the revolt besides announcing a series of relief measures and a promise of non-interference in religion.

The proclamation was made at Allahabad as the city's fall to Neill's advancing columns on 16 June 1857 had proved crucial in the battle. Akbar's fort at Sangam housed the biggest Company arsenal of north India and Allahabad's revolutionary leader, Maulvi Liaqat Ali, had almost captured the prized possession. The defeat of British defenders inside the fort would have meant the sure fall of Benaras and the beginning of Bahadur Shah Zafar's manoeuvre towards Calcutta. Maulvi Liaqat mounted his cannons on the roof of the city's Jama Masjid, lying westwards to the fort, hoping to breach British fortifications. The keys of the fort were held by a prominent Khatri banker of Allahabad. He belonged to the pro-British big trader-banker league now under pressure to side with the Mughal house, the original benefactor of the Khatris.

The banker first promised help to the maulvi. But when a Hindustani contingent advanced to take the keys they faced the British guns. It was obvious that they had been betrayed. Soon Neill arrived and the maulvi had to retreat. The Jama Masjid was then razed to the ground; its bricks were later used as construction material for the Allahabad-Jamuna bridge. The proclamation was read out, deliberately, at the previous masjid ground; its 'olive branch' shook with the settled issue of British fascism.

As a political weapon, the proclamation was meant to break the back of native resistance. British logic ordained that the 'rebels' would buckle before the sophistication of approach and language which indicated a departure from the old regime.

But the British were in for a surprise. Only a couple of weeks later, there was a counter proclamation from Baundi. In it, the queen of Lucknow, as head of the provisional government took up each and every point of the British declaration. Independent provisos and observations were also added which confounded neutral observers and active enemies.

Begum Hazrat Mahal's counter political weapon revealed the real dimension of 1857 to the world. In one stroke it summed up something which pro-landlord and pro-British intellectuals residing in Bengal did not understand at that point in time. And what historians of present day India, hailing without exception from outside Avadh, have not understood till date — that the future of modern India lay at that critical juncture with the 'rebels'. There was no repeat performance of 1857's tevar, literally attitude in action and ideas, be it the freedom struggle of Nehru-Gandhi or the radical posturings of non-Congress socialist-communist nationalism.

The counter proclamation attacked the master coup of the British — 'transfer of power' from the Company to the Crown. It stated clearly that the change was only in name with no commitment forthcoming on the policies of the Company — the Doctrine of Lapse, territorial aggrandisement, usurpation of sovereignty and financial loot. The queen's direct rule would still be an alien rule, that of one foreign nation over the other, and thus unacceptable. Likewise, 'non-interference in religion' rang hollow — the revolution began in the name of religion for which so many men and women laid down their lives. What kind of a religion would the British protect now?

The begum's proclamatory manner was strikingly original and prophetic. 1857 represented the ethos of composite culture for which Pathans and 'vilayatis', or Arabic horsemen, gave up their lives under Rani Lakshmi Bai's flag in Jhansi. The predominantly Hindu peasantry of Avadh looked at the young begum of Lucknow as their ruler. Post-'57, separate and divisive Hindu-Muslim identities came up as part of a conscious colonial design, set into motion way back in the 1780s, to redefine the culture and tradition of Hindustan. Its chief contours emerged during the heat of 1857 in Henry Lawrence's 12 May speech at Lucknow's 'grand durbar', called to placate and 'divide' recalcitrant Hindus and Muslims:

> 'It is a lie to say that the English Government interferes with the religion of Mohammedans and Hindus. Under Mohammedan rule, Hindus were taxed, and slaughtered and converted by violence and force — bullock's flesh was crammed down their throats — you all know that in this city, no Hindoo could at one time enter a temple, and I can tell you that in the Punjab, under the Sikh ascendant, the blood of pigs was spilt over the tombs and mosques of the faithful. But has the British Government done these things? No. These villains who enjoy the liberty of worship under the British have the audacity to accuse the English of doing that which Mussalmans and Sikhs used to do when they had the Government[1].'

Here was reproduced, neat and clear, that communal sense of history which Clive, Warren Hastings, Bentinck, Macaulay, James Mill, and the whole school of British Orientalists and Anglicists, wanted desperately to sell to India. And which today, Indian and expatriate intellectuals, like Bhartiya Janata Party (BJP) spokesman, K.R. Malkani[2], V.S. Naipaul[3] and Sanjay Subramanium[4], propound with scholarly impunity. In a recent interview, Patrick French, the author of *Liberty or Death*, denied the presence of tangible proof that indicts the British for deliberately following a communal policy. He forgot, perhaps, that academic scepticism is still no match for hard facts.

Henry Lawrence was not only trying to divide the Hindus, Muslims and Sikhs on a temporary basis, but was telling them that their history was one of mutual religious wars and the British were the only just rulers. Communalists in modern subcontinental politics always followed this line, the greater tragedy being that the secularists too never really tried repudiating its premises. The whole of Bengal and Hindi-belt renaissance grew up on the basis of Muslim, Hindu or Sikh atrocities against another religion. The Hindus and Muslims of 1857 were greater 'Hindus' and 'Muslims' than any renaissance leader or latter day communalist. Yet they not only ignored Lawrence but blasted his argument by invoking the history of the Mughal secular space as a joint compendium of Hindus and Muslims. In 1857 it was Bahadur Shah Zafar who ordained the raising of the Mahavir flag. Lawrence went overboard concocting untruths such as bullock flesh being forced down Hindu throats and Sikhs desecrating Muslim tombs. Such instances had no locus standi in native history but Bahadur Shah did order the ban of cow slaughter in Delhi. Lawrence said that no Hindu was allowed entry in a Lucknowi temple whereas this was the city where Lord Hanuman's cult grew under the patronage of the begums. Hazrat Mahal in her counter proclamation mentioned the philosophical unity of Hindus and Muslims against the white Christians. A revolutionary pamphlet entitled *Fateh Islam* said,

'The Hindoos should join the Chief with a view to defend their religion. The Hindoos and Mohammedans as brethrens to each other should also butcher the English, in as much as formerly the Mohammedan kings protected the lives and property of the Hindoos with their children—'

The British tried desperately to instigate Hindus of Bareli against Khan Bahadur Khan but they refused saying that Hindus and Muslims built the land of Hindustan together which, in Mughal times, shook the world with power and wealth. Pro-British pundits were chased away by pro-Hindustani pundits in Gwalior with the cry that deen was common to Hindus and Muslims, and their faith rested with the king of Delhi. Lucknow sepoys cried 'Bom Mahadev' in Hazrat Mahal's court, played with Birjis Qadar as Krishna and shouted Ya Ali! Din! Din! Allah O' Akbar! Jai Mahavir! along with Muslims in a unity of faith and culture.

But by the late nineteenth century Indians were participants in the cruel joke being played upon their destiny. While initiating social reforms, forming renaissance clubs, talking about the revival of India, praying and fighting as Hindus, Muslims, Sikhs, Shias or Sunnis, they stood on a religious and social ground which was not theirs at all. It was a result of a long process of British 'social engineering', effected with the help of native men of resources.

The begum's genius recorded another pressing detail of the coming regime. The queen of England had promised roads and public works for the native public. The begum replied — 'Let it be known that the British see us fit only to build roads and public works. If our countrymen do not realise this, all is lost'[5]. Prophetic words indeed; for decades on end Indians pushed files and worked as labourers under British rule. A whole civilisation with achievements far outstripping the 'West' was reduced to the status of a clerkly country groaning under the iniquitous weight of the white man's burden. Its people were not considered fit for representative government, industrial enterprise or municipal management late into the nineteenth century. All this after armed peasants of Avadh and Bihar ran governments in Delhi and Lucknow through elected councils, the primitive forms of which were followed in the west during the course of the German peasant wars of 1523-24, the English Glorious Revolution of the seventeenth century and the French revolution. These very events laid the basis of what was later called 'western democracy'. Success in 1857 thus would have created an India free of the communal issue, en route to capitalist democracy and enterprise. In that sense, 1857 heralded a struggle not between 'new' and 'old' but between the 'colonial new' and the 'indigenous new'.

The modus operandi of the sepoys was simple: to smash the

colonial state and build a new, alternative state. By this one act the soldiers ended up creating the possibilities of a contemporary Hindustani nation. They also came close to enacting nothing short of a fourth episode in the great India saga of Maurya, Gupta and Mughal empire building. 1857 was later replicated, on a lesser scale as the Meiji Restoration of 1867, Japan. Here the samurai-peasantry alliance revived the 'original dynasty' to worst foreign designs and lay the foundations of a modern Japan.

Every single uprising of the regiments in '57 was a highly disciplined and organised affair. After shooting British officers, the sepoys attached the arsenal storehouses and the treasury. They then broke open the jail, the centre of police power, and took control of the district office, the centre of administrative power, assisted often by local constables, chaprasee, clerks and deputy collectors. Their final movement was towards the centre of revolt or alternate power, be it Delhi, Lucknow or Kanpur.

The science of civic management was matched by the professionalism of military conduct. Strict norms were laid down for the behaviour and remuneration of the soldiers, business transactions, departmental work and the modes of representation. Specific orders were issued even against ill-treating peasants and women, and misbehaviour during festive occasions. Regiments followed hierarchy of rank with brigadier-major, subedar-major, havaldar-major, jamadar, naik and soldiers calling the shots in that order. Doctors and superintendent surgeons followed regiments according to protocol and information was circulated via newsletters.

Sepoys or 'telingas' of Avadh were new men with fatal memories of Mughal, Maratha and nawabi rule. In the days when they were employed with the British, they had invested in East India Company bonds, like small, capitalistic shareholders. Dismayed by the abatement in economic opportunities following the slide in the Company's fortune and business initiative after the 1830s, they saw colonial capitalism losing its drive. The rule of Manchester cloth was not beneficial to them and just before the outbreak, the sepoys actually surprised the British by withdrawing their bond investments.

On the eve of '57 the leading revolutionary forces, the telingas, civilian officers, small landlords, upper tenants and artisans, represented the Indian middle class. Inheritors of the great commodity class — the petty kings, revenue and military entrepreneurs, great bankers, service gentry and warrior peasant lords of the eighteenth century, they now embodied potential forms of indigenous capitalism. Sections of the old eighteenth century middle classes were either wiped out or had emerged as feudalised and 'baniaised' ruling classes under British rule.

The sepoy gave another shock to the firang. He was the one who nursed his master to health and in whose presence British ladies always felt safe. As an individual he did not pose a threat because of his image as a poor tiller of the soil, remote from the city culture of Delhi and Lucknow. This meek character was now suddenly inspired by a new vision of his own rule. The sepoys of Meerut, who landed at Bahadur Shah Zafar's court on 11 May carried a simple message: we created the empire for the Company, now we have come to offer our services for you. We will bring the treasuries to your doorstep and together we will throw the British in the Arabian sea and the Bay of Bengal.

This self-realisation was born out of his position as a member of a modern peasant army, breaking loose from its foreign masters. Shifts from one regiment to another had already shattered the local, village horizon of the Rajput, Pathan and the Brahmin. He was now in a new brotherhood bound by exchanges between widely flung cantonments. In this set up, he came to exercise responsibility and command companies on detachment as a native officer who had risen due to merit and hard work. He had an entirely Indian organisation in his hand, whose loyalties stretched wider than any post-Mughal Indian state. This organisation was superior to any caste or religion, tied as it was, by an impersonal professional code. It also had under its control all equipment required for war ranging from magazines to artillery. The army was isolated from politics and had stirred into action only on local grievances of pay, promotion and racial abuse. But once it became the target of ideological propaganda and learned to defy the white master, it held an explosive political potential to act on an all India, nationalistic scale.

The telingas became natural leaders of the restless Indo-Persian elite, comprising the Sheikh, Mughal, Pathan, Saiyyad, Thakur, Brahmin, Kayastha, Khatri, Jat, Gujar, Mewati, Ahir, Kurmi, Maratha, zamindar, trader, courtier, noble, vakil. They also guided the labour class turbulence encompassing again the Sheikh, Saiyyad, Pathan, Thakur, Brahmin, Bhumihar, Jat, Gujar, Mewati, Rangar, Banjara, Behna, Gaddi, Ansari, Ahir, Kurmi, Dhanuk and Pasi.

When the hour of revolution arrived, the Avadhian peasant was found instigating the tribals of Peshawar, Santhals, Hos, Meos and Cheras of South Bihar and the Adivasis of Chattisgarh under the slogan: 'Kaley, kaley ek hain' (all dark men are equal). He acted not for a region but the whole of Rajasthan, Madhya Bharat (Central India) , Bihar, Delhi, Haryana, Punjab. He also reached beyond the Hindi-Urdu belt to Gulbarga, Madras, Kolhapur, Hyderabad, Gujarat, Assam, Bengal, exhorting local kings, chieftains and peasants to take up arms against the firang. The sepoy also unleashed before the revolution a propaganda war. 'Rotis' and 'lotus flowers' were distributed village to village. In market places puppet shows were interrupted with the sudden appearance of a cruel British 'puppet' officer perpetrating atrocities on the people. In the night an 'ominous' slogan passed through regiments: 'Sub kuch laal ho gaya hai (Everything has become red). Revolutionary agents, fakirs and sadhus sneaked through markets preparing the mood of the uprising. Soldiers organised secret meetings in villages to discuss economic and political issues and bind the tiller in a vow against the firangi. After the fall of Lucknow, the begum herself addressed villagers in tumultuous meetings with the assistance of soldiers.

A sophisticated ideological propaganda accompanied the effective use of rumours. There was no attempt to displace politics, passion and sense of power with ideological-moral dogma. After deen and iman, power was the ideology of 1857 — the power of the weak over the strong and of the natives over the English.

In villages of Unnao a saying passed from village to village — 'The sister should protect the brother', literally to say that the time had now come for the meek to rise, conquer and rule. Women of Unnao were exhorted to give up their veil and plunder the rich zamindars. The recognition of the bold, unconventional power of women politicised, in a unique way, another inviolable Indo-Persian impulse. Similar incidents and slogans in Bundelkhand perplexed the white sahebs. In Panna raj, an unexpected demand arose for diamonds, the produce of the region[6]. This strange, beautifully sinister happening — almost like a chapter from a sensational Indo-Persian tale, reverberated throughout the Indo-Gangetic plain.

The exclusive concentration on north India in the initial military phase was a well-thought out tactic. In the American War of Independence, the northern regions led the anti-British war move, with the south supporting the 'enemy' on occasion.

A religious battle also raged in Avadh as part of the larger class and political struggle. British reforms were packaged under one slogan: the progressive role of Christianity. Debates on these lines had been conducted in places like Agra before 1857 between Christian missionaries and Indian modernists[7]. Britain may have had a representative democracy with a rule of law at home, but these political props also acted as tools of the British Empire's larger hegemonic-colonial design whose natural, 'civilisational' ideology existed as Christianity. Officers of the Company, including Henry Lawrence, were all god-fearing, white, Christian men for whom religion, ideology, modernity and politics were one.

The cry of religion on the Indian side was in the same way, a cry for the re-establishment of a Hindu, Muslim and Sikh[8] empire, civilisation and modernity. When the opportunity arose, the sepoys used the same Enfield rifles with the greased cartridges.

The Avadhian sepoy was caught in a dramatic historical moment when suddenly, the entire weight of history was thrust upon his shoulders. It gave him that special energy before which the Union Jack trembled and collapsed in one sweep, from Rohtak to Danapur, Gonda to Indore, Neemuch to Chota Nagpur.

The British were taken aback; the intensity of the hour chilled them to the extent of regarding the sepoy as acting in a drugged state. In cantonment line after line, the cry went up:

'The Pandies[9] are drugged, the Pandies are drugged!'

And the Pandies replied: 'Yes, we are drugged; we are drugged by the potion of power, we are drugged by the prospect of revenge: 'Jai Telinga Raj!'

It was this spirit which made the sepoys supremely confident of their organised struggle. Many of them embraced death without a hint of regret while encouraging the people not to get disheartened at temporary British victories as their friends would come back to settle scores. A British trooper of the 9th Lancers, recording with sadistic glee the degradation of 10th Native Infantry sepoys, being made to kneel, crawl and lick human blood with throats stuffed with cow and pork meat and pockets of shit tied around their noses, was struck by their still defiant attitude:

'Upon arriving in sight of the gallows I was surprised to see the villain of a sepoy salaam the gallows by bowing his head and touching his forehead with his hand. He was now taken into what is called the slaughter house and the bloody mat was brought out. The culprits were now ordered to kneel and to lick up the blood, at the same moment the lash fell heavily. This is carried on for about 10 minutes, that is if the prisoner took all things quiet, if not the lash was again plied freely. He is then brought to the gallows. These men were daring brutes and no dought by the way they took death had been guilty of some atrocious deeds. The man of the 10th before being hung spoke to the crowd, which was immense of both natives and Europeans. He made use of the words that he was satisfied to die and we need not think we were going to beat the sepoy's because they would yet beat us[10].'

All through the cruel spectacle, British officers like Neill, the 'butcher of Allahabad and Kanpur', kept invoking God's name and the fact that they were doing all this under his 'guiding finger'. Like everything else, God too was split in 1857.

The dehatis under their charismatic begum and the fireband maulvi had actually livened up the sedate bourgeoisie atmosphere of Lucknow. In 1857-58, the city become an early replica of the civil war-infested Spanish republican, 'fiesta' cities of the 1930s. There were shootings here, brawls there with ordinary peasants presenting themselves as princely republicans. Mirza Shauq's suppressed khangins came out on roof tops to solicit love and war. The courtesan salon had the amusing, bucolic sepoy, speaking in a mix of Avadi and Urdu, as the new paramour. A history of style simmers beneath the surface of 1857 — a mnemonic narrative of dashing looks, sensational raiment, valour, killer instinct and aesthetic liberation. The *tour de force* of style took place in Bundelkhand where a fleeting posse of British officers was met by a half clad native. He stood over their heads, as if in commemoration of the sensuality of the land of wild ravines, dark rivers, the martial Aalha, voluptuous sculptures, ferocious Thakurs and the black soil, with a drawn sword and bent gait. This was the un-Gandhian, non-comprador, authentic and valorous Hindustani pose of freedom recognised as such by an officer:

'One man — drew his sword — in a very fine attitude. He was quite a study for a painter. It was an admirable declaration on the nation having drawn the sword to free themselves. I had no idea a Hindustanee could assume so grand an attitude[11].'

The Indian army's retreat from Lucknow thus, also marked the end of a shortlived cultural revolution. Wajid Ali Shah and Amanat actually came to life for the first and last time in history. The fall of Lucknow was the end of an irreverent, boisterous, peasant-soldier-aristocrat, urbane carnival recorded disapprovingly by author of the masnavi:

'Thousands of rebels began pouring in the city — they put up their beds wherever they found a place in a jiffy. The zamindars wearing their todhidars — also kept coming in their thousands. Like this also the Pathans — they too came increasing their marks — they think of themselves as belonging to one line — upon those who rule they heap their laughter. The rebels are proud of their rebellion — they stand without a fear in their mansions even when surrounded. Even the urchins went a step ahead in their urchinism — and extended their reach upto Macchi Bhawan. They went and brought a cannon from somewhere — and fired a volley by bringing it close.'

This festivity displaced tradition and upturned convention! It was almost as if an apocalypse had struck!

'At this hour it became so festive — that limits were crossed by a crowd that was restive. People with wealth just acquired became one — the traditionalists were shocked and became numb. The Kotwal Mohammed Ali was killed by the 'rogues' without so much of a pity. Those who did this do not recognise any master — those who were in power are not respected by them.'

After retreating from Lucknow the begum called for intensifying the struggle further in the plains and the forest areas. The countryside was galvanised into insurgency geared at retaking Lucknow. Several attempts were made in this direction, the most notable being the two-pronged attack on the city in June led on the one side by talukedars of Bahraich and Barabanki and on the other by a name that was soon to become a legend for all times — Rana Beni Madho of Shankarpur. The Rana belonged to an illustrious family of Bais Rajputs, the pioneer entrepreneurs-traders-aristocrats of the eighteenth century. His warning to Sleeman about the Avadhian countryside came true as moving British columns got stymied in the hope of quickly subduing the region. The Rana enjoyed the confidence of the begum and won appointment as the nazim of southern Avadh. Azamgarh's stewardship was given to another legendary figure, Kunwar Singh of Arrah, who had come to Lucknow from Bihar. Kunwar Singh was to proceed to the east, Rana Beni Madho was to control the centre along with Mehndi Hussain in Jaunpur and Sultanpur, Raja Devi Baksh Singh was to oversee areas of the terai and Thakur Balbhadra Singh of Chahlari was to command forces near Lucknow in Barabanki. Other leaders like Nana Sahib and Prince Firoz Shah operated in the west while maulvi Ahmadullah Shah was busy organising forces in Sitapur and the revolutionary strongholds of Rohilkhand.

Balbhadra Singh lost the battle of Nawabganj, Barabanki in an attempt to retake Lucknow. Before breathing his last, he left behind the chivalrous trail of the last Rajput prince charming who abandoned his marriage half way in response to the begum's call in arms. This was not recorded in a history book but in an Aalha:

> In the field of Obri the British pitched their tent
> The princes of the land gathered together on the other
> side taking the name of Ramachandra
> The guns of the British blazed and the ground spewed
> fire
> Those who got the ball of cannon had their bodies
> running about without the head
> Those who were hurt by pellets had their bodies broken
> piece by piece
> O' Gosain, the earth shook that day, even princes ran
> showing their back
> Thus ran the prince of Baundi who was called Hardatt
> Singh
> Thus ran the prince of Charda who was called Jot Singh
> The real prince was that of Chahlari who is called
> Balbhadra Singh
> Tucking the bangle of marriage under the side he picked
> up the sword
> When the prince's elephant got surrounded from all
> sides the mahout got perplexed
> Said he to the prince —
> That if I get your permission I will take you to
> Chahlari as soon as possible
> On hearing this the prince got angry, the black eyes
> went red
> Then spake the prince of Chahlari —
> This is not the religion of Chattriya
> To run away by showing his back

Then the prince summoned a special horse and mounted
Like a wolf which chases a flock of sheep he charged
the force
He killed on the east, he attacked on the west, the
prince on north and south
He killed eleven officers in one go and there was no
count of other white men killed
In three hours he shook the earth —
Then the name of the king of Chahlari became famous
all over the country
He became famous even in London—

With Balbhadra Singh died Parvan Nau, Jangi, Bhikhari
Gadivan, offsprings of courtesans and several Ahirs and Pasis. After
the battle of Nawabganj the character of the revolt changed as
aristocratic values were taken over by the lower sections of the
peasantry. A folk song of Rajasthan spoke about how the values
of chattridom were now safe in the jhopdis, or huts, of the poor[12].
As big talukedars began submitting, the fight was led by the loyal
talukedars, small landlords, sepoys, tenants and farmers. At
Sultanpur, Chamars mislead the British and helped the 'rebels' even
as Beni Madho refused the British offer of surrender by the words
— 'I can serve only one king and that is Birjis Qadar'.

It was now that the true meaning of Birjis Qadar's proclamation,
made when he held the throne of Lucknow, struck with full effect.
After the 'mutiny', the British were to make much of the fact that
they established the 'rule of law' in India and rendered Brahmin and
Sudra equal before the magistrate. British equality was like a mirage
in the desert — on being approached it vanished for both the
Brahmin and the Sudra. But Birjis Qadar produced a scintillating,
unparalleled, Indo-Persian 'bill of rights' which stated:

'All the Hindoos and Mohammedans are aware that four
things are dear to every man; first, religion, second, honour,
third, life, fourth, property. All these four things are safe
under a native government. Everyone is allowed to continue
steadfastly in his religion and persuasion, and to possess his

honour according to his worth and capacity, be he a person of good descent, of any caste or denomination, Syed, Sheikh, Mughal or Pathan, among the Mohammedans, or Brahmin, Chhuttree, Bais, or Kaith, among the Hindoos. All these retain their respectability according to their respective ranks, and all persons of a lower order such as sweeper, chumar, dhanook, or *passee*, can claim equality with them[13].'

In Birjis Qadar's words, Indo-Persianism finally found the appropriate ideological-republican sign commensurate with the Hindustani form of Asiatic modernity, *al fresco*, since 1206.

All through 1858, the begum kept collecting land revenue and the officers of her army plunged headlong into destroying British chowkies and thanas. Districts were retaken and the begum's rule re-proclaimed with the beat of drums. The British even lost control of areas around Lucknow; in Taluka Mahona, talukedar Drigbijai Singh set up his administration under the begum's name. In Ruiya, Hardoi, Raja Narpat Singh defeated Walpole and his Scottish Highlanders in a decisive engagement. Harprashad Chakladar, the robust officer of Hazrat Mahal, occupied Sandila and boosted the morale of Thakur Gulab Singh, the victor of anti-British skirmishes in Laxmangarh and Rahimabad. Bodies of slain British officers were paraded in towns and qasbas. The battles in Sandila, Ruiya and Ayodhya proved that the rural forces of the begum could push back the British in open combat. Rana Beni Madho also won a couple of battles before getting down to harassing the enemy by hit, stay and run tactics.

Avadhian plains were ablaze till the begum crossed over to Nepal in 1859. People fought for every inch of their land, each hamlet threw up its band of fighters and the British had to reconquer Avadh village by village. About 1,50,000 Avadhians laid down their lives in active combat between the years 1857-59. Of these an estimated 1,00,000 were villagers and civilians. Beni Madho was defeated only in late 1858. The maulvi was killed by treacherous means adopted by Raja Puwayan in Shajahanpur and his severed head was hung from a tree by the British. Other talukedars were either brought over or made to submit, but their men continued the fight, even as it became evident that the open plains of Avadh were not suitable geographically for sustained guerrilla warfare. Perfect for Chinhat or Ruiya type of confrontations, or skirmishes stretched over a wide area for sustained periods leading, ultimately to the capture of Lucknow, they became disadvantageous as per the requirements of a rural, liberated zone out to encircle a city.

As an internal revolution, 1857 was a resounding success — in fact, even without colonial intervention, India would have seen, as had become evident by the rise of Walliullahism and scores of eighteenth century landlord-peasant-tribal-soldier revolts, a complete inner shake-up in the nineteenth century.

Avadhians were able to crush the British onslaught in the initial stages as they combined two lethal improbables: the power of ancient glory and the impersonal, ruthless, pulverizing energy of a revolutionary awakening. They also possessed that mixture of stoicism and ferociousness which came naturally to people of a 'hot', tropical climate. Their ruling elite were the most astute amongst all Asiatic ruling classes, perfectly adept at assimilating and adopting a range of Western or indigenous postures and logic.

But the British were the worst enemies, as they combined the survival instinct of a 'cold', island people with the impersonal, ruthless arrogance of a world colonial power. Their dogged, 'barbaric' perseverance easily ratified a rational brutality capable of seeing the destruction of a whole people without any qualm.

Talukedari capitulation did not dampen popular support but brought the begum face to face with the choice of fighting her old allies. The woman of steel that she was, there was no question of backing out from this challenge. Man Singh of Shahganj had fought bravely with her in Lucknow till February 1858, retreating to his fort just before the fall of the city. Friction between the leading talukedars and the lower classes under the leadership of the maulvi had increased leading to internal skirmishes in December. As in most insurgencies, the explosion of social forces led to implosions as well but unity was soon restored with the begum and maulvi agreeing to stick together. But Man Singh saw the changing nature of the struggle and the revolution in land rights it was bringing about. Unlike Beni Madho Singh he could not make the transition from a royalist freedom fighter to a revolutionary aristocrat.

By late 1858, the begum's army besieged Man Singh in his fort with active help from his own men. A civil war began in earnest as the Raja of Tiloi, who too crossed over, was cut off from British aid and surrounded with burning villages and armed men. The Raja of Balrampur[14] had sided with the British from the beginning; his estates were confiscated by the begum. On the other hand, the Rani of Tulsipur made his life quite difficult by constant harassment.

This phase saw the rise of a 'peoples order' in several zones of the Gangetic basin. People elected their kings and leaders and fought with matchlocks, spears, scythes and axes. They destroyed all symbols of British authority in parganas, tehsils and districts, burned the anti-peasant records of banias and mahajans and attacked pro-British landlords. The British courts of injustice were plundered and munsifs made to pay back the fines levied on people. The return of the old order was resisted more vehemently after the fall of major cities. The 'kings' and governors chosen by the people invoked the names of Bahadur Shah Zafar, Nana Saheb and Birjis Qadar and saw their 'rule' as complementary to the main centre of alternate power in the region. Where there was no such power left, the peoples order transformed itself into a national order in waiting.

The begum now selected the terai of Gonda and Bahraich, an excellent ravine and forest area, for insurgent warfare. But here she got hemmed in from the east, west and the south. The only way possible for the revolutionaries was to break the encirclement and strike out in other areas. This process began with the departure of Prince Firoz Shah to central India in a bid to join forces with Tantia Tope. Kunwar Singh's brother, Amar Singh, began his sustained fight in Bhojpur, Bihar. Bundelkhandis too inaugurated an anti-feudal uprising near the Chambal and the Kali Nadi which was to carry on till the 1870s.

The begum's entry in Nepal created quite a stir for she immediately began working on the king of Nepal's army and courtiers for a possible joint anti-British front. The rana of Nepal was a British ally and his army had participated heartily in the sack of Lucknow. But that did not prevent the begum from stoking the embers of revolution in Nepal. Public opinion forced the rana to grant asylum to Birjis Qadar's fugitive mother, even as he handed Khan Bahadur Khan over to the British and had Beni Madho killed in a bloody. engagement. When the begum was last heard of she appeared 'troublesome' to the rana of Nepal, now deep in the midst of a domestic political crisis.

Back in Lucknow, Mammu Khan was tried and sent to the Andamans. Raja Jai Lal Singh was hung at the Chini Bazaar gate near Qaiserbagh. Before dying he bid farewell to the people of Lucknow and kissed the rope. With him ended the tale of ordinary men, of Kurmi or agricultural origin, coming to the city and making it big. Raja Balkrishna, the last example of the glorious Kayastha-Indo-Persian tradition was also hanged to death. Other Kayastha notables like Raja Imam Baksh were looted as arrests and torture became the lot of Vajpeyis related to Wajid Ali Shah's court. In an unprecedented move, the ancient Vajpeyi tola was razed to the ground for involvement in the 'mutiny' prompting large numbers of this Kanyakubja sub-sect to migrate towards Kanpur. The whole area stretching from the Chowk to the Gomti in the west of the city was also demolished. The great Imambara was turned into a stable for horses and its glistening rooftop now sported grimy cannons pointing menacingly towards the city. The Bara Imambara was looted repeatedly, even after Queen Victoria's proclamation. Areas such as Sarfarazganj and Rajjabganj were demolished in the west and east with Sarai Mendu Khan, which had housed the maulvi, coming in for particular rough treatment. Amjad Ali Shah's maqbara in Hazrat Ganj was turned into a church — deliberately, it appears to assert British supremacy — by none other than the 'moderate' and 'considerate' Colin Campbell.

The town elite had fled, the middle classes were either dead or absconding in the bazaars of Kakori and Mohan and the lower classes faced a constant threat of being chased, caught and punished. There were casual suggestions to raze the city itself to the ground.

The best men of the royal household, who had not left for Calcutta with Wajid Ali Shah, were imprisoned and their property confiscated. Right after annexation, the British had interned notables like Muhammad Hasan Khan, a brother of Saadat Ali Khan, and Nawab Mustafa Ali Khan, a brother of Wajid Ali Shah, along with Raja Tulsipur, Mirza Muhammad Shikoh and Mirza Haider Shikoh, the descendants of Suleiman Shikoh. Muhammad Hasan Khan and Raja Tulsipur died but the rest were freed only after immense harassment when Campbell was retreating from Lucknow in November 1857. After the revolt was crushed, courtiers and relatives of the Nishapuri dynasty were hunted down like dogs. A brother of Wajid Ali Shah, Suleiman Qadar, had to leave the city and go into hiding. Family members of the Shia religious guru, Dildaar Nasirabadi, fell fighting to British bullets. Some survived only after leaving Lucknow. Earlier, Maulana Muhammad Baqar, the Shia scholar and notable was killed brutally after the recapture of Delhi. Poets and artists like Imam Sabhai and his sons were shot from a point blank range. Nawab Mustafa Khan Shefta, a disciple of Momin and Munir Shikohabadi, a close friend of the 'rebel' nawab of Farukkhabad, was packed off to the Andamans. The Delhi cycle was repeated in Lucknow: the house and imambara of Mir Anis was razed to the ground. The great marsiya poet had to flee for his life and hide in Kakori. The Machliwaali Baradaari near the Gol Darwaza chowk hung body after body for days on end for people to see and fear.

People were arrested on the slightest suspicion, a camel being remanded because he was found carrying an English stocking. But resistance also simmered below the surface in the whole of Lucknow. Soft British targets remained susceptible to acts of sabotage. Amongst the earliest people brought to trial were a number of tradesmen — shopkeepers, plate makers, bakers, an oil merchant a cloth merchant and a rice seller cum moneylender[15]. Sheikh Damur, the oil seller, was actually caught carrying guns. A number of labourers, munshis, domestic servants and 'Christian' drummers of Wajid Ali Shah's band were also caught in similar circumstances. Hunts were launched for the 'renegade' Europeans who had sided with the begum, and 'rebels' with no specific calling or occupation received quick 'justice'. One of them called Jamshed Beg had killed two British officers while his three sons died fighting for the king of Avadh.

In the interiors of the city, the British directed their wrath towards tailors, hakims, maulvis and sportsmen. The Jhawai Tola, which once boasted of physicians like Hakim Yakub and Hakim Abdul Aziz, was attacked and a number of residents killed. Mirza Mehndi, a great swimmer of the nawabi period, was shot during a British charge against a locality. Famous marksmen, sabre rattlers, carriage drivers and jockeys were also hanged. Maulvi Abdul Rahim of the Firangi Mahal lost his life while saying his prayers, bringing to an end the revolutionary chapter of this Asiatic centre of letters. During 1857, Firangi Mahal produced fighters and propagandists who designed and put up posters against the British. These people were still active in 1858 and British troops conducted many raids on its premises to flush out 'rebels'.

Men of influence, like Maulvi Pir Ali Khan, were common soldiers in the armies of Rohilkhand before settling down in Lucknow. Here they became typical locality based entrepreneurs, investing earnings from trade and shopkeeping into public works in the locality. Pir Ali built a 'garhi' in the western part of the city, then constructed a baradari in the nearby locality of Karim Ganj and laid out a garden, Salar Bagh, which became famous as Haathi Chingadh. In his bagh there was a bamboo forest called Kajli, where the maulvi kept his weapons. In 1857, this Lucknowi 'forest-garden' became the centre of revolutionary activities. The maulvi had a team of forty followers and enjoyed the confidence of both Ahmadullah Shah and the begum. Most of his followers like Mehboob Khan, Rajjab Khan, Yasin Khan, Muhammad Ali Khan, Thakur Singh, Suraj Singh, Tahseen Khan — all respectable men of the localities — were killed in the battles of Lucknow. Pir Ali also lost his 14-year-old son.

There was amongst his followers a man called Shamsuddin Khan who had laid out smaller localities in the city. These were the elites who stood between the royalty, the nobility of the city and the lower middle classes of the localities and they fought till the end —

again, neither showing mercy nor asking for any. Many of them were buried at Ambarganj, not very far from the main theatre of their operation.

Journalists of *Lucknow Akhbar*, workers of city presses became suspect in a war of vendetta which destroyed Saadat Ganj, Bibiganj, Rustam Nagar and dargah Hazrat Abbas. Veiled women had taken shelter in the dargah, but they were taken out and insulted in full view of the public. Some members of the royal family also lost their lives while trying to hide in the holy place. Hazrat Abbas kept passing in and out of British hands and the whole of the south-western portion of the city remained intractable.

By this time the new men seeking British favour had begun to rise. During the uprising they had maintained either a middle position or had submitted reluctantly to the begum.They included begums of Wajid Ali Shah, old nawabs like Mohsin-ud-Daula, people like Jaganath Chaudhari, Husain Baksh Chela and Ali Hasan Thanedar. These elements occupied various posts in the administration of the begum, though Maulvi Ahmadullah Shah had reportedly cognized and put to death some of them in the last phase of the war. Native treachery created mutual suspicion amongst the leaders of the revolt leading to the death of Sharf-ud-Daula in mysterious circumstances.

The turbulent situation produced Meer Wajid Ali, the daroga of the zenana. A former employee of the royal household, he had used the insurrectionary period to consolidate his own position. In conjunction with other begums, he built up an anti-Hazrat Mahal faction and supplied the British with information about revolutionary activities. His testimony led to the death sentence of Raja Jai Lal Singh for which he was duly rewarded. Outram gave him a sum of Rs. 1 lakh and extensive property in the city. He soon married the begums, acquired immense wealth and became a 'post-mutiny' neo-rich of Lucknow. Someone who was not even a genuine, comprador, profit-seeking middle man of the 'pre-mutiny' times, but a faceless figure of the old dispensation without any proper class or social identity. A 'chutbhaiyya' or a small man, now styling himself as the rais of Lucknow. It was as if someone had planted a resounding slap on Lucknow's cheek — Mir Wajid Ali now occupied the chambers of Qaiserbagh and cohabited with the queens of Wajid Ali Shah.

An imitator-impersonator of the first order, he once 'bettered the old elite' by wearing the Shaluka with both arms missing to remind people of Nasiruddin Haider's elegance! 'Khansamas' were ordered to be addressed as 'butlers'; and paltry awards given to the best servant of the month, in a cheap imitation of firang aristocratic benevolence!

The Mir Wajid phenomena raised the theme of the 'illegitimate-'nakalchi' 'elite', or illegitimacy and plagiarism as a way of post '57' upper class Indian life. Its ghost haunted the literature, cinema and the social history of underground rumour of the twentieth century. 1857 gave wealth acquired in the 'aftermath' an unwashable stain — the 'man of property' remained suspect, always, of a dark, hideous, bastard origin. There was no guarantee that he was the 'son' of his 'soil', or of his father.

When old elites returned to the city, they found a devastated environment and a culture shut indoors in shock. A renowned musician of Lucknow, who later formed the Farukkhabad school of the tabla, saw people shying away from music conferences and festivals for fear of British reaction. There was an unofficial moratorium on celebrations, and marriages were not held for years in ashraf households. Musicians began migrating in droves — the disciples of Ghulam Rasool and Nathan Peerbux left for Gwalior where they laid the seeds of a new music gharana. Thumri singers also left for Benaras and sitariyas stopped playing even for matam. On his return, Mir Anis found Lucknow completely devastated. He asked with painful irony:

Waraq ulat gaya duniya ka yak-bayak kyon charkh
Ye kis tarah ka zamane ne intaqam liya
Ulat gaya na faqat Lucknow ka ek tabaqah
Anis, mulk-i-sukhan men bhi inquilab aya
(How did the leaves of the book of the world get thus scattered?

The times have exacted revenge for which happiness?
Not only was an order destroyed in Lucknow
Oh Anis! Poesy's kingdom too suffered convulsions)

Worse was in store for courtesans, some of whom had left with Hazrat Mahal for Baundi. There they turned the qasba bazaar into a bustling chowk reminiscent of Lucknow. In the few days that the begum headed a provisional government, maulvis[16] and courtesans were her most ardent supporters. Umrao Jaan Ada was with the begum in Baundi[17] and did not return to Lucknow for fear of reprisals. When she did limp back after unfortunate experiences in Faizabad, the connoisseurs had left while a strange attitude had set in amongst the Madams. They were no longer concerned with maintaining themselves or embellishing boudoirs. An unspoken sadness clouded their manner and appearance and suddenly they began greying.

The British on their part wreaked personal vengeance on the courtesans and the bhatiyarins. A famous song of the tawaif highlighted the 'unsaid story' of 1857:

'*A hundred years have gone and past*
When India groaned under England's rule
The avenging hour has come at last and the Hindoo sepoy
is not such a fool to eat the salt of his great tool Company
John ——

Wah wah Vajeeran! Wah wah Vajeeran!
You were fond of the Captain Saheb of my Company then
But now times are turned old gel
You must sing to no one but your soobadar, Vajeeran sing
again.

The topee wallas were great assess:
Who drew their tullubs and said their masses
And after dinner filled their glasses
Then left the country to Chuprassees
But now we shall be the Sepoy's lassies
No more John Company,

Ali Khan hai John Company
Ali Kahan hai John Company oh[18]!'

During the revolt, tawaifs attached to British officers in Company stations switched loyalties to the 'inferior' sepoys. Acting as fighters, diplomats and spies for the 'Pandies', they deserted the English in politics and love. Courtesans financed the provisional governments of many areas with a specific eye on the prospect of power. Under the new British regime they were degraded systematically. For the Victorians the concept of a courtesan salon as a place of etiquette was in any case a French monstrosity, doubly intolerable in a non-European context.

After the uprising, courtesans were referred to as 'prostitutes' under the direct control of the town criminal officer. An anti-flesh trade act was slammed on their profession which brought such shame that they stopped functioning altogether. They were also degraded before their paramours. Previously, few courtesans desired to become respectable wives — their profession had enough of an aura of distinctiveness. If they did desire so, there was no dearth of suitors willing to take their hand in marriage. Many of the courtesans were close to kings, who admired their intelligence. Wajid Ali Shah had a special relationship with a courtesan named Mushtari — the habitually amorous king shared a platonic, friendly relationship with the 'intellectual' tawaif. She composed verses in Urdu, advised the king on various issues and was an accomplished calligraphist. She followed a tradition which traced its roots back to the time of Haider Jan and other tawaifs, who had played a prominent part in Avadhian affairs from Ghaziuddin Haider's period.

But now, these same personalities were made to crawl before pimps and less than noble figures. At a time when the queens of Wajid Ali Shah were being humiliated who was there to speak for the tawaif? Men, who in the past did not dare to climb up the stairs of the kotha, now lured her with promises of marriage, and then discarded her on the slightest provocation. Deprived of a voice in politics and social power, she was reduced to economic and moral destitution.

In Lucknow, a class of professional women had emerged to take up employment in government departments. This blossoming took a backseat in British Lucknow — Persian and Urdu educated women professionals were of no use in the white administration while women in arms were an embarrassment.

The emergence of a new elite class was accompanied by a large scale transfer in property. The loot collected by the British was valued at almost a million and a quarter sterling in estimable figures, the unofficial accumulation not known even to British officers. Lucknow was drained of valuable capital resources, and plunder was followed by whole scale appropriation and redistribution of property. From a city where property was shared by a vast variety of social forces including the labour class, Lucknow became a feudal-urban estate where whole areas were apportioned off to one or two individuals and families. Earlier in localities like Aminabad, the rights of every household were registered and guaranteed. After 1857-58, all rights of this nature ceased as middle class homes were auctioned off or confiscated. Wajid Ali Shah's brothers were forced to give up their mahalsarais, the family of Suleiman Shikoh was displaced and the former ministers and courtiers told to leave their mohallas. The localities established by insurgent traders and maulvis were annexed and distributed between those who had been loyal to the British — the faithful talukedars, the princes of Punjab, and later, the aristocracy which submitted.

It was through this process that a man whose family did not occupy an exalted position in the old talukedari system became the biggest property holder of Lucknow. Raja Digbijai Singh of Balrampur, the leader of the loyalist wing of the talukedars, emerged at the expense of the raja of Tulsipur who suffered in the British land settlement of 1856. The latter became a 'rebel' at an early date — his lineage was higher than that of Digbijai and his queen laid down her life fighting for the begum. Tulsipur was handed over to Raja Digbijai who became a big talukedar in the post-Mutiny period.

The knave was then dressed up as a king and introduced to Lucknow as the new master. In the nawabi days, talukedars like him seldom got to play a role in the city — Digbijai Singh had to wait for several days to get an audience with Wajid Ali Shah's official only a few years before the annexation. Talukedars had come to dominate the city and wear the silken, nawabi robe for the first time in 1857 itself — but that was a mast, rooted aristocracy displaying revolutionary power, not a conservative country bumpkin culture vulgarising royal splendour. The pain which the old, sensitive elite felt at this counter-revolution was expressed in a late century tale. Raja Digbijai Singh had once tried overtaking the bagghi of one of Wajid Ali Shah's brothers. This gentleman was known for rubbing shoulders with the 'low' in his youth; but he was unable to tolerate the pretensions of the neo-rich. He got down from his bagghi and went after Digbijai Singh with his whip — the raja drew up his weapon in combat but lost. The favourite boy of the British was ultimately saved by a leading officer of the queen who had to plead with the ex-king's brother to stop. Digbijai Singh was severely reprimanded but before the incident was over, the ex-prince turned towards the officer and said: 'You took away our kingdom; now you and your lackey will take our pride too?'

Raja Balrampur's real problem rested in the failure to do anything substantial for the cultural upliftment of Avadh. He built hospitals and schools and was the foremost amongst the talukedars to at least imitate the Bengal renaissance into opening a British India club at Lucknow. Only, in the circumstances prevailing now, this club could never become the nucleus for an Avadhian renaissance.

The talukedari club actually initiated a backlash against the old Lucknowi-Avadhi culture. One of the acclaimed acts of Digbijai Singh of that time was the publication of Kamalluddin's Haider's *History of Avadh*, commissioned before 1857. Submitted for publication after the fall of Lucknow, it was sent back to the author with express instructions from the British authorities that the work fell short of the 'expected respect for authority'. After that, the book vanished only to re-surface with a preface by Digbijai Singh in the 1870s which warned the readers not to publicise anything about

Avadhian history or about the book which they had seen or heard 'otherwise'. Even at that time it was widely suspected that Haider's book, begun during his tenure as an employee of Nasiruddin Haider's observatory, had been tampered with in the interregnum. The book was not approved by Wajid Ali Shah and in no way represented the kind of history which the British might have found offensive in normal circumstances. But such was the chill of '57, that the most important pro-British talukedar had to issue an unprecedented warning on its publication.

An offensive was also launched against Lucknowi sensuality and valour. The city soon became a dull place — while Balrampur controlled major areas in the western and central side, the trans-Gomti portion was handed over to Maharaja Kapurthala, the obstreperous and cowardly Punjabi prince whose army had helped the British during '57. This region turned into a barren land under the maharaja, the pond and garden of Aishbagh, the Kerbala of Talkatora and the bridges named after various nobles wearing a neglected and deserted look. Asaf-ud-Daula used to play Holi at Aishbagh, which now was home to stray animals. The city had crossed the seven million mark in population density before 1857, but after the Mutiny the numbers shrank dramatically with old areas remaining uninhabited as late as 1947.

Nothing equalled the disaster that accompanied the reconstruction of Lucknow. It was, to put it mildly, the dismemberment after the rape. When the city was being burned down, the first war correspondent of the world, William Howard Russell, had asked — 'not Rome, not Athens, not any city I have ever seen, appears to me so striking and so beautiful as this. Is this the capital of a corrupt and effete dynasty?' Even an objective journalist like Russell was swayed emotionally.

The express plan drawn up to restructure the city envisaged no continuity with the Lucknow of yore, no respect for the logistics of geography, not even a token understanding of civic standards. Its main concern was to control the city in a way that fulfilled the needs of a British military-administrative outpost; to build, in effect, a convoluted version of Hanssmann's post-1848 Paris. For this it was required that roads should facilitate, rather than hinder, the movement of troops. The most logical way to achieve this was to run straight pathways through the heart of the city so that armies could be rushed from the southeastern end, where new military cantonments were to come up, to the western end which had proved so resistant during the revolution. Work had to progress quickly and with precision — even in 1859 the British were not sure of their position.

The plan[19] was followed methodically and whatever posed to be a barrier was demolished. The whole strip along the south bank, from the far west to the Qaiserbagh, was straightened out. This area had a row of buildings which gave the city an elegant skyline of turrets, cupolas and pavilions all of which vanished without a trace. Similarly, on the eastern side, all buildings between the La Martiniere college and the Gomti were razed. Formerly, the city existed within an irregular and curved parallel formed by the Ghaziuddin Haider Canal with the Gomti. The areas and localities which bordered the canal were also demolished to make way for a new railway station which came up on the battle scarred ruins of Asaf-ud-Daula's Charbagh. Many other gardens were similarly turned into trenching pits and distilleries or just closed down.

The roads that came up cut through the old pattern. Earlier, the area from Qaiserbagh to Golaganj marked a series of neat rows with straight roads running parallel and horizontally. These small streets were open compounds in their own right connected by alleys to the main road. Under the new plan, a wide road ran through Qaiserbagh, the heart of the 'rebel' resistance, while Golaganj was linked vertically to the palace complex. This reduced the exclusivity of both places while literally ghettoising their localities. It was like creating a maze of airstrips around dwelling places — the so-called 'esplanades' around dense mohallas. In old Lucknow, where gigantic mohallas with gateways and imambaras ran in parallel directions, there was a majestic blend of gaiety and utility. These areas had their main roads which never impinged upon their inner structure. Now, streets broke through their centre cutting it into various portions and reducing the localities into strips of houses standing besides pavements. Alleys which were earlier a place of social activity now functioned as backyards of dirty roads, cut off from the small chowk or even from the centre of their locality.

Thus, while Golaganj remained, it became more of a gali than mohalla. The imambara of Mallika Zamania, which stood contiguous to its inner portions in one single block, was separated from a road which went vertical to the Qaiserbagh. It now became a real backwater with traffic pressing on its inner segments. It was this 'British modernisation' which really gave birth to the congestion of the alleys.

Hazrat Mahal's success too would have changed Lucknow. The military and civil requirements of the new Hindustani government might have necessitated the building of wider roads. But this could have taken the form of further expansion towards the east, west or north or of extending the extant roads. The old localities would have died a natural death or re-fashioned without disturbing the essential structure and logic on which they had been built. There was, ultimately, no plan or vision in the British re-structuring of Lucknow. A haphazard and opportunistic move, it threw the city off gear into civil anarchy and chaos. The areas towards the north and the east remained depopulated with no use of their healthy civic role.

Confusion propelled the re-ordering of the drainage, municipal and police system as well. The seven drains of Lucknow, built in accordance with the topography, were closed down. Instead, a single uniform canal system came up which played havoc during the rains. Hazratganj was a low lying area and a drain was needed to link it with the Gomti. But no such facilities were available under the new system which laid drainage pipes only near the wider roads. The result was waterlogging and flooding during the rains which posed a major problem for all localities. A new police corp and penal code with an explicit ideological commitment to hold down an insurgent population was established which distorted the very idea of civic police and law for all time to come.

By the time a new elite began to make its presence felt, a pale colourless hue was already settling down on Avadh. The Gomti, a repository of beauty, passion and pride, was being polluted. During the nawabi days, buildings like the Chattar Manzil faced the river. Now in another act of unexplained British monstrosity, its rear became its front. The same happened with Moti Mahal and other riverside buildings. As the city turned her back on the Gomti, it became a place of filth and refuse. With this ended the lustre of the bagghi, the sheen of the ashraf walk and the romance and smell of henna wafting on the waters.

The new elite came to inhabit a ghost city where elegant manzils, palaces, garden complexes were giving way to small rectangular makanats, resembling faceless encampments of the British cantonments, and bland, squarish baghs on the pattern of British parks. These men operated in the context of the great change sweeping the Avadhian countryside, the restoration of the status quo in the post-Mutiny period.

The nawabi talukedari system had revealed its radical potential in 1857. There were many talukedars who saved the lives of British ladies and children and then calmly went to battle British armies even at later stages when victory seemed difficult.

As Avadhian Rajputs ran from village to village raising armies, they got more and more remote from their old social origin. In a village, Beni Madho encountered a Pasi mother telling her son:

'Go and take the pigs to the field, this is what you have to do all your life.'

The son replied that he would not follow his old, caste occupation.

'Then what will you do?' the mother asked.

'I will join the Rana's army.'

On hearing this, Beni Madho planted a punch on the boy's heart to test his endurance. The boy faced the blow bravely and was inducted in the army.

Avadh was actually witnessing a social upheaval. Pasis were becoming fighters, while the Ranas were becoming proletarians. In 1857 the 'Pindari' also reappeared. A freebooting, mercenary fighter, this Indian samurai arrived from Afghanistan as a Pathan adventurer. He fought in several provinces with a Persian sword, a twelve-foot spear and a pistol atop the gold laced saddle cloth of the Deccani charger. After the sack of a city he could marry a fiery Brahminee and take her on an adventurous tour. The badge of courage, loyalty and dare devilry worn by this wandering Muslim warrior complemented the hardy, industrious, 'certitudinal' ethic of the settled Hindu peasantry.

By the 1830s, British anti-adventurous laws had tied this section to the land, but these untamed, ex-urban upper peasants never forgot the basic fact of colonial rule. British reforms were unimpressive, for they took away the sword, the symbol of native power, and replaced it with schools, the symbol of colonial subterfuge! The basic British instinct of intolerance behind a mask of civility was also noticed with unconcealed contempt:

'There goes my lord the firangee, who talks so civil and bland,
But raves like a soul in Jehannum, I don't quite under stand —
He begins by calling me sahib, and ends by calling me fool,
He has taken my old sword from me, and tells me to set up a school.'

The smart and clever Pindari found firang modernity in the countryside 'inferior', a cover for loot, and fit for a counter subterfuge:

'There comes a settlement hakim to teach me to plough and weed.
(I sowed the cotton he gave me, but first I boiled the seed)
He likes us humble farmers and speaks so gracious and wise
As he asks for our manners and customs, I tell him a parcel of lies[20].'

This warrior-peasant knew that no matter how much his grand-sons may learn to read and write, they will never be 'man'. There was something fatally wrong with colonial rule; it turned Indians into babus, mahajans and banias, after which they jogged away to the cutchery swaying from side to side without, as if, *a spine.*

It was against this colonial attack, not only on economy or polity but native traditions and male potency as well, that proud men became 'Pindaris', or those who lived by adventure, in the early nineteenth century and revolutionaries in 1857. Rohilkhandi ghazis and Afridi pathans of Malihabad, who initiated the qasbai-rural uprising of Avadh, were all Muslim warriors with the Pindari-cowboy badge. They had a well defined code:

'—— there is no god but one
Muhammad is his prophet, and his will shall ever be done—
Ye shall take no use for money, for your faith for lucre sell,
Ye shall make no terms with the infidel, but smite his soul to hell.'

They knew that the full-blooded values of Islam were no longer safe with status quoist Muslims who had all become 'banias'. While 'namaaz' is alive, pride and honour have taken a back seat:

'Tell me, ye men of Islam, who are living in slavish ease
Who wrangle before the firangee, for a poor man's lost rupees —
Are ye better than were your fathers, who plundered with old Chetoo,
And squeezed the greedy traders as the traders now squeeze you?'

This warrior had his own economic and cultural philosophy. He nourished the idea of making money but was antithetical, by 'gut' and 'logic', to the bania culture. Much before the intellectuals of Bengal and Bombay came on the scene, the Avadhi-Rohilkhandi warrior outlined the 'drain of peasantry' alongside the drain of wealth. He knew that there could be no compromise for an authentic patriot with the 'colonial-bania' philistinism which was to rule the roost as capitalism in India:

'Down there a mahajan lives, my father gave him a bill,
I have paid the man thrice over, and here I am paying him still,
He shows me a long stamped paper, and must have my land,

must he? If I were twenty years younger, and my life before
me to choose I wouldn't be lectured by kafirs, or bullied
by fat Hindus, But I'd go to some far off country, where
Mussalman are still men,
Or take to the forest like Chetoo, and die in a tiger's den'.

In the new British Raj, all such modern, elemental desires were
wiped out from the countryside as servile landlords and dalaals were
restored with a vengeance[21]. Those who had fought and later surrendered were separated permanently from the peasantry and any
sort of entrepreneurial role by the new British land' settlement.
Reversing the earlier Oudh proclamation, issued after the fall of
Lucknow, the British gave talukedars permanent right over their
land. In one stroke, the erstwhile adventurers and semi-capitalistic
trustees of land were converted into masters of run-down Avadhian
versions of Spanish haciendas. The immediate sufferers of the new
regulations were the middling landlords, the village landholders of
Company records, and the upper peasantry-tenncy who had worn
the British down in 1857[22].

By 1857, sections of Ahirs and Kurmis too had graduated to the
position of middling landlords and rich peasants. 1857 threw up
many leaders from their ranks. Rich men like Khushal Chand
Kurmi of Salempur[23] were important enough to be considered at
par with talukedars and harassed the Britishers till the end along
with Muslim warriors of the Lucknow countryside. All these forces
vanished into ignominy. They were reduced to the position of a
renteir tenancy whose voice was not heard as late as the 1920s. 1857
had brought forth the peasant issue as revolving around the question
of power and privilege to small landlords, middle peasantry and the
upper tenancy class. Confiscated land of pro-British talukedars was
also distributed amongst the poor and landless peasantry who took
up arms against the infidel power.

Amongst the elite the shift was no less painful. The real Digbijai
Singhs (the talukedar of Mahona), who fought vehemently for the
begum were eclipsed from the scene, to make way for the pro-
British Digbijai Singh of Balrampur.

There was an almost cataclysmic change within the Rajputs. Valorous talukedars, like Lal Beni Madho of Amethi, who surrendered, could never regain their lost position and died broken and dispirited. The capitulationist rajas of Tiloi, Tirwa and Shahganj could never regain their status. Aalhas ridiculed them as men who had left the battlefield in the hour of decision.

The Muslims faced a more drastic change. Personalities like Khan Ali Khan of Sitapur, Nabi Baksh Khan of Bhutwamau were killed. The property of Musahib Ali, Afridi Pathans, Sayyids and Sheikhs of Bilgram, Chaudharies of Sandila, Maulvis of Khairabad, Khanzads of Sultanpur were either confiscated or reduced, while insignificant pro-British clans of Salon and Rae Bareli were raised to prominence. Middle ranking households like Salempur were rewarded for their loyalty even as the house of Faqir Mohammed Goya sank back in prestige. Farzand Ali, the raja of Jehangirabad, had once enjoyed the confidence of Wajid Ali Shah himself. In 1857, he submitted early to the British who allowed him to expand his Barabanki possessions. This Indo-Persian family initiated the genteel upper class compliance to British authority — a behavioural trait differing fundamentally from the aggressive 'upper class independence' stance taken by Mahmudabad.

The post-'57 Muslim tragedy and defiance was embodied 'in person' by the Mahmudabad 'house'. This talukedar family had pre-Mughal origins, arriving in Avadh as sardars of Muhammad-Bin-Tughlaq. Mughals awarded them the vast jagir of Mahmudabad in Sitapur which had got reduced by the time of Burhan-ul-Mulk. In the eighteenth century, the family became the major pillar of nawabi rule and in 1858, Muhammad Nawab Ali Khan, who bore the title 'Qaim Jung', lost his life while helping the begum escape to Nepal. Revolutionaries of Sitapur flocked to his standard in 1857 and his own troops took part in the battle of Chinhat under the leadership of his naib, Khan Ali Khan. His influence was widely responsible for some sepoy regiments of Avadh sticking to the besiegement of the residency instead of proceeding towards Delhi. The possessions of this most ancient and prestigious of all Muslim families were annexed after '57.

Nawab Ali's son was a minor at that time — he was restored to the reduced domains of his father because of family prestige and British design of using him at a later date.

But Amir Hassan Khan was not cut out for British munificence. One day, he was called to the viceroy's durbar at Lucknow. From 1861 onwards these were held occasionally in order to gauge the pulse of the Avadhian countryside, which still aroused a state of nervousness in British minds, and to test talukedar loyalty. In one of these meetings, the viceroy passed some uncharacteristic remarks about Nawab Ali. The young Amir Hassan listened for a while and when he could bear no longer, he took out his sword and threw it towards the viceroy.

Amir Hassan's lands were again confiscated. He was reinstated only after some of his friends had him declared insane. But he was interned for life in Mahmudabad and seldom ventured out for fear of detection of his 'sanity'. The talukedars were then outbidding themselves in obeisance towards the British. But the young chief's turbulent personality could barely contain the contradictions of the post-Mutiny aristocracy who had fought in 1857 and were now forced to play second fiddle to the British.

This tragedy was more agonizing as now they did not have even the satisfaction of sporting arms. The British had disarmed the population of Avadh while taming the aristocracy to such an extent that there was a drop in the volume of hunting in the terai jungles.

During Amir Hassan's time all living symbols of Lucknow perished one by one. Wajid Ali Shah passed away in the 1880s at Calcutta much after the death of Bahadur Shah Zafar in Rangoon. After getting released from prison in 1859, he recreated a mini Lucknow at Matiyaburj. This dream enclave of manzils, baghs, palaces, thumri, kathak, sitar and sarangi compensated for the ex-king's beloved city to which he never returned. His mother and brother died unsung in Europe and during the turbulence of '57, one of the king's servants was caught enticing a guard of Fort William to join in an attack on Calcutta. The British never trusted him and his last years were spent reading and writing — unlike despondent old men of royal blood, who take to asceticism when dislodged from power, 'Jan-e-Alan' remained indulgent to the end. So much was lost and yet so much survived to live for. In his last years, Wajid Ali Shah theorised on music, dance and theatre and extended his linguistic interests to the mixing of dialects and gestures. Till his death his social contribution remained singular and consistent. He was the one to popularise the arts amongst the people, to discover new forms of light music which later became standard traditions. Developments in modern dance and theatre can be traced back to him and politically, he was perhaps the only 'peoples king' who gave a new dignity to 'lesser' men and women of merit.

As the last Indo-Persian, he carried its throbbing multilacedness and intensity in his toes which kept twitching, as if to the thaap of a tabla, in the midst of a political meeting. The same seriousness made him keep a tab on the political affairs of the world in the heat of a musical moment. No wonder he was never understood — not by his contemporaries, not by his adversaries, not by those who thought they knew better, years later.

About a decade earlier Begum Hazrat Mahal had passed away in Nepal. She too died like she had lived and fought — without regrets, as the last Indo-Persian warrior-heroine.

Till her last days, she held her head high and had only one question to put to the British: after surrender what would be her future status? That of an equal and respected opponent? She also did not give up hope — commentators were fearing that the begum might be plotting to attack Calcutta from Nepal, free her husband and march to Lucknow. In Nepal she married off her son, Birjis Qadar, into a revolutionary family of Delhi. In her last years she had grown wiser, more beautiful and a trifle amused at the way things had evolved. The politician in her kept a watch on Lucknow and the rest of the country. Even with her meagre resources she had a masjid and a few other buildings built in Kathmandu.

A British painter happened to visit her at Kathmandu for her portrait. She readily agreed — the painter went further and suggested to her that quite a period had elapsed since '57 and a 'respectable' means of salaried livelihood could be arranged for her at any place in Lucknow or Faizabad. The English would indeed be pleased if she decided to come back, the only condition being that she would not be permitted to have too many servants. Sensing obvious British interference and a future life of glorified prisonhood in Avadh, the begum dismissed the suggestion with a line of typically wry, aristocratic, Avadhi 'kataksh', or biting satire — 'Of what use will be the salary then, if I am not allowed to keep and spend on servants[24].'

12

❧❧

A Ramayana in Urdu —
and an Engineer with a Courtesan

Jo karna tha yeh
To kyon kiya woh
Jo banana tha yeh Hindustan
To kyon chedi woh Avadh ki taan

(If you had to do this
Why did you do that
If you had to make this Hindustan
Why did you play
That note of Avadh)

Before the dust could settle on the graves of Wajid Ali Shah and
Hazrat Mahal, the last light of Avadh was also extinguished. Birjis
Qadar had gone to Lucknow in the 1890s to claim his father's
inheritance. There, some relatives with vested interests invited him
for a feast. The last ruler of Avadh returned home a sick man and
died soon after, leaving behind a pregnant wife. Some versions
report that his son who went with him met a similar fate.

Behind Birjis Qadar's murder allegedly lay the hand of British
rulers, who it seems, had perfected all East India Company methods.
The 'rebel' nawab was the last living testament of 1857, his death

imperative by any logic. In between, the first stirrings of post-1857 nationalism, the first 'nationalist' died ignominiously. Salar Jung, the well known prime minister of Hyderabad, may have built a private paradise of Greek sculptures, Chinese porcelain and Italian paintings, but he had forfeited the noble traditions of the land by making the nizam of Hyderabad side with the British in 1857. His beauty carried a stain in tandem with his guilt ridden heart. Like Rajasthani and Maratha princes[1], he had freedom within his reach, and yet he threw it away. This cost him dearly, for Indo-Persians like Salar Jung ultimately failed the test of the secular Muslim legacy. Muslim identity in India was identified exclusively with the Ganga-Yamuni tahzeeb, Walliulahites invoking Islam as a common nationalist-political weapon of Indian people. Leading Muslims who betrayed '57 thus betrayed their own history.

Lucknow's post-1857 siege was led not only by firang generals in queen caps and striped trousers, but men wearing the Turkish cap and loose, colourless robes. In place of the imported Enfield rifle and howitzers, a sharp sniper fire of ostracism and perfidy was put to use. Behind the barricades of a foreign power, upstart Indians, Hindus and Muslims emerged to voice their discomfort with the sensual, aristocratic and composite elements of their own culture.

They had not forgotten that this culture had produced 1857 which had jolted the indigenous status quo. Avadh, the land where privilege was protected by divine sanction, upset the apple cart. Royal houses of Delhi and Lucknow, the guardians of faith and religion, raised dehatis to power. The status quoists were bewildered by the turn of events. In their heart, they felt sympathy for Bahadur Shah Zafar or Wajid Ali Shah, but they found the peasant-sepoy upsurge nerve rattling and a threat to property and privilege. This dilemma produced the contradictory voice of Lucknowi courtiers like Agha Hajjo Sharaf, the author of *Afsan-e-Lucknow*[2].

The men who expressed this fear belonged to an intelligentsia drawn from conservative Indo-Persian and Brahminical currents. Amongst the former, a major trend did not identify itself with the secular achievements of the Mughal house. They perceived it, at best as the upholder of a conservative social order and a pan-territorial Islamic religion. To them, *Ain-i-Akbari's* express injunction that the *acclaiming of reason and the rejection of tradition is so blatantly clear as to stand in no need of argument*[3], was dismaying. No less disconcerting was Walliullahism or the progressive measures of their 'orthodox hero', Aurangzeb, who expressly stated on more than one occasion that religion has got nothing to do with the affairs of the state.

Status quoist Hindus also did not appreciate Akbar and Asaf-ud-Daula creating a Brahmin aristocracy or re-galvanising Hindu secular learning. Remote from the world of Uddalaka Aruni, Bhaskargupta, Aryabhatta, Bhaskara, and Kanada, they had no empathy with an ancient India which discovered the zero and formulated the 'pell equation', algebra, trignometry, 'Gregory series', differential calculus, besides the earliest atomic theory. An identification with the long history of democracy, rule of law, institution building and the potential of Ayurveda and Unani to still outsmart Western medicine was positively ruled out. For these well-educated Hindus and Muslims, the 'thought' that medieval Hindustan had beaten Europe in cannon, gun barrel cleaner and military rocket invention, was not alien. But they knew that the public knowledge of Fazlullah Shirazi's 'Yarghu', which cleaned sixteen gun barrels at one time, Sawai Jai Singh's Jaivani cannon and Hyder Ali's rockets was dangerous. These technological breakthroughs were now part of the European body of military practice and scientific thought. The idea of their Hindustani origin was too subversive.

For the native status quoist, the Mughal and nawabi period was good so long as it did not go far in composite culture to include the synthesis of women and lower classes. But Mughals and Lucknowi rulers violated this ideological-political contract with impunity. It was fine so long as Asaf-ud-daula played Holi with Hindu courtiers and Wajid Ali Shah performed Rasleela in Qaiserbagh. But Jan-e-Alam encouraging the setting up of the 'takhat' and the parda and encouraging women to act on stage? Bahadur Shah Zafar organising mushiaras and encouraging the subtle use of rekhti? This was disaster. The kings were actually bringing the arts to the masses, opening the hallowed doors and minds of the princely confines to the commoners.

This sacrilege was committed in great abundance in 1857. The uprising began in the name of religion but religious zealots, opposing the West on a superstitious, supernatural and religious level, held aloof. On the contrary, men and women who spoke in the name of reason and raised the banner of insaniyat and sensuality, came to the forefront with sacrifices. After '57 people holding a traditional view of the sciences and arts became the greatest supporters of Western sciences, while enlightened men linked to Delhi and Lucknow were projected in outmoded colours. For Urdu shairs, Bahadur Shah Zafar remained a poet of lament. The younger generation was not told that the last king of Delhi, on being showed the severed heads of his sons, did not shed a tear for 'kings do not cry'. And patriotic valour, not tragic despair, made him exclaim even in the hour of defeat:

Ghazion men boo kahegi jab talak imaan ki
Takhte London tak chalegi tegh Hindustan ki

In debates preceding 1857, two figures represented two poles. One was a descendant of Khwaja Fariduddin who entered British service as a well known loyalist holding obscurantist views. He wrote a book on the traditional monuments of Delhi and a treatise which opposed the scientific view that the earth moved around the sun. He was Syed Ahmad Khan, an uncovenanted Indian officer of the British administration in North West Frontier Provinces.

Another man, a poet and a writer, held different views. A bigger figure than Syed Ahmad, he reprimanded the officer for basking in old theories when the tide had turned and it was more relevant to know how ships were run on steam power in Calcutta. This man was not enamoured by the British. He belonged to Delhi, a den of anti-British feelings, and yet he looked beyond the immediate horizon to appreciate the modernity of Western civilisation. His name: Mirza Ghalib.

When 1857 broke out against the 'West', the former opposed the struggle as the Sadr Amin of Bijnore in Rohilkhand. The latter stood by Bahadur Shah Zafar and then recorded the horror of British plunder and raids on Delhi. Soon after the revolt was suppressed, Syed Ahmad published a book which charged 1857 of being a movement of the governed — what had the Muslim aristocracy got to do with it? Another charge indirectly blamed the British for merging two *antagonistic races*, Hindus and Muslims, in one regiment[4]! Bahadur Shah Zafar was proclaimed a heretic, in whose mosque Muslim devouts did not offer prayers[5]. He could not have led a jehad, whose cry was raised by 'vagabonds' and ill-conditioned men.

Syed Ahmad was criticising 1857 in the name of reason and progress which stood with the British. And yet he invoked Zafar's hereticism, a progressive quality as per Western modernism, as a negative, irreligious, condemnable trait. From today's point of view, he ended up affirming his secular, modern character; the opposite of what he intended! In the same vein, Syed Ahmad gave '57 the unintended 'dignity' of a European revolt — his description of 'vagabond' revolutionaries are strikingly close to twentieth century accounts of modern revolutions[6].

In his anti-'57 tirades, Syed Ahmad was also informed by an anti-Pathan strand, peculiar to a certain section of high caste Muslims. Their view of history was arraigned against the eighteenth century rise of Pathans and Marathas, the prime movers behind the decline of the old Mughal nobility. Rohilkhand, where Syed Khan was posted in '57, was the hotbed of a Pathan, urban renaissance. This was also the place from where the British were routed out completely during the revolution.

In the aftermath, Syed Ahmad began showing the 'new light' to Muslims. They were told that their civilisation had fallen far behind a glorious past, that Islam needed to be modernised by complete identification with British civilisational values.

Pre-'57 progressivists too approved of Western ideologies. But their appreciation was a critical one based on selective assimilation of, not identification with, Western knowledge and fashion. They knew that the earth's movement around the sun was discovered by Islamic science much before Galileo. While the Bible taught the geocentric view, the Koran spread the original new light through the concept of a heliocentric universe.

These men were the last to carry, anywhere in Asia, the memory of Arabs laying the foundation for the scientific spirit of European renaissance. French and English 'barbarians' learned the way of romance, chivalry and bathing from Islamic crusaders. Long before Descrates, Nazzam and Ghazali enunciated the principle of doubt as the fountainhead of knowledge. The Europeans' pursuit for a rationalist methodology, for 'reaching truth through facts' ended with the discovery of Arabic traditions of experimental enquiry, detailed observation, and positive, factual knowledge. Bedil's poeticisation of pre-Darwin evolutionism harked back to Ibn Maskawaih's explorations of evolution as a process from plant life to civilised man. Mathematics owed the concept of space as an infinite continuum to sufi mystics like Iraqi. Geometry was reinvented by the reveller poet Omar Khayyam.

Asian scientists and artists were not bitter, sad, humourless, morbid creatures in the mould of their Western counterparts. They loved the power of the grapes as much as the energy of the compass. Their world view was based on a negation of classical Greek thought and culture which sought proportion, order and a singular perspective in the universe. It posited infinity, concrete patterns and the epic perspective in contrast. Greek theoreticism, speculativism, absolutism, and the consequent tendency to mystify processes when faced with a mental cul-de-sac, always hung hard on Western thought. Its spectre haunted, like a doomsday talisman, even the 'breakthroughs' of occidental dialectics and relativism. Asia, as led by Islamic Arabia and presupposed by ancient India, thrived on practical, empirical reasoning, visionary perception, the here and now and relativity of all phenomena. Instead of just 'being' in Space, it thought about 'becoming' in Time. Notably, Lucknowi scientists had already rediscovered the Asian origin of many European innovations, 'the truth', by the eve of '57.

In the 'new light' that now emerged, people like Ghalib or the surviving personalities of Lucknow had no role to play. The Lucknow of Wajid Ali Shah, also, could not be accepted as a reality.

She had to be condemned or concerted into an 'afsana' — a fairy tale of an old era. Lucknow started becoming the last city of an old culture, not the emerging beacon of a new one, as she was seen before '57. The light which she had shown then was considered embarrassing in an era where the primary emphasis was on the 'modernisation' of Islam.

In her day, Lucknow had no need for modernising, purifying or reforming Islam. She had emotionalised belief, showing the fundamental tenets of religion as perfectly capable of growth and transcendence by living practice. For her, modernity was not about buying Western goods or showing off oneself as a 'good', 'modest' Victorianised woman. It meant, first and foremost, the materialisation of emotion and secularisation of the sacred where the 'this worldly' was proclaimed in public as a hardboiled, mass issue. There was no secularism to beat the invocation of love, wine and Wajid Ali Shah's tongue 'n' cheek sexuality on the 'chauraha' of a public place in a qawwali, ghazal or marsiya with the masses dancing in ecstasy. The ghazal, marsiya and qawwali became suspect in the 'new light'. Their multilayered and intricate, 'Bara Imambara-Kalidasa type', 'tahdar'-'pechdar', sensual quality, was immoral to dour, colourless, self-obsessed, and yet secretly voyeuristic, eyes of the firang.

Syed Ahmad Khan, soon to be called Sir Syed, was not a pro-British reformer without a plan. He had a team of litterateurs who set about re-fashioning the taste of their times. The three principles figures in this were Shibli, Hali and Ismail, a fourth dissenting dimension added by the pen and mind of Muhammad Hussein Azad, the son of Maulana Baqar. They, like Sir Syed, were talented men with great ideas — only their objective and sense of history was confusing. They wanted to modernise but on the basis of purifying the past of subversive content. They looked down upon not only the poetry of Nasikh and Atish but also Hafiz and Rumi, the Iranian Sufis and the medieval masters of ghazal. What sort of a modernity was this which opposed sensuality and subversion? They disapproved of Sufis, eclectic Hindu practices which had seeped into Islam and other 'evils'. At one time, Sir Syed used to call himself a puritan Muslim. But what kind of a traditionalism was this which looked down upon religious humanism and refused to pick up the sword in 1857?

These questions were put forward in Lucknow and answered in Allahabad. A hat-sporting civil magistrate painted first, a chilling image of post-'57 north India when mention of the 'ghadar' was still taboo:

Jo guzro ge udhar se mera ujda gaanv dekho ge
Shikasta ek masjid hai bagal men gora barik hai

(If you should pass that way you'll see my devastated village:
A Tommies barracks standing by a defeated mosque)

He then wrote on Sir Syed:

What do you mean? 'Progress,' 'association'-
Listen to me. I'll tell you how it is done.
He owns the buffalo who wields the cudgel
(*Jiski lathi uski bhains*).
Ti-tum ti-tum ti-tum ti-tum ti-tum

Akbar Allahabadi minced no words in saying that this 'new light' was a colonial weapon of power. Its modernity had English fashion but little by way of new ideas. Its tradition too comprised prayer but no faith.

He was supported ably in Lucknow; there the proponents and opponents of 'new light' turned the whole movement on its head. The supporters interpreted its meaning literally; Ratan Nath Sarshar was a Kashmiri Brahmin and belonged to its Persian speaking mainstream. Part of the nawabi bureaucracy, this mainstream had lost considerably in 1857. The aftermath left them with another titanic struggle — whether or not to retain the 'Muslim' influence. Led by Brahmins, Khattris and Kayasthas of west 'United Provinces', the British administrative unit of captured Indo-Gangetic areas formed in 1836 and sustained in the 1860s with the exclusion of the special commissionary of Avadh, this movement was similar to Sir Syed's. But there was no 'new light' here. Major strains pulled backwards to the Vedas or 'Sanatana Dharma' in the name of Arya Samaj and Dharma Sabhas.

The Kayasthas and Khattris were closer to the Vedic reformism of the Arya Samaj which began to make its presence felt in Lucknow from the late nineteenth century. The Aggarwals and Banias inched towards Vaishnava reform, but Kanyakubja and Saryuparin Brahmin affiliation with Sanatana Dharma posed a problem. Lucknow had a rich, macho Brahmin culture with a different vision of the sanatan (eternal). For sons, the religion of their fathers was Sanatana Dharma and this religion shared a common value system with Muslims and Rajputs.

Products of western UP and Punjab, the new, post-'57 sanatanis were blessed in the east by Madan Mohan Malviya, a Malavi, outsider Brahmin now residing in Allahabad. Madan Mohan Malviya was financed in Allahabad by the same trading-banker family which had helped the British in the crucial battle of the fort. This family now owned nearly half of Allahabad city held firmly by a league of pro-British big traders and landlords. These very forces had betrayed the revolution almost everywhere with the exception of Avadh. Allahabad thus represented the post-'57, 'Bania-Zamindar-Babu-Pandit-Mulla' status quo, which later supported the Congress in the district, in the most perfect form.

Sanatana Dharma did not propound militant ideologies and encouraged bania, rather than aristocratic, values. In the beginning Kannaujias, found it amusing and a threat to their position. The puritanising movement tried reshaping Avadhi Brahmins along anti-meat eating, anti-Muslim lines. When this did not work, non-vegetarianism was given an anti-Muslim colour! The meat eating Ganjmuradabadi Misras were depicted as warriors who devoured goat flesh in the past for protecting Hindu religion against Pathans! This too did not work beyond a point. Even in the early twentieth century, Ganjmuradabadis were introduced, with respect, fear and trepidation, as those close to the 'bade jis' or Muslims.

Aggarwals and native Vaishyas of Lucknow too found Vaishnava reform problematic. It attacked the composite life familiar to them and proposed an 'alien' Hindu identity. In effect, it 'Victorianised' the bania aristocracy. Bhartendu Harishchandra, a Vaishnavite reformist and the father of Hindi literature in Benaras, got little support from Lucknow when he ridiculed and parodied the Indar Sabha as a 'Bandar Sabha' (assembly of monkeys).

Bhartendu's real personality was much more vibrant but he soon became the 'renaissance' father figure of the social force that gained ascendency in the late nineteenth and early twentieth century north India — the Hindu-colonial middle class. This section now filled government posts and private offices following the complete elimination of the revolutionary middle classes of 1857.

Bhartendu might have personally enjoyed the earthy, elitist and stylistic performances of the 'low' and 'high', 1857 cultural strand. His political responsibility, on the other hand, rested in the creation of a conservative, Hindu middle class morality. The most potent symbol of this endeavour was theatre; just as the pre-'57 period spoke in the language of the theatre of Wajid Ali Shah and Amanat, post-'57 attitudes would be informed by the theatre of Bhartendu Harishchandra: a theatre distancing itself from the aristocratic, peasant and middle class culture of yore.

Hindu reformism was partly a by-product of the anti-'57 mood in post-'57 forces. It produced both the genteel Hindu liberalism of Benaras traders and the conservative Hindu backlash of the Hindu Maha Sabha. But there was something grotesque about the reformist attempt to rediscover Hindi along lines which had nothing to do with the origin of the language. Hindi was Amir Khusro's discovery and got invoked in 1857 as a form of Urdu with a script close to Kaithi, the language of the scribes. Urdu, Hindi and Kaithi formed a common linguistic Hindustani league, hung on the walls of north Indian towns in the form of revolutionary posters.

Around the time when the Hindi-Urdu controversy was just gathering steam, Ratan Nath Sarshar wrote the 'new light' Lucknowi manifesto — *Fasaine Azad*. A work of classic Urdu prose, it had little in common with the characters of Deputy Nazir Ahmad, the ardent intellectual supporter of Sir Syed. Harking back to the old dastan tradition of Lucknow, its tale recalled the late medieval, post-chivalrous, early bourgeois mood of Arabia and Europe. In Lucknow was created a story of an enterprising Don Quixote represented by Azad, a doyen of the new light. His servant Khoji stalked him constantly as a superstitious, irredeemable Sancho Panza. Even while talking about modern values and ridiculing traditionalist Muslims, Azad is constantly the gliding hero of the dastan. Unlike Don Quixote, he is not a deluded medieval knight but an individual with a quest.

When other men like Nazir Ahmad were displaying examples of good, subservient behaviour before the Muslims, Lucknow produced a work where realism and romance blended to show the contradictions of the age. *Fasaine Azad* reflected those aspirations of modernity which were never realised by the moral didacticism of the official new light. The canonical criticism of Muhammad Hussein Azad and Hali also spoke a lot about producing something beyond the ghazal, with Hali writing the mussaddas to explore fresh ideas in a new, form. But Lucknow produced Braj Narain Chakbast who blended the nazm with the masnavi and the marsiya to create an original Ramayana in Urdu.

This grand project was never completed. It remained buried in the volume of patriotic and social poetry which this Kashmiri Brahmin churned out in the early twentieth century. But it was perhaps the last Lucknowi document which continued the trend of reciting Hazrat Ali's dohas in Avadhi and Krishna ras in Urdu. It also presented a radical, modern Ram a 'man' expressing fulsome feelings in Urdu, the ultimate material language Replying to a question posed by his mother, he starts speaking about his personal emotions. This was not what a 'Maryada Purshotam' did on such occasions. His mother, Kaushalya, the epitome of patience, the ideal Indian woman, breaks down to express that if she spoke out, the whole social order might break down.

In its high and lows, and the passionately charged monologues which swing from pathos to anger, complain to rancour, intensity to resignation, this scene from Ramayana has only one post-Tulsidas parallel: the Rama Katha written by Ahmad Baksh Thanesri of Haryana. Chakbast brought a Shakespearean passion to play when he made Ram speak, Hamlet like just before his fourteen year exile:

Rukhsat hua voh baap se lekar khuda ka naam — Rahe
vafa ki manzil avval hui tamaam
Manzoor jo tha maa ki ziyarat ka intzam — Daman se
ashk poch ke dil se kaya kalam

        Izhare bekasi se sitam hoga aur bhi
        Dekha hame udaas to gam hoga aur bhi

He bid farewell to his father taking the name of God —
the path of loyalty achieved its destination with a top mark
Agreeing to preparations for the final meeting with his mother —
he wiped his tears and spoke in his heart

        Expressions of anguish will only increase the pain
        Seeing me sad she will feel more bad

Ram's meeting with his mother Kaushalya is described in passionate detail. The mother is besides herself, in intense belovedness—

        Jumbish hui labon ko bhari ek sard aah,
        Li gosha hai chashm se ashkon ne rukh ki raah

(lips trembled, she took a cold breath, from inside the eyes tears marked the direction of their path)—

and refuses to give permission, throwing convention to the winds. She goes on to say:

        Kis tarah ban men ankhon ke taren ko bejh doon
        Jogi bana ke raj dulare ko bhej doon

(How do I send away into the forest the star of my eyes
Send away my darling prince as a mendicant?)

How is the blood of this world turning white
that the hope of wealth and money is making people blind

What will be the result no one knows this secret
if a human being thinks the body will shake like a thin stick

> Has this life been written for them?
> For which day are they extending their net?

If I had taken birth in the house of a poor mendicant — my
beloved would not have faced this conspiracy against him

This splendour which ought to have been my servant would
not have bit me like a serpent —
you were my son less than which kingdom for me

I'll be happy if someone burns down this throne and
crown
Without you I'll consign this kingdom to the flames

Ram then replies after a series of exchanges:

The world has seen revolutions much bigger than this
the lives of innocents were destroyed much due to which
Repeated destinations of sorrow roasted the heart like a
kebab some lost their age some lost their youth

Nothing could be done as fates were disturbed
Such a lightning fell that well-to-do homes were
destroyed

Chakbast depicted Ram as the troubled soul of the contemporary age. In this period, Iqbal had also begun calling Lord Ram, the
Imam-e-Hind of India. But Chakbast's Ram was no ideal Imam; he
was a sensitive mirror of the contradictions tearing apart the elite
society of north India. When literature veered more and more
towards a morality in which religion was smuggled in the garb of
modernity, Chakbast gave a humanistic, portrait of a godly figure.

Yet, Chakbast was no woolly-eyed humanist. His poetic stance
oozed with the solidly hard, penetrating, smug and brilliantly stolid
attitude of Indo-Persian orthodoxy. Uncomfortable with facile romanticism, this highly professional trend of the bureaucrat or the
lawyer crushed soft poetic sentiments. The metaphor of the night-

ingale 'en-captured' by the muse, or something equally delicate, was common in love stories and tragedies. Someone tried to bring the same attitude to the impersonal, 'real world' environs of the lower law courts. Chakbast's smugly, stately reply took the wind out of romantic pretensions, trying to tie the wings of the 'metal world nightingale' by veins of flower:

Khafifa adalat men ullu ke patthe
Rag-e-gul se bulbul ke par bandhte hain

Moral of the story: The world, or beauty, is not won over by delicacy. Revolution is not a dinner party.

Difficult to find the poeticisation of this superiorly terse, contemptuously humorous, 'aliberal', didactic airfound only amongst orthodox revolutionaries or orthodox conservatives — in world poetry.

When the ghazal was being thrown out of favour elsewhere in the country, Lucknow gave the sad, ironical muse — reflecting upon sorrow but asserting hope in pessimism. New school Lucknowi poets, Aziz Lucknowi, Sakib and Safi, wrote without inhibitions even in depression:

Jalwa dikhlaye jo woh khud apni aarayi ka, Noor jal jaye
abhi chashm tamashai ka
Rang har phool men hai husn khud aarayi ka, Chamne
daher hai mahzar teri yaktai ka

(If she shows off the sheen of her dressed up demeanour, it will burn the light of the roving eye
There is colour in every flower, beauty of the very
demeanour,
the eternal garden is present as the proof of your
unparalleledness)

— Aziz

Aziz and Sakib were also known for their satirical, strident tone, perfected by Yas Yagana Changezi. Though originally not belonging to Lucknow, he received both and fame notoriety in the city.

Attacking the soft tone of his contemporaries, his outspokenness led to a show of public humiliation. The growing intolerance of the times was utilised by conservatives forces and power groups to make artists toe their line. Men like Changezi were caught in the web of changing circumstances where the independent shiar, who doubted, questioned and believed, was losing his autonomy:

Adab ne dil ke takaze uthaye hain kya kya
Hawas ne shauq ke pahloo dabae hain kya kya

(How many demands of the heart the tradition of
learning has had to bear with
How many aspects of fondness have been suppressed by
lust)

Khuda hi jane yagana main kaun hun kya hoon
Khud apni zaat pe shaq dil men aye hain kya kya

(Only God knows yagana who am I what am I
What all suspicions have crept in my heart about my
own caste)

Changezi's was ignored by affirmative writers like Abdul Halim Sharar who wrote about past glories of Muslims in Arabia and Spain and tried opening a reformist front against customs such as the purdah. But Sharar was hampered by his post-'57 education which made him look outside for political and social inspiration. He also regarded the composite Lucknowi flowering of the eighteenth and nineteenth century as carrying only a limited, aesthetic relevance. This was a running theme with most Urdu writers, including Chakbast. Indeed, between the Lucknow of Mir Anis and Chakbast much had changed. The upwardly pointed, curled moustache — the original Indian lesson, taught valiantly to the world, in manliness — had drooped at the sides. The warrior-intellectual had turned into an intellectual-warrior.

Munshi Newal Kishore's press, which emerged as an institution in post-Mutiny Lucknow, was also part of the British restructuring of Lucknowi culture. But when everything was in the danger of being subsumed by the British new light, it kept alive Urdu and Brahminical traditions by printing old manuscripts and commissioning new versions of plays, poems and history. However, the Munshi himself reflected on how much things had changed — he was an outsider with few connections to pre-'57 Lucknowi press magnates such as Mustafa Khan, Haji Harmain, Ali Baksh Khan and Hunarmand Sheikh Nisar Ali. Pre-'57 Lucknow had a thriving industry of private printing presses[7] where new typesets and constant technological innovation spruced up the play of the black ink. Heavily constrained by the British presence, the Newal Kishore press could never cross the boundary from reproduction to originality.

But two prominent rivals did view for that spot. Sajjad Hussein's *Avadh Punch*, established satire as a reporting genre in India. And an engineer cropped up from nowhere to revive secular Lucknow in prose. *Avadh Punch* carried irreverence on its sleeve; critical of neo-rich pretensions, it ensnared Newal Kishore and his *Avadh Akhbar* in its net of pawky humour. Putting together a team of writers — Ratan Nath Sarshar, Pandit Tribhuvan Nath Hijra, Munshi Jwala Prasad Bark, Akbar Allahabadi, Munshi Ahmad Ali Shauq, Munshi Ahmad Ali Kasmandvi, Mirza Macchu Beg, Nawab Saiyyad Mohammed Azad — the editors encouraged the style of 'writing in jokes. Invoking unconsciously the traditions of Rijal, Danda and Phabti, *Avadh Punch* teased the 'white' and 'brown' sahibs with devastatingly caustic relish:

> *Congratulations to those black natives who are oppressed*
> *because only the shelter of skies exists for them. Congratula-*
> *tions to those who are desperate for the Civil Services*
> *because the government will no doubt give them lip service.*
> *Congratulations to those who are thirsty for the blood of*
> *their own community because they will be praised by the*
> *guardians of official religion. Congratulations to those who*
> *have hearts of stone because some sycophant newspapers will*
> *call them hearts of mercy.*

The paper further developed the realist-burlesque traditions of

Mazahiya journalism which actually began with Malik Hakim Ahmad, Reza Lucknowi and Abdul Jalil Nomani of Rampur. Soon the *Sarpanch* and the *Indian Punch* were also established and other cities too started throwing off their 'punches' — *Benaras Punch* and *Baba Adam Punch* came up in 1881, *Meerut Punch* and *Jariful Hind* appeared in 1886 to be followed by *Katra Punch* (Allahabad), *Kannauj Punch*, *Kashmir Punch* and *Gorakhpur Punch* in successive years.

Avadh Punch's counter foil, Mirza Hadi Ruswa 'engineer's' claim to fame as the author of *Umrao Jaan Ada* found place below his other great accomplishments. He drew little inspiration from the west and showed indifference to developments going on in Delhi and Aligarh. His genius lay in assimilating lessons of modern research in physics and learning the art of riding a bicycle, even if it meant breaking bones in zeal, with as much gusto as solving an algebraic equation. His open ended aestheticism was informed by a non-judgmental jest for life. It noted the development of events, the struggle of emotions, the passage of good into bad and the making and destruction of lives. Mirza Ruswa recalled much of the past — the tradition of Mir Londoni, the Lucknowi citizenry of Amanat, even the 1857 personality of Engineer Muhammad Ali Khan. Part of a lost middle class tradition, his humanism and democracy existed within the four walls and the inner courtyard of the 'house', encouraged and nurtured by the wisdom of women.

There is a strange peace attached to Ruswa's prose. It is as if a fresh sensibility, clear but not simple, still alive after so many travails, is seeking something — very much like the flow of the Gomti in the last quarter of the nineteenth century. This sensibility combines decades and episodes dipped in pain and pleasure. And yet it is almost casual about what happened, without a hint of stoicism or melancholy. Umrao Jaan, the central character in *Umrao Jaan Ada* the novel, feels a stab of regretless pain:

Kisko sunaye hale dilezar ae'ada
Awargi men hamne zamane ki sair ki

(To whom shall I tell the story of heartburn O' Ada
I travelled the world in drift and wanderlust)

And removed from the realism of Balzac or Flaubert, Ruswa's 'dastaan' summons the involuted charms of Goethe's travel stories. There is no objective landscape, but an inner, sensual journey stretched out through known and unknown signs and checkposts, recording information, mood and humour. *Umrao Jaan Ada* recreated scintillatingly, the symbol of Lucknow in harf — the image of a candle or 'chirag', slowly extinguishing itself behind exaltations, incitations, complaints and exhortations, with words completing the journey of the mind content at temporary rests but restless to reach the final destination.

13

The Fragmented Sunshine

On 20 August 1916, the Charbagh railway station was the scene of frenzied activity. A train carrying a famous national leader had just arrived. He belonged to the garam dal of the Congress, formed in 1885 to impress upon the Britishers the need for moderate reform, and was in the city to attend its national conference. Allan Octavian Hume, the brain behind the original Congress, was the 'liberal' ex-British officer who suppressed 1857 in Etawah. He designed the forum as a safety valve to let off the immediate post '57 steam engulfing various parts of the country in the form of peasant revolts, tribal uprisings and urban restlessness. The Congress changed course midway to go beyond British expectations. But the anti-'57 birthmark never paled.

In a span of thirty years, the Congress had grown from a platform of petitioners to a movement demanding autonomy or self-rule from the British Raj. It had tested the power of the British police while protesting against the division of Bengal. The inevitable split, into moderates and extremists, had come on the issue of method, rhetoric and statement of goals.

In the 1910s, it faced a new acid test. Till now an agitational party centred in the coastal towns of Bombay and Calcutta, it was looking for a transition to a Hindi-Urdu heartland based all-India mass movement. This phase was accompanied by the rise of a new leader who had gained fame as a political agitator in South Africa.

Opportunity came knocking at Mohandas Karamchand Gandhi's door. By the 1910s, the long experiment with constitutionalism was over

The attempt at repeating 1857 during the First World War had also failed. At first, the Ghadar party, formed by lower middle and working class expatriate Indians, succeeded in formulating a strategy of armed revolution. Their work followed the Turkey backed Reshmi Roomal movement of young Indian Muslims. This tahreek added a sensational chapter to the history of Asiatic revolutionism. It brought politics close to the pulsating Avadhi world of Zafar Umar — the father of the then evolving Indo-Persian detective genre. A police officer by profession, Zafar, who belonged to Unnao, filled the dark, lonely, existential world of the 'pioneer' French detective with the full bloodied, sansanikheism of the Persian-Urdu dastaan. He proved, in this 'pop' genre, the virtue of sensationalism existing 'as a way of art' in India.

The Ghadr party filled in the missing link of 1857 — most of its activists were Hindu, Muslim and Sikh Punjabis who sacrificed everything for the 'line of 1857.' The army revolted at certain places but the movement was nipped in the bud by effective British counter intelligence. Ghadar leaders were also unable to conduct the necessary propaganda war in the Hindi-Urdu belt.

With the defeat of anglicised elitism and petty bourgeoisie Indo-Persian revolutionism, a new situation arose. The deck was cleared for India's destiny to oscillate between Gandhi's ex-bania, Anglo-Orientalist,* Hindusim and Pandit Jawaharlal Nehru's 'ex-Indo-

---

* The premise here is that Gandhi's basic impulse, his independent understanding of India, was drawn from Western schools of the late nineteenth century, attempting to redefine India into an image of the 'good Orient'. This reformulation was different from the one peddled by the British and followed by the post '57 autochthonous Sanatana Dharma, the latter day Hindutva, whose chief, independent, exponent was Madan Mohan Malviya.

Orientalism painted India as a rambling, anarchic, spiritual civilisation, a place where strength presented itself as weakness, with little or no inclination towards power, order or institution building. It thus revolted fundamentally against India's image as represented by the Mauryas, Guptas, Mughals, Sufism, militant Bhaktism, and 1857, which remained conspicuous shockingly enough, from the discourse of the Managema, a supposed leader of a third world nationalist movement.

Edward Said has mentioned India's re-fashioning as the 'good Orient', in contrast to the near east and the Middle east, the Confucian and the Islamic lands, which resisted the stereotype of non-ambitious Asia, in his works. While comparing Malviya and Gandhi, the British historian, C.A. Bayly, wrote in the 1970s: 'Much of Malviya's character is out of range of European experience. This was less true of Gandhi who, consciously or unconsciously, had an eye to a place in the Western pantheon. Gandhi's spirituality masked a character more deeply impregnated with western values.'[1]

Persian', bania-babu anglicism. The making of modern India was thus influenced from the very beginning by Western-liberal-reactionary ideological influences. These were seen to be posted against Indo-Persianism at one level and Western radical-republicanism, of French origin, at the other.

On reaching his home turf, Gandhi was immediately faced with the task of bringing the agenda of a 'national' movement close to the social fabric of British India. This fabric was now split 'officially', as part of the British census carried out in the late nineteenth century, into warring castes and communities. A further schism in the army under-wrote the decisive proof of British communalism and policy of sectarian division. In a convention unseen and unheard of before, the Indian armed forces were organised along caste and ethnic lines. Avadhians and Biharis, the 'original martial people', were ignored and a racial myth constructed about their non-martial character! To ward off the spectre of 1857, the British made a mockery of Indians and their political and social milieu. They ensured that never again would the one armed Indian institution rally around a single cause.

The British also dealt a mortal blow to Avadhian-Hindustani strength by disarming the population. A direct result of 1857, the move to replace the sword with the pen, the jewel with the chain, terminated men's style, fashion and politics in the subcontinent. Carrying arms ensured the subconscious release of the individual, the very formation of a valorous and thereby free personality and nation. Always uncomfortable with true grit, the British shopkeeper mentality short circuited Indian literature and cinema. Heroism was not allowed to play in the warrior-Pindari, 1857, Wyatt Earp, Doc Holliday, Billy the Kid and Akira Kurusawa's Samurai league.

It was also pre-determined that an Abraham Lincoln will not emerge on the dusky side of the world to sculpt 'liberty'. The Indian lawyer politicians of the late nineteenth, early twentieth century were more 'banias' than courageous warriors, uncomfortable with both 'people' and liberty.

Post-'57 native tradition presented a dilemma unseen anywhere else. The unquestioning obedience of sons to parents, wife to husband, sister to brother was demanded by a priori right. This in itself was a violation of Indian-Maurya-Gupta-Mughal 1857 traditional family values which had once asked the sister to protect the brother. But even while asserting an abstract, conservative view of tradition, fathers did not teach their sons to become men, to achieve success by mettle, to respect women, stand up for justice and to live and die with honour. Fathers themselves lost their individuality and potency as babus under colonialism. They turned their sons into babus who went to work, like the Pindari had said, without a straight spine.

For women the catastrophe was total. Mothers turned up from nowhere to abuse Indian culture and teach daughters the virtue of soft compliance to authority. The British discontinued the great north Indian-Lucknowi tradition of military training for women. In one move they made them powerless. Indian heroines were barred entry in the Hazrat Mahal, Lakshmi Bai, Azeezun Bai, 'Queen Christina' league. Devalorisation was combined with desexualisation. The path was clear for the emergence of the weak, cloy, submissive, undignified, now-faithful, now manipulative, 'ideal', Victorian-Indian woman.

Indian family culture thrived on the very un-Lucknowi, 'essential weakness and decadence of being'. Combining orthodoxy with a backward but egotistical philistinism, this tendency impaired the militant tone of the freedom movement. Suppressed manliness then found an outlet in typically un-noble, dangerously weak, fascist postures which became, subconsciously, a part of Indian social life. This murder of cultural representation, social ambition and the spirit of a nation was unprecedented in the history of world culture. How and why did post '57 Indian leadership agree to disarmament[2] will have to be answered one day by those who follow the way set by them in the late quarter of the twentieth century.

The area which once stoutly resisted colonial redefinition and social engineering, now the conjoined provinces of 'Agra and Oudh' after the separate chief commissionership of Avadh ended in the 1870s, succumbed to a communal holocaust in the 1890s. The decade saw internecine religious conflicts which brought to the fore the phenomena of mass level communalism in north India. But even though Avadh had turned into an economic backwater, the fire of tehzeeb ensured a very slow intrusion of the communal menace. Conflicts of the 1890s found a fertile ground in the more strongly British influenced area of eastern United Provinces.

The Congress was still a small force in Avadh in the first quarter of the twentieth century but much worse was the position of the Muslim League. Set up in 1906, the League was struggling to evolve as a forum of petition for Muslim bigwigs and aristocrats seeking separate electorates. The League's conference too was scheduled on the same day in Lucknow when Bal Gangadhar Tilak stopped at Charbagh.

The League and the Congress had chosen the same venue to give shape to a unity of Hindu and Muslim forces. Both formations were also getting weary with the politics of petition — Tilak had actually come to effect a patch up between the tough and the soft parties. Tilak's entourage was blocked as a number of students belonging to Avadh and Rohilkhand. They wanted the national leader to lead a procession. The police became nervous — the First World War had started, an anti-war mood prevailed amongst the people and the League and the Congress had yet to commit themselves to the war cause. The local leaders of the Congress too were upset — a procession was not part of their schedule and they had a car waiting outside for Tilak's transportation.

But the boys were adamant. Led by vocal leaders, including Ram Prasad Bismil, they made Tilak sit in the car and pulled it towards the conference site. The procession turned towards the city while touring the main areas, alarming the local police further by deafening slogans. It was cheered on its way from within the Qaiserbagh by participants in the League conference who were busy initiating a monumental change.

The presidentship of the League was passing onto Amir Hasan's son, Raja Muhammad Ali Muhammad of Mahmudabad. The two trends of post '57 talukedari Avadh had diverged to the point of Farzand Ali's nephew, Raja Tassaduq Rasul Khan, taking up a permanent anti-Mahmudabad position. In Ali Muhammad, the 'word' had long replaced the 'sword', just as the achkan and the shervani had supplanted the long khillat between two generations. Lucknow had already evolved the shaluka into the chapkan — a native coat with a round collar, but with slits on the side forming a ghera from the waist and falling just above the knees. Despite being a a full coat, it bore no resemblance to any

Western design. Buttons were draped with embroidered cloth and the sheen of the collar blended the splendour of nawabi days with the elegance of modern taste.

The dominant talukedars tried, for a while, to revive the old traditions of the city. Around the first half of the twentieth century, the Chowk again became abaad. The old kothas were reinhabited by courtesans coming from the rural areas of Avadh and Benaras. With faint memories of the Lucknow of Haider Jaan, Umrao Jaan, they recreated the courtesies taught to sons of wealthy families in the salons. But they occupied an isolated respectability and specialised mainly in thumri and the mujra, a modified, popular form of the Kathak. Classical dance still retained that special, Wajid Ali Shahi element now not in any court or open stage but a small, decrepit room in Aminabad on Jhau Lal's bridge.

In the unusually 'black' atmosphere of a whitewashed interior, two brothers sat for hours re-fashioning Kathak. In the dead of the night, when the watchman's voice and the darogah's whistle silenced the locality into slumber, a flicker of flame would arise in a deorhi. Then a male ankle with painted fingernails would slowly put on ghungroos. A 'thaap' of 'addha tala' on the tabla and then the words:

> *Kahe ko mere ghar aaye ho*
> *Pritam tum, bin sauten sang*
> *Jage naina ratiyan re paiyan main padu re pyare*
> *Unhai ke ghar raho*
> *Jaao nahin bole mose*
> *— Binda suno yeh nahin mane jiya jare dare*

> (Why have you come to my house
> O' my love, without the other woman
> The whole night my eyes were awake
> I fall at your feet in request, my love
> Go and stay at her house
> And Don't speak to me)
> — listen 'Binda', he is not agreeing

Here, the thumri did not sway to the rhythm of emotion. Its melody remained constant, feelings of pain and complaint forming part of a sustained mood, laced, impeccably with aristocratic restraint. After singing, Bindadeen used to get up to remember the night when he danced for thirty-six hours under the tutelage of his court dancer father while standing on the edges of a 'thaali' with Wajid Ali Shah nervously twitching his toe.

Binda had one more speciality — he was the master of sadra, the light classical extension of the dhrupad, analogous to dadra which occupied a similar position vis-a-vis the khayal and thumri. Ustad Dulhe Khan was sadra's author in Lucknow; it was said of him that he had one eye fixed firmly on Jaunpur and one on Lucknow and was able to develop a thoroughly compositional form with an exhortative style totally opposed to thumri. Arousing the passion of war, it 'pulled back' after raising the pitch to a high, stopping 'to think' before exhorting once more.

Sadra adopted the attitude of Aryan and Brahminical valour, part of the official nawabi pantheon. If dadra represented the sensual, Sufi dimension, the sadra came forth as the 'ghazi', valorous strain of Lucknow. Adept at physical and intellectual war, Bindadeen's compositions dealt with fiery debates, the exhortation of Mandodri against Ravana or the invocation of Durga in a fast track.

Binda's obstinacy kept the sadra alive even after 1857. In keeping with the versatile vocation of a Lucknowi genius, he fought, cooked and mused. Rasiyas of his type played the tabla in the mornings, had their fill of roasted quail at noon and wrestled in the evening. Exercise, cuisine and music went together — the one who did not combine the three was considered effeminate and 'thas', incapable of conquering the wife's body, mind or manner on the first post-wedding night.

In between soft performances Binda would suddenly think of something else. The audience would get edgy, the talukedars a bit apprehensive. In a ten beat rhythm, the 'jhaptaal', Binda would cry out.

Shesh fan dagmagyo Lank hal chal padayo
(The hood of the serpant god wavered, the plough ran through Lanka)
Kahat Bindadeen jab Ram dhanu tankor

(Says Bindadeen when Ram's bow twanged)
Chalat sar ladat bhat kadat bin mund bhayo
(People were moving along fighting, heads were being severed from bodies)
Sarit shonit bahi veer mahi gir gayo
(Rivers of blood began flowing, the valorous fell on the earth)
Kahat Mandodri sunahu mere Lankapati
(Then said Mandodri, listen my Lord of Lanka)
Jeet nahi sakoge Ram sang jhagjhor
(You will not be able to win this war against Rama)

Bindadeen softened the harsh tone of sadra chaupaiyan, or four line verses, by using the 'tarana' playfulness which, by Wajid Ali Shah's time, had evolved into the chaturang. In this, the first line was sung as a sargam, the second as the tarana, the third in bols of the pakhawaj and the fourth as a dadra. This was Wajid Ali Shah's response to Amir Khusro and the ultimate 'explosion of genres'. Bindadeen also experimented with the 'thematic' thumri which Wajid Ali was himself trying to evolve during his last days at Matiya Burj. He began separating, as per the demands of the new era, the elements of pure dance and emotional narrative, the tap dance and the ballet, which had existed in a playful unity in early Kathak.

But the efforts of Bindadeen and Kalka, nephews of Thakur Prasad, the great and incredibly handsome Kathak-Rahas exponent and confidante of Wajid Ali Shah, were underwritten by the pathos of isolation. All through the latter years of the nineteenth century they had no fixed patron. They shifted from place to place, sometimes knocking at the door of the nawab of Rampur. The nawab had sided with the British in 1857 and his court attracted artists and musicians fleeing from the ravages of Lucknow and other north Indian cities. But like the Raja of Benaras, the other great pro-British aristocrat, the Nawab of Rampur could never emerge as a connoisseur of the Ganga-Yamuna tehzeeb. The raja tried becoming the secular protector of Muslims and the traditional master of the Hindu culture of the east. The nawab attempted the same with Hindu and Muslim traditions of the northwest. The Rampur house was, after all, a part of Hafiz Rehmat Khan's lineage whose legacy in Bareli had sacrificed all for the cause of 1857.

In both places, the memory of Lucknow, Bareli and Bhojpur proved strong. In Benaras the Raja of Ramnagar was upstaged by the courtesans of Dalmandi and the traders of Assi Ghaat as far as cultural patronage was concerned. The proud musicians of Avadh too did not flock to the largesses handed down by Rampur. Though gratified by the magnanimity of successive nawabs, they found the spirit of freedom missing in the city. Rampur was a restrictive durbar propped up by the British straining hard to maintain rituals and traditions which Lucknow had already bypassed.

The musicians, therefore, preferred to set up their own gharanas. Proceeding from Lucknow and Delhi they arrived in Gwalior, Agra and other regions of the United Provinces with nothing but memories, a bag of instruments and lots of pride. Things were not easy and the Miyan Bakshu gharana of Lucknowi tabla almost closed down due to economic difficulties. But that did not deter Miyan Bakshu from giving a final shape to the qaida and the peshkara — two modes which set the basis of modern tabla. It was akin to introducing manner and style, nafasat and ada, to the tabla's thaap. Tabla's severance from the mridang and pakhawaj was complete. In a lane not far from the Kalka-Bindadeen deorhi, Munne Khan and his brothers sweated out to carry forward the legacy of Wajid Ali Shah, Salari Khan and Mammad Khan, his father and the direct descendant of Miyan Bakshu. They refined not only the gat, the compositional element of the tabla, just as the peshkara stood as its alaap, but also the rela — an open system based on the playing of open bols, such as 'dheneghene'. Haji Vilayat Ali Khan, a disciple of Miyan Bakshu, left Lucknow to create his own gharana in Farukkhabad. He had to suffer more before giving the peshkara a very native, Farukkhabadi-Kannauji sound where every gat and tukra acquired a pose of its own, so that the bols sang, talked and struck an attitude at the same time.

But the fate of Kothiwal gharana, the house of tabla patronised directly by Wajid Ali Shah, was tragic. The gharana was responsible for turning Delhi's band baj — where the sound came out in muffled tones — into the khula baj, or the open hand, of Lucknow. In this the full impact and elaboration of the thaap was as important as the mood, a bit like the openness of the khayal distinguishable from the muffled sombreness of the dhrupad. It flourished on the unusual combination of restraint and arousal, setting a style which was followed later by the Benaras Gharana of Ram Sahai. Modhu Khan, the founder of Kothiwal, made even the chandeliers dance with his performance. His tabla was still alive in the late nineteenth and early twentieth century when the drawing room or the hall was fast replacing the baradaris of yore. The earlier clustering of chandeliers, jhad, fanus and the handi was giving way to the separateness and singularity of objects. In the drawing rooms of the talukedars, the jhad and fanus stood afar, one near the mirror, one atop the mihraab, one on a table of Burma teak wood and one besides an almirah of Belgian wood. The tabla of Modhu Khan played in the haunting loneliness of these places where romance went hand in hand with recurring stabs of pain. Behind perfect etiquette, patronage was slowly being withdrawn; the Kothiwal gharana soon vanished from the scene to leave behind a forgotten memory.

The glorious days of the freedom struggle were also underwritten by a note of sadness. Muhammad Ali Muhammad was the last figure common to both the League and the Congress. He brought Jinnah to the League but also persuaded Annie Beasant to stay on in the Congress. While still a Muslim League President Muhammad Ali Muhammad was offered the presidentship of the Congress. Annie Beasant and Sarojini Naidu even came down to Lucknow to convince the politician who, however, succumbed before the man.

By that time, the United Provinces had a new lieutenant governor — a figure steeped in the brooding love of aristocracy that informed the lively, decadent British humanism of the early twentieth century. But there was politics in Sir Harcourt Butler's emotions. The chosen man of the moment was, of course, enamoured by the lifestyle of mannered aristocrats who had an ancient history of adventure and enterprise. But his drooping eyes also saw the possibility of cultivating them as a distinct constituency when the national movement threatened to make inroads into the 'dreaded' Indo-Gangetic plain.

One of his first moves was to transfer the capital of the United Provinces from Allahabad to Lucknow. Allahabad, the capital since

1867, was by then an established anti-British bastion. The native, post '57 professionals, centred around the High Court and led by the Nehrus, had taken over the leadership from Madan Mohan Malviya and his Khatri patrons. The Nehrus belonged to a patrician breed which stood neither pro nor 'anti' the British side during 1857. They also constituted the new elite from within the post '57 middle classes. This section came to dominate the national movement in north India. It initiated an Allahabadi brand of modernism, liberalism and socialism which later developed into an 'all-India' Nehruvian liberal-left current. Its early mentors emerged as Dadabhai Naoroji and Surendra Nath Bannerjee. Their Parsi-Bengali, conservative modernity soon merged into the Allahabadi strand of feudal sophistication and liberal accommodation. Lucknow, however, was not the perfect vehicle to check the tide of nationalism. Sir Butler may have been a nineteenth century man sent to hold back a twentieth century reality, but his favourite talukedar did not rise to the occasion.

The Raja of Mahmudabad became a maharaja; he also refused Annie Beasant's offer as Harcourt Butler offered him the prestigious home ministry in his executive council. This was at least how the situation appeared. Harcourt's family had done great favours for the Mahmudabad house in their hour of tribulations and now the young raja wanted to oblige him. But there was something more in his refusal; he was a personal friend of Motilal Nehru but not closely associated with Gandhi.

To Muslim intellectuals and aristocrats Gandhi presented a strange paradox. They first supported him wholeheartedly; an unexplored aspect in the 'making of the Mahatma' was the role played by Muslims and Urdu speaking Hindus in South Africa and India. Chakbast even wrote a poem calling back the South African satyagrahi to India. Ferverently anti-British, they were in support of any idea which could start a new movement and break the silence of post '57 years. Muslim intellectuals began building up Gandhi as the apostle of the new age — Akbar Allahabadi talked of 'Gandhinama' replacing *Shahnama*.

But disillusionment was not slow in coming. For a people bred on memories of an armed conflict with the British, the politics of satyagraha, peaceful agitation and moderation held little strategic appeal. They soon began to despair — Akbar himself said in his last days that Gandhi's charkha will remain in operation but 'angrez sahib' will never go:

> *'Let acclamations sound, and keep on spinning all you will. But mark my words: When all is done, the sahibs will be here still.'*

This chilling voice of opposition came from that Muslim elite of Avadh and Allahabad which had never reconciled either with the pro-British policies of Sir Syed, or the anti-Sir Syed, but backward looking policies of Muslim traditionalists. They stood opposed to post '57 religious schools of Deoband or Bareli and showed little enthusiasm for Allama Iqbal's pan-Islamism.

Punjab's fiery poet was then writing much that spoke of anti-colonialism in contemporary jargons. As one intellectual giant of the early twentieth century Asia, he wrote a mind blowing treatise which compared the 'non-positivist', anti-classical scientific spirit of Islam with the 'backward' and idealistic scientism of Western-Greek thought. Marxists were surprised at this comparison for they had always posited positivist materialism against Western idealism. Where then were they to place Islamic Arabia and ancient India which were material and yet fell in neither slot? Many years later, Derrida and Foucault did not even dare to mention this real, guiltless 'post-modern' world which celebrated a metaphysics of dialectics, a classicism of anti-classicism, and a 'nihilism of scientism. In it, Western modernist and post-modernist oppositions between the organised scientific spirit and the anarchic nihilistic attitude, broke down completely and clearly. But politically, Iqbal lacked an understanding of Ganga-Yamuni tehzeeb and 1857.

At the height of the pro and anti Sir Syed controversy, Lucknow produced the seminary of Nadwa which tried effecting a midway course between Aligarh and the traditionalists. But the Nadwa was still eclipsed by Mulla Nizammuddin's old college which launched journals such as *Ans Nizammiya*. Several dissenting individuals were given a platform in *Ans Nizammiya*. Major contributors included Abdul Halim Sharar, Akbar Allahabadi, Hasrat Mohani and Sir Kishan Prasad Shad, the Hindi writer and former prime minister of the state of Hyderabad. Hakim Shams-ud-din, Maulana Sayyid Ali, the descendant of Dildaar

Ali Nasirabadi and a leading light of the newly formed poetic society of Lucknow, and Khwaja Abdur Rauf carried forward the tradition of enlightened theology. Articles dealt with philosophy, politics, science and history. The famed professor of the Osmania University, Hyderabad, Maulvi Muhammad Yunus, practiced his amazing genius in *Ans Nizammiya* to quote classic Islamic scholars, Leibniz, the French educationists Gustave Le Bon and J.W. Draper in one breath. His death in 1923 cut short the blossoming of a Lucknowi intellectual who was talking about bridging the gap between science and religion and reforming education by evolving a 'non-rote' system of examination. The journal was funded by the Lucknowi Ulema, leading landed families of Paisar and Satrikh, as well as by Qidwais and the Mohanis of Barabanki and Unnao.

Politically, the Maharaja of Mahmudabad never stated his explicit position. He was a thorough moderate who pleased everyone from the British to the League to the Congress. But like Akbar Allahabadi, he belonged to no one. He funded the Mohammedan Oriental College and contributed immensely to the setting up of the Lucknow University and the KG Medical College. Prior to this, he had made a financial contribution to Sir Syed's Aligarh Muslim University. The Ulama group opposed him on this issue but Mahmudabad was adamant. A true aristocrat, he knew that whether Shia or Sunni, the traditionalists were always better off under the sword of the 'secular' monster. The traditionalists had, after 1857, escaped from the control of the aristocrat, asserting their version of Islam or Hinduism. But they were helpless before Mahmudabad. Akbar Allahabadi, whose time was now spent as much in Lucknow as in Allahabad, the town of the 'three' wonders, the guava, Nehrus and Akbar himself, could not help commenting —

Raja sahab se sheikh ji ne kaha, ab bharosa huzoor par na raha
Mujh ko choda imambare mein, pahunche khud natureri
akhade men
(The religious heads said to the Raja, now we have no faith left in his excellency
You left us in the Imambara, and landed yourself in the arena!)

Mahmudabad remained in search of something elusive, probably a politics and culture where the League and the Congress could survive together. For a man who was the home minister of the province, and who virtually led the Muslim League, he died a dissenter. The Congress-League pact was broken in the 1920s after the withdrawal of the Non-cooperation Movement — the charkha kept on spinning but the Hindu-Muslim unity, virtually cemented in the Lucknow pact of 1916, was despoiled. The city which had transformed the Khilafat movement, begun to oppose the post First World War British dismemberment of Turkey, into the freedom movement, was now pushed out of the national agenda.

The Khilafat Committee elected here included a long line of Muslim and Hindu leaders who needed no mediation to unite. They were together almost by habit, as naturally as the shaved chin of Lucknowis. In fashion since the days of Nasiruddin Haider, this style became the cause of immense amusement for Lucknowites in the early twentieth century. At that time, in the rest of the country, shaving off one's beard was being considered revolutionary and 'Curzon-like'. To emulate Viceroy Curzon's clean looks was supposed to carry a distinct advantage with the ladies and Lucknowites scored here even while ridiculing Curzonism and brushing their moustaches.

When the Congress was reconstituted as an organisation in the city, the charismatic Khalliqulzaman served as president and the quiet, methodical brain of the Naubasta Kayastha, Mohanlal Saxena, handled the secretaryship. Balmukund Vajpeyi looked after treasurery matters in the Congress's Golaganj office. The District Committee (DC) had Sheikh Shaukat Ali, Harkaran Nath Misra and Beni Prasad Singh as president and secrataries respectively. Other members included Khwaja Ahmad Khan and Usman Khan of Malihabad, Izzat Ali of Kakori, Gopal Narain Saxena and Ramchandra Sinha. This period saw a short revival of pro '57 forces in the Congress with foreign returned brown sahibs or the influential men of the old city, like Ganga Narain Verma and B.N. Dhar, who had dominated the organisation earlier, receeding in importance.

At Kanpur in 1922, just before the Chauri Chaura incident in Gorakhpur, Gandhi got a taste of the Avadhi 'mizaj' in a Congress conference. While deliberations proceeded on the 'nature' of freedom, a young man got up and challenged the Mahatma. He opposed the idea of limited freedom and advocated purna swaraj or complete freedom. Hasrat Mohani, the poet and adib from Mohan, Unnao, the same area which had resisted Havelock's advance towards Lucknow, went beyond the war cries of Tilak. Hasrat's poetry was romantic but 'punned' to devastating effect. The inscription on his Lucknowi tombstone was to call him both a man of deen and duniya. And his encounter with the Congress, in which he expressed 'too much', must have made him quip:

Tere karam ka sazavaar to nahin hasrat
Ab aage teri khushi hai jo sarfaraz kare
(Hasrat is not the best fitted person for your work
Now it is upto you whether you are pleased enough to
grant me the proper respect)

In both the Congress and the League there was discomfort with Lucknowi radicalism. In 1921 another young and fiery speaker read a poem in the Avadh Khilafat Congress held at Lucknow under the chairmanship of a famous Ali brother, Muhammad Ali. It excited the same level of consternation in League ranks who advised caution and the poem was confiscated by the British.

Earlier, Maulana Abdul Razaqq Malihabadi and Maulana Abdul Bari of Lucknow had persuaded Abul Kalam Azad to declare himself Imam of the Muslim community and lead an anti-British jihad in alliance with the Hindus. An Egypt returned scholar-turned-revolutionary, Maulana Malihabadi was perhaps the last Avadhian to originate from a small town and cross international borders while conquering hearts and minds. He took up residence at Maulviganj and began propaganda work as Maulana Azad's Khalifa. Assisted by Abdul Bari Firangi Mahali, he published a newspaper, *Albayan*, which kept churning out anti-British propaganda for quite some time.

During Gandhi's movement, several schools and self-reliant institutions came up in Lucknow. A pathshala began operating from Chutki Bhandar in mohalla Tilpurwa and in Saadatganj, in a number of Kayashta mohallas, small schools dished out nationalist education. League and Congress leaders ran the institutions in unity and Gandhi's dictat of non-violence was violated with impunity. The early arrests connected with the independence struggle in Lucknow were of people like Maulvi Jafrul Mulk and Khwaja Ahmad Khan who represented the turbulent intelligentsia. Even small incidents, such as opposition to the Indian tour of the Prince of Wales, used to take on a militant colour with sedate district Congress officials, some of them trusted Kayastha and Brahmin men of Gandhi, talking in the language of subversion. As a result, Congress party organisation was constantly reshuffled.

Following communal disturbances elsewhere in the province after the withdrawal of noncooperation, Khalliqulzaman was removed from the city presidentship. The post went to Kishan Lal Nehru. Balmukund Vajpeyi and Mohan Lal Saxena too had to bow out making place for Shyam Sunder Kaiser and Raj Narain Khanna. This was a shift from the middle class of the traditional Lucknowi sections to the middle class of the commercial castes of recent origin considered close to the Nehrus. The factional fight between these two sections ultimately paved the way for the assertion of the Hindu business community in the Congress under the leadership of C.B. Gupta.

But before that, small towns of Avadh passed through a different sort of upheaval as the qasbai youths took to the gun. The 1920s in general saw the rise of a new Indo-Gangetic middle class. Inheritors of the 1857 petty bourgeoisie, they emerged from within the 'lower middle class' of the late nineteenth century after the decline, or the elitisation, of the post '57 middle classes. By then the qasbai maulvi had lost its role after the end of the Khilafat movement and the revolution in Turkey where Kemal Pasha overturned the ancient regime and proclaimed a modern, secular nation. The need for a new, post-radical Islamic ideology became evident. Kemal Pasha himself showed the way by linking ancient traditions of Ṭurk-Islamic chivalry with demands of secular, capitalist modernisation.

On 9 August 1925, a couple of boys drawn from various districts of the United Provinces stopped a train near the Kakori railway station and looted the government treasury. They were led by Ram Prasad Bismil and Ashfaq Ullah who represented two factions of the Rohilk-handi-Avadhi qasba. One was a Brahmin of Shahjahanpur, inspired to change the world by the Bhagwad Gita. The other belonged to a trend where Pathans and Ansari youngsters from established and declining families went to the mazaar of Shiekh Uns in Bilgram and thought — the Babas were all heroic people, they died for a cause; why not lift the gun and die for a cause too?

These youth soon became part of the Hindustan Republican Army, a revolutionary organisation with headquarters in the Punjab. They saw little in common with Gandhism and the Congress, and yet invoked all the symbols of Indian tradition. Their banner was not the charkha and the half-naked body, but the kurta and the turban. Their language also did not extoll patience or the eternality of Indian spiritualism but celebrated its philosophy, militancy and exclusivity. In the months during which the Kakori conspiracy case hit the headlines in India and Britain, something fundamental emanated from Avadh. The youth began defining an alternative current of nationalism. Their terrorism was a not a fringe act — it came from the depths of mainstream society and posed a serious threat to the Congress.

Ram Prasad Bismil and Ashfaq Ullah were hanged along with Roshan Singh and Rajendra Lahiri. Scores of Khatri and Bengali boys, including Manmath Nath Gupta, were arrested and sent to jail. But the attempt to suppress the generation of 1925 failed, as patriotic action developed into a consistent trend of revolutionary terrorism in north India. Different from the more religiously oriented Anushilans and Yugantars of Bengal, this current succeeded in breaking away from the extremist practice of using traditional symbols for political appeal — a tactic established by Tilak. It shifted to a sophisticated and modern analysis of socio-economic issues along Marxist lines. This backdrop led to the emergence of Bhagat Singh, the future leader of the Hindustan Republican Army, re-named the 'Socialist Hindustan Repulican Army' under his influence. Bhagat Singh himself came from the depths of a Punjabi, Indo-Persian qasba and went on to formulate an indigenous form of 'atheism' ('Why I am an Atheist'), an alternative form of political tactics ('the philosophy of the bomb') and an alternative social base (the peasantry and the working class) in the freedom struggle. He came close to evolving an indigenous brand of revolutionary socialism, which, if developed further, could have provided a real challenge to the Congress — something which the Communist Party, founded at Kanpur in 1925, was unable to do.

Bhagat Singh's distinctiveness rested in his charisma as a modern 'son of the soil' which unnerved the British as it came close to rivalling Gandhi's mass appeal. Contemptuous of established Congress leaders, he said on one occasion that their much touted understanding of India and its villages extended only as far as the reach of Birla's car.

The Birlas, along with the Tatas and Bajajs, were the leading industrialists of India; they were also the 'mind' of the growing big bourgeoisie of India. Baptised under British influence, they were now building up their own constituency in the national movement. The post '57 trader-comprador bourgeoisie did not have the entrepreneurial-aristocratic mindset. The Tatas had set up a steel industry while the Birlas and Bajajs were into jute and textile production. But neither of them made any attempt to revive Mughal-Tipu Sultan-Avadhian traditions or striking out boldly as explorers in the European renaissance-bourgeois manner. Real capitalism arrived in the West from the ranks of restless seekers, artisans and aristocrats. Avadhian portfolio capitalists too were made up of similar stuff. In contrast to the Tatas and Birlas, they chose a risky path to money making. The post '57 Indian capitalists lacked a will to gamble in the manner of Almas Ali, Darshan Singh, Tikait Rai or the great American entrepreneurs of the nineteenth century. Darshan Singh and Tikait Rai were masters of local R&D, the litmus test for a bourgeoisie mind. Bombay club entrepreneurs transformed research and development into a non-functional *nom* de plume. Because of this choice India was faced with the dilemma of a 'lack of capitalism' in the growth of capitalism.

By the late '20s and the early '30s, an invisible cleavage appeared in the national movement over the issue of leadership. Articulated as a 'left'-'right' division, it drove a wedge between the national bourgeoisie (a term used to categorise anti-British, anti-landlord, medium sized capitalists), middle class, peasantry and the working class on the one hand and the pro-British big bourgeoisie and landlords on the other. Bhagat Singh groped towards a non-Congress brand of left nationalism. He was supported, organisationally and ideologically by Chandra Shekhar Azad, the well built, sacred thread bearing proud and secular Brahmin — the same stock which produced the Pandies of 1857 — of Unnao.

Bhagat Singh was hanged for the killing of a British officer accused of having a hand in the death of the 'garam dal' Lahore leader, Lala Lajpat Rai. Azad too died in a police encounter at Allahabad, allegedly betrayed by members of a prominent Khatri family and Punjabi friends. A tussle between the authentic Uttar Pradesh middle classes and the Punjabi-bania middle and elite forces underwrote another complex social and psychological Indian sub-history of *treachery as a way of life*.

Bhagat Singh's execution in the early '30s was condoled by massive, spontaneous demonstrations all over the United Provinces. Lucknow observed a total strike organised independently of the Congress. The role of Gandhi and the Congress leaders in the entire episode was highly 'controversial', to say the least. They adopted a position of silence, neither supporting or opposing Bhagat Singh. At that very moment, talks between Gandhi and Viceroy Irwin were taking place. The consequent Gandhi-Irwin pact led to the winding up of the Civil Disobedience Movement and several concessions for the Congress. It was widely speculated that if Gandhi wanted he could have made Irwin repeal the death sentence on Bhagat Singh with the threat of another round of agitation or he could have at least made a political issue out of the affair. But he kept silent leaving behind one of the most enduring mysteries of the freedom movement.

By the early '30s, Maharaja Mahmudabad was once again embroiled in controversy. Due to post-noncooperation communal tensions, the industrial city of Kanpur, was burning. Its singularity rested in remoteness from an advantageous coastal backdrop along which centres of economic growth came up not only in British India but other Asian nations like China and Japan as well. A potential mainland powerhouse, it presented a classic case of British bourgeois growth atop an antiquated Hindu social structure. After 1857 and the removal of Indo-Persians like Nana Sahib this structure had lost its inner dynamic impulse. British mishandling and under-modernisation saw economic tensions finding an extra-economic outlet. Solidification of Hindu and Muslim identities proceeded at pace with the growth of the freedom movement as the city became a home to class and communal tensions. It had already seen the mysterious murder of the journalist, Ganesh Shankar Vidyarthi, in a riot and was on the edge of another conflagration.

Help arrived, again from Lucknow. By that time Mahmudabad had become known as a builder. He constructed the courtyard of the Qaiserbagh. This sparked off the new trend of courtyard building in 'front of the verandah', a brilliant innovation which became part of the twentieth century Avadhian bungalow.

In Lucknow the bungalow evolved in response to both the 'Indic' and the foreign-Imperial designs of the British. It also stood in contrast to the 'bania haveli' as opposed to the older 'thakur haveli', of the late nineteenth century. Thakur havelis of Benaras, Bhojpur and Bundelkhand were insular, grand and aristocratic and had huge enclosed walls. The bania havelis of Agra, Mathura, western Uttar Pradesh and Allahabad were patronised by British officials as representing an authentic, anti-aristocratic, 'Indian', trader tradition.[3] They were graceful, but stifling. Closed, arcaded corridors abounded on the exterior in a straight line, storey after storey, with no open verandah. Anand Bhavan, the house of the Nehrus in Allahabad, followed an innovative, anglicised, verandah pattern of this very formula.

The 'Indic' pattern could never become an integral part of Lucknow. Its use was limited to Mathura, Bikaner, Gwalior, Ajmer and Allahabad where the white sahib tried to blend the Gothic arch and neo-classical pillars with the Indo-Persian dome to present a version of authentic 'Indianness', untainted by foreign influences! This was a political statement in architecture, the ultimate language of power. The 'Indic' asserted politically that the British knew better than the Mughals and Avadhian nawabs about Indian traditions. First an attempt was made to distinguish between 'Moslem' and 'Hindoo' styles which backfired, for the Deig-Bharatpur architecture of Jat 'Hindu'-Indo-Persian rulers turned out to be Mughal-Rajput in inspiration[4]. British architects then began favouring the architecture of Rajasthan and Maratha princes because they chose the 'right' side in 1857 over the 'heathen', 'debased', 'impure', un-Indian architecture of Lucknow[5]!

Lahaul-a-vala —
Yahan bhi Lucknow se he khas khunnas?

The world knew at that time that true 'Indianness' rested in Chattar Manzil and Qaiserbagh. But the firang, like a true philistine, kept on building the 'true' Indo-Saracenic style for its 'model princes'. Victorian-bania-religious fundamentalism and eclecticism was Indianness in his vision. Any deviation in this line was a foreign travesty. The Brits even tried teaching the Mughals a lesson by building, 'in marble', the Victoria Memorial in Calcutta — an exercise, actually, in the worst type of synthetic eclecticism and knave architectural superciliousess.

Indicism's 'non-start' in Lucknow compelled the British to accommodate Lucknow in Lucknow. They built the King George's Medical College (KGMC) on the ruins of the Macchi Bhawan with domes, pavilions and arches to produce a white washed, British version of Indo-Persianism.

The architecture of the Medical College bore little resemblance or continuity with Lucknow. Built on a general, abstract, almost medieval and pre-Lucknowi understanding of Indo-Persian patterns, the structure combined philistinism with folly. Its follicular, modish and squarish look appeared gaudy and characterless with the passage of time. More elegance was sought to be attributed to the Council House in which Indic pretensions were rigidly subsumed, controlled and subordinated, 'within a European classical idiom to create an architecture expressive of the ideals of the British Empire.' The real, Imperialist intention behind their espousal of 'authentic' Indian tradition in the Indic phase became clear. The half-baked Orientalism having fulfilled its purpose, it was now time for a naked assertion of Anglicist-architectural politics. Herbert Baker, the messiah of the new period, had already designed the union buildings at Pretoria, South Africa as an imperial statement of apartheid. He reproduced the same pattern with the same statemental motifs of columned porticos in the New Delhi Secretariat[6]. He was commissioned to build a 'New' Delhi, as the Indian capital or British Imperialism, by subordinating Indo-Persian Delhi. It was to embody 'the idea of law and order which has been produced out of chaos by the British Administration.'

Edwin Lutyens, Baker's comrade-in-design and the master builder of the Viceroy's House (ironically, today's Rashtrapati Bhawan), ridiculed Saracenism as 'Mughal Tush'. In the Council House at Lucknow 'Hindu-Muslim' elements were subsumed in the grand semicircle of pillars and the Christopher Wren style dome. Hindu brackets adorned the junction of the walls and the motif of the two fishes was slammed as the link to the past. This early twentieth century colonial backlash looked good from a distance but a closer view gave away the fact that Hindu and Muslim elements were present as alien structures touched up by alien hands like the shikharas of modern Hindu temples, which, despite appearing ancient bore no mysterious or mnemonic quality. Compared to the Council House, the nawabi Hayat Baksh, now working as the governor's Government House, blended Western and Indian motifs successfully without appearing eclectic.

In the Lucknowi bungalow, the courtyard in front of the verandah drew parallels more with the pillared verandas and frontline gardens of nawabi country houses. Old motifs returned. The burjs of Khurshid Manzil were transformed into side rooms with a window while old pavilions were converted into study rooms and private libraries. The pillars of some pavilions were rolled up spirally like the toffee of the Kannauji 'gatta'. Roofs, adorned with festoons and gilded banners shone like gold and silver. The baroque curve also returned. In the new locality of Lal Kuan, the Bengalis sacrificed Greek pillars and porticos of Calcutta for twisted walls and frilled verandahs.

The winning over of the Bengali to Lucknowi ways was by far the greatest triumph. They were the first to dominate British professions in the post '57 vacuum and remained exclusive and remote till the 1920s. A current of native hostility also ran against them as some prominent estates of big 'rebel' talukedars, like those of Rana Beni Madho, were given over to Bengalis in exchange for their loyalty.

The ice was broken by Rabindranath Tagore himself. A thumri fan, he applied its compositional elements in the evolution of Rabindra Sangeet. However, the Bengali voice of Lucknow was not Tagore but Atul Prasad Sen, an ardent Lucknowi wanderer of the twentieth century. He reformulated the thumri into a linear, dhun pradhan following the singularity of the 'tune' in place of the waviness of the melody — 'lyric'; something which Tagore was trying to bring about in Rabindra Sangeet. In Tagore's scheme of things the taming of the thumri and its baroquian, rococo element was important to evolve a true lyric form. In Atul Prasad Sen's rendition the thumri itself became a bit straight to absorb the singularity of the lyric without shedding traditional features or accommodating the spiritual and emotional aspects of Bengali folk. It thus became the perfect vehicle for the new, more puritan cosmopolitanism of Lucknow — an influence which spread to the bustling bazaars and kothas of Calcutta.

The return to indigenous ways, however, did not alter the structure of the city. The jhaanki was disturbed forever and houses represented caged gems behind the impersonal concrete of British roads and buildings. No longer was there the sight of a garden and a unwalled manzil, separated by friendly paths, where antelopes roamed in the backdrop of parapets and domes. Such features were kept alive only in Mahmudabad, in the maharaja's Naya Makan which combined elements of the twentieth century bungalow with old scenes. In his last days, the break with the British finally approaching, the maharaja became more and more innovative in taste. He began resenting the prominence given to lowly talukedars, like the raja of Bhinga. At the same time he voluntarily abolished nazars and other forms of feudal exactions from his domains.

He also played host to the making of the Nehru report which drafted the first Constitution of a future, dominion India. Motilal Nehru was a guest at the very house which was later surrounded by the police when the Simon Commission came to Lucknow. There was a big protest during which Khaliqulzaman took to the novel idea of writing 'Simon, go back' on balloons and kites. Almost a century ago, when gas balloons were still a curious novelty in West, one of the earliest demonstration of the sport was held by Asaf-ud-Daula. Indian kites were of course a typical Delhi-Lucknowi invention and competed with Chinese lanterns and dragons of the sky as patangs, tukkals, guddis and kankavas, sometimes flown in the night with silken thread. But in contemporary Lucknow, the ground drew blood protesters as fell by the dozen and the maharaja faced his first violent confrontation with the British.

The authorities already disliked their former blue-eyed boy; they hated him when he helped diffuse communal disturbances in Kanpur. During the 1910s, the maharaja had outsmarted the British in the famous Kanpur mosque issue. At that time confiscation of Mahmudabad property was being considered in official circles. This time around, the maharaja was left alone from the beginning to mend his growing differences with the League and the Congress.

Motilal Nehru's death at the Kalakankar house in Lucknow made Mahmudabad face a new generation of politicians who spoke a different language. Jinnah's Western cosmopolitanism lacked a Ganga-Yamuni background, while Nehru's modernity did not carry an emotional bonding with the past. Motilal's bonding with Mahmudabad had once stretched from politics to lifestyle. It was laced with seven course meals at Qaiserbagh and billiards and tennis at the Rifah-e-aam Club. The club had been set up by the maharaja in retaliation to the exclusively British, United Services Club at the Chattar Manzil. The British had a Muhammad Bagh and Cantonment Club which barred entry to Indians as late as the 1930s. In the United Services Club, officers of the Indian Civil Service (ICS), the Indian Police (IP), Indian Veterinary Services (IVS) and Indian Engineering Services (IES) gathered for social events. By that time, the club culture was fully entrenched in the United Provinces. The trend of the Moradabad Club Ltd., Meerut Club Ltd., introduced a current of 'non-bania' Westernisation which was soon taken over by natives and transformed into an Anglo-Indian brand of fashion and way of life.

It is significant that Anglo-Indianism acquired the widest possible base in small district stations, railway colonies and army and air force messes of north India. In western and eastern India it remained confined to the metropolis of big cities, rarely penetrating deep into 'mofussil' culture. Even during 1857, northern India enjoyed the best possible cultural relationship with the west. This was the place where Azimullah Khan and Nana Sahib, to name just a few flamboyant 'rebel' leaders, had roaring love affairs with British ladies. They were also on best of terms with men of intelligence and senior officials of the British administration. Before being executed, the engineer Muhammad Ali Khan was asked to remember his god. The Indo-Persian hero of '57 replied that he was remembering Dante and the heroes of the French Revolution. This was not possible amongst the less confident and more dependent elite of Calcutta and Bombay. They did not participate in 1857 but were more inward looking, rarely attracting the European mind. When war broke out it was evident that there was nothing personal in the whole affair; human emotions were subsumed with just a wreath placed on the grave of the 'best of enemy' in remembrance.

In Lucknow, the maharaja's friends were once refused entry in the British clubs on account of their Indian dress. So he went ahead and converted his plot of land near Golaganj into an imposing building with flying festoons. The Indian elite gathered here in churidars, achkans and Hyderabadi sherwanis to discuss the latest happenings in England and Turkey, circulate the local gossip in sophisticated monosyllables and have a shot at the sport of their liking. The Rifah-e-aam played host to nationalist leaders, combining politics with pleasure.

The talukedars had their own British India Association whose functions remained formal. The focus of Lucknowi life shifted to the Golaganj hub and its ittar shows, sherbet parties and tennis games. A great, synthetic, liquid yarn, exclusive to the Middle East and South Asia, sherbet summed up the history of Indo-Persian brewing. Spun with sugar, water and a host of orange, lemon, khas, leechi, apricot flavours, it did not fizz like Western soft drinks of later years. The colours shimmered, cooled and excited passions in the typical fashion.

Rifah-e-aam was frequented by vakils, doctors, engineers, businessmen and the high ranking employees of the talukedars. Their rank boasted of barristers, judges and litterateurs some belonging to Ali Zaheer's family, vice chancellor of the Lucknow University Sr. Habibullah and his glamorous wife, Khaliqulzaman, chief justice of the Avadh Chief Court, Ghulam Hussein and Iqbal Ahmad, the first chief justice of the Allahabad High Court. This Lucknowi beau monde included the Lakhimpuri Misra family of Harkaran Nath, Gokaran Nath, who combined official service with business, intellectual and political activity, an advancing leitmotif of the larger Kanyakubja families.

Shyam Behari Misra and his brothers from Sitapur were bureaucrats and litterateurs. Occupying a building with the 'courtyard in front of the verandah' in Golaganj, they inaugurated an independent current in Hindi literature. When leading personalities like Mahavir Prasad Dwivedi and Ram Charan Shukla were busy creating a non-sensual, puritan, canonical history of Hindi literature in Allahabad and Benaras, the Misra brothers of Lucknow re-opened the debate on erotic Braj poetry of reetkala. Hailing from an aristocratic Kanyakubja lineage with solid Persian impact, they wrote their own history of Hindi literature against Ram Charan Shukla. This version revived interest in the most 'un-Brahmin' (as per the conventional logic of the twentieth century), erotic, 'Brahmin' poets of Jehangir's time.

The spirit against literary philistinism was kept alive by dissenting and refined elites in the Gangetic plain. The Urdu-Hindi controversy, introduced the communal bias in the 'word'. During the entire debate script was equated with language and language with religion so that both Urdu and Hindu had to search for pure and distorted Sanskrit-Arabic-Persian, mazhabi roots. The evolving interdependence of Urdu and Hindi, as 'Hindustani', was pushed aside.

The Devnagari form of non-Kaithi Hindi became the official language in 1899 but pro-Hindustanis did not keep silent. In Bhartendu's time, his rival, Raja Shivprasad, needled Benarsi trader complacency with 'Hindustani' ripostes. Babu Devaki Nandan Khatri, the entrepreneur of Benaras and Mirzapur whose *Chandrakanta* played a pioneering role in popularising Hindi, too wrote in a mixed, Urdu-Persian-Hindi-Hindustani style. Even within the Benaras based 'Nagari Pracharni Sabha' (NPS), the penultimate and orthodox propagator of Sanskritised Hindi, Pandit Laxmi Shankar Misra advanced the cause of Hindustani. In a 1902 minutes, this ex-president questioned the very foundations of the sabha by saying that script may be Persian or Nagari but language has to combine Hindi and Urdu.[7]

Individuals who reshaped Hindi were actually doing the work of the British. This farcical attempt to invent Hindi as a national goal for 'Hindus' was at first not accepted by the Hindus. Way back in 1847 Dr. J.F. Ballantyne's (president of the English Department of Benaras College) students of Sanskrit weared his patience. The 'gentle' professor was trying to improve their 'Hindi' style by urging an exclusion of Urdu and Persian words. But the students were not listening. The professor lost his patience and ordered them to write an essay on 'Why do you despise the culture of the language you speak everyday of your lives, of the only language which your mothers and sisters understand?'

The topic was amazing. An Englishman was telling Hindus why they talked their natural language Urdu and Hindustani, as it was 'unnatural' (according to whom?)! He was telling them what their mothers and sisters spoke i.e. Sanskritised Hindi! A student was equally blunt in his response: 'We do not clearly understand what you Europeans mean by the term Hindi, for there are hundreds of dialects — and there is here no standard as there is in Sanskrit. If the purity of Hindi is to consist in its exclusion of Mussalman words, we shall require to study Persian and Arabic in order to ascertain which of the words we are in the habit of issuing everyday is Arabic or Persian, and which is Hindi. That you call the Hindi would eventually merge in some future modification of Ordoo, nor do we see any great cause of regret in this prospect'.[8]

The student also mentioned the fact that English words were also being naturalised in the village like Arabic and Persian so that it was impossible to invent a pure Sanskritised Hindi. Later, Gandhi himself advocated 'Hindustani' with a deliberate feebleness.

The elite Avadhian dissent also produced the science fiction of Dr. Neval Bihari Misra. This Sitapuri Kanyakubja improved upon the magical and scientific elements of Arabian tales to implant the H.G. Wells universe in Avadh. Misra's novels were dramatic and original as they combined latest technological developments with native sensuality. The explosive presence of this genre and trendy mind in an Avadhi qasba remained unknown to ordinary Hindi readers. Probably the 'social' aesthetics and ethics of the pure Hindiwallahs had no use of the basic scientific qualities of quest and adventure. And all this while Mahavira Prasad Dwivedi and Ram Charan Shukla were being advertised as humanists and men of science and reason.

By the '30s, another 'new light' was in the making. Inspired by the worldwide impact of the Soviet revolution, the growing communist movement at home and the general atmosphere of a national liberation struggle, a cultural revival shook the Lucknowi social scene. A churning of ideas produced new poetry, new stories, new painting and new dances in the form of a progressive art and literature movement.

A film industry also grew as part of a general revival in Bombay and Lahore. The progressive movement emerged from the efforts of a single figure, a rationalist whose first short story read like a miniature *Candide*. Sajjad Zaheer belonged to the Jaunpuri family of Ali Zaheer and worked up his ideas for the formation of a radical writers group in London with a team of like-minded friends over coffee and curry. In 1936 this group held a conference at the Rifah-e-aam in Lucknow which formally announced the setting up of a Progressive Writers Association (PWA). The Indian literary scene was never the same again. In 1932 Sajjad Zaheer published a volume of Urdu short stories which created such a storm that its publication was banned. Titled *Angare* or 'Burning Coals', it had five stories by Sajjad himself, two by Ahmad Ali, one by Mahmudu Zafar and two by a woman who belonged to Aligarh but had married into an elite Lucknowi family. Rashid Jahan's stories, *Dilli Ki Sair* and *Parde Ke Peech*, hit Lucknowi society like lightning. She was not the first woman to write prose in Urdu but with her a feminist and modern voice became established for the first time in twentieth century Urdu literature. Exposing the callousness of men against women with a refined bluntness that came naturally to Urdu, Rashid Jahan made 'burquawalis' speak out against their husbands. The indifferent world of men, who think they have done a great service to womenfolk by marrying, came in for scathing criticism. Sajjad Zaheer questioned blind belief in *Garmiyon Ki Ek Raat* and *Phir yeh Hungama* — the atheism and agnosticism of his themes came from Ghalib himself who had written many years ago referring to the existence of God —

'When all is you, and nought exists but you, Tell me, O' Lord, why all this turmoil too?'

But conservative society was not interested in what Ghalib had said. There was a polarisation in Muslim society over *Angare* of a type not seen since the days of Sir Syed. Only this time, the traditionalists were in western United Provinces, the modernists resided in Lucknow.

The '36 conference was also attended by Munshi Premchand, by then the foremost author of Hindi prose. He belonged to Benaras but had shifted his base to Avadh when the national movement began acquiring a mass-peasant character. While he wrote about the middle and lower classes of Benaras he was a Gandhian. When he came to Avadh his novel *Godan*, about the trials and tribulations of the backward caste peasantry amidst the backdrop of a changing elite society, was termed a modern classic. It also typified his genteel departure from Gandhism.

In the 1920s, Avadh saw a milltant peasant uprising which occupied a unique position amongst the variety of similar movements emerging elsewhere in India against the feudal system. Issues revolved around the removal of feudal cesses, nazar, security of tenure for the ryot or the dependant, largely non-occupancy, rentier peasantry. Leaders came from the backward castes and the affected areas spread all along the 1857 route — Rai Bareli, Pratapgarh, from where the legendary leader Baba Ramchandra hailed, Unnao, Hardoi, from where another leader Madari Pasi óriginated, Gonda, Bahraich, Barabanki, Sitapur. In Baba Ramchandra's movement, Lord Rama áppeared as a benefactor of the backward castes. Most of the Rajputs were either in the opposite camp or stood aloof — the post-1857 situation now struck the countryside with added agony. In some places the descendants of the heroes of '57 sided with the peasantry at great risk of opposition from their caste brethrens. But the memory of the revolt also ensured that most Rajputs were not in the direct line or target. The peasant ire was directed at the post-1857 landlords, many of them Sikhs and Bengalis.

In Premchand's writings there was no direct mention of the struggle; there was also no description of the force which benefited from the battle. The British government passed a rent act giving the peasant a limited security of tenure. But when the ryot returned to his field he found that in the fight with landlords, the fence sitters, i.e., the Brahmins and Banias belonging to the Congress, had gained. In the following years Baba Ramchandra became a wandering Congressman while Avadh remained a solid peasant bastion of the Congress. It proved resistant even to communist and socialist influences which swept aside the Congress in many areas of neighbouring Bihar and eastern Uttar Pradesh. Unlike these two areas, which became prominent in the '30s, a class shift had already taken place in the Avadhian countryside in the '20s. A peasant struggle had been fought without the aid of Marxist propaganda and the new power brokers of the countryside had consolidated their hold over the outcome of the movement.

Yet, an unexpected sort of reaction emerged from within the depths of the countryside. A foreign returned aristocrat, who had spent most of his adolescence and early youth in London collecting French Can miniatures, watching Rudolf Valentino and admiring the latest models of Isotta Fraschini, arrived in Kotwara, Lakhimpur Kheri. He was just twenty-six years of age and belonged to the Abhan lineage of Muslim Rajputs: the lineage of Raja Loni Singh of Mithauli, the great talukedar of Kheri who fought for Hazrat Mahal and was sentenced to the Andamans. His arrival in his home estate coincided with the Government of India Act of 1935 and the decision of the Congress to participate in the first ever elections held on the basis of a limited franchise. The young Avadhi with sharp features, who spoke the rough 'bangar' sub-dialect of Avadhi, Urdu and English with the same flair decided to enter electoral politics. His first, pro-peasant manifesto described the Congress as the party of the 'bania' and the sugar barons of Avadh.

Raja Sajid Hussian won the elections from Lakhimpur. The sugarcane farmers had fought from the begum's side; now they sided with the surviving legatee of that struggle against the neo-rich. History repeated itself strangely; the handsome figure who brought the Isotta Fraschini because Valentino did it too was as smug and proud in his Avadhi gesture as the old modernist-aristocrats of Avadh. This combination of style and rusticity proved too much for the Congress. The British authorities, who first tried to use him against the Congress but then found him too hot to handle, were also stumped. The raja rode home in jubilation celebrating his victory achieved without any help from the Muslim League. Brimming with energy, he began schemes of self-employment in the region and advocated an agricultural policy favourable to sugarcane farmers. A few months before the elections in 1937, Jawaharlal Nehru had announced at Lucknow an intended pro-gramme of agrarian development and abolition of landlordism. Such a stand would have benefited the peasantry but in places like Lakhimpur it sided with the raja rejecting the Congress. Why? Because it had a realist, grassroot view of the new face of the Congress — a party that was now coming to be dominated increasingly by middlemen and agro-traders struggling to emerge as leaders of rural society.

The raja was probably the last of the Lucknowi-Avadhi aristocrat-entrepreneur. His palace in Kotwara was built like the Khurshid Manzil, his life in Lucknow spent in a spell of perfect romance. He married a Turkish princess, a descendant from the family of the Khalifa, and for four years, till her death in Paris in the early '40s, she was the perfect

Joan Crawford to his Gablian demeanour. Their drives by the Gomti in the Sunbeam, Studebaker, Citron, Hupmobile, Ford and the Wolksol, their apparel which recalled costumes from a Hollywood film, took the city by storm.

As a follower of the Indian marxist, Manabendra Nath Roy, the raja had leftist sympathies. He was founder member of the Scottish Communist Party — one of the many adventures he indulged in while in England. But his brand of an aristocratic, rooted leftism did not find favour with the middle class leftists of Lucknow, more inclined to the Congress brand of nationalism. Prisoners of the Aligarh brand of modernity, they carried neither a rustic gesture nor an Indo-Persian style.

In a society like Avadh, where high and low cultures intermingled in unity and struggle, the Victorian middle class values of left-modernists isolated them from the history and culture of the Indo-Gangetic plain. This proved fatal to the Indian Communist movement as it was evident from the very beginning that the whole issue of 'power' in pre and post-independent India would be decided by the United Provinces.

Leftists lost out to Gandhi on the issue of the peasants. The Mahatma became the authentic voice of rural tradition even when his ideas and gestures revolted against the ethos of the Hindi-Urdu belt. The bastion of Indian ancient society, this was a region waiting for a peasant revolution since 1857. During '57, an officers corp, capable of leading successful bayonent charges against fixed British positions in open combat, was greatly missed. Seventy years later, communists could have acted as professional 'officers corp' of the Indian peasantry. They knew that the entire Indian status quo of contemporary times was based on a negation of 1857. Its blind and politically intimidating invocation of tradition hid the insecurity of the parvenu. It actually lacked the cultural and moral legitimacy necessary for political hegemony. 1857 was central, more important than general socialist-modernist ideals, to the establishment of a counter moral authority and hegemony.

But for years the communists did not even formulate a party programme let alone a policy for a moral-cultural war of position. Therefore, they kept missing a focus on agrarian change, the natural turf of this war. The peasant question was approached without the armour of 'quotes' from *Panchatantra*, Shukracharya and Brihaspati, Nizamuddin Auliya, Tipu Sultan, Hazrat Mahal and Beni Madho. In the end, the Indian leftist subconscious did not the carry the ada, andaz, mizaj and methodology of the *Arthashastra* or the *Ain-i-Akbari*.

A cultural challenge to the British also came from a friendlier source in Lucknow. When British ladies were still dancing the waltz and discussing the misadventures of Miss Becky Sharp in the Chattar Manzil, the dance floor of a club, surrounded by rows of plush, green grass, and shades drawn like hats, was resonating with the voices of the young. They caroused to the beat of the swing and the jive, playing out latest jazz numbers. In dim lights young boys and girls read the more whackier stuff coming out from the 'underbelly' of Western literature. These 'masters of culture' had a white skin which glistened with native heat. Their English was immaculate but the accent was Urduish with the 'Q' and 'GH' coming deep from within the throat. Looked down by the British these Anglo-Indians* of Lucknow had more style than many a sahib.

They kept alive city bars and patronised Chinese shoemakers in Hazratganj. Girls in their new found skirts with a faint knowledge of the 'roaring '20s' in the West became the perfect 'Colonel's daughter' while struggling for a life beyond the Sunday visit to the church and the roll call of the school. But their aspirations for bobbed hair, silk stockings and love did not lead necessarily to tragedy. Everything from imported watches, raincoats, purses, shoes, umbrellas, clothes, right down to the prickly needle then in vogue, was available at Whiteway Ladlow & Co. at Hazratganj. Owned by a British proprietor this departmental store had branches at Delhi, Shimla and Mussoorie as well.

For boys, it sold the best ties and flannel trousers and they, with their culture of handshake and the curtsies to the 'miss', brought Lucknow close to a native version of Bohemian, anglicised etiquette.

---

* This refers to the Anglo-Indian 'community'. Earlier, the term 'Anglo-Indian' was used to denote the social-cultural trend, applicable to Hindus, Muslims and Indian Christians as much as to people of the Anglo-Indian community, born out of a fusion of British and Indian influences. This term has been used interchangeably in this and other chapters.

Anglo-Indian families encouraged individual freedom though most of them hailed from a lower middle or working class ethos. Living around places like the Lawrence Terrace, they were the sons and daughters of railway foremen, head clerks and station masters. Some of them occupied high ranks and a position of pre-eminence in education and medicine, the women amongst them becoming pioneering principals of leading colleges. This section gave Lucknow a 'non-colonial', Western feel — the West of cinema and pastry shops, the tweed jacket and the muffler, Benny Goodman and the Fax and the Crow series.

During the extremely hot summers, the Gomti was no longer the only haven for repose. Led by Anglo-Indians and native Christians, the roads of pleasure led to a site of dusty romanticism — the race course. Built on the far side of the Dilkusha, away from the city, British ladies appeared in its shades in hats, ribbons and frilled skirts. They reflected an unihibited sophistication which converted the sprawling complex of grass into an Ascot of north India. There the Indo-Persian aristocracy, in gold and silver robes and swords, rubbed shoulders with high ranking British officers and the Anglo-Indian elite.

Nurtured in a culture of convent education this elite was drawn from Sindhis, Punjabis, Parsis and Muslims who had done well in business and other professions. Races were held twice a week with special events organised for the army cup and the civil service cup day. A band dished out tunes to the regalia in display and after the races the stewards used to retire to the committee room with their wives. The room had a bar and a verandah where a dance would end the evening.

Race horses were imported or brought in from Bombay and the jockeys became the *enfant terribles* of the city with their wild escapades and pluck. They were superseded in this only by the tennis stars. Ghaus Mohammad of Malihabad and his doubles partner Iftikhar Hussain turned the grass court lawns of the Avadh Gymkhana at Qaiserbagh into the breeding ground of Indian tennis. India's number one Ghaus Mohammad was a true Lucknowi. Known for his precision and etiquette, he never let go of the killer instinct. He belonged to the early generation of sportsmen from the Hindi-Urdu belt; individuals coming from the middle class, rural families who dominated Indian sports with their combination of earthiness and novelty. These 'sons of the soil' included Dhyan Chand and Lucknow's very own hockey captain, K.D. Singh 'Babu'.

The race course was also a place where star crossed lovers conducted their affairs with elan. Here, intellect met with pleasure; *The Pioneer* was read with zest which Kipling would have found amusing in his fair 'Nacklau'. The paper moved from Allahabad to Lucknow in the 1930s and was being financed by talukedar houses like Jehangirabad, as well as by a self-made industrialist of Kanpur, Sir Jwala Prasad Srivastava.

The Pioneer, functioning for long under the genial patronage of S.N. Ghosh, was soon challenged by a newspaper which, while enjoying a wide readership in the older areas of the city, was still out of bounds at the race course. This was the *National Herald*, the paper of the Congress and the Nehrus with Firoze Gandhi as the manager and Chelapati Rao as the editor. Rao and Ghosh were poles apart. If one saw himself as the fiery nationalist, the other reflected more on language and the British mode of 'interesting' advertising. If one was geared towards elaborating ideas, the other went into planning to create the value of sensational news. *The Pioneer* rivalled the *Times of India*, Lucknow being the only place from where any competition appeared to the Bombay based monopoliser of Indian news and views. *National Herald* competed with the *Leader* and the *Northern India Patrika*, the other two nationalist papers being published from Allahabad. The United Provinces had a very significant section of English newspaper readers, a majority of whom were avid Urdu and Hindi speakers as well.

The National Herald was also served by Babu Mohan Lal Saxena who, by 1942, had turned into an underground revolutionary with a price of Rs. 10,000 on his head. Along with C.B. Gupta he was one of the first legislators from the city and became a minister in the Govind Ballabh Pant ministry which came to power in 1937. By the early '40s, the ministry had resigned. It had failed to deliver on many fronts and its popularity was in doubt when the Second World War and British intransigence in yielding to even a modicum of Indian demands led to the hardening of the Congress stand. A call of 'do or die' came from Mahatma Gandhi who began the last and the most radical phase of his life.

The Quit India call on 9 August saw a massive movement in

Lucknow. Most Congress leaders were arrested before Mohanlal Saxena's 'illegal' entry into the city on 1 September. At that point Lucknow had already changed socially and demographically with the regaining of some lost areas of 1857. The Dallybagh was now inhabited and new colonies had come up in the eastern side. Aishbagh was still embroiled in deep silt and dirt but new shops stood prominently in the demolished areas of the Chowk. The Carlton Hotel owned by Shah Najaf along with the Royal Hotel, catered exclusively to a British and elite-Indian clientele. The Burlington Hotel owned by Jaan Muhammad was more amenable to Indians. The Carlton, however, had the best bar which sold the White Horse whisky and the Blue Riband gin. Its flamboyant British owners ran hotels in Mussoorie as well. Apart from the Carlton, the best eating out place was the Kelners' at Charbagh, part of a chain of railway restaurants spread out in the eastern sector of the Indian railways. There were similar chains in the northern and southern sectors known by the brand names of Spencers and Brandons. They laid out excellent four course dinners in the best crockery and heavy silver cutlery. The bearers served the best whisky and cocktails in starched uniforms and turbans and the bar man could outwit a gentleman of calling with a joke or two. In Hazratganj, Vikajee's car showroom housed the latest Chevrolets, Fords and limousines. The Council House had a number or roads running towards the Gomti and the heart of the city, named after British officers, parallel to the complex of parks and offices that had come up in the eastern and the southern part.

It was this Lucknow which saw the flaring up of buildings during 1942. Railway stations at Alam-Nagar and the city were attacked, post offices burned and the university closed down after the arrest of a number of students. For a brief moment, the memory of 1857 came alive, albeit on a much smaller scale — just as the era of Indo-Persian, Bohemianism had preceded the great conflagration, one of Anglo-Indian elegance was still in action when the first shops were set ablaze. Like 1857, local sarais became suspect — the Mahavir Hotel was thought to be the centre of revolutionaries where posters in Hindi and Urdu were stuck. Lucknow became a formidable base of the Revolutionary Socialist Party (RSP) which openly indulged in violent acts in order to dislodge the British.

One of the more daring acts was the looting of the Calcutta Commercial Bank in broad daylight. On the day of the attack, boys in dhotis, vests and shirts were seen running here and there giving cover to attackers. From the old parts of the city, girls in their long plaited hair, and the full sleeved salwar kameez, came out with threatening postures. Even school boys came forth with their quota of armed activity by serving as 'tamancha' bearing conduits. At places Anglo-Indians also extended spontaneous help to the revolutionaries.

Soon the Mehboobganj office of the RSP was confiscated. Repression and destruction began anew in the old areas and there was a semi exodus from the city. Not many were killed but such was the memory of the repression of 1857 that psychologically, people went into a state of shock at the threat of another round of savage reprisal.

14

❦

A Deadly Game and a Tragic Consequence

Bathed in blood
The land of Bailey Guard
Tells a tale
That the war of independence
Was first fought
In this place

— Fazal

Even before the uprising of 1942 could let off anti-British steam, children from Golaganj and Chowk had developed their own favourite past time and sport. Cautious of the watchful eyes of their parents, they would sneak out from their lanes towards the Residency, known in folklore as 'Bailey Garad'. The symbol of the historic battle of Lucknow was now desolate. The main buildings were left in their state to commemorate the 'heroism' of British men and women. A Union Jack flew constantly over the central tower — it was the only flag in the whole of the British empire not lowered at dusk.

A living symbol of foreign power and Indian humiliation, the Union Jack rankled the Lucknowites. The British had constructed several monuments and plaques in memory of their dead inside the Residency which disparaged the 'rebels'. The land around the place, on which stood graves of old and venerated Muslim figures, was also in their possession.

For the Congress, the Residency was a burning issue. It was too dear to British sensitivity and invoked a memory which went beyond Gandhian non-violence. Till Subhas Chandra Bose stopped with the 'rebel' Indian National Army (INA) at Bahadur Shah Zafar's grave in Rangoon to remember 1857 with tears and anger, the great uprising was not part of the official, nationalist iconography. V.D. Savarkar's angry biography[1], which termed 1857 as a war of independence and not a mutiny, was surreptitiously sidetracked by Nehru. While endorsing Savarkar's title, he preferred to term the uprising the last flicker of 'feudal India'.[2] Here, as elsewhere, Nehru preferred to ride on two horses.[3] Lucknowi aristocrats too were fond of commenting, in private, upon 'Nehruvian doublespeak' — which doled out platitudes and 'words of wisdom' about the entire world from Anand Bhavan, Allahabd.

A personality like Nehru was certainly out of touch with the Hindustan of the Ramayana, Mahabharata, *Ain-i-Akbari* and Arthashastra. He single-handedly defined a half-baked, positivist, intellectualist agenda for the post-independence academic establishment. Lacking the subtlety, openness and grandeur of their leader these liberal-left minds could not produce a consistent theory of the ancient Indian state or medieval socio-economic structures in fifty years. Habituated in seeing the Ramayana as 'mythology', and Mughals as lacking the potential of a capitalist development, they might have been better off writing commentaries on the Bible or the British Constitution. Their reign could not even demolish the colonial propoganda about the British uniting India.

The only exception to this rule was the pre-independence Allahabad school of history. Emerging much before the blanket rule of Nehruvian brown sahibs, it revived focus on Mughal history in opposition to the anti-Indo-Persian bent of the Bengal school. At that time. D.D. Koshambi too was beginning his study of ancient Indian history. But the Maharashtrian Brahmin-pioneer-Marxist could not cross the social, cultural and historical barrier from the 'ancient to the medieval'. While dealing with the ancient too, he could not see the dialectical materialism of power in mainstream Hindu-Brahminical thought. Indo-Persianism remained remote and 1857, 'non progressive'. Yet, Koshambi's rooted renaissance mind traced the problems of the twentieth century, 'Bombay club' capitalists to their late nineteenth post '57, comprador origin as 'go-between dalaals'.[4]

While the older generation in Lucknow brooded over the Residency issue, the children evolved their own method of revenge. Once inside the Bailey Garad, they played their favourite game. One became a rebel while another an Englishman; the gulels, or slingshot, came out and a shooting match ensued. Whoever 'shot' the maximum number of 'Englishmen' was declared the winner in the contest and donned the mantle of a hero till the next round.

The Residency came back to haunt Lucknowites soon after 15 August 1947. The British had left and the country was free. Earlier, the 1946 elections had seen the installation of another provincial Congress government led by Govind Ballabh Pant with C.B. Gupta and Mohan Lal Saxena as ministers. Political happenings at the national level, like the coming of the Cabinet Mission, the debate over the Muslim League's demand for a separate state of Pakistan, and radical upheavals in other parts of the country led by the communists, took precedence over local sentiments and issues.

After Ali Muhammad's death, the Muslim League lost its base in Lucknow. The formation remained weak in the city till factional politics in the Congress drove Khaliqulzaman into its arms. In the '46 elections, the League scored impressive gains in the United Provinces. There were other shifts in the Congress — Kanyakubja Brahmins and Khatris were now more conspicuous by their absence. The family of Jai Karan Nath Misra had entered the field of education and social services and Lucknowi Vajpeyis withdrew into professions and dissent. Old Congress Muslim leaders had either died or been pushed away from active scene.

During the decisive years of 1946-47, when north India was buring with communal frenzy, not a single riot occurred in Lucknow. League-Congress politics went on as usual but religious passions were not instigated by even a single fiery statement. The Maharashtra based Rashtriya Swayam Sevak Sangh (RSS) and other militant pro-Hindu parties too changed their tone when it came to the city. Instead of rabid

The ruined late eighteenth century gate of qasba Newalganj -
the gateway to mofussil capitalism.
(top) Kothi Bibiapur in the late eighteenth century.

(top left to right)
Burhan-ul-Mulk (1722-1738) - the sensation begins.
Asaf- ud - Daula (1774-1798), lets make a culture!
Saadat Ali Khan (1798-1814) - science, administration,
leisure and pleasure.
Nasiruddin Haider (1827-1837)
Wajid Ali Shah (1847-1856)
(courtesy, Picture Gallery)

Sham-e-Avadh.

The Sat Khanda - Lucknow's leaning tower of Pisa,
unfinished like Lucknow's possibilities.

'To the sacred' memory of
the 'British dead'.
(below) The sensation and
passion of Moharram.
(courtesy Ravi Kapoor)

Hollywood in Lucknow.

The Tikait Rai bridge, Kakori.

The ceiling of the Bara Imanbara - early '60s restaurant decor!

*Avadhian revolutionaries -
even then the
Thakur - Brahmin - Sheikh
- Saiyyad Pathan 'ada'
is perceptible.*
(courtesy Residency Shed)

*Havelock's grave at
Alambagh.*
(courtesy Residency Shed)

*The seige train passing
through Shahnajaf.*
(courtesy Residency Shed)

16

anti-Pakistan propaganda, the Hindu Mahasbha and RSS pamphlets printed in Lucknow called upon Hindus to exercise daily to improve their physical and mental health for the coming independence. The RSS was overshadowed in the city by the Hindu Mahasabha. Led by Maheshvar Dayal Seth, Kunwar Guru Narain Seth and the anti '57, Sidhauli family of Talukedar Raja Rampal Singh in Lucknow, its 'Hindu Rashtravaad' fed upon Malviya's Sanatan Dharma. Both Santan Dharma and Hindu Mahasabhaism were given a Western-fascist dimension by Guru Golwalker, the 'first' RSS ideologue. Golwarkarism was indigenised into Rashtriya Ekatmvaad by Deen Dayal Upadhyaya, the 'second' RSS ideologue. Rashtriya Ekatmavaad was historicised and anglicised by the Jan Sangh, the political arm of the RSS, as India's non-Ganga-Yamuni tehzeeb civilisational identity — or Hindutva.

When the moment of destiny arrived, Lucknowites did not mix celebration with fear and apprehension. Unlike other cities of the United Provinces, there was very little foreboding of independence being marred by mayhem. The real issue before Lucknowi crowds was a different one. Driven, as if by instinct, their feet turned towards the one spot which had long excited their suppressed imagination — the Residency. People began gathering at the site and numbers swelled as cries went up for the pulling down of offensive British plaques and the installation of the Indian flag at the central tower.

The fact that historical revenge would be sought was amply clear to the British. GOC Eastern Command Francis Tuker's job in August 1947 was well-defined and clear. He was to operate from the capital to extend help in combatting and controlling the spread of communalism in the United Provinces. But Tuker's mind was somewhere else; on the night before British withdrawal, he ordered British troops into the Residency, removed the Union Jack and demolished the flagstaff.[5]

The crowds, however, were not deterred by Tuker's trickery. They crossed the gateway and forced their way into the main compound, proclaiming 1857 'rebels' as national heroes. They were almost about to fulfill their intention of hoisting the tricolour when a grand old figure intervened. He stopped the crowd, told them to go home, and leave in peace a spot so sacred to the 'British dead'. His name was 'Dhadhu', better known as Govind Ballabh Pant. As a Congressman he had led the independence movement. Yet, on that fateful day, he stood firmly with a tear for the sacred memory of the British. He did not utter a word about the thousands of Indians sepoys, Ahirs and Pasis who died shooting arrows and placing mines around the Residency.

Ninety years ago, another Brahmin and Pant, 'Dhondu Pant' Nana Sahib, led the Hindu and Muslim society against the British. He was a pucca Hindu, in whose name the Brahmins of Kanpur used to swear. Yet, he spoke and behaved like a Muslim and his proclamations during the revolt, which began with bismillah, were fine examples of Indo-Persian popular propaganda. Now Dhadhu Pant, who bore Nana's caste mark much more zealously, toned down the pitch of historical passion. Pant's action proved that Congressmen were not true bourgeoisie or aristocrat nationalists. Part of a rentier, dependant intelligentsia, they played out an Indian version of comprador nationalism common to many third world liberated countries.

The leader of this nationalism. Pandit Jawaharlal Nehru, gave India a republican constitution and a democratic system on the British Westminster model. He also kept the RSS in check, not by Indo-Persianism but a soft interpretation of the post '57 'Hindutva' and Western style bureaucratic legalism. But Nehru could not separate the state from religion, nor could he become a legatee of pre-'57 traditions of religious and secular humanism.

In free India, imperial laws, penal codes and administrative struc-tures were left untouched. So was the British system of justice which concentrated on arbitrary, unaccounted power in the hands of the judges. Under this system even a simple matter of granting of bail was left at .the judge's discretion with no clear-cut-laws defining the issue. British laws were vague, ponderous and highly personalised, suited to imperial designs. Their continuance in independent India undermined democracy, civil rights and the very praxis and theory of the rule of impersonal law. The British ethnic system of army oganisation was also not reversed. This prevented the Indian army from emerging as a symbol of India's cultural heritage and national pride. Under the garb of Nehruvian pacifism military energies were caged in a prison of inferiority complexes and diverted towards anti-Pakistanism.

In the '40s, the navy had 'mutinied' against the British at Bombay and their movement was joined in by the working classes and ordinary people of the city. Congress leaders, however, condemned the revolt going against all established conventions of modern nationalism. Their negative attitude towards Subhash Chandra Bose and his attempt to defeat the British through an armed combat also smacked of a strange, conservative attitude. Yet, there was no justification of not changing the army structure once independence was attained. Did the Indian political class fear the political potential of a united army?

In Lucknow, the Council House became the Vidhan Sabha and the United Provinces, under the new name of Uttar Pradesh, dominated India politically with its large contingent of eighty-five Parliament members. Lucknow was still the capital where nothing much changed after 1947. Muslim families did not migrate in large numbers and people who left for Pakistan were motivated more by the prospect of getting away from the dominating shadow of their fathers than any League propaganda.

Stories revolving around migration spoke of a cultural despair at the new India than any communal hostility. In a leading Lucknowi family, there was a young man whose father typified the Muslim angst. First a Congress sympathiser, he switched over to the League and then found a place midway between the two. Even though he supported the formation of Pakistan he never summoned the will to migrate. He was also unhappy with his son — a product of the Aligarh Muslim University, the boy was in love with an Anglo-Indian girl. The son was a progressive; unlike his father he liked Majaz and Josh and spent time in the hills of Mussoorie and Nainital.

From the late nineteenth century onwards, the aristocracy of Avadh had patronised these two hill stations of Uttarakhand. There was something wildly mysterious about Mussoorie and Nainital, which was not evident in Kashmir or the British and Punjabi Rajput stations of Himachal Pradesh. Kashmir was the paradise of royal splendour; Simla and Manali, islands of classic 'peasant' love. But Garhwal and Kumaon formed the perfect backdrop for aristocratic, 'knightly' adventure between the king and the peasant. Their winding paths, dense jungles and curvaceous hills possessed a dryness' similar to the soil of Avadh and common to tales of risk and achievement. They were centres of romance and war during the days of nawabi Avadh. The hills of Almora and Garhwal witnessed bloodshed during 1857; post-'57 they became the hunting and resting ground of the caged aristocracy. Here, cottages were built in the style of the Chota Imambara and stories of tragedy, heroism and valour added to the mystery of the local landscape.

In them, the aristocracy fought with British contractors and the local lass, herself a daughter of some Garhwali Rajput, gave her heart to the young adventurer from Lucknow. The denounement of their love story arrived usually on a dark, stormy night atop the four-storey manzil which gave the raw beauty of the hills a Jaunpuri-Lucknow sheen. By the early years of the twentieth century, glamour was added to aristocratic remoteness with the opening up of Anglo-Indian restaurants, bars and the adventures of Jim Corbett.

But by the '40s, the high society life was on the wane. Garhwal and Kumaon were fast becoming tourist attractions for the middle classes and perpetual retiring spots for English authors. The young Indo-Persian gentleman of Lucknow had his last ball at Mussoorie's Savoy Hotel with his Anglo-Indian girlfriend. When he returned to Lucknow parental pressures and the uncertain conditions of the time, which made inevitable the later migration of both the Muslim and the Anglo-Indian to separate destinations, prevailed. He got engaged to a prospective bride of his parents choice even as his girl prepared to leave the country. The son got to know of this when her train was about to depart for Delhi. He wanted to give her a memento but his father had manipulated even the knowledge of departure. He reached the station only to see the final glimpse of his beloved — it was of remorse and contempt. He glanced at the memento — the glow of the 'khooni neelam', tied to a ladies' ribbon in the typical '40s style, had faded.

He never forgot that look. Outwardly, he followed his father's biddings and got married, but inwardly, he was getting ready for defiance. He knew that his father was emotional about Avadh and would never leave India. And yet he had scolded and humiliated him in front of friends for speaking out against the League. As predicted, when the time came, the father stayed back. But he got the news that the son had left for Pakistan leaving his wife behind. The father never recovered from the shock.

The Muslim diaspora of Lucknow treaded a different path. Ali Muhammad Mahmudabad's son, Amir Ahmad Khan, who had evolved into a trendy 1940s version of his father, did not wish to go to Pakistan. But Jawaharlal Nehru was no Motilal to him — he felt alienated and lost in the '30s and the '40s, retreating to the pleasures of his brother Mahmud Hasan Khan's marriage in 1939. This was the last of Lucknowi style weddings and played out grandeur in a moving silhouette. Dolis and taifas of dominis and mirasins arrived from all over Avadh with musicians of Lucknow. On the day of the main festivity, the city was hit by a thunder bolt. Three big names arrived to entertain the guests — Akhtari Bai Faizabdi, Wahidan Bai and Jaddan Bai regaled the aristocracy with the last grand performance of the old mujra. Years later, Nimmi and Nargis, the daughters of Wahidan and Jaddan, were to make a great name for themselves and their mothers in the Bombay film industry. No wonder Lucknowis remained condescending towards Bombay's glittering pretensions.

For each of the seven days, the cuisine followed a different pattern. One day, everything was prepared with gram flour as the base; the next day, two kinds of salan, two kinds of korma, six kinds of pulao, even the sweetmeats, had something of colocasia in them. Dishes such as the murg badam, shikhampur kebab, noor mahali pulao were heard of, and eaten, for the last time. Kebab kofte had meat balls dressed up like burning, brown coals — they melted in the mouth leaving an aftertaste which combined the sweet teekhapan of the bayleaf, the mustiness of pulses and turmeric and the raw refinement of cooked mutton.

Guests at the wedding were served with an extraordinary dessert invented originally by Wajid Ali Shah. The last king was a great cook and gourmet fan. Even Bahadur Shah Zafar had prepared a sweetmeat concoction which left an aftertaste of pepper and bittergourd.

In the night colour and fragrance was added to the cuisine by clothes, jewellery and perfumes. Kundun work with diamonds and pearls bung on slender necks and the lapels of the farshi gharara rustled the floor with vanity and elegance. Made up of charm, wood and flower, perfumes excited exotic and erotic passions. The charm could be of 'mushk', drawn from the belly of the deer, possessing the special quality of keeping alive the lovely smell for more than twenty to thirty years.

The wood could be of khas, kevda, agar, ud and ambar and flowers of the bela, chameli and genda as per the seasonal mood. For summers the wood was khas, the flower, rose; wild trees and the motiya flower was used for monsoons and winters produced the exquisite 'shamam tulamber' combination. But during the wedding, seasons mixed to produce a kaleidoscope of sensations.

When a lady smoked a hookah with restraint in the karvati pose, she embellished it with a range of sweetened tobacco. At such times, she wore dresses laced with zardozi work and studded gota falls, covered herself from head to toe with chandanhaar, karn phools and pazebs. The jamboree of precious details produced a throbbing, overpowering smell exclusive to a physical assembly of women. Sexy, material, salty and divine, the odour combined the scent of sweat, perfume, female skin, hookah, gota, silver, gold, henna and missi.

Only one other event matched the dream wedding and that took place way back in 1935. In that year an industrial and agricultural exhibition was organised by Sir Jwala Prasad at the pond of the Muhammad Ali Shah's baradari, now functioning as a park and picture gallery. A British made Hussienabad clock tower, built in the quasi-Indic style, also stood in the old nawabi complex. Sir Jwala Prasad reclaimed the site to launch an Avadhian 'fair' for a few days. Valerios, Lucknow's best cafeteria, shifted shop beyond the Rumi Darwaza and the whole city followed suit. Fashionable ladies set up their stalls, the men put on their best suits, achkans and shervanis and miniature boats sailed in the pond. Imported greyhounds ran races for the first and last time in Lucknow. Evenings ended in a dance — couples waltzed in the background of the Daulat Khana with the Bara Imambara and the baradari standing at a panoramic distance, the sound of the violin intermingling with the fading glory of the lakhauri. A meeting of Indo-Persian sheen with Anglo-Indian style, the temporary uion was cut short by the events of the '50s.

In that decade. Amir Ahmad left for Pakistan, disillusioned about the new India. Propitious circumstances could have turned his drive and ambition towards playing the role of an industrialist, statesman or a cultural ambassador for India. But these slots were going over to other forces — business to marwaris and the banias, politics to babus and

Brahmins and statesmanship to the 'yes men' of Congress leaders. Far back, in the late nineteenth and the early twentieth century, the British had thwarted the industrial ambitions of some enterprising talukedars. They had conspired to close down the industrial enterprise of Salempur and were alarmed when anyone bearing the legacy of 1857, like the raja of Bhutwamau, dared to extend forms of entrepreneurship in Avadh. Neither allowed to invest or divest, the talukedars paid a heavy price for Sir Harcourt Butler's romanticism.

Amir Ahmad's voyage to Pakistan did not rattle the new rulers of Lucknow but dealt a death blow to the city. The business enterprises of Kanyakubja and Kayastha families folded up by 1947. Kanyakubja Brahmins had factories of indigo and salt in partnership with Thakurs and Muslims. They also flirted with the idea of opening cotton mills on the pattern of Kanpur.[6] These pandits were big egoists and individualists; they travelled first class and beat up racist English fellow travellers and rangroots. But their initiatives and dreams collapsed when influential and disillusioned Misras of Ganjmoradabad and Meerasarai migrated to England, America and Scandinavian countries in the '50s. Only the perfume and sandalwood industry of Kannauj reminded one of the lost age of Brahmin entrepreneurship.

In the post-independence period, Madhya Pradesh and Vidarbha in Maharashtra emerged as new Kanyakubja Brahmin bastions. A literary, professional and political revival followed but the post-'57 re-definition was now complete. Brahmins were transformed into role model government servants — honest, flexible and bloodless with a lost memory of a warrior history.

Ironically, this very decade saw the coming of age of the 'Bombay club' Indian bourgeoisie. At times like these it became understandable why members of Benaras and Agra merchant families, who had sided with the British during the decisive battle of Lucknow, were in the habit of burning their British marked 'rupee' in the late nineteenth century.[7] Consciously or unconsciously, they were expressing remorse at a lost opportunity, the full realisation of which could have seen entrepreneurs and magnates of United Provinces emerge as the dominant bourgeoisie of the country.

At the northeastern end of Avadh, the raja of Kotwara relived another kind of a tragedy. By the early '50s the romantic prince was fast turning into an internal recluse. He had opposed the Congress and the sugar lobby and now the opponents bayed for their pound of flesh. In 1952, zamindari abolition was announced in Uttar Pradesh. But no large scale transfer of landed property followed the move. The UP agriculture minister and the chief architect of land reforms in the state, Charan Singh, had already written in 1947 that the manifesto of the Congress 'does not seek the elimination of the zamindar. Abolition of zamindari' simply means, and ought to mean, abolition of the landlord-tenant system and no more.'[8]

When abolition did come amidst talukedari and zamindari opposition, only the intermediary role of the landlords, between the government and tenantry, was scrapped. The tenants were allowed to buy back their land from the government which favoured the privileged few amongst them. Theoretically, the political and economic role of the landlords was over. But practical policy ensured the endurance of the old order. The old aristocracy was broken, but power did not pass on to the peasantry. Middle men-Congress office holders, sugar lobby power brokers and the henchmen of old landlords reaped the maximum benefit. Writing in the *National Herald* under the pseudonym Shekhar, a radical Congress intellectual exposed the Uttar Pradesh land reforms: 'One is forced to draw the conclusion — that landlordism is not being abolished but the zamindari system is being replaced by new forms of landlordism. The land hunger, the symptom of acute agrarian crisis, is left intact and the insolvent rack rented undersized ninety-five per cent peasants do not draw any benefit from this abolition scheme. Politically it is a device to extend and stabilise the social base of the present government.[9]

In Avadh, the abolition of the zamindari system was also underwritten by a subtle communal policy. The Muslim landlords were asked to pack up and retire to Lucknow, while the Hindu zamindars were allowed surreptitiously, without anything ever entering the records, to keep huge portions of land. The loopholes in the act, which allowed the zamindars to keep their 'sir' and grove lands plus retain a large area under false and genuine names of relatives, friends and servants, advantaged the Hindu ex-talukedars. They took full advantage of their proximity to local officials of the government in an atmosphere vitiated by the sectarian ill will of partition. The only pro-'57 element to gain from the process was the Kalakankar house of Pratapgarh, the complete list of post-'47 Avadhian landlords reading like a 'whose who' of 'betrayers' in the revolt. Later, some Muslim landlords too got the benefit of being close to the Congress or staying quiet in the hour of changing equations.

There was also a section which opposed the Congress while asserting its Hindu identity, or others who were not very big landlords earlier but became so on the strength of their economic status and relations with the ruling party. The Raja of Mankapur fell in the former slot. He joined the right wing Swatantra Party and defeated the Congress from his district in Gonda in the early '50s. His son, however, joined the Congress and spread his hold to become a fish exporter. Earning huge sums of money, he emerged as a landlord-capitalist, using his vast resources for profit. But he did not introduce modern farming or agro-industry in Gonda, retaining, quite artfully, the culture of extra-economic extraction and semi-feudal land relations. Mankapur became a model for others following a similar, parasitic, landlord path to capitalist development. Vast amounts of land were held in unproductive holdings leading to a huge waste of national resources. The development of regions was kept in check by these landlords who controlled elected bodies by force and created a very efficient network of corruption throughout their domains.

Old aristocratic culture was turned on its head. New uncultured men from amongst the Rajputs, like the raja of Kunda in Pratapgarh, a 'little man' before independence, emerged as real tyrants, who now treated courtesans as 'kept' women. Inventing new forms of torture, such as crocodile ponds, and punishment by whipping became their favourite past time. Noble individuals drifted into a wandering life — the offsprings of Kalakankar became ambassadors, politicians and men of style attracting beauty, brain *and* the daughter of Josef Stalin.

The Brahmin Kanyakubja aristocracy of Avadh and Doab also folded up in the wake of the Congress-Bania-small men onslaught. The Sukul, Pandey, Misra, Vajpeyi and Tiwari families of Balan, Khor, Majgaon, Vajpeyi Khera and Jehangirabad lost their 100, 200, 500 village zamindaris getting as little as Rs. 2,000-Rs. 4000 in compensation.

Hereafter, 'the pandit' became permanently typecast as the fanatically puritan, vegetarian, 'anti-Muslim' maharaj of Bania households with the notoriously 'inert', poori-Kondha taste bud. His alter ego appeared as the parasitic and wily purohit.

The fiery Brahmini became the fat panditayan; women born in the 1890s or the 1900s, who remained alive till the 1980s, were the last in the line of chabeeli-great grandmothers who quoted the Ramcharitmanas and lines from Shakespeare in one breath. They seldom stepped out from the four walls of their houses and yet were more modern than the educated daughters-in-law of the '40s and '50s by then firmly under the conservative, Arya Samaji, Sanatan Dharmi grip of the 'new Hindu woman' image. Taught at home by Maulvis, Pandits and English teachers, they were the ones who asked their daughters-in-law to remove their veils and sit on the bed, above the ground, with the mother-in-law.

The old Brahmini made and unmade unconventions whenever she liked. Once an Arya Samaji, a man schooled in the teachings of the Hindi-Bengali literature, approached a grand old woman of Lucknow. He wanted proper sanction for the pure Indian woman concept then in vogue from a traditional 'amma', but on being informed about the purity of Indian women, she drew a blank expression, looked upto the man and said:

Jano beta koi videsi soch laye ho. Apni zindagi mein hi ham kabhau naye suna. Aurat, aurat hot hai; uhme pavitra aur apavitra kya? Unke jiyae naye hot kaa?

(It seems, son, that you have brought home a foreign thought. Never heard of such a thing in my life. A woman is a woman; what is pure and impure about her? Don't they have a normal temperament like everyone else?).

This Brahmini had a superior colleague — the high cheekboned Muslim aristocratic housewife-mother with haughty brows. This purdah woman seldom flinched from smoking a cigarette. And healthy sons grew up in her shade with the moral courage to face the world and appreciate innately, a lady's aroma of freedom.

In their days, it was customary to beat errant husbands. Kanyakubja families played out a humourous 'aside'. There were plenty of hot headed men who were in the habit of beating their wives to prove their manliness. On reaching home, they often encountered an army of women with household utensils in their hands. The issue of manliness settled, the husband got back to being a docile lover. Dowry too was taboo in Avadh and Lucknow. It was considered valorous for men to actually give the wife's family gifts as the 'father was parting with his daughter who must have been the jewel of his eye.' Those who violated this code were looked down upon and ostracised from civilised society. So were fathers who struck their grown up daughters and sons. Individual will and right to choice were respected in marriage and societal approval overrode family conservatism if lovers opposed the evil designs of the scheming uncle. Like everything else, a love marriage too was an issue of power in north India. Love stories of this belt documented unsentimental social protest; they also gave lessons in physical lovemaking and violent warfare.

The moral of the story came back to haunt UP when television serials of the '80s and the '90s initiated a backlash, nay, the beginnings of a cultural counter revolution, against the values of dying great-grandmothers and grandfathers. They put forth sick and demeaning portrayals of ideal and 'pure' Indian women. Pig headed 'panditayans' and pathologically superstitious, mazhabi Muslim housewifes further typified this stereotype. Wife beating was extolled as a virtue in movie after movie. Dowry became a compulsive instruction, negating the Hindu-Urdu belt code. Mainstream family and societal radicalism in love and marriage disappeared without a trace.

This inversion of traditional values was astounding, suddenly, the ethics of the old ladies of the late nineteenth century became outside Indian tradition! And those of the late twentieth century became eternal and traditional!

Zamindari abolition spelled disaster for Khatri, Kayastha and Aggarwal aristocracy as well. They were forced to give up traditions of wine drinking, card playing and meat-eating with Muslim friends. The erstwhile sophisticated Bania and Kayastha ceased to exist and his kind became permanently typified as the rapacious mahajan or the prurient lala.

The abolition of the zamindari was a signal for another transfer of property from the old elite to the neo-rich. This prompted the real exodus of Avadhi Muslims to Pakistan. Much after 1947, Lucknow now saw families leave for reasons related to changes in class and economic position. The Muslim aristocracy understood that besides taking away their land, the abolition had also done something fundamental — it had cut off their link with the peasantry, their watan and soil. Thereafter, the raja of Kotwara was never able to win an election. He was defeated in 1952 in a totally changed atmosphere where he suddenly became a Muslim zamindar while his opponents turned up as patriotic patronisers of the peasantry. This was something the raja found difficult to handle as an individual. His family was a trustee of the ancient Hindu shrine of Gola Gokaran Nath in Lakhimpur Kheri. According to old practice, prayers still did not begin without the blessings of the Kotwara head, but the link of religious composite culture with secular, political life was impaired. Communal identities were openly invoked in Avadh by Congressis, as part of a conscious policy, during Nehru's time. The RSS later expanded on this very base to become a major ideological and political force in northeastern Avadh.

The communists too, were slowly edged out from their limited areas of influence. The Lucknowi 'commune' stopped functioning after the transfer of prominent leaders to West Bengal and Bombay. Sajjad Zaheer's PWA closed down in the early '50s following internal strife and failure to function creatively. The only solace for both the Muslims and communists, ironically, was the figure of Pandit Jawaharlal Nehru who provided a healing touch by respecting men of personality. He brought back Sajjad Zaheer who had left for Pakistan on the instructions of the Communist Party as part of a failed political game plan. The raja of Kotwara became his personal friend but Nehru did little to prevent the confiscation of Mahmudabad property. The family which produced a freedom fighter like Nawab Ali and was threatened thrice with confiscation by the British, got the label of a 'traitor' in independent India.

15

❧

Crimes, Smiles and Misdemeanours—1
The Early Years

Lucknow in its hey days
approximated to the culture of
aristocratic France
with the difference that there
it was destroyed by an internal convulsion
while here it was colonised by an external power
while an internal convulsion
arose
to save it

— Josh Malihabadi

Muslim cultural and political alienation was prevalent in the '50s. But it was left to an Avadhi and a Malihabadi atheist to speak out on the issue from the Red Fort in Delhi. Once, during the independence day celebrations, Josh Malihabadi, Nehru's personal friend and the most prominent Urdu poet of his age, was called upon to recite something in honour of the republic. In a moment of revelation he read out, instead, a 'matam-e-azaadi'. One of its verses said —

Chaati gayi lugat se jo lafzen thee kaam ki
Guddi se khich gayi jo zaban thi avaam ki

(Each word of importance was removed from the dictionary.
The language of the people was pulled out from the nape)

These two lines summed up for posterity the post-independence pain felt not only by the Muslim but the cultured nationalist as well. Josh expressed anger at the systematic efforts on at that time to change the subconsciousness of the Indian subcontinent. Begun in the late nineteenth century in the name of creating a perfect Hindi language free from Urdu and Persian influences, the exercise assumed bizarre proportions during the '50s. By then partition, designed and executed meticulously by Lord Mountbatten, had finished everything built so strenuously by Sher Shah Suri, Akbar, Shivaji, Aurangzeb, Asaf-ud-Daula, Maharaja Ranjit Singh, Wajid Ali Shah and the heroes of 1857. By agreeing to and participating in the dismemberment of the country, Jawaharlal Nehru and Sardar Patel violated the Gupta and Maurya mandate as well. 'The British united India', so there was nothing wrong in their breaking it up too. Lord Mountbatten was also the last English G-man* in India. The flexibility of his ancient, insular caste underwrote division with the concession of freedom or vice versa, at the right time. Insured from possible upheaval, the British Commonwealth ensured continuing Western patronisation of 'two' hostile populations.

Resisting partition would have meant affixing the red rose atop a soldier's armour, but Nehru was no warrior. The Congress leadership was too tired to even go to prison on the eve of '47.

Gandhi, despite eminence, cardinal political contribution, 1942 and late pangs of conscience was no less guilty. In the field of culture he remained close, but yet very far, from the Indo-

---

* government man

Persian subtext. His unique, 'anti-communal' experiment of Muslim integration under an Anglo-Orientalist, Hindu shade failed miserably. The post-'57 Hindutva forces used and discarded him away as per their changing needs; his influence checked and reinforced their aggressiveness. In progressive distinction, the valorous, Hindustani Hinduism of militant bhakti and 1857, limited echoes of which were found in the Bengal and Punjab of C.R. Das, Subhas Bose and Lala Hardayal, was for more secular and republican by temperament.

His sexual experiments too seemed to inch near the great Asiatic, Lucknowi and Japanese tradition of yogic abstinence in face of a naked body. But the 'purposes' of the old aristocracy and the Oriental Hindu differed widely. For the former, abstinence and suffering in the time of passion was a means of acquiring unbeatable strength for the eventual moral and physical battle of the sexes, power and inner 'selves'. For the latter, it was an approach to shun battle and potency for the misplaced haven of ascetic, abstract and weak spiritual power.

Jinnah's legitimate grievances against the sectarian, 'Hindu' politicking of the Nehru-Patel combine were drowned in his un-Indo-Persian political act. Jinnah could have emerged as a bourgeosie-aristocrat nationalist, the Kemal Pasha of India. But he chose to become an official 'Lawrence of Arabia', confusing independence with division. The only figure who brought back unconscious Mughal-Avadhian-pre-1757 Bengal traces on the dark Indian palimpsest was the Bengali warrior-hero, Subhas Chandra Bose.

Nehruvian India began censuring Urdu words in the All India Radio, set up in the 1930s. A 'perfect' dictionary of the Hindi language came into being, shorn of Braj and Avadhi influences. This highly misplaced legacy of Ram Chandra Shukla and Mahavir Prasad Dwivedi now had the support of the Congress, socialist, and even a section of communist politicians. The national leaders were talking about secularism in the political realm, but Urdu, the very language of Indian secularism, was being erased. Since the Kaithi-Devnagari Hindi of 1857 warriors carried the diction, words and lehza of Urdu, the toady* Devnagari Hindi of independent India betrayed the linguistic mandate of the great uprising. It also betrayed the semiological mandate of Indian tradition.

The new Hindi dictionary would have no word that corresponded to the experience of sensuality. The Sanskritised Hindi translation, 'endriya', or of the senses, was too literal, flat and abstract. Similar was the case with the word 'style'. Ada remained out of bounds from the toady Hindi consciousness which ultimately, had to look towards the West for 'style'.

People like Josh knew that the days when deen, ilm or hunar held more importance than religion were gone. He was given a job in Delhi and a lot of respect by Nehru; yet he left for Pakistan. For Josh, India and Pakistan were still not two separate entities; despite the 'two-nation' theory, people on both sides of the border were one. When the rulers of Pakistan, quite a few of them from Uttar Pradesh like Liaqat Ali, Qasim Raza, Muzaffar Ali Naqvi and Mazir Ali, invited him saying that India has many national poets but they had none, he could not refuse.

But Josh became unwelcome in Pakistan after Liaqat Ali's death in the era of Punjabi generals. His importance in India too declined after Nehru passed away. A proud man of Faqir Muhammad Goya's lineage, Josh had once shown his Pathani temper to Maulana Azad, the then education minister, in Delhi. On a personal visit, he found a delay in Maulana's response to his calls. So he asked for a paper and pen and scribbled a note to the minister. On receiving it, the Maulana froze — there in bold Urdu it was written:

Na munasib hai khoon khaulana
Phir kisi aur roz, Maulana

---

* A 'slang', used by Bhagat Singh and his friends to define the attitude of those Indians who supported anything by 'rote'. This was Brechtian 'crude thinking', a hardboiled, street smart way to express moral indignation, at its north Indian best. The revolutionaries expressed here the very Indian philistinism seen in the brown skinned 'rai sahabs' or the toady bacche (kids) of the British. The RSS cadres parading in half pants were also reportedly called 'toady' Hindus.

(It is not proper for blood to boil
Let us meet some other day, Maulana)

At another time in Allahabad, Urdu men of letters including Josh and Firaq Gorakhpuri, the great Allahabadi progressive Urdu poet, were out on a boat cruise on the Yamuna. There, in the middle of the river, an argument began over the existence of God. Josh kept denying it, while Firaq, the agnostic, known for his caustic comments, took up an ambivalent position. At one point, to tease Josh, he affirmed the existence of God. Suddenly, Josh caught hold of Firaq and dipped his body in the river — he then asked him: now who is your God, me or the guardian of heaven? The hapless Firaq replied that at that moment it was of course ·'him'.

For a man preserving rebelliousness and anger even in everyday happenings, a confrontation with the military government of Pakistan was inevitable. Josh's atheism invoked the aristocratic traditions of Avadh and the radical humanistic beliefs of Sufism. No Maulana ever dared to pass an injunction against him even as they made life miserable for the academic atheists of Lucknow.

All this must have deeply disconcerted the rulers of Pakistan — they could have coped with a Soviet backed communist, a West inspired secularist and rationalist. But how to undermine an Asiatic modernist? Josh himself never complied with the wishes of the new dispensation and preferred to slide into slow oblivion. He also did not show much enthusiasm, unlike other progressive poets with roots in Pakistan like Faiz Ahmad Faiz, for the Bhutto years.

In the '50s, Lucknow was jerked out of post-independence complacency by another tragedy. One of the foremost poets of the progressive-romantic age died a stunning death. A run down desi bar of the city opened, one day, to find an ardent customer lying motionless. Majaz's demise left behind a lot of heartache and mystery. Despite his sensitivity, he was not a frustrated, self-deprecating man. His was, probably, the kind of end which happens at the height of creative release; when rancour dissolves into personal bliss and there is just the way to go forward towards a fatal void. Thus in dying too, Majaz the poet, immortalised vazadari, individuality and non-conformity which made the period when he was alive the 'period of Majaz' in Lucknow.

Hailing from a middle class family, he signified the intensity of the shuriefa sensibility. From this background emerged the archetype shair — a being involved in himself and the world, getting hurt by the most trivial of things but also loving the whole universe, a darling of women but a loner in death. Majaz once told Josh that you may have the vocabulary but I have the speech; he was also the kind of guy whose pictures were kept under pillows by girls of the Aligarh Muslim University. A student of the institution, Majaz composed a nazm which is still sung at university functions as 'Aligarh Ka Tarana'. Majaz had a heart which went out to the poor and the underprivileged. His non-conformism compelled him to question faith in decisive brush strokes—

> *Zindagi kya hai gunahe Aadam*
> *Zindagi hai to gunahgaar hun main*

(What is life, a sin of Adam
If there is life, then I am a sinner)

He carried a 'dimension of love' which gave the left movement in literature a rare feel of inner grace. His pet themes were combined in famous lines which exemplify modern symbolism in Urdu poetry. In it, the white moon, a symbol of beauty, has turned pale; instead of being comparable to splendour it is now akin to a Sufi's imagination, a lover's thought, a mulla's turban, a trader's account book, and still further, to a 'poor man's' youth and a 'widow's' prime of youth:

> *Ae game dil kya karun ae vahshate dil kya karun*
> *Ek mahal ki aad se nikla voh peela mahtaab*
> *Jaise sufi ka tasavvur jaise ashik ka khayal*
> *Jaise mulla ka amama jaise baniye ki kitaab*
> *Jaise muflis ki jawani jaise beva ka shabab*
> *Ae game dil kya karoon ae vahshate dil kya karoon*

After Majaz, Urdu poetry did not produce a comparable individual voice. The moustache was trimmed further and altogether vanished. Smug didacticism gave way to contemplative rhetoric. In and beyond the world of Urdu, the intellectual-warrior had turned into a 'pure intellectual' or a 'tellectual-in'.

The poetic space was occupied by silent and sedate whispers, both in India and Pakistan. These were the women poetesses of Lucknow and Avadh. Some of them had begun their life behind the veil and went on to become scholars of Arabic, Persian, Urdu and English. Some were the last amongst the great courtesans, some the first modernists. There was Tasneem Rai Barelwi who announced, hesitatingly:

Tumhari aal men ek khaaksaar hum bhi hain
Chaman men ek shajre khardaar hum bhi hain

(I too am a small being in your generation
I too am a thorny plant of your garden)

She died in 1973; similar to her in poetic temperament were Akhtar Jayasi, Husn Jahan Begum, who belonged to Kanpur, Zeba Kakorvi, Alam Lucknowi and Ismat Lucknowi who supported the Khilafat movement and the independence struggle. Her poetic debate with Khaliqulzaman's wife, Zahida, revived for a brief moment the memories of intellectual and artistic exchanges between literate women of the 1840s and '50s. She expressed pain with ravangi, or an 'emotional wanderlust':

Har saans zindagi ki kati yun kisi ke saath
Jaise koi safar men hon ek ajnabi ke saath

(Each breath of life was spent in such a way with someone
As if someone was with a stranger during the journey)

Others like Fakra Naqvi, Vafa Lucknowi, Vasiya Jayasi and Shajahan Bano made more muffled statements:

Daste talab daraz ho duniya ko fikr thi
Lekin na khul saki meri mutthi bandhi hui

(The world wanted that my desires should be big

But the untying of my tied fist could not come about.)

— Vasiya

Vafa to unse hui na umar bhar hogi
To phir hina tujhe kyon aitbaar aaj bhi hai

(Acts of loyalty could not have from his side
Then why 'Hina' do you still have trust?)

— Hina Lucknowi

Across the border the Lucknowi tone was voiced even more
ardently. In Pakistan, Zahida Lucknowi, Shamim Malihabadi, Haya
Barabankvi, Makhfi Lucknowi and scores of other brilliant poetesses kept on writing unnervingly direct lines. In later years, they
fell victim to the subtle ethnic policy followed by Pakistani powers.
Great talents of Lucknowi and Avadh, drawn from the qasbas, were
suddenly labelled as Mohajirs and ostracised. The political dimension of this problem became acute in the '80s but its social aspect
was seen in the '60s and the '70s by Haya Barabankvi:

Sharabe naab mein ab rango boo nahin baaki
Vo rabte sheshao jamosubu nahin baaki
Gale to milte hain ahbaab ae haya ab abhi
Magar dilon men sadakat ki boo nahin baaki

(In the purest of wines colour and smell are no longer
left
That sequence of wine and water served in a glass is no
longer left
Friends exchange greetings even now O' Haya
But in the hearts the smell of righteousness is no longer
left)

Something else happened in the Pakistan of the '50s. Amir
Ahmad once again entered into the eye of the storm. He was asked
by Ayub Khan's military regime to become, reportedly, the president of the country. But like Josh, the ex-raja of Mahmudabad was
bereft of friends and thus the cause for feeling an affinity with

Pakistan. The ascendancy of the army had seen the eclipse of the north Indian Muslim elite in Pakistan. The new Punjabi elite kept alive the Urdu language but eroded the base of Indo-Persian culture. For them Mahmudabad was little more than a symbol to be used — they were therefore incensed when he refused to toe the official line on political and social issues.

Mahmudabad was soon declared persona non-grata in Pakistan and his property confiscated. He became, literally, a man without a nation, roaming the world in search for a home. Back in Lucknow, his family went through a catharsis — one of the brothers had to sell off the house that had been the hub of nationalist activities and the great wedding of '39. The other swore never to set foot in the lane again till he had recovered the family possession.

That house had the highest gateway in the entire city — its arch was unmatched by the new houses of the Rastogis, Aggarwals and the wealthier refugees who began a construction boom in the outer reaches of the east and the west. They had gained a lot after the departure of the British, by which time the Rastogis had risen from their status of petty traders to that of big moneylenders. Some of them had become small talukedars by the closing years of the nineteenth century. Expanding from their old quarters in Raja Bazaar they had spread out to the larger mohallas of the Chowk and by the twentieth century were monopolising the chikan embroidery trade.

Independence and partition meant a windfall as the departing Muslim aristocracy, British officials and businessmen sold off their property for a pittance. One of the great moneylenders acquired a number of cars for as little as below a thousand rupees and others did the same with regard to houses. Much of the property around Aminabad was purchased by refugees. Many beautiful shops in Hazratganj, belonging to Muslim families, had new bewildered Punjabi owners.

The old cosmopolitan character of Hazratganj underwent a change. On the eve of 1947 it was like a cafe-market resort of Egypt or Morocco. Coffee and tea shops abounded besides the pastry shop and dance floor of the Valerios, which specialised in the creamy layered, dry walnut cake topped with dry fruits. Its combination with a bottle of soda was an aesthetic experience as it left behind a pungent, musty, dry sweet aftertaste. Standing there one got a feel of Bogart's drawl or Robert Taylor's stylish angst, both of whom could be playing across the street.

The Mayfair cinema at Hazratganj received the best of film noir and romantic Hollywood, *The Big Sleep* and *The Waterloo Bridge*, in the '40s. The foot tapping heartaches caused by the American soldier, who had crowded its seats and dance floor during the Second World War, were over. They were replaced by the first flush of that native identification with the West which looked for adventure on the streets while still reading *Zehr-e-Ishq* and *Tilism-e-Hoshruba* on the sly. Sensationalism creeped in the sexual heat of Lucknowi houses. Here, between hurried bites of khutia,* the aching desire of young girls aroused the virgin passion of middle class boys in the upper room atop the zeena near the dalaan. These rooms and objects, which smelled of north Indian seasons and sweat, became aestheticised emblems of sensual lust in the surviving history of pornography, now forced to go 'cheap' on roadside stalls.

This was a time of great discovery for youngsters. The departure of the British had lifted off a great weight from the shoulders and elite spoils were his or hers for the picking. So was cinema, the Mayfair dance floor and the China bar. Here the swing and the jive could be improvised without the fear of the white daddy or the stern, British college principal; a glass of beer could be gulped down just after having fun with the suave tongawala asking or refusing money in chaste Urdu and eating paan regally at the end of the journey. This tongawala had a female counterpart, the tongawaali of Lucknow who could abuse, beautifully, in Urdu after her introductory knock: '*Huzoor, aap ki shaan ke khilaf kuch arz karoon?*' (Venerated gentleman, should I speak something against your honour?)

For the angry, young Lucknowi man of the '50s there was a

---

* The Shahajahanpuri-Lucknowi sweetmeat-toffee, or 'revari', made of sugar, khoya (in some cases) and white sesame. Once the favourite ' candy' of young boys and girls.

flip side too. He was already facing an identity crisis which exploded in the '60s. This archetype came from a Hindu background but was not connected, in the beginning, to the world of Hindi literature. His schooling may have taken place in the Colvin Talukedar which, unlike the convent schools of Allahabad, did not excel in British literary traditions. In the new Indian Administrative Service (IAS) examinations which replaced the British ICS as the most prestigious grade for a young man, it was, however, the latter which counted.

In the literary arena, the tales of Bhagwati Charan Verma, Amrit Lal Nagar and Yashpal, the three chronicles of the middle classes of Lucknow, became familiar to the man of the '50s only on entering university. This was a strata different from the authentic Uttar Pradesh middle class of Chandrashekhar Azad variety. This, by then, was either finished or had merged into the renewed triumph of the post-'57, modern bania-Brahmin culture. In the spiral cycle of changing middle class equations, this trait, which had transformed itself into an elite current under the Nehrus by the '20s, re-emerged as the eclectic cosmopolitanism of the '40s petty bourgeoisie. The Hindu-Victorian lower middle class of the puritan-Bhartendu variety got recast in the Gandhian, liberal-oriental image. Madan Mohan Malviya's Sanatan Dharma current was now part of the small, Hindu Mahasabha or RSS-Hindutva inspired middle strata.

Classification amongst the Muslim propertied sections was less fragmented. The Sir Syed trend had reconstituted itself as a League middle class-elite current, which switched over to the Congress after partition. In Pakistan, this section defined the standard of bhadralok taste and lifestyle in the absence of a similar impulse amongst the Sindhis and Punjabis. The Maulana Azad current survived as an idealist outpost of qasba service and trading class. The PWA intelligentsia formed the advanced guard of the Nehru-Gandhi-Jinnah, petty bourgeoisie train.

In Allahabad there was no synthesis between those who read Premchand and Agyeya and those who took singing lessons in 'Que Sera Sera' singing lessons, but the vernacular and the 'English medium' world was not so rigidly separated in Lucknow. They had been fused as far back as the late nineteenth century through institutions such as the La Martinierc, the first true boys 'convent' of north India.

The literature from Allahabad in the '50s leaned heavily towards an anti-elite strand. Characters were caught up in the vicious circle of drab 'homewardness' and the lure of the outside world, quite unable to cope with both. The men more proficient in Hindi struggled to get a foothold in the upper strata environs of Kashmiri Brahmins and Allahabad University English Department snobs. Lucknow's literature, by contrast, was one of quiescence, rebellion or love in a drawing room with the harmonium or an old piano. In Allahabad, things ended in a critique of the system; in Lucknow they took on the contours of a revolt or a life away from the system. There was less misery, even in the Marxist novels of Yashpal, who came from Punjab to settle down in the city with his wife Prabhavati Paul sometime in the '40s.

Of the other two literary personalities, Bhagwati Charan Verma's Kayasthism and Amrit Lal Nagar's Gujarati Brahminism sipped luxuriantly, the rich feel of a city, 'nagar' culture. Amrit Lal's social naturalism broke down into fleeting moments of torment and pain while Bhagwati Charan's realism stoked freely the liberated picture of ancient India. In it a philosopher-courtesan, holding the view that it is involvement in life which gives true insight and wisdom, triumphs over on ascetic. The sadhu values renunciation and high ideals over the low exegesis of material life, but succumbs to courtesan Chitralekha's charms. His spiritual quests take a backseat and his long suppressed physical and emotional needs, including a human penchant to lie and control by power, come to the fore. The wise courtesan rejects the sadhu and goes back to her amorous lover. It did not pay, after all, as Sahir Ludhianvi's song in the second version of the film *Chitralekha*, directed by Kedar Sharma reminded, to try and strive for God when one has always been running away from the world:

Sansar se bhage phirte ho
Bhagwaan ko tum kya paoge

Chitralekha was a happy document of a belief in this world, in the ripples of the river, in the sound of a koyal, in the beat of the drum. Religion, if too remote, was out; it was more important to love the beauty of one's fellow being. This message from ancient times spoke in the language of a contemporary sensibility in Lucknow's discreet family world. Here inter caste love marriages were embraced by the middle class. A traditional woman, used to cleaning her kitchen each time after a meal, had no qualms in accepting a sophisticated Bengali girl for her Kanyakubja Brahmin boy, or in changed circumstances, a Christian lady for her shy, Kayastha offspring.

These pictures of upper caste sensuality appeared way back in the '30s, in the novels of the Hindi litterateur and Baiswara Brahmin, Suryakant Tripathi Nirala. Laced with the sheen of the sindoor, the resonance of the jhanjhar and the richness of the pooja ki thaali, this feeling understood the spark of merit in struggling, dreamy, young and manly eyes. In Nirala's montage of intellectual sensations, the Lucknowi bhadralok woman played tennis in a salwar kameez, stole a note of the piano beneath pictures of Raja Ravi Verma and manipulated a date in the thick of a family ceremony.

Nirala received his baptism in literature and politics while working as an editor of a Lucknowi journal. In latter stories and novels he depicted the Kanyakubja fall from ex-elites to backward, dual, whining, complaining, women baiting, conservative petty landholders. The sensitive Brahmin hero became an outsider who feels, in the novel *Nirupama*, the passing away of time, moment by moment, in bursts of fragmented, existentialist purity, during a train journey. He prefers to polish shoes than wear the badge of his caste. In another setting he gets transformed into an iconoclast threatening to severe the head of his favourite deity because 'humanism died in the Gods'.

The characters of Yashpal and Amrit Lal Nagar represented, more consciously, the modern facets of Lucknow — the artiste, the shair and the revolutionary looking for an identity. If there emerged a native literature of throbbing identity in India, it did in Lucknow. In these novels even rooms, chardivari (boundary), gusalkhana (bathroom), alleys, cafes, avenues lined by shops, stomped noisely for attention. The prose could be faulty, the form too verbose and the 'stammer' before the 'full, constructed sentence', too long. But the novels succeeded in portraying the reality of Hindi-Hindu families passing through a crisis of trust, betrayal, drift and agnosticism.

As a communist theoretician and playwright, Yashpal wrote *Nashe Nashe Ki Baat*, performed by the Lucknow branch of the Indian Peoples Theatre Association (IPTA). This theatre movement, begun in the '40s in Bombay and Calcutta under the direct tutelage of P.C. Joshi, general secretary of the Communist Party, revolutionised Indian theatre. It's impact on the performing arts was similar to PWA's impact on literature and many latter day talents, who defined mainstream Indian cinema, were groomed on IPTA's makeshift stages. Prithvi Raj Kapoor performed *Deewar* at Lucknow in 1940. By then the city had a couple of theatres, the Nari Natya Kala Kendra in Qaiserbagh and the Bengali club of Dwijendra Nath Sanyal, which organised drama competitions on the pattern of Calcutta.

The '40s also saw the edging out of the Parsi theatre, a post-'57 Bombay development, built on the ruins of the Urdu theatre of Lucknow. In the twentieth century, 'Benarsi Lucknowis' like Aga Hashra Kashmiri kept alive the jaanbaaz, dramatic legacy of Amanat in sensational 'Bombay-Indo-Persian' interpretations of Shakespeare. Othello and Hamlet spoke Urdu with the akkhad, Indo-Gangetic plain gesture in a grand epic of rising and falling emotions. But this was a stigmatised, bastardised Indo-Persianism — a semi-Westernised, semi-traditional Bombay merchant ethos trying to ape aristocrat art; bungling and muddling through with humour and parvenu magnificence. Gestures of Urdu theatre were taken over by purer intent in the peasant dramas of north Indian tamasha which retold stories of revolt and heroism as per the stage instructions of Wajid Ali Shah.

Bombay Hindi cinema stole the emotional substructure of Parsi and Lucknowi theatre in the '20s and the '30s. The social-realists gave it a Western-Bengali dimension in the '50s. The golden years of Indian cinema thus came into existence but Lucknowi emotions existed in an uncomfortable unity with filmi sob stories of the Indian social genre. Still carrying the feel of Bahu Begum and Hazrat Mahal, they responded uneasily to the screen canonisation of the 'ideal Indian woman' as a sado-masochistic paragon of a priori virtue and suffering. Edged out from the 'middle level' mainstream, Lucknow echoed in the '50s either in the big commercial film or the small, Sheikh Mukhtar-Shakeela led the 'B' cinema where emotion existed as power.

Indo-Persian values galloped freely for the only time on the Indian screen in the '40s 'B' image of fearless Nadia: an image of adventure, voluptuousness, speed and individuality, untrammelled by sentimentalism. This was tomboyishness with a vengeance: a reinvention of the sensual, avenging, martial princess, courtesan or working class girl, who gave up her throne, salon or home for a life of personal freedom and social justice, of eighteenth-nineteenth century Indo-Persian literature. Contrary to current, fallacious wisdom, which cannot see the location of a liberated image* in India, this female Robin Hood was not inspired by Hollywood. Put on screen by the Parsi team of the M.N. Roy sympathiser-businessman, J.B.H. Wadia, she also invoked the folk memory of fiery heroines and jaanbaaz goddesses of Pauranic literature.

Feared by the Victorian-Hindu middle classes, Nadia was turned into a hit by the ordinary working people. They perhaps understood better, the aristocracy of adventure. Her Bohemianism, and the typical, non-romantic, aristocratic tendency to shun sentimental love even while winning over a man of style, created a storm in female circles. Her war cry went out against the weak, often hypocritical, colonial-Hindu modernity of high society 'Congressi women'. Her kind came breathtakingly close to Amrita Sher Gill, Ismat Chugtai and all those young chabeelis of Urdu literature and Lucknow society.

Deewar inspired Babulal, Santram and Kunwar Kalyan to inaugurate IPTA in the city. In keeping with the practice of the day, eminent personalities distributed communist party literature in the

---

*An image carrying the autonomy of gesture, opinion and character.

morning and physically acted in the evening — they included Yashpal, Krishna Narain Kakkad and the poet, Raghuvir Sahai. IPTA's leftist affiliations led to a clampdown on civil liberties by the government — posters were put up so that people could be arrested for attending or participating in IPTA plays. Prime Minister Jawaharlal Nehru was then proclaiming a progressive, pro-left foreign policy for the new nation. But in Bombay artistes like Balraj Sahani, who had communist-IPTA affiliations, were attending film shootings in handcuffs. In Lucknow, Raghuvir Sahai and K.N. Kakkad had to cancel the performance of the play, *Neelam*, due to governmental pressure.

Lucknowi artistes replied by floating new platforms, the Lucknow Writers Association and the Lucknow Natya Sangh. The modernist poet, Naresh Mehta, was part of this attempt which strove to break away from the stereotypes of progressive art as well. The crisis in the left cultural movement, then caught between the outdated social-realist podium of the '40s and demands of the '50s modernism, was spotted early by Lucknowi artistes. Behind hot leftist debates over cultural issues also lurked a political crisis, especially on the issue of developing an adequate response to Nehru and his democratic experiment.

The Lucknow group evolved as a heterogenous entity, incorporating Marxist and non-Marxist trends from theatre to painting to sculpture. Similar quests led to the formation of a Progressive Artistes Group of painters in Bombay and the mainstream theatre of Shambhu Mitra, an ex-IPTAite, in Calcutta. An Art's College was built in Lucknow in 1911 representing both the Bengal and the Academy School of Painting. The two trends were led respectively by Asit Kumar Haldar and L.M. Sen. After winning affiliation with Lucknow University, the Arts College went on to produce painters, sculptors and graphic artists such as Ranveer Singh Bisht, Madan Lal Nagar, Avtaar Singh, Srikhande and Jai Kishen. Though they blended abstract patterns with traditional realism, there was no continuity with the native minimalism and impressionism of the Avadh school of painting.

In north Indian art, there was a break between 1857 and the

1920s. Modern schools were informed by trends evolving in Bengal and Europe rather than Mughal-Avadhi traditions. These appeared, surprisingly, in the figurative perspectives of Raja Ravi Verma in Kerala and Amrita Sher Gill in Punjab — two states and cultures where an event like '57 had not snapped links with the past.

In theatre, stultified Sankritised gestures of Hindi literature cut off city drama from creative trends of rural Uttar Pradesh, Bihar, Madhya Pradesh and Rajasthan. The only exception was the Benarsi trader-aristocrat-poet-dramatist, Jaishankar Prasad, who revived the anandvaad, or epicureanism of motive, and valour of original Sanskrit plays. In the land of Rahas and Indar Sabha, no vibrant modern theatre, based on the gestures of Uttar Pradesh, came to the fore. *Aalha,* which had enormous dramatic possibilities, was not translated into epic drama or opera. Modern-progressive activity in Uttar Pradesh was always dogged with the accusation of being rootless — of being either too Hindi-ised, cut off from the living traditions of Urdu and Hindustani, or too anglicised. Lucknow was not Benaras or Allahabad, the centres of Hindi-ised and anglicised currents, and the failure to carry forward the Indo-Persian ethos led to modernist isolation. After the '70s, especially when religious revivalism began within the erstwhile liberal middle classes and elite, whatever little flowering that did take place just caved in. Lucknow's relationship with modernist art and literature remained ambivalent:

> *Hue hum tumhare sanam*
> *Kuch na ho sake tumhare sanam*
>
> (I became yours my love
> Some what could not
> become yours my love)

But before that happened, the Lalit Kala Academy was established in 1962 along with the Sangeet Natak Academy. Its magazine, *Kala Traimasik,* achieved national fame under the editorship of K.N. Kakkad. A Rashtriya Kala Kendra also came up which gave a further fillip to the movement of modern art. In theare, there was a big, nationwide explosion during the '60s inspired by the new, worldwide attitude of revolutionary criticism. The plays of B.V. Karanth, Badal Sarkar and Girish Karnad arrived with a bang; they were followed by the explosion of a student and peasant movement in Bengal. Led by a new Communist Party, the CPI-ML, the movement raised the issue of land reforms and independent left assertion away from the pro-Nehru policies of the two Communist Parties, the CPI and the CPM, which had become separate entities in 1964. The 'spring thunder of Naxalbari' (as the movement came to be known) took place in the backdrop of a turbulent situation of food riots, two wars with Pakistan in 1965 and 1971, and severe economic and political dislocation. It had a profound impact on Hindi-Bengali literature and Indian art. For Lucknow, the importance of the CPI-ML rested on the fact that it was the first movement since independence to establish tentatively, an indigenous, revolutionary line of non-Congress nationalism. 1857 and Bhagat Singh were invoked on the pages of the party's magazine, *Liberation*, and Bengali youths condemned leaders of the Bengal renaissance for betraying the first war of Indian independence.

B.V. Karanth performed his famous play, *Hayvradan*, in 1971 in the city at Ravindralaya, a new swanky auditorium. The event was organised by Raj Bisaria who established the Theatre Work shop in 1968 and Darpan in 1969. Badal Sarkar came down to the city in 1973 and Lucknow played a role in grooming the post-Naxalbari, angry young men of Indian theatre. It was a happening city where the theatre organisation, Meghdoot, came up in 1973 and the Bhartendu Natya Academy was established in 1976. Both these institutions enlisted the services of Hari Mohan Samson, Ranjit Kapoor and MK Raina, besides manufacturing artistes like P.N. Srivastava and Vishwa Nath Misra. Theatre activities also produced Bhuvneshwar, a noted playwright, and Anupam Kher, the actor who made a name for himself by giving a villainous touch to comedy and a mimic's twitch to the evil eye.

Away from the tendencies of contemporary art, the characters of Lucknowi Hindi literature still lived in Aminabad, Sarai Maoli Khan or Rani Katra. Evenings were spent around Sahu, the new post-independent movie hall with a large, straight forward, modernist perspective of nationalist motifs. Ranjana and Kwality entertained avid restaurant-goers returning after long family walks in Victoria street. On dusty summer mornings, boyish angst ran deep in the campuses of Lucknow University and the Kanyakubja degree college. The same feeling predominated the stuffy but well stocked libraries of Agha Mir 'deorhi' and Amir-ud-Daula apart from creeping in the premises of the Urdu Academy. Named after prominent nawabs, talukedars and intellectuals, the library culture of Uttar Pradesh saved Indo-Persian documents from complete extinction. Shibli Nomani academy in Azamgarh housed rare manuscripts of Khusro's time and Ali Raza's library in Rampur was now the biggest Qutubkhana of Asia. Ali Raza was a reforming Rampur nawab of the early twentieth century who was keen to wash off the anti '57 stain through a rigorous patronage to art and literature. His institution boasted of a Persian 'Ramayana', officially sanctioned by Aurangzeb, which began with customary Islamic-Arabic invocations.

On the other side of the Gomti, students of Nadwa read modern interpretations of traditional texts. Post-independence baghs bore a nationalist, utilitarian look while serving as favourite 'love spots' of love-lorn men and women from Lucknow and Uttar Pradesh. But by the late '60s, people had begun migrating from the cities of Uttar Pradesh to metropolitan centres. Old professions had already reached a plateau, no new industries were coming up and employment was hard to find. The ruling powers of the state dithered and fumbled at the task of development and industrialisation — it would have meant implementing schemes such as land reforms which Charan Singh had opposed for class reasons:

'— the drafters of the legislation were cognisant of the need to ensure political stability in the countryside. By multiplying the number of independent land owning peasants, there came into being a middle of the road, stable society and a barrier against political extremism. It is fair to conclude that agrarian reform has taken the wind out of the sails of the disrupters of peace and the opponents of ordered progress.'[1]

But this ordered progress was achieved at a heavy price.

Without land reforms there was little hope of increasing the purchasing power of the peasantry and extending the sway of the market economy. Because of this, the initial spurt in agricultural production could not be sustained. The state of Uttar Pradesh was best suited to the development of a modern peasant economy which then would have laid down the basis for the agro-industrialisation of the qasbas and the large scale industrialisation of the cities. Mughal-Avadhi political economy was geared in this direction but its basis was almost completely eroded in the colonial interregnum. The task of the national state was now to re-establish a mnemonic link with the economic past in light of contemporary thought and technology.

This the state refused to do; it then went back even on the traditional role of 'big government' in the third world by not irrigating the villages. The feudal superstructure dominated sound administrative logic, making Uttar Pradesh fall behind Punjab and Haryana by decades in this sphere. Peasants were soon caught in the vicious circle of ploughing small plots of land without an incentive to take up cash cropping. Sugar mill owners and agro-industrialists, who should have worked as agents of capitalism in the countryside, preferred to form a nexus with state officials and the landed gentry to loot the peasantry.

The depression in the villages began hitting the cities. No entrepreneur of Avadh was encouraged to set up industries. On the other hand, the great promise of the state making up for the weaknesses of Indian capitalism never materialised. Public sector industries, the temples of modern India, were geared to create an infrastructure of power and steel for the burgeoning private, monopoly sector, not to industrialise the poorer regions. State investment in local, small scale industries remained poor under the laws of this Nehruvian mixed economy. Direct foreign control gave way to a tardy process of import substitution which provided growth at a slow 'Oriental-Hindu' rate.

In Avadh, however, even a major public sector industry was not established. Here Nehru's 'milk and water' socialism exposed itself early as an instrument of bureaucratic state-private monopoly capital. The British had extracted the maximum amount of revenge from Avadh for '57 by keeping it thoroughly backward. This was the crucial political point, missed by historians and economic analysts, which demarcated the region from Punjab, Haryana and western Maharashtra. These areas were no less prone to being poor and backward, but they had not seen a momentous event and its aftermath in the form of a wilful suppression of even those potentialities which fell within the ambit of the British system. Here even conservative reform was not pursued for fear of disturbing the status quo and unleashing revolutionary tendencies in the countryside. The Indian large bourgeoisie and the post '47, intellectual-political ruling class continued the subtle, anti-Avadh policy. They used the region as a conservative base for their 'all India', semi-feudal hegemony. Lack of opportunities saw the labour class moving out of Lucknow. Chamars were forced to give up their old partnership with the Chinese, which had sustained the local shoe industry.

The famed shoe industry of Hazratganj declined as a consequence. Artistes and men of talent moved over to Bombay, the city of the spunky, compradorish market sensuality, unlike their brethren from Allahabad and Benaras who preferred Delhi.

Bombay's composite, multi-odoured khichri formulae of art, life and economy was not as palatable as Lucknow's original cultural, commercial and gourmet khichri dressed up with badaam, kishmish, and the singular saundhi, bhini mehek. Acchan, Lacchu and Shambhu Maharaj, Kalka Prasad's sons and Bindadeen's nephew's, revived its scent in the heart of pre-independence Bombay through Kathak. The dance became, all of a sudden, the perfect vehicle for the communication of the contemporary ada; the same way in which the Bharatnatyam influenced choreography of Uday Shankar became a votary of contemporary ideas. Kathak as a dance style, an operatic ballet run by Madam Maneka, the Mata Hari of Bombay, was part of a city en route to adopting ways of wild, raucous European capital of the '20s and the '30s. Actresses appeared in the nude and kissed on screen for the first time. Films with fancy titles. *Handsome Blackguard, Telephone Girl* and the *Wild Cat of*

Bombay, had equally fancy stars: Raja Sandow, Ruby Myers, Yvonne Wallace, Zebunissa and Ermilene.

Madam Maneka eroticised Pauranic tales under Lacchu Maharaj's able choreography. Shambhu, the younger brother, was the master of abhinaya and thumri while Acchan, the elder, perfected the nritta. Acchan's school encompassed Vikram Singhe from Sri Lanka, Sitara Devi from Benaras and Kartik Ram and Kalyan Das of Raigarh. Lacchu, a man of vision, blended nritta and abhinaya to choreograph *Malati Madhav, Mausam-e-Bahar,* and *Amrapali.* The irreverent, Wajid Ali Shahi element in him came forth in stage performances called 'gokul ki gali sankri' — the alleys of gokul (where Lord Krishna grew up) are 'narrow' — and Radha Piya Pyari (Radha, loved by her lover).

After independence, the Lucknow Gharana of Kathak, though formally retaining a singular identity, actually split into two trends. The one followed by Acchan and Shambhu Maharaj found a base in Delhi where they, along with Acchan's son, Birju Maharaj, got recognition as Kathak maestros. They formed the Delhi School of Hindustani Music and Dance, later renamed as Sangeet Bharati.

Lacchu, the man of the masses, established his own Nutan Nritya Niketan in Bombay and came to Lucknow as the head of the Kathak Kendra, set up as late as 1973. More than Lucknow, in fact, the Jaipur Gharana of Kathak was popular at that time. It merged Lucknowi technique with Rajasthani dance forms to create a distinctly vibrant, folksy, regional form. The dramatic, courtly and urbane dimension of Lucknowi Kathak was in the danger of extinction when Lacchu Maharaj produced a set of trained disciples. They carved out their own niche, separate from the achievements of Birju Maharaj, and kept alive the trend of Avadh-Braj-Urdu thumri sung in dances. Lacchu's thumri subverted the common, sound alliteration of two entirely dissimilar words — say sham (evening) and Shyam (Krishna) — and two entirely separate levels of emotional and semiological 'rhythms' residing in the alternate lines of Avadhi-Braj and Urdu. Two levels of mood, as dissimilar as a song on a swing near a riverside and a poetry recital on a pavement near a lonely road, were intertwined in the complex structure of emotions. This Lucknowi innovation recalled the intellectually 'alliterated' conversation between Amal and Charulata, the brother-in-law and sister-in-law on the verge of a relationship, in Satyajit Ray's *Charulata:*

Charu: Jabe age Bardhaman, tarpar Bilet, tarpar barrister
(First it's off to Burdwan, then Britain, then Barrister —)
Amal: Uhuh! age Bardhaman, tarpar biye, tarpar Bilet, tarpar
(Not quite! first Burdwan, then marriage, then Britain, then)
Charu: Tarpar?
(Then?)
Amal: Tarpar Bristol.
(Then Bristol.)
Charu: Ar Bouthan?
(and what about sister-in-law?)
Charu: Bouthan baje? Birir? Beha?
(Is she no good? A bad girl? Shame?)

Only in Lacchu Maharaj's renderings, intellectual subtlety was replaced by a variety of stances and ambience by changing attitudes. The difference between Uttar Pradesh and Bengal, the dramatic and the lyrical, got summed up, thus:

Sham bhayi, ghanshyam nahi
Kaho shyam bin sakhi, sham na aaye

(Evening arrived, not Ghanshyam) (another name for
Krishna),
What say you, my friend, without Shyam, evening
(sham) won't come)
(Urdu) (change of rhythm)

Main woh naghma hun jo khamosh hai ek muddat se
Hastiye naaz ko cheda jo bikhar jayega

(I am that song which is silent since a generation
If you will disturb my delicate identity it will fall to pieces)

(Back to Braj, change in rhythm)

Shyam hi shyam pukar rahi
Sham bhayi ganshyam na aye

(Only Shyam and Shyam I call
Evening arrived, Ghanshyam did not)

(Urdu) (Change in rhythm)

Dhire dhire inhi rahon se guzar jaunga
Rafta rafta kisi manzil pe pahunch jaunga

(Slowly and steadily I'll sift through these paths
Steadily and slowly I'll reach some destination)

After the deaths of his father and uncle, Birju Maharaj became
the leader of the Delhi branch of Lucknow Kathak. He went on
to evolve his own style of concentrating on the exhibitionist and
'simple sentimental' aspects. The gestures of Wajid Ali Shah were
subsumed under colour and festivity existing for performance
rather than thematic elaboration. The dramatic element too was
transformed into a soft and often bloodless lyricism. This became
popular as the 'national Kathak style' in the '80s, the same time
when the tabla of Zakir Hussain edged out the moody thaap of
Lucknow.

After the death of Abid Hussain, Wajid and Afaque Hussain in
Lucknow and Ahmad Jaan Thirakwa in Farukkhabad had kept alive
the Lucknowi tradition of the qaida and the peshkara. Benaras
competed with approbation in the form of Kanthe Maharaj introducing the 'uthan', or the tidal wave of bols or lyrics, as a new
technique. But Ahmad Jaan Thirakwa died in the mid-'70s and
Afaque Hussain was left alone to carry on the 'theme and variation'
style. Sometimes, Zakir Hussain, presented an interesting blend of
differing schools. But eclectics, rather than dialectics, became the
norm in modern performances. The percussionist was not free to
explore each step, the qaida, rela, tukra and the chakkardar, sepa-
rately and yet make everything fall in place with attitudinal connections[2]. This turning away from theme, mood and sensual mathematics to abstract and exhibitionist instrumentation affected the

pakhawaj and sitar while extinguishing the sarangi. With Afaque Hussein's death in the late '80s, the Lucknowi tabla once again faced the threat of extinction.

A school of music was established in Lucknow in the' 20s by Pandit Bhatkhande with help from the British government and talukedars like Rai Umanath Bali and Rajeshwar Bali. Bhatkhande attempted a post-Khusro codification of Hindustani classical music to make it respectable for the Hindu middle classes. Once he tried pruning the khayal and the thumri, products of the now decadent Delhi and Lucknow 'Muslim' courts and heathen, courtesan influences, to establish the purity of the 'Hindu' dhrupad. But Bhatkhande erred, for dhrupad itself was a product of the Mughal court and Hindu-Muslim interface of central India.

The Maharashtrian Brahmin ended up puritanising khayal — a move resisted by Ustad Faiyyaz Khan of the Agra Gharana and Ustad Khurshid Ali Khan, a disciple of the great Lucknowi khayaliya, Ustad Sadiq Ali Khan. Away from Bhatkande College and official patronage, Ustad Mohammad Hussein Khan (son of the great sadra singer, Ustad Dulhe Khan), Ustad Raza Hussein Khan, Khalifa Ahmad Hussein Khan and Ustad Rahmat Hussein Khan codified rare gats. The compositions of Faiyyaz Khan highlighted a 'mood filled' romanticism over the abstract bhakti of Omkarnath Thakur, striving then, for a strange, 'Hindu mode of singing' in Benaras. In the pakhawaj, a struggle arose between the mandir and the non-mandir, style while in the sitar, the Raza Khani tradition of Lucknow was called into question. Evolved by Ghulam Raza Khan, the sitariya of Jaunpur and Lucknow during Wajid Ali Shah's time, this style soon got established as a gayaki, lyrical-epical mode of instrumentation. In the twentieth century, Ustad Vilayat Khan popularised Raza Khani along with Basharat Hussein Khan, Ustad Yusuf Ali Khan, Ustad Hamid Hussein Khan and Ustad Ilyas Khan of Lucknow.

Opposition arrived in the form of Ravi Shankar, Uday Shankar's brother. Ravi Shankar's sitar imparted an intellectual dimension to the instrument but then went on to incorporate a context less devotionalism. Playing the sitar in this form revolved around the technique of 'question' and 'answer' and the unsensual, mathematical elaborations of the gats. The pure gayaki style flowed like a tempestuous river; the new style was more like a contemplative, placid lake which made ripples but did not allow the rise and fall of passions or the play of subtle, ironical gestures. The same phenomena occurred with the sarod with Allauddin Khan setting the pace for the tradition of Ravi Shankar and Lucknowi sarodias, like Ustad Sakhawat Hussein Khan, maintaining the courtly, urbane stance. Traces of this style were also found in Hafeez Ali Khan, the non-Lucknowi rival of Allaudin Khan. Disciples of Bhatkhande, Ratjankar, Mohan Lal Kalyanpurkar, Dinkar Kaikini, Ginde and Hiralal, tried mediating between the two camps, but a deep cultural chasm and understanding of modernity separated the Indo-Persian style and the new redefinition.

In non-film popular music too, Lucknow added a third dimension. While influences from Bengal and Lahore straddled the musical productions of the major studios, singers from Lucknow, Benaras, Allahabad and Azamgarh cut records of thumris and ghazals giving Kanan Devi and Co. a real run for their money. Known as Gauhar Jaan, Mallika Jaan and Janaki Bai 'chappan churi' these courtesan-songstresses were free, sinuous and aware on the 70rpm HMV disc. They were also the last of the great Indo-Gangetic belt, robilee women who sat on their couches like tigresses even while acting out their role as agents of fashion and culture. In keeping with the 1857 tradition of financing causes, they gave money to Congress conferences on several occasions. In later years they were led by Akhtari Bai Faizabadi, the 'respectable' siren of Avadh.

Akhtari Bai, even before becoming Begum Akhtar, was a colossus. She possessed the natural grandeur of the petite, heavy gait and was usually unconcerned about negative gossip. When told that someone was being personal or derogatory, she would ask with mock disbelief — *Accha ! aisa farma rahe the* (Oh ! was he really speaking this way). And then would call that person over and give such a powerful dose of the 'clever, magnanimous chiding' that by the end of the encounter, her aura stood redoubled in the eyes of the offender. She also had an eye for khandaniyaat and recognised the noor of a face irrespective of economic status. Her life was spent in developing her proteges and searching for differing states of emotion — the heartbreak of a girl of seventeen, the search of a mature damsel for an ideal man and the tragedy of the woman of experience. She also expressed several forms of love — adulation, deceit and passion of soft, cunning and valorous men.

This modern touch cosmopolitanised the Avadhi-UP woman. Akhtari Bai, along with Siddheswari Devi of Benaras, gave thumri a solid theme, a psycho-sexual sub-text and an emotional, sophisticated punch line. Akhtari Bai even brought the reflection and observation of the ghazal to bear upon the form. She struck out with her nasal, husky voice, as the last woman with the manly touch, when the middle classes were building up the image of a puritan songstress, in the white saree and the womanly, squeaky voice, in Bombay. During the earlier part of her life, Akhtari Bai broke away from traditional lyrics to sing the kalaam of Ghalib, Mir Taqi Mir and Atish. In her later life, as the wife of Dr. Abbasi, and a Lucknowi high society lady of grace and adab, she expressed the intellectual tone inherent in the poetry of contemporary masters such as Firaq, Jigar Moradabadi and Faiz Ahmad Faiz.

Lucknowi pride and talent also wrote and composed the great hits of Bombay — *Ganga Jamuna, Mother India* and *Mughal-e-Azam* — during the trail blazing reign of Mehboob Khan, Raj Kapoor, K. Asif, Bimal Roy and Guru Dutt, the original five rifles of Indian cinema. Brain and brawn met in Wajahat Mirza to give India the first example of the action-social script. Mixing drama, simplicity, passion and the grand narrative, this Lucknowi firebrand spread the smell of Indian soil in Bombay. He wrote *Ganga Jamuna* and *Mother India* and co-authored *Mughal-e-Azam* with Kamaal Amrohi and Amaan Sahab, the Indo-Persian father of Zeenat Aman. But Wajahat Mirza was the master of the macabre; of the point where drama turns into the darker side of human emotion in the best Lucknowi, zehr-e-ishq tradition. Sunil Dutt's dark, negative character in *Mother India*, Dilip Kumar's chase sequence in *Ganga Jamuna* where he is hunted like a dog by the villagers baying for blood, Madhubala's torture in *Mughal-e-Azam*, are examples of sensational writing. In them, vain, wounded and off beat elements acquired a 'charge of the adrenalin' which writers of parallel Indian cinema were unable to convey.

Naushad's Avadhi music in these films too wasn't always sweet. It reverberated with the jhankar, not only of the payal, but the harsh kamarband as well. There was sentiment but loneliness too. Lucknow's forte in music was the emotional 'epic' even when the age of lyric dawned in the twentieth century. All music directors remotely connected with Lucknow epicised emotion. Roshan overturned the filmi, lyrical qawwali (more suited to the epic form) in the '50s — *carvan ki taalash hai (Barsaat Ki Raat)* — by making it sound like Amir Khusro's tarana. Madan Mohan hammered home the pulsating voice of the north Indian-UP and Punjab-qasba. His songs were like odes and elegies sung at Sufi mazaars. They aroused a deep emotional commitment and a dizzy, hazy state of mind — *Tum jo mil gaye ho, yeh jahan mil gaya (Hanste Zakhm)*.

Avadhi musicians and lyricists, like Majrooh (wounded) Sultanpuri, kept alive UP's individuality in Bombay. The same way in which O.P. Nayyar overturned the conventions of commercial film music to create the modern sound of the late '50s and the early '60s on basis of old memories of Punjab. The notes of Madan Mohan were imbued with a brooding but charged sensuality; they created the night of murder, (qatal ki raat) or a mood of violent passion, a structure of feeling common to Urdu literature and to films with a Lucknowi backdrop — *Bahu Begum, Mehboob Ki Mehndi* and *Pakeezah.*

From Amir Khusro to Madan Mohan, Indo-Persian art delyricised and gesturalised love, poetry and music. While un-emotionalising and un-sweetening aesthetics, it went beyond the non-emotional, gestural traditions of Western art and music. Western jazz came closest to the 'South Asia according to Lucknow' mood. Both celebrated the lack of sentiment and the ideal melody' with attitude and sensation. Beyond heart and soul, the troubadours of Western classical, they introduced mind and 'gut' to music. But jazz 'beboped' sensations in unaccented notes. Masters of Hindustani style 'full bloodied' sensations in charged notes. They gave the only example of the sensationalisation of the epic, dramatic style of the mind, or, for that matter, of the classicisation of the passionate style of the gut — resplendent elsewhere in South American, Spanish and Arabian art.

Bahu Begum and *Pakeezah* had Meena Kumari dimly lit in white, red and purple, an ocean of mystery, subterfuge and emotion behind the veil. *Bahu Begum* and *Pakeezah* were stunning — the latter was shot in a real manzil near the Raja Bazaar and there never emerged a kotha which looked so ornamental. The film had pauses lasting for a life time — the wind that blew and separated the generational tale of two lovers, the flame that flickered and transformed a tawaif into an elusive figurine, the whistle of a train that brought back the memory of a past encounter. Meena Kumari in *Pakeezah* was the last Asiatic heroine who read a letter while bathing her hair in the fountain and who danced on a carpet worth Rs. 36,000.

Pakeezah was the story of a tawaif's love for a man of high society. The fatal encounter with the heart condemns her to ostracisation and self-imposed death. Her daughter too grows up to become a tawaif of repute and falls in love with a dashing forest officer belonging to the same high society family. Familiar circumstances are repeated but for the unexpected climax wherein the daughter's wedding doli is lifted in front of the very kotha from where her mother had departed disgraced and forlorn.

Pakeezah's bold theme had a chivalrous hero. Lucknow with its Victoria Street, fountains at the crossings, small time nawabs and the tonga, evoked an early twentieth century environment. Yet the central theme of love was not based on premeditated, eternal emotions. It was ishq of the fleeting aroma, existing for a passing moment — a love which begins with the hero, the forest officer played by Raaj Kumar, eying the still sensuality of his future beloved's legs —

Aapke paanv dekhe, bahut haseen hain, inhe zameen par
mat utariye ga, maile hon jayenge

(Saw your feet, they are very beautiful,
Do not put them on the ground, lest they get soiled)

Despite being set vaguely in the Lucknow of '20s and '30s, *Pakeezah* was a late '60s film. It summed up hundred years of post-'57 courtesan life — a time when the tawaif struggled hard to retain her institutional relevance. She enamoured the world while carrying that special feel for style, romance and sacrifice. The film gave the last glimpse of a vanishing code — the scene of a nawab shooting down the pretensions of the neo-rich contractor daring to show off his money before status and culture.

Pakeezah was also the last film to show the old mujra — *Thare rahiyo o banke yaar* — orchestrated specially by Lacchu Maharaj. The mujra stood apart from the rest of the songs composed no less brilliantly by Ghulam Muhammad. It began with the theka and the bhaav and then erupted, without warning, into a tatkar; a filigree of notes and emotions deviated with a break and then returned to the theme — a sudden eruption and calm. This pattern was carried over in the background score, composed by Naushad, where on occasions the organ suddenly interrupted the drone of the sarangi. When personal, dramatic feelings came to the fore, Western style notes, filled with foreboding and longing, took over. Naushad had never done this type of music before; it went beyond his more famous interpretations of folk and classical to capture the elusive mood of the bungalow type '30s and '40s havelis .

Pakeezah ended happily for the tawaif, but far away from the world of cinema the real Sahibjans and Nawabjans packed their bags to leave. In the '70s, the last of the connoisseurs departed. The middle classes too stopped flaunting conventions for a courtesan. Upto the '60s, the kotha culture of UP was respectable to the point of Hindu marriages being arranged under its shade. Even in villages and qasbas of Sultanpur and Azamgarh it was customary and traditional for the Bhumihaar, Kayastha or Brahmin uncle to initiate his nephew in the ways of this world at the kotha. But by the late '70s, the alleys of chowks in Lucknow and other Avadhi-east UP towns began to get filled with those who flock to empty havelis to scavenge the leftovers — the dregs of society who now descended upon empty courtesan houses to rob and steal even the corpses of remembrances.The end of the kotha symbolised the end of a way of life in UP. *Uske baad,* (after that) as they used to proclaim in the heavy, sonorous *(Mughal-e-Azam)* type voice, *savarna Hindu aur Mussalman bacchon se tahzeeb chali gayi,* (Hindu and Muslim kids lost their culture).

Away from the culture of the chowk, C.B. Gupta died in 1978 after ensuring the defeat of Mrs. Indira Gandhi and her son Sanjay Gandhi from Rae Bareli and Amethi in the 1977 general elections. The elections saw a non-Congress government at the centre for the first time in the history of independent India. Avadh, the trusted countryside of Nehru's daughter, dented the fifty-five year old Congress monopoly in UP. C.B. Gupta, the most well-known chief minister of UP after G.B. Pant, had parted ways with Mrs. Gandhi in the late '60s. He finally reacted to a situation where people like him, who had done many a good and dirty work of the Congress, were becoming obsolete for a Congress which was then well on its way to becoming the party of the dictatorial big bureaucracy and the anti-civil rights Emergency.

With C.B. Gupta, the last rooted politician of the post-independence era also passed away. Lucknow had produced great Muslim freedom fighters but none of them acquired a major ministerial berth after '47. The shadow of exodus, especially the departure of Khaliqulzaman, who had vowed not to migrate, broke their back. Khaliqulzaman was the one figure who carried secular values up his sleeve and an attitude which came easy to the aristocracy. His beautiful wife had long given up the purdah. Intimate with women rights, he betted at the race course, sat with radical youths and understood Muslim fears and apprehensions. Figures like him had no reason to leave but perhaps the Uttar Pradesh of G.B. Pant and Sampurnanand was too much handle. The only other option left for the aristocracy and the Muslim elite was to go to the villages, a la 1857, and join up with the peasantry. Some of them did do so and for many generations a well-read Urdu gentleman was thought to be a communist, both in India and Pakistan. But by and large, the peasantry, or any future beyond the Congress or the League, could never become part of the post-1857 Muslim aristocratic vision. This choice of the elite, also a result of forced circumstances, crippled them mentally and physically while crushing their creativity between India and Pakistan. Their fate was echoed by other sections as well. There were very few Lucknowites in the successive ministries of the Uttar Pradesh government — Mohan Lal Saxena, one of the few prominent personalities to sustain his position in the post-independence period, ended up as a dissenter. Another principled politician, Gopi Nath Srivastava, was appointed the chairman of the Public Service Commission but he wrote a scathing annual report criticising G.B. Pant. Gopi Nath, known in official circles for his uncompromising integrity, was also peeved at the caste based nepotism then gaining ground in government institutions. Pant complained about Gopi Nath to K.D. Malviya and the honest Kayastha was never again able to rise in public administration.

After C.B. Gupta, politics in Lucknow came to be dominated solely by outsiders. Places like Allahabad produced their own leaders who became national figures — Lucknow became the field where national and state leaders came to play out their innings. It became a sort of stop gap political capital while Avadh was reduced in importance as eastern and western Uttar Pradesh began exhibiting the more interesting features of agrarian restlessness.

The peasant question now touched the peasant-proprieter of the west and rural-proletariat of the east. But in the middle man-feudal gentry dominated Avadh, the price for the failure of the 1920 movement and the consequent Congressisation of the peasantry was heavy. Markets which once fed the cities of the state began wearing a deserted, depressing look, as if someone had turned the clock back to the time of the barter system. Qasbas, those great centres of learning and industry, became ghost towns with a graveyard, a few dilapidated buildings, and the devastated ruins of 1857 and 1947 lying about in heaps. A great chasm emerged between the upper and the lower classes, slowly a gulf also began to separate the communities. This was exacerbated by the landlord class which began turning away from the composite culture of yore — the Mankapur family of Gonda sponsored the activities of the Jana Sangh and those advocating sectarian, Hindutva values.

Underdevelopment marked the city itself. Chief ministers came and went but the Gomti grew dirtier, rain, flood water logged the streets and the drainage system fell far below the standards of the British era. The main contribution of C.B. Gupta included the building and repairing of bridges, the opening of libraries and the construction of a dam on the Gomti. One of his other plans involved the resettlement of the city by creating accommodation for the burgeoning service sector and locating areas for outsiders to pitch in their tents.

Any far-reaching plan of industrialisation too, would have included the influx of outsiders in the city, the way Bombay developed in the late nineteenth century, drawing men and material from the hinterlands of Maharashtra. That would have brought the dehatis of Avadh with historical memories of the city and its past to the environs of Lucknow. But the opposite happened. Employment opportunities in the city were severally restricted to the secretariat and governmental offices, and here what mattered was the clout of the political leader and the number of men, normally from outside Avadh and Lucknow, he could fill in his name.

The people of the region were faced with a different choice — migration at a mass level. This fate struck home with particular poignancy in Avadh as there was no adventure or sense of seeking new opportunities in the whole affair. Avadhians belonged to an old civilisation — they had seen a bourgeois and a working class culture which included concepts like dignity of labour much before it made an appearance as a Western concept at the national level. They also had an aesthetic attitude towards work and differed in their ethics from the working people of eastern Uttar Pradesh and Bihar who inhabited, after '57, a rootless historicity moulded by the British. The Biharis and Balliatics were able to adjust more fully in the factory conditions of Calcutta and Bombay. They brought their folk music along and gave a lyrical, Bhojpuri idiom to the language and culture of Bombay. But the Avadhian working class tryst with the Indian asphalt jungle produced an unrequited love and an absymal pain. From this experience emerged the feeling of the exhaustive, working class 'alienation'.

When Raja Sajid Hussein's son, Muzaffar Ali, stepped into the world from Kotwara he was a nobody. His father had long since receded from the mainstream. The now old man had stopped writing articles and letters to the editor in *The Pioneer* or giving patronage to new ideas and individuals in Lucknow. Still a respected figure in the city, his name did not 'sell' beyond Avadh.

Muzaffar Ali occupied that existential state which his first film *Gaman* set out to portray — that of an Avadhian alien in Bombay. From deep within his heart came a voice — *'Is shahar mein har shakhs pareshan kyon hai'* (Why is everyone so upset in this city?). From unusually sunken eyes arose a pain which saw dimness in the brightness of neon lights, squalor of the mind in the city of immaculate opportunity, tears on cheeks made for joy. *Gaman's* picture of working class angst was new to Indian cinema. The fact that this image came not from petty bourgeoisie intellectuals of Bombay and Calcutta, the Meccas of the Indian proletariat, but from an Avadhi ex-aristocrat added to contemporary incomprehension.

Muzaffar looked back in *Gaman* at the decay of rural Avadh where valour and festivity had turned inwards. The beating of one's chest in Moharram was now also a form of social-sadomasochism. Beauty too had wilted away in unsung isolation. The story of an Avadhian taxi driver's dismal travails in Bombay was as provocative as Avtaar Kaul's *27 Down*, the first 'angry young man' document of north India.

In the late '70s, Lucknow was visited by Satyajit Ray, then making his maiden Hindi film. Based on a short story by Premchand, *Shatranj ke Khiladi* spoke of 'Lucknowi decadence' just before annexation in 1856. As such it followed the stereotype of chess-playing nawabs, cock fights, licentious women, political inaction and gratuitous opulence set by the Hindi-Bengali renaissance. Nirala too could not help raising the anti-Hindustani bogey of 'Islam the aggressor' in *Ram ki Shakti Puja*. For all their progressivism, Premchand and Nirala were tragic prisoners of the post-'57 redefinition.

But Ray was able to alter the stereotype by adding a sensitive touch and a humorous brush to his portrait of Wajid Ali Shah. 'Jan-e-Alam' was now a much abused figure outside Lucknow, almost a pebble in the eye of the petty, moralizing intelligentsia. Even Ray could not desist from portraying him as out of sync with his time: as a childlike 'feminine', brooding figure unable to confront cool and adult British machinations. Earlier, Ray had sketched a sympathetic and 'correct' picture of the Bengali aristocracy in *Jalsaghar*. The film had the talented zamindar playing the esraj, north Indian classical music by Vilayat Khan and a free wheeling mujra by the dancer Roshan Kumari. It also gave the timeless symbol of Indian culture: the image of the neo-rich, 'bania thekedaar' failing to imitate, despite best efforts, the style and sophistication of the old elite.

But when Ray came to Lucknow he did not explore the drama behind the dance, the brain behind the opulence, the brewing revolution behind 'decadence'. Ray's Wajid Ali Shah did not come remotely close to the politician who tore to pieces the British 'blue book'[3] or the man who symbolised social-sexual power. An authentic child of the Bengali renaisance, Ray's academic aristocratism just could not measure up to the heat and dust bound Avadhian vision. *Shatranj ke Khiladi* attempted a decent, honest portrayal of Lucknow but it missed the point completely. It forgot that history was not about placid irony, especially when it came to Avadh. It was about spectacle, imagination, sunlight and broken columns: usually, about the stories of Attia Hossain and Qurratulain Haider.

Both these women actually belonged to the generation of the '40s — to the bindaas, post-purdah (whose mothers had discarded the veil) women of the city. Attia hailed from the family of Shahid Hussain who had married into the Habibullas. Her sister, Razia, was a lady of charm, wit and enlightened ideas; she was also one of the best hostesses in town. Her uninhibited garden parties made every guest feel special. But what remained in memory was her dream like image — the white gharara, white kurta and the jewellery, garlands, bracelets, earrings, pearls all made out, singularly, from white jasmine flowers.

Attia herself was part of that circle which broke conventions and loved before marriage, never allowing, however, to let the bold descend down to the base. In keeping with her fashionable ways, she married and left Lucknow to settle abroad with her husband. There she suddenly came up, in the early '60s, with an English novel which spoke about the wisdom of grandmothers and the rebellion of young Avadhian lasses.

Sunlight on a Broken Column, shattered the unchanging picture of Indian tradition. Qurratulain Haider's pen went even further back in tradition. Originating from a Shia background, Haider belonged to the fiery, feminist trend of Ismat Chugtai. But it was she who created the true, adventurous picture of Buddhist-Indian phase. Her epic canvas cut across periods to universalise the phase as a complex and valorous struggle of morals. *Aag ka Dariya,* written in the late '50s, was recognised as a Urdu classic but the author got the Jnanpith award only in the early '90s. Its true merits wait, yet, a proper recognition by the non-Urdu world.

16

.⋆.

Crimes, Smiles and Misdemeanours—2
The Final Phase

The return to history saw Muzaffar Ali exhibiting his other side. *Umrao Jaan* was released in 1982 and became a cult film. It was not a copy of Hadi Ruswa's original and neither fell in line with the Muslim socials of H.S. Rawail. Basically about dress, gadgetry and manner, *Umrao Jaan* spoke through ugaldans, pyjamas of 1840s and the shy, lovelorn, tragic Rekha. The film was ornamental to the point of working as an 'album of style'. But it had a soul which guaranteed box office success to this 'art' project; designer clothes mouldered with a gamut of emotions and 'items' knew how to stay within the 'frame'.

Muzaffar Ali's *Umrao Jaan* had irony and sentiment but no attitude — she was more, a static object of circumstances. Hadi Ruswa's Umrao Jaan 'Ada' carried a stance even in pain — she was an unrepentant subject of the narrative. Muzaffar Ali's frame was already establishing, unintentionally and evidently, the non-attitudinal foundations of late twentieth century Avadhian nostalgia.

In *Pakeezah* it was the mood which set the tone of content. *Umrao Jaan* assembled the mood through fragments and pieces. *Pakeezah* closed the 'subject' of Lucknow: *Umrao Jaan* showcased the dwindling reminiscence of her apparel and persona present, invisibly, from early '60s to mid-70s in the great age of cinematic style. When

Asha Parekh and Hema Malini wore 'rust cenna' and 'mehndi green' in *Aan Milo Sajna* and *Raja Jaani*, Lucknowi tints flashed in instinctive strike. Sporting their sharara, kundan, shaluka, salwaar kameez, dupatta tied to the chignon, beloveds of Nasiruddin Haider smiled posthumously from lost tracks of repute. This sartorial coup came to the aid of the effervescent, warm, outgoing and sensitive Indian woman of the '60s, angling for a revolution of attire.

Male envy and spunk reappeared in shards of style in the '60s: the coloured pant, striped muffler, loose coat, the short collared, embroidered kurta, the mauve wood, crown blue, gun metal, sand, plum, forest, old rose 'achkan-sherwaani', the laced churidar pyjama, the men's earring. Worn with easy fascimility by Shammi Kapoor, Biswajeet, Joy Mukherjee, Dharmendra, Sanjeev Kumar and Rajesh Khanna, the garment upheaval bred an attitude of tough sincerity and existential flamboyance. The last phase of the Lucknowi race course glimmered with similar looks with black glasses punctuating further the inflamed vehemence of the Avadhian summer.

But *Umrao Jaan's* maker was not allowed to savour the gall of his achievement. He returned to Lucknow in 1993 from Bombay, a broken and embittered man. The city was in flames over the demolition of the Babri Mosque at Ayodhya on 6 December 1992 by a Bhartiya Janata Party (BJP) backed mob. The act resulted from the 'mandir-masjid' dispute raked up by the BJP and the Rashtriya Swayam Sevak Sangh (RSS) from late '80s onwards as an anti-Muslim political movement.

· The matter stretched back to ages without ever becoming a communal issue. In 1856, just before the great uprising, Avadh saw a separate Ayodhya based mandir-masjid controversy. A portion of Hanumangarhi was claimed by a section of Muslims as their masjid ground which led to violence and Hindu-Muslim polarisation. But there was no political campaign to define Hindus and Muslims as the social, cultural, historical 'other'. Sectarian, violent passions did not spill over to a pan-regional, anti-Muslim or anti-Hindu propaganda war on separate identities and eternal grievances.

This was a confrontation in the nature of past struggles, untouched by British redefinition, where caste and religious battles were essentially ideological, political or emotional affairs. In keeping with the best traditions of Islam, Hinduism and Sikhism, religion was still a means to stir a community into social, political and spiritual action. None of the great religions were ever interpreted as defining an ethnic-racial enemy for the chosen community. All jihads were 'non-other' based wars for establishing a fastidious outer and inner order.

Even the mandir-masjid demolishing drives of the kings and zamindars were temporary exercises aimed at breaking the opponent's symbol of power. The same kings and zamindars also nurtured mandirs and masjids. Indo-Persian culture had run so deep that revolts against the Mughal rule took place in Indo-Persian regalia, their 'Hindu' elements itself part of an earlier composite synthesis. Moreover a counter religious faith often worked as a correct or incorrect ideology behind an attack on places of worship. This was something fundamentally different from tearing down a mosque 'in the modern way' on the basis of a cold and calculative cultural nationalism.

In 1856 Muslim zealots organised a march for liberating Hanumangarhi. But Wajid Ali Shah suppressed the movement. He had said once: *Hum ishq ke bande hain, Mazhab se kya vasta* (I am the slave of love, what has religion got to do with me). The next two lines further elaborated the idea: 'If he dwells in Kaaba, I care not. If in a household of idols, so what?'

During the current Ayodhya controversy a Hindu prime minister and chief minister, belonging respectively to the Congress and the BJP, ran the show under the shade of a secular state. A zealous Hindu mob, not religiously-politically but ethnically-politically inspired, marched on to ransack a Muslim shrine, built, supposedly, by Babar's officer at the spot of Ram Janambhoomi. The evidence for this charge was sketchy and mythical: Babar did not mention the incident in *Babarnama* and Lord Ram was venerated by both the Mughals and the nawabs. The issue was raised for the first time by officers of the British resident of Avadh sometime in the 1820s.

But the secular state did not popularise such obvious truths. It also took no cognisance of the fact that the 'dispute' stood sub-judiced in a court of law and the BJP had no legal right to start a movement on the issue, let alone lead the kar sevaks threateningly close to the Babri Masjid. As part of an almost wilful conspiracy, the state kept quiet as outsiders drawn mostly from the south and west vandalised the mosque. A riot began soon after leading to the murder of several Ayodhya Muslims. But the Hindus of Ayodhya proper did not show a ready penchant for violence. Some mahants supporting the Ram Janambhoomi movement came out to prevent attacks on hapless Muslims when they saw that things were getting out of hand.

They were too late, however, to prevent the so called 'Ram sevaks' from dishonouring Ram and 1857. During the revolution, Baba Ramcharan Das, a priest of Hanumangarhi and the leader of the local uprising, was hanged by the British at Kuber teela on a tamarind tree. Who hung along with the Baba on the same spot? Amir Ali of Hasnu Katra, Faizabad, Baba's right hand, and Acchan Khan. The latter belonged to Begumpura, Ayodhya and led the Faizabad uprising along with Pandit Shambhuprasad Shukla, the priest of Ayodhya's Vasudev Ghat temple and the right hand of Devi Baksh Singh. Acchan Khan and Pandit Shukla were also sawed from the head by the British. As worthy sons of Henry Lawrence, the 'Ram sevaks' sawed the heart of nationalism on 6 December. They were helped gleefully by Bal Thackeray's Shiv Sena, a pan Indian-Hindu but anti Avadhian-Hindu organisation. BJP leaders accepted responsibility and yet distanced themselves from the event, claiming that Hindu mobs got out of hand due to pent up (read anti-Muslim) grievances. The Baba, Shambhuprasad Shukla and countless Hindus of Ayodhya, before whom the BJP, RSS and Shiv Sena pale into dwarfish insignificance as far as true Hinduism is concerned, defined pent-up Hindu, 'cultural-nationalist' grievances in anti-British terms. On the eve of '57 they were also on the point of resolving the British fanned Ram Janambhoomi dispute. Who gave toady Hindu parties of today the right to will otherwise?

Secular opposition to 'Ram sevaks' was comic. The ex-Prime Minister VP Singh, was arrested on 5 December while trying to march on to Ayodhya against the BJP programme. Yet, all through, he exhibited historical amnesia apropos the dynamite episode of Ayodhya: 1857.

The build up to the ugly face of the '90s began in the immediate post-CB Gupta years. UP, the land of turmoil and stability, was a solid Congress bastion till the '70s. The cross-class-caste-community, Brahmin-Muslim-Dalit, combination forged by Nehru worked like magic. For years, at least till the early '70s, UP was the best governed province of India, the all India model of class and caste peace. But deep underneath, the composite culture was dying a slow death.

Muslim support to Congress was unconditional and laced by genuine affection for Nehru. But in the Congress scheme, the Muslim question worked to balance the party's soft-Hindu face. Crucial in this policy was the upkeep of the community as a depressed, isolated lot dependant on the Congress. For forty years after independence, till the Gulf boom of the '80s, the majority of Muslims remained poor and ill-equipped to cope with other communities in jobs and businesses. They did not get the benefit of any affirmative action as well. A small pro-Congress faction, many of them convertees from a Muslim League background, cornered most of the economic and political benefits.

The Maulana Abul Kalam Azad trend of pro-Congress, middle class Muslims became figureheads as ambassadors and even presidents. The Muslim power broker and big mullah emerged as the spokesperson of the community. This shift made the Congress kowtow to conservative-fundamentalist interests leading to Rajiv Gandhi's historic compromise in the Shah Bano case. The young prime minister could have easily helped Muslim women get proper divorce rights and due share in property, precedences of which abounded not only in early Islam but the Hanafi school of jurisprudence followed by the Mughals. Indeed, post-independence India was much more illiberal towards Muslim women than the best days of Mughal and Avadh rule. This cynical manipulation of Muslim conservatism allowed the BJP to level the charge of 'Muslim appeasement' on the Congress and prepare the 'justifiable ground' for the 'Hindu' backlash.

The post-independence ruling class of UP faced severe problems from the late '60s onwards. The green revolution fostered the rise of economically and socially backward castes plus a section of neo-rich upper castes. A battle of hegemony began between these two forces with the landed gentry of Avadh siding with the latter. The region's business class was cornered by sugarcane farmers demanding an end to the 'sugarcane baron-state' injustice. Crores of rupees, owed by state and private sugar mills to the farmers, were not paid back. When a movement began on the issue it was suppressed by police bullets and goon terror.

Harried and misrepresented in politics, Muslims too began moving away from the Congress's protective shade. Their grievances were articulated in Lucknow through Dr. Faridi's political and social forum, the Muslim Majlis. The party tried reforming the ghettoised conditions of the community through electoral action in the late '60s. It aligned with the socialist movement of Dr. Ram Manohar Lohia, led in the city by Babu Triloki Singh, in order to challenge the Congress. Socialists were then full of energy having unnerved Nehru by fighting his 'Western myopia' with indigenous symbols. Dr. Lohia also tried avoiding the communist folly by linking left-wingism with the Indo-Gangetic reality of caste.

For years Dr. Lohia defined anti-Congress political opposition in UP but he was not a politician in the Indo-Persian mould. His sense of tradition did not go beyond the post-'57 Hindi-Hindu pantheon; despite invoking images of India's past glory Dr. Lohia could not smell revolution in the 'roti'. Averse to Mughal and Lucknowi traditions, his petty bourgeoisie socialism paled before Nehru's Westernised 'rais' grandeur. This 'defeat symbolised the larger weakness of the post-independence Hindu-Hindi middle class before the Indian big bourgeoisie.

The Hindu upper castes began swerving towards a form of political conservatism, away from even the post-'57 liberal interpretations, by the late '70s. Later, liberal Hindu figures were pushed aside from active social life by the rising tide of communal polities. Lucknowi Rastogis, Aggarwals, Punjabi Hindus, Brahmins and Kayasthas had little hold over those who descended on the city in December '92 shouting 'Jai Sri Ram'. The Ram Janambhoomi movement and the rise of the BJP actually saw a profound but silent shift within the Hindu community of UP. Its Avadhian tale hid a brooding saga of neglect and decline — there was not one math, mandir or social institution where older, shudh Hindiwallahs were not edged out from an erstwhile position of prominence by their aggressive 'sons'.

In the Khatri and Aggarwal sabhas, a tradition of literary and cultural activity proceeded apace with religious and moral teaching. Patronised by the 'rais' and led by idealist men of respective castes, these assemblies were slowly taken over by rank criminals and lumpen elements. They even removed the portrait of the old Aggarwal, Khatri or Rastogi patron from the central office. Under the evil shade of the new dharma, property was grabbed at random and charitable institutions of the old rich were turned into commodities sought eagerly by the land mafia. This 'commercialisation of charity', under the cry of 'Hindu religion in danger', slammed all dissent and established the new Hindu-lumpen Raj. Neo-lumpenism also edged out the colourful, streetsmart history of Lucknowi shohdes and bankes, the lumpen aristocrats, who had resisted yuppiesm in the '80s.

When Avadh was consigned to fanatical religious slogans in the late '80s and early '90s, followers of Bhartendu Harishchandra and Ram Chandra Shukla were caught in a trap. Appalled by the communal frenzy and irrational anti-Muslim attitudes, they found themselves crippled by their own teachings. They had created the liberal myth of a pure Hindu-Hindi identity standing against the 'Muslim other' whose fascist ghost now came to haunt them.

The extended 'Sangh Parivar' of the BJP, comprising the RSS, the Vishwa Hindu Parishad (VHP) and the Bajrang Dal, painted the Indo-Persian age as an age of darkness. Ordinary people resisted this distortion from their common sense, intelligence and political interest. But the secular intelligentsia failed completely to come to their aid. The Sangh Parivar was after all giving a more militant and political form to the anti-Urdu, anti-Muslim attitudes of the official liberal cultural discourse.

The Ram Janambhoomi case was re-opened by Rajiv Gandhi, the grandson of the secular Nehru. It was his administration of the late '80s which unlocked the 'disputed site' at Ayodhya, closed down and almost forgotten since the since the '40s under court orders. Earlier, Mrs. Indira Gandhi began a subtle communal policy after she lost power in 1977. Unable, politically, to go back to authoritarian politics, she chose the democratic way of dividing society along religious lines. Her game plan rested in building up a new equation of right wing communal and caste forces, glimpses of which were seen in her come-back electoral victory in 1980. She then played the Sikh card and fell to an assassin's bullet after Operation Blue Star. The anti-Sikh riots that followed, which saw innocent Sikhs being butchered on the streets of Lucknow as well, anticipated the new mood.

Soon the Muslim dominated Kashmir valley was in flames. This place, like Lucknow, had not seen a riot in 1947. Its Muslim masses had agreed to stay with India while its Hindu raja was once plotting to join Pakistan. But the autonomy demands and special status of the region fell victim to Nehruvian 'small thinking' authoritarianism. In his daughter's time, Kashmiris were deprived of democratic and civil rights, the administration of Rajiv Gandhi's time going as far as to rig state elections in 1987. Facing a blind alley, the Kashmiri youth picked up the gun for the independence of his land. The matter was delicate and could have been handled in the early stages by an honest political class, sincere, in principle, to the right of self-determination and, in practice, to authentic decentralisation and autonomy within the Indian Union. But the political struggle of the Kashmiris was first given a religious, communal colour and then sought to be suppressed by the Indian state. Pakistan also followed the same policy from the opposite side and reduced a secular battle to a sectarian proxy war. This dangerous political fire was stoked by America and other Western powers, happy to see the subcontinent fall apart as per their re-definition.

The upper castes thought they were protecting their power by encouraging criminals and bringing religion into politics. But the policy backfired as many festivals in and around Gonda, Balrampur. Bahraich, Faizabad and Barabanki were either stopped or taken over by criminals. This trend led to the lumpen ferocity of the Gonda riots of 1990 and the decline even of Congressis like Raja Mankapur. His henchman, now a big mafia don, joined the BJP and defeated him from the same constituency.

Socially, Lucknow was the city which, after Bombay, Calcutta and Delhi, saw the growth of the middle class culture of the '70s, exemplified in *Rajnigandha, Choti Si Baat* and *Jeena Yahan*. This was the Bohemian decade of freedom, when past spirits of the '20s and '30s rolled up with spunk, and the endgame of Indian city cosmopolitanism. The last epic reel of movie halls and radio songs, rebellious love and postcard memories, cute heartbreaks and summers of '42, film society and the university magazine, the benevolent father and the romantic son, the genial babu and service-sector bending. The mis-en-scene of the decade also framed, in deep focus, the traditional housewife and her mysterious aura, the girl next door and the wistful 'colony', family get togethers in the party on the balcony, conventian-boarding school angst in dreamy hill stations, Bombay victoria and the Calcutta saloon, BHU* times and the Allahabad nostalgia. During the zoom-out the edges shook with strechlon pants and the nylon sensuality, mini skirt cheek and the check orange bell bottom, neon city lights and the Coca Cola zing, secret girl adventures, Anglo-Indian hip hop, twist and shake.

The big, decorative belt, the ornamental shine on loose garments, the maxis and midis with tropical colours and designs of sea animals, all symbols of national fashion, were inspired by Lucknowi patterns. Lucknowi middle class girls of the '70s rode on bicycles, played hockey at the newly built KD Singh Babu stadium and bashed up 'ishmart' boys who had a trick or two up their sleeves. The Avadh Girls Degree College, now receiving the best talent from all over UP, formed the nucleus for this mini explosion of girl power. A new institution, the 'Sainik School', thrashed out the literary, scientific and practical 'funda' of Lucknowi high school and college boys in clear, unambiguous, competitive terms. This institution was different from the old convent schools of UP in being closer to the more advanced

---

*Benaras Hindu University set up by Madan Mohan Malviya in 1916-BHU times, or the glorious days of liberal Hindu modernity

public school culture of west and north India. Many of its teachers were able scholars with Ph.Ds who attained fame as authors and sportsmen.

By the late '70s and the early '80s, Lucknow was also producing national heroes in men's hockey. Mohammad Shahid, the last wizard of Asian hockey, dribbled through the uncertain '80s with uneasy perfection trying to keep alive the skill, mastery and dash of the forward line. These Asiatic techniques were slowly losing ground to the International Hockey Federation backed power of astro turfs, European technology and penalty corners.

The great debate in Indian hockey then was over the adoption of the European technique or the modernisation of the Asiatic style; as often happens with other things Indian, a 'middle path' was evolved which left the game neither here nor there. But the Lucknow, Aligarh and Bhopal school of Indian hockey, the school of wisdom and the 'final kill', of suburban north-central India and the Indo-Persian sporting ethic, favoured the modernisation of the Asiatic style. This school dominated pre-game planning and the punchline goal, while the more sturdy Punjab school commanded the back field in the best days of Indian hockey. Partition divided Indian hockey as well but both these influences went on to form part of the great Pakistani hockey renaissance of the '80s.

Lucknowi pre-eminence in hockey supplemented her thriving book shop culture, already an institution by the '80s. In north India, Allahabad was the classic city of book shops. But it was the haven for the browser than the chatter, the mind than the heart. Allahabadi book shops were eerie; they carried the cold sophistication of a laboratory where a stalker searched for new concepts. Lucknow's 'Ram Advani', tucked away in a small corner of the Mayfair building beneath the wooden dance floor of yore, was 'warm' by contrast. It had the intimacy of a private library where one retired for rest and poetry. The Mayfair area, which bore the flamboyance of the Thadanis, the original Sindhi owners, was bemused, pleasantly, by the sedate Advanis. Their bookshop opened out into the field of sociology and modern research inaccessible, for long, in the more heavy, literary-encyclopaedic bent of Allahabad. Its cosy interior groomed talents who went on to become short story writers and editors.

The Urdu bookshops of Lucknow too wore a majlis look, in contrast to Rampur and Aligarh, the other two great cities of Urdu bookshops. Ameenabad's Danish Mahal symbolised the Urdu book shop culture of Avadh — well stocked stalls in small but airy rooms could be found everywhere from Rudauli and Khairabad in Hardoi and Sitapur to Akbarpur in Faizabad. They were the breeding grounds of Urdu journalism, alive in UP at least till the '80s.

A product of the entrepreneurial drive of small elites and individual dreamers, the book shop culture acquired attitudinal shape in the coffee houses of north India. These steamy dens provided the best backdrop for the cooling off, or the heating up of the energies of the 'enterprising intelligentsia' — the section behind the brilliant sprout of Hindi magazines in the '70s.

At one time all KAVAL (Kanpur, Agra, Varanasi, Allahabad, Lucknow) towns had their singular, coffee house ethos. In them, men of letters rubbed shoulders with the man of action and true grit — the north Indian politician. Later, the canopy-roofs, littered tables and sullen stately chairs of coffee houses would record the last testament of this vanishing breed. Till the late '60s and the early '70s, it was customary for Dr. Lohia to share fried cashewnuts and a cup of coffee with Ila Chandra Joshi. Points were scored in literary as well as political debates; in such instances the UP politician revealed his hidden knowledge of poetry, architecture, manners, painting and science.

The Avadh of the '70s recorded another last testament — the story of the individual, rural 'rebel'. 1857 actually closed off with the end of the 'Barsaati' saga in a famous 120 hour police encounter. Barsaati of Savangi Sultanpur, defied, along with his seven brothers, the might of UP police and the local status quo for a decade. A proud Pasi, he combined the certitudeness of the Hindu peasant ethos with the flamboyance of the Pindari-cowboy, thus merging the two individual types of UP. His revolt was against local Thakur-Brahmin injustice. The Dalit movement of UP, which invoked Barsaati in the '80s, never went beyond rhetoric to challenge old customs and traditions. But Barsaati harangued against anti-women, anti-lower caste double standards of the Hindu society and blasted a bomb in a 'holika' celebration. That day conventional values about caste and gender lay strewn and tattered in blood. Barsaati's actions mocked the pretensions of big city angrez brown sahibs. Conditioned to regard indigenous society as a hotbed of ethnic kitsch, their fulminations fumbled fantastically when it came to understanding caste in action. They could not comprehend how touchables turned into untouchables and vice-versa.

Barsaati's right hand man turned out to be a 'chandan dhaari' Pandit and his chief advisor, a Thakur. As the hero of 'all' Savangi, he confirmed Avadh's Birjis Qadarian, democratic history. A few decades ago, another 'Barsaati', Mehndi Hasan of Pratapgarh, similarly emerged as a Avadhian hero against local landlordism. A protector of women and the weak, this daredevil was dubbed a dacoit and killed in a police encounter. Barsaati and Mehndi Hasan were the last link in the great UP class-social banditry chain set into motion in the early twentieth century by Sultana Daku, the flamboyant hero of Jim Corbett and the UP tamasha. In the 80s, the rise of Phoolan Devi brought the caste-political-criminal element of the dacoit saga to the fore. Phoolan Devi's personality was more complex but she did not carry the grandeur and moral weight of Putlibai, the original 'Bandit Queen' of UP.

This great democratic undercurrent was also alive in the spy-detective novels of Ibn-e-Safi and Raizada, legatees of Zafar Umar. Published respectively from Allahabad and Delhi, their stories stood out for their 'non-James Hadley Chase' Indianness. Stoic but passionate characters stalked the 'asocial' world of untainted, 'unpoliticised' crime, making and breaking rules as profound symbols of the 'opportunism of good intent'. These Captain Hamids, Colonel Vinods, Rams and Rahims peopled a red, dark, blue non-religious universe of composite culture where criminals and heroes were bound by a common code of power, individuality, survival and victory. In the battle of 'good' and 'bad' both were equally grand, the latter more so in the best Hindustani tradition of the 'secularism of villainy'.

In Lucknow the rolling back of the '70s began from the Lucknow University, established in the 1920s at the nawabi site of

Badshah Bagh. Unlike Allahabad University, Lucknow was never the classic ground of elite level caste-interest group polities. Here it was not the Brahmin and Kayastha 'power group' which jostled for the spoils of office. Instead, the government of the day kept a tight control on university affairs through the 'official group' in the Senate. But while the University remained free from the worst features of caste politics, it fell a victim to bureaucratic interference and 'outside' politics. Vice-chancellors, beginning with Bisheshwar Dayal Seth, were all political appointees. A Khatri talukedar, Bisheshwar Dayal's participation in the First Round Table Conference prompted CY Chintamani, the wry political commentator-editor of *The Leader,* to remark: 'he is the true representative of the dumb millions of India because he never opened his lips.'

But beneath the official shade, campus life followed the fate of all things Lucknowi. A garden of romance and gaiety grew up within the university premises: scientists, social scientists, historians, economists and English language masters like Birbal Sahani, DP Mukherjee, Radha Kumud Mukherjee, Radha Kamal Mukherjee, NK Sidhant and Dr. DN Mazdoor spent their best years cultivating concepts and manners. Riding to classes in Chevrolets, these teachers were quite popular amongst the ladies of the city. They had a university club and often the Baradari of Badshah Bagh was lit up to host dances and parties.

Official strictures were also unable to check the growing appeal of leftism which, with its emotional, aesthetic and inquilabi appeal, enjoyed a strong tradition in the University. Painting exhibitions were held in the union hall of the students union and the liberal-left legacy encompassed shairs and learned maulvis.

The university became a center of anti-government dissent in the '50s when CB Gupta, the then education minister, created his Bania lobby. He appointed Acharya Jugal Kishore as the vice-chancellor in 1953 and following this move, a wide chasm appeared in the Executive Council. A major section regarded the VC as unfit for the job; an anti-VC students movement began which faced severe police atrocities leading to the death of a medical student. Around this time, the city walls echoed with a new slogan:

Lucknow ke teen chor
Munshi, Gupta, Jugal Kishore

KM Munshi, the ex-socialist, was the then state governor and the dissenting trend led to the election of a leftist as the students union president in the mid-'70s. Even the Medical College was not free from radical influences. Regarded as a highly politicised campus, the KGMC had heads of departments of medicine and surgery playing tennis, billiards and sharing tips on style. The KGMC students of the '70s were famous all over north India for their theatre troupes, talent competitions and uninhibited behaviour.

But the clamping down of Emergency in June 1975 ended this short honeymoon — the students union was suspended and remained so for several years. During this time, whatever cultural and political awareness existed was systematically eroded by successive governments. When political activity became permissible in the '80s, the whole atmosphere had changed. Various political parties had begun giving protection to anti-socials inside the campus. The Jugal Kishore episode was repeated with the appointment of HK Awasthi as the vice-chancellor in the '80s at the age of seventy-two even when the official limit stopped at sixty-five. Executive council members with integrity, like Prof. SK Narayan, opposed the move but the governor endorsed it.

Within a year, the campus turned into the den of a shady 'Brahmin lobby'. Corrupt practices led to a 'gang war' between rival elements now finding easy recruits in students coming from east UP and the more backward areas of Avadh.

This change came in the wake of Lucknow Municipal Corporation's decline. Set up in the late nineteenth century, its leaders followed a tradition of debate, and active participation in town planning and politics till the 1930s. The corporation was in the real sense a 'multifaceted' organisation where the famed botanist and town planner, Sir Alexander Galex, aired his views on the 'city and its culture'. Picture galleries, badminton courts and libraries adorned the inner rooms, well maintained till VC Sanwaal's mayorship. Successive mayors after him reduced the place to a pathetic site. The corporation sold baghs and buildings for the private gain of officers. A rare collection of ninety-two paintings, purchased at a cost of Rs.11,000 by Mr. Sanwaal, was also vandalised.

The larger process of flux underway also saw new areas of Rajajipuram, Indira Nagar, Nirala Nagar virtually encircling the old areas in a zig zag semi-circle. They accommodated the ex-'rurban'* middle class of the '60s, now on the ascent through official and unofficial means. Their numbers were swelled by the emerging neo-rich; the retired bureaucrats, contractors, political middlemen and executive engineers who carved out a separate enclave beyond the Gomti.

These forces brought their own style with them. A lot of concrete, cement and brick hung out of proportion in their houses with a religious symbol stamped for respectability. There was not even a pretence of continuity with Lucknowi architecture: big, fat railings, large, static, convoluted designs, lawns and the encaged verandah replaced the world of the '20s and the '30s. In the area around the Gomti, only a dilapidated mansion of the elliptical arch and the Kamkhari dome, near Dally Ganj en route to the Gomti barrage, remained to remind people of past magnificence.

When the agitation for the temple began in Ayodhya it was the new Lucknow which responded. As late as 1989 the white collar employees had ensured the victory of a centrist party candidate in the parliamentary elections. But after that the city moved over to the right wing. At the time when hordes were marching on to Ayodhya the Imambara of Golaganj was being littered with cow dung, its frescoes were torn and bruised and appeared like a skeleton ripped naked of flesh. Roshan-ud-Daula's kothi was crumpling in the backyard of a dirty bus station. And buildings like the Chaulakhi, once the pride of Qaiserbagh, had given way to the brutal impersonality of the real estate developer.

BJP's rise was a watershed for Lucknow for another reason too — suddenly, new mosques, bearing the dubious fame of Gulf money

---

*a cross between urban and rural, a product of the colonial, not Indo-Persian 'qasba'.

and the faceless designs of Kuwait and Dubai began rewriting the flamboyant art of mohalla mosque building. Muezzins with Japanese tarpaulins, Topakapi type roofs and gates with the Romanesque arches stood interned and isolated from view. The culture of shady money penetrated Muslim religious and educational establishments, both Shia and Sunni, now controlled by powerful caucuses.

These caucuses, despite making a show of leading the community, did not make the necessary contribution towards bridging the Shia-Sunni gap. Shia-Sunni riots became a reality only in the '70s despite the existence of a 'Shia court' in Lucknow for more than a hundred years. The Shia procession on the eighth day of Moharram was objected to by some orthodox Sunnis back in the '30s and the '40s. The matter went to court which decided in favour of the procession.

After many years in mid-'70s, some Sunni leaders decided to take out a new 'Khalifa' procession involving those early Muslim religious heads who, barring Hazrat Ali, did not belong to the family of Prophet Mohammed. As followers of Hazrat Ali, Shias did not follow the other Khalifas; the dispute had acquired a military colour in ancient Arabia with the slaying of Hazrat Ali's son, Imam Hussein, in the battle of Kerbala by Yazid, the son of Maviya and the leader of the Bani-Ummaya tribe.

The religious dispute revealed a deeper ideological and political debate between two trends of Islam. Over time both trends interpenetrated in ideas and beliefs — Ummaya rule was overthrown by Sunni Abbasids who patronised Shia scholars during the great age of the Arabic-Islamic renaissance. Sunnis enjoyed a peaceful existence during most part of Safavid-Shia rule in Persia and Shias were quite prominent in the Turkey the Sunni Khalita.

Hot Shia-Sunni exchanges were common during nawabi rule but they never spilled on to the streets. Secular kingship also ensured an indifferent attitude to sectarian differences expressed potently for the last time by Akbar Allahabadi. When asked by Munni, his 'perturbed' maid, about whether he was a Shia or a Sunni, he replied:

Mazhab ka haal mujhse kya poochtee ho Munni
Shia ke saath Shia, Sunni ke saath Sunni

(Why do you ask from me the state of religion Munni?
I am Shia with a Shia, Sunni with a Sunni!)

By the '70s, however, the elite of both sects carried a fractured face. A dubious intelligentsia, encouraged by the British, had come into existence right after 1857 which set about re-interpreting the history of Indian Muslims. Their most obvious targets were 1857 and Lucknow — the city had seen the Shia begum and the Sunni maulvi leading the struggle jointly with even their dispute never taking on a religious colour. At many places during 1857 there were pro-British Shia administrators who faced Sunni 'rebels', as in Moradabad, and pro-British Sunni zamindars who became targets of the Shia followers of the Mughal and Avadh house. In Allahabad, where Maulvi Liaquat Ali was locked in a furious debate over the interpretation of Jihad with Shia scholars, Ali Qasim, the head of the most respected Shia family of the district, was killed at Bilgram while bringing aid from Delhi.

Later it became a fashion to distort history — Sunni scholars began constructing a past which followed British models in defaming the Nishapuri House and character assassinating Wajid Ali Shah. In reaction, Shia scholars began attacking Maulvi Ahmadullah Shah. These were basically petty-bourgeois elements interested in taking over the leadership of their respective groups by supplanting liberal elites. But even they were unable to check the slide into anarchy when power brokers encouraged by political parties excited people over trivial issues.

The procession of the Khalifa was stopped by the court; this created the fertile ground for propagandists, drawn mostly from outside, to excite passions. A big clash took place during a Moharram procession in 1976 near Patan Nala which proved very damaging for Lucknowi Muslims. It left them helpless before the communal offensive of the '80s which cleverly exploited Shia-Sunni differences. In 1997 Shia leaders of Lucknow and Sunni Ulama of Delhi made a commendable effort to sink divisions and solve the dispute. But this time they were stopped short by the secular establishment led by Mayawati, the Bahujan Samaj Party (BSP) chief minister. Maulana Bukhari of Delhi was arrested along with Kalbe Jawwad, the Shia leader of Dildaar Nasirabad's family. Then the police attacked Muslim areas; previously in the '80s, before the mandir agitation, the Provincial Armed Constabulary (PAC) of the UP government had unleashed a reign of state terror on Muslims in Moradabad, Meerut and several other cities. The 1997 police-Muslim show down was labelled, falsely, as a Shia-Sunni riot by the establishment. But people of Lucknow did not buy the story and maintained calm amidst great provocation. Ironically, the ban on Moharram processions was lifted during the BJP's 1998 tenure.

While people are bogged down with issues of survival, Lucknow is facing effacement after the rape and dismemberment. The British had performed the last two acts with precision, patience and meticulous planning. Now the native ruling classes are carrying forward the task with haste and haphazardness. And for this, it is not just the contractors and the estate developers who are to blame. The Begum Kothi, which should have been kept intact as a memorial to 1857, was pulled down to make way for a market centre, the Janpath, by Hemvati Nandan Bahuguna, the liberal, 'pro-Muslim' Congress chief minister, back in the '70s.

After Charan Singh and Hemvati Nandan Bahuguna, Mulayam Singh Yadav of the Samajwadi Party (SP) emerged as the secular leader of UP. A disciple of Dr. Lohia, he highlights both the ecstasy and denouncement of his movement. Mr. Yadav fought with the BJP for many years and became the chief minister twice, in 1989 and 1993. In 1990 his police stopped the kar sewaks from attacking the Babri Mosque during the early phase of the Ram Janambhoomi movement. His 'pro-Muslimvaad' earned him the title 'Maulana Mulayam' from Lal Krishna Advani, the then president of the BJP. An 'akkhad'mizaji UPite, it was in his interest to revive the old cultural symbols of Lucknow. But he preferred to call himself a 'sanatani' Hindu and wear the piyari dhoti to covet Brahmins and the upper castes. His Ahir-Yadav constituency was made up of true sons of UP's soil who possessed a history of composite culture and involvement in 1857. But Yadav secular reserves were not invoked to revive Indo-Persianism on a new basis.

Modern cultural proposals, like the building of a film institute in UP, were also brushed aside by Mulayam Singh. The proposal had a historical basis; when Baburao Painter, Chandulal Shah and Dhirendara Nath Ganguly were laying the foundations of Indian cinema in Bombay, Lucknow poineered the Ideal Studio. Sets were located in a building near the Vidhan Sabha and the first production emerged as *Yadein Raftagaan*. Directed by Devaki Bose, the film starred Pahadi Sanyal and Leela Desai. Sanyal was an early product of the Marris Music college, later renamed as the Bhatkhande College, and Leela a Kathak dancer of the city. Both achieved fame in Bombay along with Kumar, Veena, Kalpana Kartik, Alka Rani, Nazneen, Ramola, Asha Tikku, Indira Panchal, Swaran Lata Syal, Kamlesh Kumari and Yashodhara Katju. The biggest of the Lucknow; stars was *anarkali* Bina Rai, the 1950s representative of the petite, buxom, household trend. She fictionalised Mughal beauty in films after films, just as Veena came forward as the stern female aristocrat and Kalpana Kartik as the fun loving lass.

Ideal Studios contributed a great deal to PC Barua's New Theatres, opening out its modern shooting, dubbing and sound recording facilities, available in a Rs. 35 lakh complex constructed by a German architect, to the flamboyant experiments of the Assamese prince and showman. Films like *Adarsh Patni, Rashid Dulhan, Muqaddar, Kaun Jane, Mahila, Kadam Bhadao, Manzil Ke Sahare* and *Bebas*, directed by the Kanpur director BS Hajale and starring Bharat Bhushan and Poornima, were mounted and finished here. Prior to independence, the talukedars and surviving members of the royalty backed the studio financially but when these sources dried up the UP government did nothing to shore up its sagging fortunes.

Sir Jwala Prasad, the last industrialist of UP, took the project under this wing and renamed it the Kailash Studio. But he died in 1951. The idea was then revived by VR Mohan, the one cultured, post-independence mayor of Lucknow. Personally friendly with stars like Sunil Dutt, Nargis, Raj Kapoor and Rajendra Kumar, he was their regular companion in the famed starry joy rides and picnics of Lucknow. Rajendra Kumar and Sunil Dutt also chose the city for gruelling shooting shedules with VR Mohan's help. On not finding a suitable atmosphere in the city, the mayor tried establishing a large studio complex in Ghaziabad. But the Mohan Nagar studio project was also scuttled down by the government. Henceforth, there was no end to migration of talent and a young Lucknowi man had to struggle hard even with a diploma from FTII, Pune to make his first film. RN Shukla got little backing from the city but went on to make the award winning *Mrigtrishna* in the '70s. Sensual and dreamy, the film used the convention of the north-central Indian adventurous-princely tale to convey a contemporary moral of desire, illusion and reality.

In the '50s Amrit Lal Nagar returned to Lucknow following a broken affair with Bombay. But the best he could find was a job as a drama producer in the Akashvaani, still oscillating undecidedly between Urdu and Sanskritised Hindi. The radio station could not enlist the services of Arzoo Lucknowi, Hasrat Lucknowi, Shama Lucknowi and Noor Lucknowi, the lyric writers who made a name in Bombay. Nor could it enroll the talent of Brajendra Gaud and Maya Govind, famous dialogue and lyric writers in their own right. The musical creativity of CH Atma, Ram Lal, Raghu Nath Seth, Talat Mahmud, SN Durrani, Dilraj Kaur, Rajendra Mehta and Kabban Mirza also did not measure up to official opinion.

· Kaifi Azmi and Jan Nisar Akhtar too preferred to migrate — the latter was known not only for his deeply sensitive and talkh poetry but for views which fought with other poets to establish the centrality of 1857 and Lucknow. Jan Nisar's son Javed Akhtar grew up to extend *Ganga Jamuna* and *Mother India* into *Deewar*. Along with Salim Khan, he summed up the history of Indo-Persian script writing in *Sholay*. The grand, gestural, non-lyrical, non-poetic north Indian epic aesthetic came alive for the last time in this enduring document of subcontinental chivalry.

Political postures from Lucknow quickened the pace of national change as UP entered a prolonged phase of instability. In nine years the state saw four general elections; in the same period the country went four times to the polls. The BJP, which had won the maximum number of seats in the 1996 parliamentary elections, suffered reverses in the assembly elections held in October the same year. After the Ram Mandir movement, Avadh was considered a bastion of the BJP but the backward castes and the dalits voted against the party. They were emboldened by two trends which proceeded apace with the Mandir issue — 'Mandal' and the rise of the Bahujan Samaj Party (BSP).

Backward caste reservations were implemented by VP Singh, the prime minister of India from 1989-90. An Allahabadi ex-Congressman, Mr. Singh broke away from Rajiv Gandhi to form the Janata Dal and inaugurate the final phase of Dr. Lohia's non-Congress centrism. His administrative move begun a political movement for 'social justice' which saw the rise of Mulayam Singh Yadav in UP and Laloo Prasad Yadav in Bihar. A necessary evil of Nehruvian India, reservations made possible the swelling of a creamy layer from within the backwards and the Dalits. It also gave them 'self respect' which the left movement had failed to provide. Yet it crippled the independent political prospect of the Indian working classes by making them parasitical appendages of the post-57 Brahminical system. Dalits and backwards became neo-Brahmins under this Faustian deal, cut off from their ada which had brought them so close to power in '57.

The BSP rose from the '80s onwards as an independent Dalit party. It weaned the Dalits away from the Congress and inaugurated a new, scheduled caste led, anti-Brahminical politics of Bahujanwaad. Dalitism, as defined by Dr. Ambedkar, the father of the Indian Constitution and a genuine modernist amongst post-'57 leaders, was a fringe trend when confined to Maharashtra and Tamil Nadu. It became a mainstream, 'mass' political current on arriving in UP. The Janata Dal broke in 1991 and its former UP unit formed itself as Samajwadi Party (SP) under Mulayam's leadership. The BSP allied itself with the SP in 1993 to stop the BJP in its tracks.

The turbulent '90s also saw the rise of the Uttarakhand movement of the hill people of UP for a separate state. First, the movement was sought to be suppressed by the SP-BSP combine; women were raped and men killed by the state police in October 1994. But soon every party had to recognise the validity of the demand. A strong, conservative 'united UP mindset' worked behind the denial of genuine rights to Uttarakhand but this thinking inched more towards British than Mughal-Avadhian traditions. During Akbar's time, UP was divided into three subas and 1857 too saw the revived king of Delhi working as a united centre of federal zones. Two years after the Uttarakhand movement, federalism became a reality when the 1996 elections did not return a majority and a 'United Front' of Janata Dal, Samajwadi party, left parties and a host of prominent regional parties emerged to form the government. The Front chose Mr. Deve Gowda, a Janata Dal regional leader of rich peasant origin from Karnataka, as the country's tenth prime minister. His government promised thirty-three per cent reservations to women in Parliament and legislatures and female power was visible to a limited degree in and around Lucknow during panchayat elections.

Surprisingly, the '90s saw the return to roots movement in Lucknow. Its genuine side unnerved the cultural mafia of the city, edgy about any new claimants to cultural power. Away from long speeches or banners, a middle aged man with a steely determination carries the real, uncensored manuscript of Kamaluddin Haider. Discouraged by official vanity, he mocks at their pretensions, knowing that perseverance rusts the hardest of opposition. A Muslim lawyer looks at the neglected frescoes of Dayanat-ud-Daula's Kerbala and laments its dying status while swearing historical revenge. In a reversal of roles, sensitive 'outsiders', those who settled in localities from the '70s onwards, exhibit new interest in the history of the place.

Far away, behind frescoed windows and tall ceilings, the surviving members of Mahmudabad, Jehanagirabad and Sheesh Mahal sit unsure but miles away from pessimism. Muzaffar Ali himself reflects the contradictions of the Avadhi '90s man — the film maker, who is also a painter, photographer and craftsman, could not make a second movie of Umrao Jaan's repute. Problem of proper state and private investment in his style is compounded by a personal lack of long-term vision. For the post-'57 Avadhi men of talent, the continuing crisis of their traditional ethos has produced an invisible sense of stasis and insecurity, especially in face of the neo-rich offensive. Going back is impossible but the way forward, towards a confident revival and renaissance is blocked by hangovers. What Lucknow needs now is not the contemplative 'sufi-sufi' prayer but the hardboiled 'ghazi-sufi gait'.

Lucknow's showcasing is now an official act, a number of agencies running pageants on the theme the year round. But this ornamental, bloodless festivity rarely crosses the 'Pahle-Aap', or 'Navabeen Avadh Ke Dastarkhwan' threshold. The nostalgia of the city represented in novels, films and magazine, is also caught in an image trap where it becomes imperative, even boring, to go on talking about the decline of the upper classes with the refrain: 'Kahan gaye woh din' (Where have those days gone). These portraits do not resonate with the sound of Begum Hazrat Mahal's armour, the burlesque laughter of Wajid Ali Shah's 'amorality of morality', the shiver of Rekhti's 'morality of amorality' and the ghee laden, ajvain smell of the paranthe of 1830s. The angular-'Ankhen tarer ke dekhna'— gesture of the old courtesan, the akkhadpan of the Avadhian peasant, the ideas of Mulla Nizamuddin and the bold chaila of the old mother get seldom demonstrated.The surviving motifs of the Lucknow mizaj, the ash brown 'gajak', the pearl shaped 'revri', are not listed in the official menu. The only authentic smell of old market cuisine is preserved in kebabs of tunde. Sold in the Chowk and Ameenabad, they arouse a sharp, 'desi' passion which complements, slightly, the nagging absence of the real Lucknowi gourmet.

The Lucknow of power, style, spunk and thought has one unlikely prospective audience — the wild bunch of the 90s. This is a class of people which wears danger up its sleeve. Its reign has seen the 'end of idealism' and the dissolution of many hallowed institutions of the past. But for the first time since the 1970s, attitude and style have become cult brands. Free from liberal and conservative prejudices, these children of materialism and the technological revolution have shown a better, though as yet adolescent, appreciation of India's real, physical past than the generation of the '60s.

Dehati akkhadta amazes the hep crowd which loves mixing high and low culture. The end of '60s style rock and roll, 'pop elitism' has seen a immediate hurrah for Hindi pop. Beyond the sneers of the anti-popular culture wallahs, Daler Mehndi, who not coincidentally hails from Jaunpur, reverberates with a desi, 'theth', 'jismani' 'thasak', or bodily twang. This pop star, as popular in the city as the qasba, is just a commercial tip of the revolution going on lifestyle and apparel all over India. All 'bad' things of the past, such as clever women, non-family individuality, taste for the spontaneous, are coming back as 'good'. If anywhere, Indo-Persian sub-culture is alive today in the new generation music of UP qasbas. Or in the comedy, the 'Danda' type irreverence, of early Javed Jafri, Nasir Khan, Sajid Khan, Imitiaz Baghdadi in Channel V, Sony and Zee TV. Indeed Bombay is still one place where style may be respected over 'looks' — an inane Delhi type invention — just as in older days sensuality and gesture, rather than a vague 'handsomeness', won over more women in Lucknow.

The '90s are both threatening and liberating — behind vice there is virtue and behind genteelness an incumbent legacy of corruption. The post-Independence, 'Anglo-Indian-liberal-Hindu' cultural aura is folding up along with its positives and negatives. The contours of the new are also hazy — 'attitude' has often got stuck in the vicious, moronish, vapid and half baked modernity of bewildered, mega rich stars, models, teenagers and TV addicts. The '90s reality includes the escalation of illiberal revivalism and renewed Westernisation in the middle classes. The latter trend has broken the stranglehold of certain feudal habits. At the same time it has created new grounds of a philistine imperialism of the mind. More frightening is the reign of the dumb, bland and bountiless as the bold and beautiful — TV stations, research institutes and print manufacturers are caught in a sudden spell of mediocrity where the stupid, the average, the ugly, the plaigarised is praised as brilliant.

The middle class has gone bonkers trying to mediate between conservation and commercialism — it produces both crazy puritans and disoriented achievers. A new section with hazy class and caste origin has emerged to establish the unhindered rule of the seedy and the shady. Ready to grab and fit anything anywhere — Dilip Kumar with Ayub Khan and Raj Kapoor with Govinda — this lumpen entrepreneur is introducing fascism in culture. Keen on degrading all values, it takes pleasure at the fall of good and the division between communities. It also glows with an instinctive, knee jerk hatred for the sensible and the wise.

In this confusion mainstream cinema lost its ada while the 'idea' departed from the art film. There is something aesthetically sick and perverted about the recent crop of pyaar or dil films. The hero in them is a wimp with no individuality or passion. Long ago, Raj Kumar was warned, in threatening tones, by his venerated elders in *Pakeezah* to desist from marrying a courtesan. The example of his uncle (played by Ashok Kumar) who had destroyed himself by loving and losing Meena Kumari's mother was put forward as an example: "doodh ka jala chach bhi phook phook kar peeta hai".

This was classic power play between fathers and sons — a theme in which Indo-Persianism excelled by arming both parties with an equal stance. Raaj Kumar replied with equal rob:

'Afsos to yeh hai ki log doodh se bhi jal jaate hain.'

In the skewed, '90s clash of fathers and sons there is no meeting of stance with stance, subfterfuge with subterfugere. Failure and surrender of the young generation is glorified. In the process the fathers too have lost their raub. These chikni, yuppie images blacken the name of the jaanbaaz Lucknowi-Hindustani hero. They are quite fashionable amongst the now 'puppieised' NRI elite: the clean shaven sons and bonny daughters of this section present wretchedly wimpy pictures of un-gestural, un-Hindustani, accented, English speaking ignorance while seeing family and Indian values in garish wedding celebrations. The liberal-left elite too seems to have lost its power of thinking in concrete concepts after the collapse of Nehruvism and the Soviet Union. The new art films are highly status quoist and dated in style while fuddy duddy daddies of the '60s are discovering epic revelations in well crafted, cloy and co-quettish texts.

The new cultural policy of the ruling powers has completely

abrogated responsibility for preserving India's heritage. Whether this is a good or bad development is debatable for culture was actually pigeonholed under the old policy. First no attempt was made to contemporise say, classical music through its original, robila, aristocratic stance even during the best days of Nehruvian patronage. Lack of experimentation and research led to the ultimate emasculation of the art form in face of Hindi pop onslaught. Folk too was patronised the way the British looked 'approvingly' at the tribal playing the drum — with a contentless, styleless and passionless gaze that turned a live image into a technical, soulless post card picture. With neo-Victorian foreign agencies coming in to preserve Indian culture, the nightmare for Hindustani tehzeeb may have only begun.

The governmental approach looks to be an off shoot of the New Economic Policy (NEP). A limited privatisation drive, launched in 1991 due to International Monetary Fund (IMF) pressure, saw the dismantling of the worst features of the Nehruvian economy. Economic growth picked up breaking the stiffing strangtehold of the 3% 'Hindu rate of progress'. New business firms emerged edging out old ones, changing the nature of the Indian corporate world. Small entrepreneurs and the middle classes also got a lift in the initial years leading to a boom in the share market. But the bubble contracted as it became apparent that benefits were appropriated by the same top monopoly houses who had gained under the Nehruvian license-permit raj. The new forces which emerged were not healthy, adventurous capitalists but unhealthy profiteers who used governmental loopholes to build' a regime of speculative money. This bourgeoification of the business underworld proceeded apace with the globalisation of big business. The small man and the dynamic individual was left cooling his heels off waiting for the promised economic miracle. Liberalisation did not reach the villages where feudal remnants stood as a barrier to the full growth of a money economy. The Indian modernists 'forgot' to implement land reforms and invest in health, education and infrastructure, the primary conditions for a genuine market ethic. The Nehruvian state had owned hotels and media which it should have disowned. And had disowned the task of teaching people to read, stay healthy and eat two square meals a day which it should have owned.

The NEP did not after this orientation go over to societal transformation along modern-capitalist lines. This line would have seen a revival of nationalism; instead India's sovereignty stands impaired more than ever before. With Cola wars of the multinationals entering the Indian cricket board, no one is sure of anything anymore. But money making is no longer a crime and the gaudy new rich with Rs. 10, 6000 springback whisky, Rs. 90 lakh Mercedes SL, Rs. 40,000 Cartier bag, Rs. 2.4 lakh Daum Ganesh, carries the half rustic, half seedy, half sophisticated, 'Mac the knife' pluck. Under the current aggressive code, the 'bad' has become besharam while the 'good' is on its way to becoming smart and crafty. In the big metropolis, crime and prostitution acquire the symbolic status of a way of life; as ordinary people turn to crime, criminals become models of social behaviour. Politicisation of crime is accompanied by the criminalisation of the society. In response, the 'killer instinct' enters the eye of the weak and the dispossessed.

The Lucknowi response to this snazzy and maddening crisis would be to re-enact Brecht, Wajid Ali Shah, and the whole history of action of eighteenth century Hindustan, to show how good things come wrapped in the bad. In the world according to Begum Hazrat Mahal's city, weak, unattitudinal 'Indian writing in English' is out while the contemporisation of Tilism-e-Hoshruba is in.

The city in the '90s produced a generation uncomfortable with the burdens and syrupy emotionalism of their fathers. Though lacking a grounding in ideas, this unpredictable and individualistic section feels free to discuss taboo topics with disarming frankness, not seens since the '70s. Whacky and reliable, they have produced famous video jockeys, scientists and entrepreneurs in India and abroad.

Despite the ravages of an almost continuing war, Lucknow's survival instinct makes it a moving city. Something new is always coming up, right from the meteoric rise of ambitious girls to the appearance of new shops serving rare dishes near the Gomti, from sudden bursts of fluent Urdu in poorer localities to top survey ratings in sexual behaviour. In between, there are unexpected spurts of the pure, sensuous nritta in Kumkum Dhar to remind one of Lacchu Maharaj's days.

The political classes set up in Royal Hotel and Darul Shafa, both ruined symbols of Anglo-Indian and Indo-Persian life, have little connection with the everyday persistence of the people. Till very recently Mulayam Singh's link with the city was Mr. Anna Shukla, a character with a history of criminal activity. His second most important backer happened to be a chit fund company owner running a national Hindi newspaper and attempting to gain a foothold in the city as part of his larger plan to emerge as north India's corporate giant. Lucknow is now the constituency of Mr. Atal Bihari Vajpeyee, the Prime Minister of India. The party once proclaimed anti-criminilisation as its political plank, attacking Mulayam Singh Yadav for harbouring anti-socials. But in 1997, the criminal phenomena of UP was Sriparakash Shukla, a protege of the Bihar coal mafia. He allegedly murdered old gang leaders of UP and was involved in two daring, day light shoot outs with the police in Hazratganj.

Then the BJP-BSP coalition government was in power, formed in March 1997 on the basis of a six month rotatory arrangement. The BSP broke away from Mulayam Singh Yadav in 1995 after a bitter round of fight between two competitors of the anti-BJP lower caste base. The SP leader failed to carry the Dalits under the leadership of Yadav power groups while the BSP could not rope in the other backward castes. A wide gulf between the mass of Dalit rural poor and the backward caste 'Kulaks', or rich peasants and capitalist landlords, also placed obstacles in the way of the alliance.

The day when the two parties seperated, BSP leader Mayawati was attacked by SP legislatures in Lucknow's state guest house. After that, the two formations never got together again. The BSP then aligned with the BJP. The alliance broke in 1996 and was reformed in March 1997 with the installation of Mayawati for the first six months. The Dalit chief minister excelled in creating new districts, named not after historical personalities of UP but Buddhist icons and post-'57 reformers of Maharashtra. This 'social revolution' bled the state dry of money while writing another chapter in the erasure of memory. Several developmental schemes were started for the Dalits which aroused great enthusiasm in the beginning. But the slogan of 'land to the tiller' was stopped midway, indicating BSP's compromise with feudal interests. Instead of making the Dalits assert independently on the basis of their secular legacy, the non-secular, post-'57ised Brahminical coots of Dalit sub-sects was sought to be traced. The UP of Prannath, Bablal and Damis, Mohan Lal Chamar, the leader of '57 in parts of Jalaun, Bundelkhand, and Jhalkhari Bai had no place in the BSP's scheme.

Criminals ruled the roost once again as BJP leaders were accused of patronising Sri Prakash Shukla. But the Dalit-upper caste honeymoon did not last — the BJP, now in power for the next six months, broke the Congress, Janata Dal and the BSP when Mayawati threatened to withdraw support in October 1997. The political instability ended to begin anew — the BJP chief minister, Kalyan Singh, formed a jumbo, ninety-two member, upper caste dominated cabinet with more than ten history sheeters as ministers, badly fracturing the 'Hindu idealism' of the RSS. His cry of providing a terror free society to UP turned into a whimper as large parts of Lucknow lay postage to the rule of the gun by mid '98. By that time BJP had captured power at the centre, outdoing their leftist and centrist rivals in tactics. After all they carried the plank of Indo-gangetic nationalism which, however distorted, appeared better than the rank opportunism and 'pseudo-secularism' of contending formations.

BJP's hidden agenda, however, turned out to be something else. Prime Minister Atal Bihari Vajpeyee and Home Minister Lal Krishna Advani were recognised as legatees of Nehru and Patel, not Golwalkar and Deen Dayal Upadhyay. History, however, is repeating itself as a farce. The BJP government appears more vulnerable and ineffective than even the previous I.K. Gujral government even as it moves towards a show of authoritarianism.

Kalyan Singh's installation led to social tension on the issue of land and social respectability. Mulayam Singh Yadav remained a mute spectator: BJP chief minister Kalyan Singh had, after all, stumped him by stealing his anti-Dalit, upper caste-backward caste plank while forming the government. This was being cultivated by Mulayam Singh in contravention of his centrist position which should have favoured a Dalit-Yadav-Muslim combine.

Beyond the Gomti, the Taj hotel came up in the '80s as a well intentioned, five star, post-modernist gift to Lucknow. With an outer structure scattered in kiosk type windows, the place looked like a cross between the Farhat Baksh and the Chattar Manzil. Beyond the entrance, a wide flight of steps led to a long winding exit path in the true Avadhi fashion. But inner halls had squarish high ceilings typical of British style hotels of Calcutta.

Though a place of sukun in Lucknow's chaotic conditions, the leading halls and bars of the Taj are not peopled by old connoisseurs or young, hep customers. These spaces of refined leisure are occupied, mostly, by LDA contractors, power brokers and government engineers. The same story is repeated in the 'Falaknuma' and 'Gulfaam' in Clarks Avadh, the hotel set up by a business family of Benaras way back in the 70s.

The Rifah-e-aam club is now a bhoot bangla. Petty gamblers scrounge about in dingy corridors at night brushing shoulders with nefarious characters. It was a healthy place till the '50s and '60s when after Ali Zaheer, Dr. Faridi, and then Athar Hussain, managed its affairs. Then it was taken over by an emerging businessman, Jaswant Singh 'Tyre Wallah', and a new board with members drawn from the commercial community. Litigation ended the remaining hangover of old days; now the place awaits the sorry fate of either sale or demolition.

The Lucknow club will, in all probability, not be pulled down. But its character has changed beyond repair — the wooden floor is still there but instead of dainty dance steps it is inhabited by lazy card players and sleazy drunkards. Before, gamblers and drunkards were happy go lucky creatures, who took risks as entrepreneurs of their world. Now they are part of the false cultural pretensions of the neo-rich. As in the Rifah-e-aam, the shift in Lucknow club became perceptible when the last of the Anglo-Indians, Mr. Sam Jordan, left and its reins passed into the hands of one Mr. Bedi.

The old timers still prefer to sit in the Ritz — the surviving relic of the zany '70s. Amongst the remaining Anglo-Indians, a healthy stoicism makes old ladies chug at their work in schools and colleges with unmitigated steadfastness. Full of pride, they express their dissatisfaction with *36 Chowringee Lane*; 'It self pitied the Anglo-Indian. We are certainly not decaying creatures forced to read Shakespeare alone on a cold night'. There is a very Lucknowi sense in them of being at the centre of things as an individual which distinguishes prominent Shia personalities as well. Elsewhere in the city painters show interest in opening art galleries and small crime magazines run with the roving eye of a detective. A descendant of Birjis Qadar sits in Aligarh still collecting rare material which, if researched upon, has the potential of exploding the stereotypes about his family. His brother Anjum Qadar died recently in Calcutta leaving behind another treasure of books and memories. The chikan embroidery workers of the city too appear restless with the middle man who exploits them with impunity.

Behind the decay and decline, the city is actually simmering; like the 'aanch', or the low but intense fire, kept alive for a long period, to prepare the Avadhian 'dum pukht' cuisine. And the heat is being stoked not only by the city dwellers. On 10 May 1994, the day of the 137th anniversary of 1857, a group of students belonging to a prominent, left wing student organisation of north India tried to march on to the Residency. Their purpose? To remove, 'once again', the plaques praising the British officers and denigrating the 'rebels'. Their method? A militant protest against the then government of Mulayam Singh Yadav. This student organisation had defeated the BJP in UP campuses right after the 6 December incident thus confirming the basic, secular underbelly of UP. Now its activists were arrested and packed off to jail but their brief sojourn created ripples amongst the city intelligentsia and Muslims living around the residency complex. They left behind important questions — why was the BJP, which made such a show of cultural 'nationalism', always quiet on issues concerning the British raj? It whips up a hysteria around the Babri Masjid issue but never talks about the anti-'57 British monuments scattered all over India, some built over desecrated mosques and mandirs, which ridicule and make fun of native pride? Why did 'cultural nationalism' never demand the bringing back of the Kohinoor diamond? Why do secular parties, like the Congress, Janata Dal and the Samajwadi Party, ignore the great revolution? Why is 10 May still not a national holiday?

The subtle cultural Hindutvaisation of the political establishment became evident during celebrations that marked fifty years of Indian Independence. Apart from a few mandatory names like Maulana Azad, Muslim freedom fighters were ignored. Badr-ud-Din Tyabji, Maulana Muhammad Ali, Hakim Ajmal Khan, Khan Abdul Ghaffar Khan and the two ex-Congress presidents, Mukhtiar Ahmad Ansari and Mazhar-ul-Haq, did not figure in the official list. 1857 was downplayed along with the 1921 Moplah uprising, as it constituted a 'Muslim subject'. Communists and socialists too became absent sons and daughters of the embarrassing 1940s which, with 1942, the Telangana uprising of 1946-51 and the naval 'mutiny' of 1946, threatened to explode the myth of communal India.

In the fiftieth year of Indian Independence, the Queen of England too landed in India. She did not return the 'Padshahnama', the panel of Shahjahani painting kleptomaniacised 'the English way'. She was not asked to return the precious ornaments and jewels of Tipu Sultan, Mughals and Avadh. She was not pressed for an apology over the Jallianwala Bagh atrocity. Issues of 1857 did not even come up for discussion.

In the fiftieth year of Independence, the political class also found itself isolated like never before. The successful conduct of democracy was advertised as its greatest achievement. But in a classic reversal of roles, the greatest strength turned out to be the greatest weakness. It became apparent if the present stage of political alienation continues, democracy would become unrepresentative of the people.

Kalyan Singh's October coup saw the naked assertion of an upper caste-class, reactionary political plank for the first time in India. During the 'test of strength' on the Vidhan Sabha floor in Lucknow, mikes and items of public use flew like missiles. Democratic pretensions were thrown in the wind to introduce the UP brand of 'Khula Khel Farukkhabadi'.

Socially, there is now a colder perception of status interests with personalities growing apart in extremes in UP. Either there are solid conservatives or modernists angling for an overthrow of the system — once again, the middle ground is shrinking. These people can be found even amongst bureaucrats, magistrates and the 'floating', 'in job' but uneasy professionals. Living in UP cities is becoming desperate as infrastructure crumples, financial collapse looks imminent and courts of law become more and more remote from the people. A psychological-social disorder has also led to an increase in everyday violence, especially against women. Contemporary religion has degenerated completely into babavaad and bhabootism with no spiritual insight left to console people in distress. A large number of the adult population has forgotten the gesture of their original Gods and Prophets while surrendering irrationally to new cults. The scenario is frightening for these people, who swear by rituals, Bhakti, Indian cricket, anti-Pakistanism, family values have no sense of patriotism. Talking about 1857 to them is like playing a flute before a buffalo; this is 'non-nationalism' at its worst. Ram, Mahadeva and Prophet Muhammad stalk the universe in lonely orbits.

The faltering but powerfully stolid establishment has stuck up an alliance with the corrupt-criminal forces — an explosive combination which may lead to unrest and revolt in the future. This theme is already being discussed in middle class drawing rooms of Lucknow, Allahabad and Benaras. Hindi and Urdu newspapers and journals, which have shown a marked revival in recent years, are also mirroring the confusing and itinerant reality. Political parties and the English language media appear dangerously cut off from the ground reality. A sure sign of things to come is when they do not find a focus in the image or the word. If the turbulent situation in UP, Bihar and the whole of Hindi-Urdu belt is not being echoed in major national dailies and magazines, be sure that something terribly positive is in the making.

Poised thus, the Indo-Gangetic plain is unnervingly exciting. There are three major, real and invisible struggles going on in UP — one, an ideological struggle between Hindutva and composite culture, two, a class struggle between the rural proletariat-poor peasantry and the landlord-Kulak combine and three, a political struggle between the middle classes of the city and the countryside and the state power. All these contradictions are subsumed consciously and unconsciously in the final battle to overcome the legacy of post-'57 forces, now working as the decadent 'will' of the post-'47 ruling classes.

Bengal school of Marxists and Bombay school of liberals find UP unnerving for it does not conform to their 'western' demarcation of caste and class, tradition and modernity. Here one can mix Marxism and Islam, talk unabashedly about capitalism as a way of future, appreciate the Yadav gesture without feeling guilty about Brahmin lineage and think about politics while enjoying the flight of sparrows and kites. The ideal woman is not just the one who serves her husband first on the dinner table, but who works as the upholder of relative social values. Not the 'adarsh Bhartiya naari' but lady 'Chengiz Khan'. This land of ancient society looks most feasible for the birth of the modern.

Urban decay too is exciting for its brings back the prospect of an Indo-Persian, 'ancient-Hindu' revival. As the urban citizen looses his moorings in face of the ascendant lumpen bourgeoisie, the dehati waits in the wing to assist him in re-launching the cultural revolution of 1857.

Splitting three way between SP, BSP and BJP in the 1998 parliamentary elections, UP sustained the spectre of instability at the national level. None of these formations were able to evolve a stable, post-congress eqvation of social forces — the roat cause behind the current political crisis. But the slight increase in BJP's seats and vote percentage gave it the moral high ground to form a coalition government at the centre. Sonia Gandhi's re-entry could not energise the Congress, further establishing the new, non-centrist mood. Even the Congress's revival, it seems, has to pass through an upheaval. How false is the picture of an unchanging, static UP-Indian society was proved by reactions to Pokharan II. The nuclear blasts first raised the phantasm of anti-Pakistanism and war mongering. But political benefits did not fall in BJP's lap and initial euphoria gave way to re-appraisal in less than a month. Somehow in India, as well as later in Pakistan, the issue became a means for the buried spirit of subcontinental pride to raise its head. There may be no going back after this; the powers in Delhi may strike a deal with America over CTBT or paint China as enemy no 1, But from a Lucknowi perspective, the controversy may well transcend the limited objectives of pro and anti bombsters to lay the basis of a new Third World vs America standoff.

The BJP has the strategic objective of building a nuclear 'Hindu Rashtra', but the anti-'57 points in its history may lead the party into the exploitative arm of the national-international, military-industrial complex. This sinister force seems eager to keep India divided in order to use it as a hegemonic tool of America in South Asia. Forces within the Sangh Parivar would like to act as an anti-Muslim ally of America on Israel's pattern.

The Israelisation-Fascistisation of India is a real possibility and not only because of the BJP. The Post-'57 forces were already building up parts of this agenda. Now, with the right opportunity, that 'mood' has resurfaced. Its strength comes not only from a favourable present but the past as well. Indian fascism, as an objective current, exercises a deep historical power — right through Maurya and Gupta times, wily, 'thus', power hungry, egotistical, charbaric and divisive forces strutted the dark corners of society. Both Tulsidas and the Mughals were opposed by this mindset, which never accepted the secular unity of India.

Last-year, in an article, a BJP theoretician[1] termed the eighteenth century Maratha rise as an anti-Mughal, Hindu 'dharma rajya' crusade. He forgot to mention that Mahadji Scindia, the eighteenth century Maratha sardar, was the 'plenipotentiary' of the Mughal empire in the 1770s. Why didn't he declare a Hindu rajya then? Why did the Muslim Ulema went on calling Hindustan 'Dar-ul-Islam' when a Hindu controlled the de facto reins of power?

These individuals know that the 'idea' and entity of 'Hindustan' is an Indo-Persian creation occurring as an indivisible, national-civilisational entity for the first time in Akbari Firmans[2]. In the light of this evidence Hindutva becomes an alien construct; the Hindu way of life and the Indo-Persian way of life are one.

Since official secularism is now reduced to the level of a 'Shikhandi', a subconscious and emotional power stronger than the fascists, efficaciously invoking and uniting all castes and communities of the Hindu-Urdu belt, is required. Who knows, the long arm of the Lucknowi-Avadhi soldier-peasant-aristocratic sword is twitching somewhere to strike back. In history two truths cannot co-exist; either India is 1857 or it is 1947 and 6 December 1992. If it is the first then Partition too will be overturned, irrespective of the will of current Indian, Pakistani and Bengladeshi political actors and their western teachers.

Internationally, the twenty-first century arrives with the proclamation of a new cultural war between the east and west, the south and the north — a war between a 'simmering flow and dead grandeur, cool intensity and cold involvement, epic immediacy and one dimensional tradition.

With the tiger economies of Southeast Asia entering a period of financial crisis, the focus within the continent is bound to shift to the south and the Middleast. These original lands of religion and science, now the brown skinned, 'Hindu', 'Muslim' and 'Sikh' backyards of the modern world, are bound to take an exclusive path in their modernisation. Their battle line will not be led by Western inspired third world, 'pink' nationalists. The '40s and '50s anticolonialism tom tommed about civilisational values without liberating the native style. As per the Pindari song, countries like India are subject to the greatest bondage of all — the bondage of ada. Indians may take pride in their culture and shun the English. Or they may beat the British in writing better English. But they fight a shadow battle for colonialism has pulverised, not, mind, identity or language, but 'gesture'.

The new war would bring forward the unchained, physical, unadulterated, khalis Hindustani ada and andaaz, capable of unravelling the modern dialectic of experience in Hindi and Urdu. In India, post-'57 family values, which extolled idealist suffering and downgraded material success, power and individuality, appear increasingly out of date. A new temper is building up which favours the return to 'Shakti'. This mood knows that in the world arena, Hindustanis are considered devoid both of the competitive, killer instinct and the necessary moral weight. More than an economic powerhouse, a 'lucrative' business adversary, the country is regarded (a perception only partially mitigated by Pokharan) as a 'goody goody', weak aspirant for international favours. Unlike China and Japan, India is not respected, feared and emulated in the West.

Lucknow's rediscovery is an agitated petition for her defence against total effacement. But it is also a dramatic episode in the final discovery of the real, tough, competitive, aristocratic Indian subcontinent. A trail that stretches back and forward from the cut off point of 1857 to Veer Pandian Kuttubonam's southern chapter of anti-British valour in 1797, and Bir Thikendra's closing, Manipuri narrative of the 'nationalism of honour' in 1886.

Last night people saw a new performer on the mnemonic stage. He/She recovered the broken hilt of Hazrat Mahal's sword, and the broken beads of Wajid Ali Shah's ghungroo and struck a 'naaz gat' pose on one of Qaiserbagh's gates: *tune mori qadar na jaani sanwariya re, main thi ras ki pyaari, Tune maari pichkaari, bhigi mori angia re* — 'You did not learn to respect me O' beloved; I was yearning for love; you just shot through the noose; and wetted my blouse'.

Before the audience could recover from the effect of this complaint, 'naaz gat' changed into the 'banke', or the flamboyant, stance. The sword replaced the ghungroo and a marsiya boomed:

Ek zamana tha hamara
Ek zamana hua tumhara
Na khao rashk
Ho jayaga ranj
Phir aayega
Zamana hamara

(There was an age which was mine
There was an age which went by yours
Don't feel proud

It might fuel a row
Once again would come
The age of mine)

(Aside): because, you see, these days, 'again' —
Galle Ki Girani Hai, Giraniye Khatir Ki Arjani hai
Khune Dil Sharab Hai, Tarje Dil Kebab Hai

References

Evenings, Gomti, Henna and the Bagghi

1. One of the many pen names of Wajid Ali Shah, the last king of Avadh who has attained symbolic status as Lucknow's eternal lover.
2. Literally, four gardens.
3. The evening of Avadh.
4. The morning of Benaras.
5. Settings of 'Heer-Ranjha' and 'Sohni-Mahiwal', the great peasant love stories of the Punjab.

A City Comes into Being

1. A move made by the Bhartiya Janata Party government in 1992.
2. *Lucknow, the Last Phase of Oriental Culture*, Abdul Halim Sharar, pg. 36
3. *The Sharqui Sultanate of Jaunpur: A Political and Cultural History*, Mian Muhammad Saaed, University of Karachi, Pakistan, pg. 203-210.
4. This fact is controversial, though Sharar mentions it on pg. 37.
5. See Muzaffar Alam, *The Crisis of Empire in Mughal North India*, (OUP) Chapter III.
6. *The Mughal Empire*, John F Richards, (Cambridge University Press) pg. 202-204.
7. Europe too was passing through the royalist phase of commercial capitalist development at that time. European and Mughal states collaborated and competed with one another. But Europe at that time was following the landlord path of capitalist development noticeable in England and Germany. For the earlier point see CA Bayly, *Pre-Colonial Indian Merchants and Rationality*, in *India's Colonial Encounter*.
8. Muzaffar Alam, pg. 64-66, 69-70.

The Making of a Culture

1. G.N. Jalbani, *The Life of Shah Waliullah*, Chapter 6
    Shah Waliullah, *Hujjatullah-ul-Balighah* (Arabic)— Chapters I & II.
2. See *One India, One People*, September, 1997, published from Mumbai, pg. 17.
3. On one occasion Mir wrote:

    Kya kahne! apne ahad men jitne amir the
    Tukdon pe jaan dete the saare faqir the
    What worthiness! all the rich of my time
    Thrived on doles were all like beggars

    Sauda was known for his satires which poked fun at the high and the mighty. See the chapter, *Satires of Sauda*, in *Three Mughal Poets* (Khurshid Islam and Ralph Russell).
4. It is unfortunate that a modern book on Khusro has yet to be published. But a collection of his Persian works can be found at the Shibli Nomani academy, Azamgarh, the Ali Raza library, Rampur and with National Amir Khusro Society, New Delhi. The society has also published a single volume *Life, Times & Works of Amir Khusrau Dehlavi*.
5. Present day Uttar Pradesh comprises of six regions: Avadh (central UP), Bundelkhand (southwest UP), Poorvanchal(east UP), Rohilkhand (north UP), *Doab* (the region between Ganga and Yamuna, northwest of Avadh) and Uttarakhand (the hilly region on the extreme north).
6. Akbar was equated with Lord Ram in Rajput dominated villages of present day Rajasthan and Uttar Pradesh. See John F. Richards: *The Mughal Empire*, Cambridge University Press, pg.23.
7. Qutubuddin Sihali has a long list of eminent contemporaries and disciples, drawn from small country towns of Avadh, who achieved national and international fame. Today, they are better known in western and central Asia than India. Shah Jahan termed Avadh the 'Shiraz of Hindustan', and the Avadhi flowering encompassed major portions of the Indo-gangetic plain including poorvanchal and Bihar. Mulla Muhibullah *Bihari* (d. 1707-08), Ghulam Yahya *Bihari* (d. 1715) and Hafiz Amanullah *Benarsi* (d. 1720-21) were as renowned as Saiyid Qutbuddin *Amethwi* (d. 1709-10), Mulla Naqshabandi *Lucknowi* (d. 1714), Mulla Kamaluddin *Sihalwi* (d. 1761), Maulana Hamdullah *Sandilwi* (d. 1747) and Qazi Mubarak *Gopa Mawi* (d. 1748). They were thoroughly regionalised Muslim scholars who gave Hindus and Muslims of their respective qasbas, a contemporary identity.

Their dominating, mainstream presence acts as a counter to commentators like Iqbal Masud and Syed Shahabuddin who reject the intellectual basis of composite culture and paint the Indian Muslim elite of the past as seeking an identity in the Islamic lands of west Asia.

8. Mulla Nizamuddin too is a neglected personality of modern history. Commendable work in this sphere is being done by Francis Robinson. See his forthcoming, *Islamic Leadership in South Asia: the Ulama of Firangi Mahal*. See also *Mulla Nizamuddin Firangimahali: Manaquib e Razzaqia* (Persian), Urdu translation by Sibghat Ullah Shaheed. In the twentieth century, Mufti Enayat Ullah wrote *Tazkira Ulema-e Firangi Mahal* (Urdu), 1930, reprint 1988.

9. In the author's ancestral village of Ganj Muradabad, Unnao, Kanyakubja Muradabadi Misras were called 'pro-Muslims'. Eating meat, worshipping a valorous cult goddess and training in warfare was natural to their calling. Goat sacrifices were made during the 'mundan' ceremony and the 'sakat' fast, which mothers kept for their sons. The author has witnessed scenes of symbolic goat sacrifice during 'sakat' in his childhood. The tradition might have pre-dated Turkish, Afghan and Mughal influences but a definite change seems to have occurred after Akbar's time. It was also a tradition amongst Muradabadi Misras to wear the Persian jama in certain marriage rites.

10. Abdul Halim Sharar, *Lucknow: The Last Phase of an Oriental Culture*, pg. 38. One of the reasons for Akbar's special interest in Lucknow was the presence of Vajpeyis, who were given lakhs of rupees and liberal grants. *Upmanyu Vanshavali*, compiled by Ambika Prasad Vajpeyi, notes the proximity of his Vajpeyi ancestors to the Lucknow court. Numerous Vajpeyi family histories allude to relations with Muslims and contributions in 1857.

11. Kannauj is part of the Farukkhabad district and lies north-west to Lucknow in the middle Doab. It is the ancient seat of Brahminical political power predating not only Mughals but the Turkish sultanates as well. As a centre of culture, it predates both Lucknow and Jaunpur. The famed perfumes of Lucknow originated in Kannauj, the original city of 'ittars'. 'Pakvaans' or household sweetmeats, a very important tradition of the Indian 'family', achieved the status of a sophisticated market product in Kannauj in the medieval age. The place produced confectionaries and salted masalas which are still not found beyond the Doab and Avadh in modern day Uttar Pradesh, let alone India. Of particular importance is the 'maath' pancake and 'bukunu', a yellow-ochre salted masala with a heavy dose of turmeric addition. Kannaujia history of cuisine includes such forgotten

memories as 'rasaje', 'panauche', 'moongchi', 'galare, 'ratre', 'sootpheni', and 'khorika'.

12. The TV actor Rajesh Jais, star of the popular Doordarshan serial 'Shanti', hails from this sect.

13. Episode mentioned in Amir Minai's, *Intikhabe Yaadgaar* (Urdu).

14. One of many of Asaf-ud-Daula's names.

15. Bahraich, Shahbad, Khairabad, Sandila, Rudauli, Bilgram, Jais, Sandi, Zaidpur, Balrampur, Gonda, Leharpur, Purwa, Mallanva, Nawabganj, Lucknow, Faizabad, Tanda. These towns had a population exceeding the 10,000 mark. Four towns had a population of more than 5,000, thirty-one towns between 2,000-5,000 and 101 towns between 1,000-2,000.

16. As a reformist movement, Satnamis shunned idol worship. They had much in common with the movement of Kabirdas and Guru Nanak. Jagjivan Das was given land grants by the nawab in Kotwa, Barabanki. He established a 'math' and a market network which became the site of Avadh's largest fair. Surplus produce was exchanged in the village market which overtook rival market centres of other areas. Special patronage was provided to the service castes, poor and the lower castes who constituted the base of the Satnami movement. See B.H. Bradley, *Jagjivan Das: the Hindu reformer*, *Indian Antiquary*, viii(1879).

A Countryside in Turmoil

1. The Hindu Singh episode is mentioned in vol. II of *Gazetter of Oudh*, pg. 450.

2. Scattered material on Faqir Muhammad Goya is available in Urdu books on Malihabad. Some of them are in possession of Mr. Ramzi Khan, a native of Malihabad who now lives in Lucknow. Author is told that Josh Malihabadi has also referred to Goya in some of his writings. See also Jafar Malihabadi, *Goya, Saheb-o-Saif-o-Qalam* (Urdu).

3. C.A. Bayly gives a good account of Baiswara in *Rulers, Townsmen and Bazaars*, pg.97 & 98.

4. Interview, Salauddin Usman, Lucknow.
   Interview, Shiv Murat Singh, Bais, 'retired man of adventure', Jaunpur.

5. *Ganj-Muradabad ke Misir* (Avadhi), handwritten, in possession of Bisesvar Misra, Kanpur.

6. This was none other than Beni Madho Singh, the later hero of *1857* in Avadh. See Sleeman: *Journey through the Kingdom of Oude* in *1849-1850* vol 1, pg. 253.

The Lucknow Bourgeoisie

1. C.A. Bayly: *Rulers, Townsmen and Bazaars*, pg. 102. Also mentioned in Munshi Faiz Baksh's *Faizabad* (Urdu), probably the first book to compile the history of Avadh.

2. A short account of Beni Bahadur appears in Michael H Fisher's, *A Clash of Cultures: Awadh, The British and the Mughals*, pg 55-57.

3. C.A. Bayly, pg.98-99. pg. 98-102 deal extensively with ganj and market formation in Avadh.

4. Munshi Ismail completed *Tarix-e-jadid* in 1773. Itisam-ud-Din's *Sigarf-nama-e-Vilayat* came out in 1785. A copy exists with Royal Asiatic Society, London. Mirza Abu Talib Khan Isfahani's, *Masir-e-Talibi fi bilad-e-afranji* was completed in 1804-1805 and translated as *Travels of Mirza Abu Talib Khan in Asia, Africa and Europe*, two vols. by C. Stewart in 1811. For details see *An Eighteenth Century Narrative of a Journey from Bengal to England: Munshi Ismail's New History*, by Simon Digby in *Urdu and Muslim South Asia*, OUP.

The Company and the Kingdom

1. Kamaluddin Haider, *Sawanehat Salateen Avadh* (Urdu), pg. 114-115.

2. Tipu called himself Khadim-i-Din-i-Muhammadi (servant of the faith of Muhammad). He built an army of Muslim neo-converts on the modern European pattern, like the Janissaries of Ottomon Turks. He followed the teachings of Sayyid Ahmad Sirhandi, the radical scholar of Jehangir's time, who provided the backdrop for the later rise of Shah Waliullah. Egalitarian in approach, Tipu once ordered his soldiers to greet one another in the simple Islamic style: Salam-o 'Alaikum and Wa' -Alaikum-as-Salam. See *Sahifa-i-Tipu Sultan*, Mahmud Banglori (Urdu), vol. II.

3. Tipu admired Napolean and his military science. He established a regular Jacobean club in Seringapatam. One night, all members, including Tipu, burned symbols of royalty and addressed one another as 'citizen'. See KM Ashraf, *Muslim Revivalists and the Revolt of 1857* in *Rebellion, 1857: a Symposium*, edited by PC Joshi.

4. Mahmud Banglori, vol II, pg. 250-252.

5. For a modern assessment see *A Very Ingenious Man: Claude Martin in Early Colonial India*, Rosie Llewellyn-Jones, OUP.

6. Michael H Fisher, pg. 97.

7. CA Bayly, pg. 102. See also Sleeman, vol 1, pg. 63.

8. Kamaluddin Haider, *Sawanehat Salateen Avadh*, pg. 199-200.
9. Fisher, pg. 125.

A Sensuality Pleases: Arts and Culture in Transition

1. *Tarikh Rekhti, Divan Jaan Sahab* (Urdu).
2. Abdul Halim Sharar, pg. 149.

A Sensuality Emerges: the Life and Times of Wajid Ali Shah

1. Fisher, pg. 168.
2. By then, Shah Waliullah's ideological current had acquired a political dimension. His son, Shah Abdul Aziz, declared Hindustan 'Dar-ul-Harb' (hostile territory), the moment Lord Lake wrested Delhi from the Mughals and the Marathas in 1803. Followers of Shah Abdul Aziz then took the path of Jihad, which was defined by Shah Waliullah to include inquilab (revolution). Led by Syed Ahmad of Rae Bareli, Avadh, they began organising the peasantry in Punjab on anti-British lines, going as far as demanding the expropriation of landlords.

   Similar movements appeared in Bengal under the leadership of Sharaitullah and the Faraizis who demanded complete abolition of landlordism. Western scholars of recent origin, like Kenneth W Jones (*Socio-Religious Movements in British India*, Cambridge University Press), confuse the issue when they call Waliullahites, 'Muslim revivalists' in the sense the term is understood today. Earlier, the British termed them, derogatively, as Wahabis, even though Shah Waliullah had nothing to do with the movement of Abdul Wahab of Nejd.

   Waliullahites were revolutionaries, conducting an underground movement with wide influence amongst Muslim and Hindu intelligentsia, especially those who had taken service under the British. Many deputy magistrates and district officers, who switched over Bahadur Shah Zafar's side in 1857, turned out to be Waliullahites. See KM Ashraf, *Muslim Revivalists and the Revolt of 1857, in Rebellion, 1857, A symposium*, ed. P.C. Joshi.
3. Kamaluddin Haider, *Sawanehat Salateen Avadh* (Urdu), preface, pg. 16.
4. Bishop Hebber, *Narration of Journey through the Upper Province of India-1824-1825*, London, 1828.
5. *Parikhana*, Iqbal Bahadur Devsare (Hindi), pg. 12-13, a novel based on Wajid Ali Shah's text of the same name.
6. He was a Kashmiri Brahmin, a munshi in the army of Amjad Ali Shah, who wrote the famous masnavi, *Gulzarè Nasim*.

7. *Avadh ki Loot* (Hindi), Chapter 9. Translated version of RW Bird's *Spoilation of Avadh.*

8. Lori is a lyric form sung by mothers to children at the hour of sleep. Khusro invented the form through prevailing practices in the Indo-Gangetic plain. His loris are popular even today, though his contribution is rarely remembered.

9. Of these, about forty are available at various official and private libraries. The more famous ones are: Hujne Akhtar, Parikhana, Masnavi Afsana-e-Ishq, Kulliyat-e-Akhtar, Bahar-e-Ulfat, Dariya-e-Tasshuk, Sautul Mubarak, Nasaihea Akhtari, Chanchal Nazneen, Risaldar Bayan, Ahle Bait, Jauhari Urooj, Bani, Nazo and Dulhan. Most of these deal with theatre, music, poetry and prose. His writings on mathematics are lost. See Mirza Ali Azhar, *King Wajid Ali Shah of Avadh*, Karachi. Amir Hasan, *Palace Culture of Lucknow*, Delhi.

10. Birju Maharaj, the famous Kathak dancer and a descendent of the courtly Lucknowi family of Kathaks, is compiling a book on family history which traces the origin of Kathak to Handia, Allahabad.

11. A form of Shia temporary marriage.

12. The early dramatists of Nasiruddin Haider's time.

13. Mithila region of north India possessed a rich history of dramatic performance, developed in the court of Siva Singh, a contemporary of the Sharquis. Maithal performers were invited and entertained by Nasiruddin Haider.

14. See *Raskhan, the Neophyte: Hindu Perspectives on a Muslim Vaishnava*, Rupert Snell, *Urdu and Muslim South Asia.*

15. *Bani*, translated by Roshan Taqi, Dr. Krishna Mohan Saxena, Uttar Pradesh Sangeet Natak Academy.

16. Walter Benjamin, *Understanding Brecht*, pg. 17.

17. Syed Masud Hasan Rizvi, *Lucknow ka Avaami Stage* (Urdu), pg. 47. Copies of *Indar Sabha* (pub: Nawal Kishore press) are available at the Hindi Sahitya Sammelan library, Allahabad, and with descendents of Munshi Nawal Kishore in Lucknow.

18. *Bhartendu Poorv Hindi Natak ka Itihaas* (Hindi), compiled edition, Hindi Sahitya Sammelan library, Allahabad.

19. Visible on Sher Shah Suri's tomb at Sasaram.

20. See, Amaresh Misra, *Padshahnama: Search for Indianness, The Times of India*, edit page, 18 March 1997.

21. Mirza Shauq was an Urdu poet of Wajid Ali Shah's time. He is credited with 'the break' from Persian and Urdu traditions of story telling and introducing hard-boiled, middle class characters.

A Sensuality Fights Lucknow: 1857

1. Edited by Narayan Aiyyash and Pandit Baijnath of Lucknow.
2. Pre-annexation, 27, 23 and 22 grams, respectively, of rice, wheat and bajra sold at a rate of one rupee. Post-annexation prices had almost tripled. Most of the money was pocketed by traders and Company officers, because of which peasants had begun sabotaging and withholding supply of foodgrains. *Gazetter of Oudh*, vol. 2, Hunnar Mandane Avadh (Urdu), *Soaring Prices in Lucknow, Freedom Struggle in Uttar Pradesh*, SA Rizvi and ML Bhargava, vol. 1, pg. 282.
3. Fisher, pg. 235.
4. After the Battle of Buxur, the East India Company was awarded the diwani of Bengal, Bihar and Orissa by the Mughal emperor. The Company thus remained the vassal of the Mughal emperor; legally the assumption of power by Bahadur Shah Zafar in 1857 was not a revolt but an assertion of his de jure position. If any one did 'revolt' in 1857, it was the East India Company against the Mughal Emperor.

   This point was made by FW Buckler, a British intellectual, in *The Political Theory of the Indian Mutiny*, written in 1923. The article was reproduced in *Legitimacy and Symbols*, ed. M.N. Pearson, Michigan (1985).
5. Lord Macaulay's statement, Christopher Hibbert, *The Great Mutiny*, pg. 51.
6. CA Bayly, *Rulers, Townsmen and Bazaars*, pg. 270-74.
7. Amjad Ali Khan, *Tarikh-e Avadh Ka Mukhtsar Jaiza* (Urdu), pg. 220.
8. *Avadh ka Antim Shasak*, Kauqab Qadar (a descendant of Birjis Qadar), Naya Daur, Avadh number (Hindi).
9. Brahmins inhabiting the area east to the Saryu.
10. Rizvi and Bhargava, vol. 1, pg. 283-4.
11. See Dr. Kirti Narain's article, *Cawnpore Before the Outbreak, A Companion to the Indian Mutiny of 1857*. PJO Taylor, pg. 75. See also Zoe Yalland, *Traders and Nabobs: The British in Cawnpore 1765-1857*.
12. An account of Ahmadullah's past appears in Intizamullah Shahabi's *East India Company Aur Baghi Ulema* (Urdu), pg. 48-49. This version is taken from Abrar Hussein, *Mahasarul Dilavari* (Urdu).
13. P.J.O. Taylor, *A Companion to the Indian Mutiny of 1857*, pg. 30.
14. Rizvi and Bhargava, pg. 308-9.
15. Resentment against the new cartidges, smeared in cow and pig fat, began from January, 1857. The issue was used by the Indian revolutionary guard as a mass rallying point. See P.J.O. Taylor, *What Really Happened During the Mutiny*, pg. 35-45, for civil and military unrest before 10 May 1857.

The planning of the revolution encompassed Assam, Madras, Bombay and Bihar, breaking the stereotype which places north India as the only organised centre of the revolt. See Rizvi and Bhargava, pg. 356-59.

16. In Meerut, civil uprising accompanied the military 'mutiny'. See Hibbert, Malleson, *History of the Indian Mutiny* and SB Chaudhari, *Civil Disturbances in India*.

17. The major native regiments in Lucknow were, 48th and 71st N.I., 7th Oudh Irregular Infantry and the 7th Native Cavalry.

18. John Pemble, *The Raj, The Indian Mutiny, and the Kingdom of Oudh*, pg. 179.

19. Rizvi and Bhargava, pg. 315.

20. Marx-Engels, *The First War of Indian Independence* (Progress Publishers), pg. 36.

21. Rizvi and Bhargava, pg. 316-7.

22. Rizvi and Bhargava, pg. 443 & 459.

23. Rizvi and Bhargava, pg. pg. 456.

24. Bundle 153, Fo. no. 16 (Persian), dt. nil. (Press list of mutiny papers, Imperial office record library, now the 'National Library', Calcutta), Quoted in *The Great Rebellion*, Talmiz Khaldun, *Rebellion-1857*, pg. 43.

25. Hibbert, pg. 91.

26. Maulvi Fazle Haw mentioned British monopoly of grain trade and a deliberate official policy of creating foodgrain shortages, as one of the main reasons behind the uprising. He wrote *Saurat-ul-Hind* in Arabic while marking time as a prisoner in the Andamans in the 1860s and '70s. The book was published secretly in the late half of the nineteenth century. See pg. 355-60. Also Rizvi and Bhargava, pg. 489-90.

27. Rudrangshu Mukherjee, *Awadh in Revolt: 1857-1858*, pg. 90.

28. Hibbert, pg. 339.

29. A walled, European style garden built by Wajid Ali Shah on the southern outskirts of Lucknow.

30. *1857 in Folk Songs*, compiled by PC Joshi (PPH), xv—

To us belongs our Hindustan
and to no one else
Our sacred motherland
dearer than heaven
The world is aglow
with the light of her soul
How old, how new
and unique of its kind

To us belongs our Hindustan
and to no one else.

Ganga and Jamuna making
our lands fertile
And overhead the snow clad mountain
our sentry towering.
Beating against the coasts below
the trumpets of the seas.
And gold and diamonds from our mines
overflow.
Our pomp and splendour evoking the
envy of the world.

And then came the firangi
and such magic spell he cast
Pillaging and plundering our motherland
he ruled.
The martyrs call you, O' countrymen
do you hear?
Smash up the chains of slavery
and pour out fire
Hindus, Muslims and Sikhs—
all of us brothers.
Hail and salute it,
Here is our flag of freedom.

PC Joshi has written in his introduction that he took the song from *Naya Hind*, edited by Pandit Sunderlal. It was first published in *Payame Azadi*, the paper which Azimullah Khan took out from Delhi under the editorship of Mirza Bedar Bakht, a grandson of Bahadur Shah Zafar, as the *Qaumi Tarana*. An original copy is kept, reportedly, in the British Museum.

31. Eric Stokes, *The Peasant Armed*, Clarendon Press, Oxford, 1986, pg. 92.
32. Pemble, pg. 231.

A Sensuality Passes Away: the Women of Lucknow

1. Male practitioners of rekhti used to adopt female titles as their 'takhallus'. See *Tarikh Rekhti: Divan Jaan Sahib* (Urdu), pg. 78-80, for this episode.
2. During the 1857 uprising at Lucknow, Begums of Wajid Ali Shah wrote

letters to the King, then interned by the British in Calcutta. These letters detailed how Hazrat Mahal was 'breaking traditions'. Shaida Begum writes: 'Your beloved, Hazrat Mahal, has become the leader of rebels through cunningness and manipulation. She is showing a rough, stubborn disposition. Lets see which way the camel turns (a proverb)'.

In another letter Sarfaraz Begum writes: 'I had never imagined Hazrat Mahal to be a grand suitor of calamity, she mounts the elephant herself and combats the English by riding ahead of the sepoys. Fear has left her and so has the water of the eyes.'

'Water of the eyes' (aankh ka paani) is an expression reserved for the timeless, 'shy' quality of Indian, household women. That quality had 'left' Hazrat Mahal; no more proof is needed for her 'break' with conventions. Shaida Begum again wrote, presumably after the fall of Lucknow, this time praising Hazrat Mahal: 'Hazrat Mahal showed such bravery that the enemy was flabbergasted, she turned out to be a fearless woman who has made your name for all times to come, that the man whose wife could put up such a brave combat must himself be very brave and strong.' Reproduced in Amrit Lal Nagar, *Gadar Ke Phool* (Hindi), pg. 232, 237-38.

The Grey Years

1. *The Historiography of the Indian Revolt of 1857*, Snigdha Sen, Calcutta, pg. 89-91, quoted originally in 'Overland Bombay Times, from *Bombay Times*, May 23, 1857

2. K.R. Malkani, *The New Age Hindu*, *Times of India*, edit page, October 20, 1997.

3. V.S. Naipaul, *A Million Mutinies*, *India Today*, special issue, 1947-1997.

4. Sanjay Subramanium, *Before the Leviathan: Sectarian Violence and State in Pre-colonial India*, in *Unravelling the Nation*, edited by Kaushik Basu and Sanjay Subramanium, Penguin, 1996.

5. Rizvi and Bhargava, pg. 465-68.

6. Tapti Roy, *The Politics of a Popular Uprising: Bundelkhand in 1857*, OUP, 1994, pg. 232.

7. This refers to Dr. Wazir Khan, an England returned surgeon who led, along with Maulvi Inshaullah Khan, a world famous debate with Christian missionaries in Agra. The debate was referred to by FW Buckler in *Political Theory of Indian Mutiny*. Dr. Wazir Khan later became a leading revolutionary figure of Agra during 1857. The debate is still invoked by the Muslim Ulema in South Africa and the United States of America.

8. Sikhs are referred here as part of the overall strategy of the revolutionaries.

9. Mangal Pandey was the first to pick up the gun for the revolution and often all sepoys, Hindus and Muslims, were called 'Pandies' by British soldiers and officers.

10. Hibbert, pg. 211.

11. Tapti Roy, *Bundelkhand in 1857*, OUP, 1994, pg. 229.

12. P.C. Joshi, *1857 in Folk Songs*, introduction, xiii.

13. Rizvi and Bhargava, pg. 450.

14. There were seven big talukedars who opposed the revolution from the very beginning: Digbijai Singh of Balrampur, Hardeo Baksh of Katiari, Kulraj Singh of Padhua, Kashi Parsad of Nigohan, Chandi Lal of Muraon, Zahar Singh of Gopal Khair and Rustam Shah of Dera. A list of talukedari troops present in Lucknow on the Begum's side is given in R. Mukherjee, *Awadh in Revolt*, pg. 94. Pg. 189-204 give an area-wise break up of talukedari and landlord participation-non-participation.

15. R. Mukherjee, pg. 105-06.

16. For maulvi participation see R. Mukherjee, pg. 143.

17. For courtesan participation and the Baundi episode see *Umrao Jaan Ada*, Mirza Hadi Ruswa (Hindi), Rajkamal Paperbacks, 1988, pg. 95.

18. PJO Taylor, *A Companion to the Indian Mutiny of 1857*, pg. 312.

19. Veena Talwar Oldenburg, *A Tale of Peril and Pestilence*, in *The Taj Magazine*: Lucknow special issue, 1994.

20. *The Old Pindaree*, reproduced in Hafeez Malik and Morris Dembo translated Sir Sayyid Ahmad Khan's, *History of Bijnore Rebellion*, pg. 204-06.

21. Thomas R Metcalf, *The Aftermath of Revolt, India 1857-70, Chapter IV, The Restoration of the Aristocracy*.

22. Eric Stokes, *Agrarian Relations, Northern and Central India*, in *The Cambridge Economic History of India*, Vol. II, pg. 66.

23. Gazetter of Oudh, Vol. II, pg. 514.

24. K.S. Santha, *Begums of Avadh*, Varanasi, 1980, pg. 250.

A Ramayana in Urdu

1. This refers to Scindias, Holkars and Bhonsles who showed pro-British proclivities in '57, even when their army sided with the revolutionaries.

2. The author of the masnavi quoted in chapter 9 and 11.

3. *Ain-i-Akbari*, vol. 11, ed. Blochmann, Calcutta, pg. 237.

4. Sir Syed Ahmad Khan, *History of Bijnore Rebellion*, trans. Hafeez Malik, Morris Dembo, pg. 192.

5. Sir Syed Ahmad, pg. 155.

6. See Walter Benjamin, *Charles Baudelaire: A Lyric Poet in the Era of High Capitalism*, Chapter 1, for the revolutionary character of 'vagabonds' and 'men floating on the surface of society' in Europe: 1848.

7. The list of leading non-royal pre-'57 presses of Lucknow is as follows: Matabiye Haji Harmain Sharifain, Mustafai Press, Matbaye Alavi, Matbaye Murtjavi, Jalaali Press, Mir Hasan Rizvi Press, Maulai Press, Ahmadi Press, Mehdiya Press, Vali Muhammad Press, Samre Hind Press, Jafri Press, Husseini Press.

The Fragmented Sunshine

1. C.A. Bayly, *The Local Roots of Indian Politics: Allahabad 1880-1920*, Clarendon Press, Oxford, 1975, pg. 216-17. See also Amaresh Misra, *Gandhi: a Critique*, in Asghar Ali Engineer edited, *Gandhi and Communal Harmony*, Gandhi Peace Foundation, 1997.

2. This point was raised by Subhas Chandra Bose during the freedom movement: 'After the failure of the revolution, the Indian people were thoroughly disarmed and they continue disarmed upto the present day. They now realise that they committed the greatest blunder in their history by submitting to disarmament in 1858, because disarmament weakened and emasculated the nation to a large extent.' See *The Essential Writings of Netaji Subhas Chandra Bose*, ed. Sisir K. Bose and Sugata Bose, OUP, 1997, pg. 287.

3. See Thomas R Metcalf, *An Imperial Vision: Indian Architecture and Britain's Raj*, Faber and Faber, 1989, pg. 169-70 for the following comment involving the architectural preference of a famous Indian civil service officer of Bulandshaher who set the trend of town building in western Uttar Pradesh cities: Only the merchants and traders, marked out by their conservative adherence to ancestral usage — put up structures Growse found attractive.

4. ibid, pg. 69-70.

5. ibid, pg. 111 for the comment of Dr. A Fuhrer, curator of the Lucknow provincial museum, on nawabi buildings and Qaiserbagh, 'the most debased examples of architecture to be found in India.' See also the last three lines of the page for British preference of Scindia's style over 'Oudh' due to 1857.

6. ibid, pg. 226.

7. Christopher R. King, *Forging a New Linguistic Identity: The Hindi Movement in Benaras 1868-1914'* in Sandra H. Frietag (ed.), *Culture and Power*

336 • Lucknow: Fire of Grace

in Benaras: Community, Performance and Environment 1800-1980, OUP 1989, pg. 189.

8. ibid, pg. 184.

A Deadly Game and a Tragic Consequence

1. V.D. Savarkar, *The Indian Independence Struggle of 1857* (Hindi), Rajdhani Granthagaar Prakashak, New Delhi, 1995. V.D. Savarkar was a modernist Maharashtrian Brahmin and a rooted intellectual. He could have emerged as the Mazzini of India had it not been for the peculiar distortion of the nationalist consciousness along Hindu-Muslim lines in the '30s.

2. Jawaharlal Nehru, *The Result of Indian War of Independence*, in Sankar Sengupta edited, *War of Independence Centenary Souvenir, 1957*, Snigdha Sen, *The Historiography of the Indian revolt of 1857*, pg. 45-6.

3. *The Essential Writings of Netaji Subhas Chandra Bose*, ed, by Sisir K. Bose and Sugata Bose, OUP, 1997, pg. 237-256.

4. D.D. Koshambi, *An Introduction to the Study of Indian History*, Popular Prakashan, Bombay, 1975, pg. 403.

5. Eric Stokes, *The Peasant Armed*, pg. 2.

6. This information is gleaned from interviews with individuals in Kanpur, Lucknow and Allahabad and the author's family history.

7. Bhartendu Harishchandra himself used to indulge in this practice. The author found similar instances in the history of Benaras trading families. See Amaresh Misra, *Benaras: the Many Splendoured City*, EPW, November 6, 1993.

8. Peter Reeves, *Landlords and Governments of Uttar Pradesh*, Bombay, OUP, 1991, pg. 285.

9. Ibid, pg. 282.

Crimes, Smiles and Misdemeanours—1

1. Peter Reeves, *Landlords and Governments in Uttar Pradesh*, p. 295.

2. James Kippen, *The Tabla of Lucknow, a Cultural Analysis of a Musical Tradition*, Cambridge University Press, 1988, Ch. 5.

3. The list of British accusations against Wajid Ali Shah who rebutted each and every point in a lengthy treatise which RW Bird incorporated in *The Spoilation of Avadh*.

Crimes, Smiles and Misdemeanours — 2

1. KR Malkani, *The New Age Hindu*, *Times of India*, 20 October, 1997.
2. *Perception of India in Akbar and Abul Fazal*, M. Athar Ali in *Akbar and his India*, Irfan Habib, OUP, 1997. The Indo-Persian idea of ancient India is richer, more comprehensive and nationalistic than either Nehru's, Gandhi's or the Sangh Parivar's. None of these three 'schools' ever described India like Amir Khusro, Abul Fazal, Asaf-ud-Daula and Wajid Ali Shah — as not merely a land of Sanatan Dharma but one with a high secular and religious culture which gave numerals, Panchatantra tales and chess to the world. Here people are able to speak foreign tongues even when the Mongols, Turks and Chinese are unable to speak 'Hindi'.

Bibliography

The list of relevant books, articles, references given at the end of the book makes for the bulk of material used in the biography. I have used a lot of material from government publications, interviews and chap books, the complete list of which could not be compiled by the first edition. A list of miscellaneous sources is given below, followed by a list of twenty-one Urdu books on Lucknow. These are part of the seventy-two Urdu books on the subject.

Kenize Mourad, *De la Part de la Princess Morte* (Robert Laffont, Paris, 1987). This novel describes the aristocratic life of Princess Selma of Turkey who married Raja Sajid Hussein of Kotwara. It presents a useful source of the mnemonic history of the 1930s in Lucknow.

Mirza Ali Azhar, *King Wajid Ali Shah of Avadh* (Royal Book Company, Karachi, 1982).

Shafi Ahmad, *Two Kings of Avadh: Muhammad Ali Shah and Amjad Ali Shah 1837-1847* (Aligarh, 1971).

Amir Hasan, *Palace Culture of Lucknow* (Delhi, 1983).

Veena Talwar Oldenberg, *The Making of Colonial Lucknow 1856-1877* (Princeton University Press, 1984).

Francis Robinson, *Separatism Among Indian Muslims: The Politics of the United Provinces Muslims 1860-1923* (Cambridge University Press, 1974. Allen Sealy, *Trotternama*.

Munshi Faiz Baksh, *Tareekh Farah Baksh* — mid-eighteenth century.

Masihuddin Khan, *Safeer-e-Avadh*.

Abu Talib Isfahani, *Tafzeelul Ghafileen* — 1797.

Syed Ghulam Ali Naqvi, *Imadut Saadat* — 1808.

Bhavani Prasad Shad, *Shad Nama* — 1852.

Azmat Ali Kakorvi, *Muraqqai Khusravi* — 1852-53.

Raaes Agha edited, Syed Kamaluddin Haider's *Tarikhe-Avadh* (under print) — 1859.

Munshi Nawal Kishore, *Nadirul Asr* — 1863.

Pandit Kanhaiya Lal, *Tarikh Baghavate Hind* — 1869.

Durga Prasad 'Mehr', *Bostan-e-Avadh* — Post-1857.

Tota Ram 'Shayan', *Sitara-e-Hind* — 1872.

Mirza Hatim Ali 'Mehr', *Ayagh-e-Firingistan* — 1873.

Nawab Syed Amir Ali, *Wazir Nama* — 1875.

Munshi Ram Sahay *Tamanna, Ahsanut Tavarikh, Afzalut Tavarikh, Ashrafut Tavarikh* — 1876.

Munshi Radhey Lal, *Tarikh Farman Ravayan-e-Avadh* — 1878.

Kamaluddin Haider, *Sawanehat-e-Salateen Avadh* (vol.1), *Qaiser-ul-Tavarikh* (vol.2), published — 1879.

Rajab Ali Beg *Surorr, Fasana-e-Ibrat* — 1881.

Abdul Halim Sharar, *Guzishta Lucknow.*

Najmul Ghani, *Tarikh-e-Avadh* — 1913.

Revised Note

There has been a lack of emphasis on Kerbalas and gourmet details in the book — these and other unintended omissions are regretted.

Glossary

abaad	–	infested
akhada	–	arena
abhinaya	–	acting
achkan	–	a form of male dress
ada	–	style
adab	–	literature
adarsh Bhartiya nari	–	the ideal Indian woman
addha taal	–	a tabla beat
adibs	–	litterateurs
ahirs	–	an Indian caste, today's Yadavs
alaap	–	opening notes of vocal music
akkhad	–	the rough edged Hindustani gesture
amil	–	officer
angrez	–	British
anguthi	–	ring
ashraf	–	Indo-Persian gentleman
ata ·	–	flour
azaadi	–	independence
bagghi	–	carriage
bagh	–	garden
baghi	–	rebel
bahu	–	daughter-in-law
balabar	–	a form of Persia male dress
bayan	–	narrative
bazaru	–	market oriented
bel-bute	–	creepers and flowers
belan	–	rolling pin
besharam	–	lit. shameless

bhadralok	– the colonial Indian gentleman
bhaand	– play actors and mimic artists
bhang	– opium
bhaav	– gesture of emotion
bhini	– soft and scenty (smell)
bhoot bangla	– haunted mansion
bismillah	– in the name of God
bols	– words
burada	– sawdust
burqawalis	– veiled women
chabeeli	– flamboyant
chamar	– an Indian low caste
chakkardar	– spiral
chanchalta	– flippant
chandandhaari	– stripes of sandal paste smeared on the forehead usually by Brahmins
chappan-churi	– fifty-six knives (or knife wounds)
chaprasies	– peons
chardivari	– boundary
charhari	– tall and lanky
charm	– skin
chauraha	– crossing
chikni	– literally, smooth
chowk	– the market centre
daasi	– female servant
dalaan	– the inner verandah
*daroga_*	– sub-inspector of police
dastan	– story
deen	– faith
dehati	– rustic
deorhi	– entrance of the house
desi	– local
dhoti	– loin cloth
dhunpradhan	– a dominant tune
dil	– one's heart
diwankhana	– High Court

doli	–	palanquin
dominis	–	courtesans (lower)
duniya	–	this world
fanus	–	wall lamp
fatwa	–	Islamic decree
fiza	–	air
gali	–	alley
ganj	–	market
garam	–	hot
garam dal	–	the 'hot party'
garhi	–	small fortress
gat	–	compositional form of tabla
gayaki	–	style of singing
ghera	–	circle
gheredar	–	circular
ghetle	–	shoes
ghungroo	–	anklet worn during a Kathak performance
gota	–	tinsel
guddi	–	nape
gusalkhana	–	bathroom
handi	–	vessel
hansli	–	choker
hiran	–	deer
hori	–	Holi
hunar	–	speciality
ilm	–	knowledge
iman	–	honour
inquilabi	–	revolutionary
ishq	–	lit. love
ittar	–	perfume
jaali	–	bracket
jaalidaar	–	bracketed
jaanbaaz	–	heroic

jadidiyat	–	modernity
janaeo	–	sacred thread usually worn by Brahmins
jhaanki	–	tableaux
jhad	–	a type of chandelier
jhanjar	–	a form of anklet
jhankaar	–	resonance
jhoomar	–	ornament worn in the parting of the hair
jogiya	–	ascetic like
josh	–	passion
junoon	–	madness
kajri	–	UP monsoon folk
kalam	–	pen
kalash	–	urn
kalma	–	the Muslim rite of injunction
kamar	–	waist
kamarband	–	girdle worn around the waist
kanhaiya	–	a name of Lord Krishna
kankavas	–	kites
karkhana	–	factory
karnphool	–	an earring
kerbelas	–	places constructed in memory of Imam Hussein's martyrdom
khairatkhana	–	alms house for the poor
khalis	–	pure
khameera	–	a filling used in paan
khandaniyat	–	good breeding
khangin	–	ordinary woman
khansama	–	chef
khatta	–	sour
khayal	–	a form of Indian classical music
khichri	–	an Indian dish of rice and lentils
kochvaan	–	carriageman
kotha	–	courtesan's salon
kothi	–	house
ladis	–	beads in a sequence
lala	–	shopkeeper

lakhauri	–	brick
lehnga	–	Indian long skirt
lehza	–	manner
lori	–	the song of sleep
lota	–	a large round mug
maang	–	the parting of the hair
mahajan	–	a money lender or small time banker
maharaj	–	Brahmin chef
maheen	–	thin
majlis	–	assembly
makanat	–	houses
mandir	–	temple
manzil	–	destination
maqbara	–	grave
masnad	–	seat
mast	–	happy-go-lucky
matam	–	lament
mazaar	–	a holy place where usually a saint is cremated
mazhabi	–	religious
mehek	–	smell
meend	–	the glide between two notes in music
mihrab	–	arch
mirasin	–	courtesan (lower)
missi	–	powder applied on the teeth by women
mizaj	–	one's nature or mood
mohalla	–	locality
muhavaras	–	proverbs
mulla	–	Muslim priest
mussaddas	–	a form of Urdu verse
mutahi	–	temporarily married (a Shia convention)
nabhi	–	belly
nafasat	–	subtlety
naib	–	deputy
nakalchi	–	plagiarizer
namak	–	salt
nastlikhs	–	calligraphers

navrasas	–	the nine emotions of ancient Indian aesthetics
nazakat	–	delicacy
nazm	–	song
nikaahi	–	married
noor	–	halo
nritta	–	pure dance

paan	–	betel leaf
pakhawaj	–	percussion instrument
parikhana	–	house of fairies
pariyan	–	fairies
patang	–	kite
payal	–	anklet
pazeb	–	a form of anklet
pechdar	–	not smooth, complex
peshawaz	–	a form of female dress
pooja ki thaali	–	a plate used for worship having flowers and other offerings
poorvi	–	eastern
poori-kondha	–	Indian dish of deep fried roti and cooked pumpkin
premikayen (f)	–	beloveds
pucca	–	solid
pukhta	–	strong
pulao	–	Indian fried rice
purohit	–	Brahmin priest
pyaar	–	lit. love

qaida	–	manner
qasba	–	small town

raand (crude)	–	prostitute
rais	–	rich and famous
rajniti	–	politics
rangroot	–	recruit
rani	–	queen
ras	–	juice
raspurna	–	juicy

raub	–	to assert
robilee	–	full of authority and honour
roti	–	chapati
ruin	–	cotton
ryot	–	peasant
sadhu	–	ascetic
sakhiyan	–	friends
salan	–	gravy
sansanikheism	–	sensationalism
sarai	–	inn
sarauta	–	betel nut cracker
sargam	–	seven note structure
saundhi	–	earthy
saunf	–	fennel seeds
shareef	–	honest
sharifzaadi	–	honest woman
shehzada (m)	–	prince
shehzadee (f)	–	princess
shudh	–	pure
shuriefa	–	respectable men
sindoor	–	the red vermilion worn by married Hindu women in the parting of their hair
sohar	–	UP folk
sonar	–	goldsmith
surma	–	kohl
sukun	–	rest
taal	–	rhythm
taan	–	elaboration of musical notes in rhythm
tahreek	–	movement
taifas	–	the courtesan's vanity box
talkh	–	sharp and harsh
talwar	–	sword
takhat	–	hard bed of wood
tamancha	–	country made pistol
tamasha	–	play
tatkar	–	the foot movement of Kathak

tawaif	–	courtesan
tehdaar	–	wavy
teekhapan	–	sharp and spicy
thaali	–	dish
thaap	–	tabla sound
thanak	–	bodily twang
theka	–	beginning of a beat (tabla)
thekedaar	–	contractor
tijarat mandi	–	centre of trade
topi	–	cap
tukkal	–	kite
tukra	–	piece
ugaldans	–	spittoons
ustad	–	master
vazadari	–	sacrifice
vazan	–	weight
veerangana	–	valorous woman
watan	–	one's motherland
watanparasti	–	patriotism
zaban	–	language
zamzama	–	the instrumental trill used in sitar playing
zeena	–	stairs
zenana	–	ladies chamber

Index